Gypsy Blood

Book 3

Best wishes!
Tonya Royston

Tonya Royston

GENRE: PARANORMAL THRILLER/YA/PARANORMAL ROMANCE

This is a work of fiction. Names, places, characters and incidents are either the product of the author's imagination or are used fictitiously, and any resemblance to any actual persons, living or dead, businesses, organizations, events or locales is entirely coincidental.

GYPSY BLOOD ~ Book Three of The Gypsy Magic Trilogy
Copyright © 2017 Tonya Royston
Cover Design by Jennifer Gibson
All cover art copyright © 2017
All Rights Reserved
ISBN: 1546927719
Print ISBN: 9781546927716

First Publication: JUNE 2017

Just when I thought things couldn't get any worse, a snowstorm blew in from out of nowhere, trapping me on the trail...

About halfway home, the memory of my afternoon with Lucian vanished when a gust of wind kicked up the snow. Within seconds, Gypsy and I were engulfed in white-out conditions. I squinted, trying to see through the snowflakes whipping sideways, but it was impossible to make out the trees a few feet away.

Gypsy planted her feet, halting as the blizzard circled us like a tornado. She whinnied, the fear in her cry sending an icy blast of panic through me.

Spinning around, Gypsy pawed at the ground, snorting angrily. She tossed her head, her reddish mane barely visible in the dense cloud of snow swallowing us up. I couldn't see a thing, let alone tell which direction was which and how to get home.

My heart pounding, pure fear taking hold of me, I grabbed Gypsy's mane, hoping she'd get us out of the woods safely. Instead of charging through the storm, she raised her head, her ears pointed forward. Without any warning, she began backing up as a wave of solid white rolled toward us. She stood up on her hind feet, her hooves striking at the snow about to topple us.

I tried to hold on, but lost my balance and fell to the ground. The snow felt soft when I landed, wrapping around my neck and wrists, sending a shiver through me.

Catching my breath, I stood up and looked for Gypsy, but saw no sign of her. I spun in a circle, the blizzard closing in on me. My pulse quickened as fear lodged itself in my throat. Feeling trapped, I froze, not sure what to do. I was about to run straight through the blowing snow when the blurry shape of a person emerged. The figure came closer and, just when I recognized Marguerite's long red curls, my world went black.

GYPSY BLOOD ~ Book 3 of The Gypsy Magic Trilogy

Gracyn would like nothing more than to return to her old life, one that was boring, but also safe. Instead, she begins to sink deeper into the mystery surrounding the murder of a young girl while defending herself against an evil witch.

Gracyn's attempt to carry on with school as usual is quickly derailed by Marguerite's threats. When her car slides off the road one morning, she realizes Marguerite isn't playing around. Not sure where to turn, Gracyn feels lost and alone until Lucian steps in, teaching her how to harness her energy and use magic to defeat Marguerite. If only it was that easy.

Putting her faith in Lucian, Gracyn trusts him to help her find her inner strength. But her world is turned upside down when she uncovers new evidence in the murder case, leading her to question his innocence. After refusing to heed the warnings about him, she starts to wonder if she'll be the next victim and resolves to fight for the truth, no matter what that might be.

1

I had always loved fall. The cooler temperatures brought a welcome change from the summer heat while the red and gold leaves painted the land with color. In Maryland where I lived before moving to Massachusetts a few months ago, autumn progressed slowly, often saving the bitter cold for December. It had been easy, inviting, a time to cherish and enjoy.

But those days were over, at least for me. This year, fall had brought mystery, danger, and heartache. First, there was Marguerite, the centuries-old witch I had unknowingly released from a crypt, who wanted nothing more than to get her hands on the dark, dangerous spells missing from a book she'd stolen from Becca. She also happened to be Becca's daughter. Cold-hearted, selfish, and calculating, Marguerite was nothing like Becca. With Lucian's help, Becca had defeated Marguerite's attempts to restore the words to the book of evil spells, but Marguerite promised she'd be back to get what she wanted.

Then there was Lucian. The moment the police officer arrested him for the murder of his sister, Cassie, I found myself slipping into a state of shock. I felt numb, not ready to believe the authorities could possibly have enough evidence to put him back under investigation. He had professed his love for her several times, claiming he hadn't hurt her, and somehow he'd convinced me he was telling the truth.

I wasn't sure what bothered me the most—the idea of an evil witch ready to stop at nothing in her quest to obtain a book of spells that, according to Becca, could cause massive death and destruction, or Lucian locked behind bars for a crime I was sure he hadn't committed. But Marguerite was far from my mind the afternoon I watched the sheriff lead Lucian to the cruiser in handcuffs. Even after the police car disappeared out of the school parking lot, I couldn't think about anything else.

Alex took me out for pizza that afternoon as though nothing had changed. I tried to concentrate on working through our Calculus assignment, but it was nearly impossible to ignore the whispers. Lucian had become the talk of the town with most people seeming relieved. The words "justice will finally be served" and "he'll get what's coming to him" echoed in every corner of the restaurant.

It was all I could do to fight back tears and swallow the lump growing in my throat. I wanted to march over to the police station and rush to Lucian's defense, but I had no evidence, only a gut feeling he was innocent. Every time he had spoken about Cassie, moisture filled his eyes, the grief buried in his expression enough to tear my heart into pieces. I vividly remembered the raw emotion in his voice on so many occasions—the afternoon we sat on the rock overlooking the town, the morning after the Homecoming dance when I woke up in her room and he shared how much she had loved church, and the day we drove out to the pumpkin farm, a place he had last visited with Cassie. The memories of her clearly haunted him, eating away at his soul, but I seemed to be the only person who noticed.

I had no choice but to let Alex drive me back to school to get my car that afternoon. After a quick goodbye, I headed home. As soon as I parked in front of the porch and shut off the engine, I slipped out to the barn, but brushing Gypsy failed to comfort me. My mind miles away and my heart heavy, I went through the motions of putting the horses in and making sure they had plenty of hay and fresh water.

Later that night after I gave up trying to write an essay for one of my college applications, I climbed into bed, knowing sleep wouldn't come easy. I pulled the comforter up to my chin and rested my head on the pillow, wondering where Lucian was. I pictured him lying on a cot in a cell, the image of him surrounded by bars built to hold dangerous criminals depressing me. I went over everything I knew, every detail of Cassie's murder I had read, and yet nothing made sense. Something had to have happened, prompting the warrant for Lucian's arrest, and I'd just have to wait to learn what new evidence had been uncovered.

I tossed and turned for what seemed like hours, hoping the darkness would help me fall asleep at some point. When that happened, I wasn't sure, but the peace didn't last very long. It felt like only minutes passed before I opened my eyes to find myself lost in the woods, surrounded by fog. I stared up at Lucian who sat on his huge black horse, my breath catching for a moment when he spoke. "You shouldn't be here."

The memory was as vivid as though I had stepped back in time. In the blink of an eye, I was straddling the horse behind the saddle, my arms wrapped around Lucian as we galloped through the woods. My eyes squeezed shut for an instant, and I opened them to see Lucian's kitchen. My sunglasses were folded on the counter next to a tray of cheese, crackers, and fruit, and my easel leaned against the wall in the corner. At once, I recognized the day Lucian had cured my hangover before we worked on our paintings for an art project. He stood next to me, his steady gaze meeting mine. "Tell me, Gracyn, do you think I murdered my sister?" he asked.

His question struck me like a knife in my heart, but I had no time to answer. The next minute, I was standing under the clear blue sky at the pumpkin farm. Children shrieked in the background, playing on tractors and hay bales, but their cries sounded muted. Instead, all I heard was the woman thanking Lucian for finding her daughter who had gotten lost in the corn maze. I watched Lucian drop to his knees to talk to the little girl. Before he stood up, she wrapped her arms around his shoulders and hugged him.

I would have cried at that moment if I had the chance. But the scene changed, putting me in front of Lucian's house where I watched him close the door two days ago. A cold glare in his green eyes, he was shutting me out, pushing me away, perhaps because he knew what was coming.

Standing on the sidewalk, I looked up to see black birds swarming in the clouds, flying above the stone mansion that rose up toward the unforgiving sky. A chill rolled through me when fog dropped to the ground, swirling around the house and smothering me until all I could see was the white mist. Completely engulfed in the thick cloud, I turned in a circle, feeling trapped, lost, and afraid.

My heart hammering in my chest, my eyes shot open and I found myself alone in my room, the familiar shadows providing little comfort. I sat up, catching my breath while the images from my dream flashed through my mind. So much had happened since I'd moved to Sedgewick, but I had a feeling more was on the way. And one thing was certain, I wouldn't find peace until Cassie's murder was solved and the real killer was punished, thus clearing Lucian once and for all.

With that thought, I leaned back on my pillow and tightened the comforter around my shoulders. Closing my eyes again, I prayed for a dreamless sleep.

— —

I barely managed to get ready for school the next morning. The black sweater and jeans I picked out matched my dark mood, making me feel like I was going to a funeral. My thoughts were focused on one person—Lucian. I wondered if he would be out on bail and back at school, but a voice of reason stomped on my hope that I might see him soon. *You might as well go back to sleep because you're more likely to see him in your dreams than at school. If his father bailed him out, he's probably going to stay out of sight for a while. And why would he want to be seen right now? Within hours of his arrest yesterday, the whole town was whispering about him.* From what I knew about Lucian, I suspected he'd hide from the world until the rumors subsided.

By the time I arrived at school, my spirits had fallen to a new low. I had just opened my locker when Alex approached, his cheerful smile failing to lift my mood. He wore a vintage Rolling Stones T-shirt under a motorcycle jacket, his dark hair pulled back into a ponytail. Normally, I welcomed the sight of him, but this morning, nothing seemed to make me feel any better.

"Good morning," he said before planting a quick kiss on my lips.

"Hi," I replied, my voice weak as I forced out a small smile. But it was short-lived when my eyes wandered to the flow of students in the hallway behind him, the realization that Lucian wasn't among them weighing on me.

"Hey," Alex said, breaking my attention away from the crowd. When my gaze settled on him, he continued. "You seem like you're miles away. Everything okay?"

I shrugged, not wanting to tell him the truth. "I just didn't sleep very well last night," I replied.

"Ah," Alex mused, his dark eyes studying me. His smile caved into a frown as he appeared to read the real meaning in my answer. "I think I have an idea of what's bothering you. And I've got some news about Lucian, in case you're interested."

Raising my eyebrows, I perked up at once. "Yes. Of course. The suspense is killing me, so spill it."

He leaned in, stopping a few inches away. "All right. I'll tell you everything I know, but it's top secret. You can't tell a single soul, although you only have to keep it quiet for today because it'll probably be all over the papers by tomorrow."

I nodded, my heart jumping in anticipation. I didn't care about sharing whatever Alex was about to tell me. I just needed to know for myself. "Got it."

"Okay, good." Alex scanned the hallway before shifting his attention back to me and dropping his voice. "Apparently, he and Zoe broke up. She wasn't too happy about it, so she ratted him out. She finally came clean and fessed up that she wasn't with him at the time of Cassie's death."

"She lied?"

"Through her teeth." Alex paused, taking a deep breath. "Everyone knew she was just protecting him, only why she did it is beyond me."

"You never believed her?"

"No. I talked to her about it once right after they dropped the case against him two years ago, but she denied lying. She was very tight-lipped and told me to stay out of it, which I did, at least until he returned a few months ago."

"Is she in trouble for lying?"

Alex shook his head. "Of course not."

"That doesn't seem right. Aren't there consequences to lying about a murder case?" I asked, my thoughts spinning. If she really had lied, then the authorities had a case against Lucian. This was far worse than I expected.

"You would think so, but she's been granted immunity. Of course, that's no surprise considering her father is the district attorney and will be leading the case against Lucian, assuming it goes to court as it should have years ago."

The idea of Lucian being shuffled into a courtroom wearing an orange jail suit shattered my heart. Fighting to stay calm, I took a moment to digest all Alex said. My attention drifting to the students in the background, I caught sight of Zoe walking down the hallway with a friend. Her black hair fell below her shoulders, blending into her dark coat. Her blue eyes remained cold, her expression void of any emotion.

My eyes locked on her as she came closer, but she didn't seem to notice me from across the hall. I was about to look away when she glanced at me, her eyes narrowing the minute they met mine.

Pure disgust filled me while I took in her stare. I saw a bitter girl full of jealousy and spite who had taken her revenge out in the most awful way possible, by putting Lucian back under investigation for a murder no one had been able to prove he'd committed.

Fury coursing through my veins, I focused on Zoe, unable to move my gaze away from her. In that instant, she tripped and fell to her knees, her books flying out of her arms. She gasped when she hit the floor with a thud, breaking her fall with her hands. Several students rushed to her side while others stopped in front of me, blocking my view of the commotion. But I couldn't bear to watch any longer. A sudden pang of guilt shot through me as I realized my dark thoughts must have triggered her fall.

Snapping my attention back to Alex who was watching Zoe, I grabbed his wrist before he could run to her aid. "Wait," I said.

His eyes remained locked on the crowd helping Zoe to her feet and gathering her books. "Okay. It looks like she's fine. Maybe now she'll stop wearing those crazy high heels. I don't know how she can walk in them."

"Maybe," I mused, thankful he thought he knew what caused her to fall. "But back to this whole thing about Lucian. So over two years ago, Zoe told the police she was with him when Cassie was killed and stuck to it even when he dropped her and left town?"

"Yes," Alex said, turning back to me.

"And now she's mad at him, so she told everyone she lied?"

Alex nodded. "That about sums it up."

"But it doesn't make sense. He left her and wandered through Europe for years. Why didn't she come clean then?"

"I don't know. What are you getting at?"

"Just that maybe she's mad things didn't work out since he moved back to town, so she told her father she lied out of spite."

"Are you suggesting she's lying now, and that she really was with Lucian when Cassie was killed?"

"It's definitely possible."

"I don't know." Alex sounded unconvinced. "I never believed her from the beginning. No one did, although the authorities had no choice but to accept her sworn statement."

"Either way, she lied. We just don't know if she lied about being his alibi or if she's lying now."

"Gracyn," Alex began, shaking his head, his tone disappointed as though he was about to lecture me. "It sounds like you want her to be lying now. Don't you want Cassie's killer to be brought to justice?"

"Of course, I do. But I don't believe—"

Before I could complete my thought, Alex put a finger up to my lips. "Please don't finish that sentence. Hearing you doubt Lucian's guilt and knowing all the time you've spent with him worries me. You're not safe with him. You never were, and I'm just thankful he hasn't tried to hurt you."

The conviction in Alex's voice cut me to the core. Like everyone else in town, he believed Lucian had killed his sister, and I suspected nothing I said would convince him otherwise. "I don't know why you're worried. He has never tried to hurt me," I insisted.

"And now he never will. I have a feeling this will finally lead to a trial. They have no choice but to reopen the case, and you never know what they'll find."

"They didn't find enough evidence to convict him two years ago. What makes you think they will this time?"

The frustrated look Alex shot my way told me I'd gone too far. He'd never believe Lucian was innocent any more than I could believe he was guilty.

"Time will tell," he said. "This year is going to be more interesting than I ever expected. Just remember, not a word to anyone today, okay? I was sworn to secrecy."

"Then why did you tell me?"

"Because I felt of all people, you needed to know. You're closer to Lucian than anyone, and I want to protect you. My guess is he'll be out on bail soon, if he isn't already since I heard his father returned to town over the weekend. So consider this a warning and please avoid him if he tries to find you."

The idea of seeing Lucian made my heart soar rather than frighten me, but I pushed my feelings aside. "Okay. I'll be careful," I assured Alex, hoping he believed me.

"Good. Because I don't want you to end up like Cassie."

"Neither do I," I said, frustrated Alex couldn't let go of the idea that I wasn't safe with Lucian. I bit back a defensive remark, forcing myself to smile as I changed the subject. "Did you start the Lit assignment yet?"

"No," Alex said with a groan.

"It's due tomorrow," I reminded him.

"I know. Guess we know what I'll be doing tonight."

"Yes, we do," I replied, my gaze drifting once again when I saw Celeste winding her way through the crowded hallway. Her dark hair had been neatly brushed, falling over her shoulders in waves. She wore a black sweater with army green cargo pants, her eyes alert and free of the haunted look that hadn't left her expression for months.

"Speaking of homework, I should get to my locker before the bell rings," Alex said. "See you in class?"

"Of course."

Alex leaned in for a kiss. When he pulled away, he caught my eye and flashed a winning smile, then spun around and disappeared into the crowd. I grabbed my book bag off the floor, stuffed it with what I needed for the morning, and shut my locker door. Planning to go straight to homeroom, I headed down the hallway, but my attention was diverted when I noticed Celeste at her locker.

Veering off to the side, I squeezed my way between a few students until I reached her. "Hi, Celeste," I said, leaning against the locker next to hers.

"Hi, Gracyn," she said, glancing at me with a soft smile.

"You look good."

"Thanks. I feel good. Actually, better than I have in a long time."

"I'm glad."

She took a deep breath. "I feel like a huge dark cloud has been lifted from over me. I can't believe how relieved I am now that they finally reopened the case against Lucian. I'm sure he'll get out on bail, but I doubt he'll try to hurt anyone else while he's being investigated."

"Are you forgetting he helped us Saturday night? Even Becca said she wasn't sure how things would have ended if he hadn't shown up when he did."

Celeste gave a flippant shrug of her shoulders. "No. I remember. But it'll take more than that to convince me he didn't kill Cassie. He's probably trying to throw us off the trail, make us like him. Well, I'm not falling for it."

Frowning, I resisted the urge to insist she and everyone else stop judging him without concrete evidence. If there was a way to convince her of what I knew in my heart, that he couldn't possibly be guilty, I would have made a case. But I had no hope of changing her mind, so I bit back the words on the tip of my tongue. "At least you aren't scared anymore, and that's a good thing."

"Gracyn, it should mean more to you than something making me feel better. A little girl's life was stolen from her. Justice needs to be served, and Lucian should pay for his crime. I'm just glad it's finally happening. He had two years of freedom, something he didn't deserve after what he did."

"Well, it'll be interesting to see how things play out over the next few weeks. They're going to have to build a case against him, and if they can't find any hard proof, they'll have to let him go like they did the last time."

Celeste sighed, a dark shadow racing across her expression. "I'd rather not think about that. I just keep hoping this leads to a conviction, because that's what this town needs."

Nodding, I kept my thoughts to myself and changed the subject. "Do you want to get together outside school again? Just no more talk about Cassie and Lucian, okay?"

"Deal," she said.

"I mean, a week ago, we almost lost you. So instead of focusing on a murder case neither one of us can solve or change, let's hang out like normal teenagers. I feel like we need to celebrate because you're back."

"Sounds good. By normal, do you mean you're not going to ask me anything more about our world?"

I felt a sly grin spread across my face. "Okay, maybe not completely normal. What about getting together for a ride one day? That would be fun."

"Sure. But you have to ride over because—"

"I know. You can't ride past the Dumante estate. I get it, and that's completely fine."

"Good. Because now that the leaves are gone, it'll be easier to see their house. And I can't—"

I reached for Celeste's wrist, stopping her in mid-sentence. "Say no more. I understand. Now I've got to run to homeroom before the bell rings. See you at lunch today?"

A wide smile broke out across her face as I let go of her. "Yes," she stated. "I'll be there."

With a wave, I backed away before turning and heading into the crowd. Conflicting emotions tumbled inside me. I liked Celeste, and I was glad her ordeal with Marguerite was over, at least for now. I wanted to get to know her better, but my allegiance to Lucian made me feel defensive every time she or anyone else condemned him. I couldn't help wondering if befriending her was a betrayal to Lucian. But the thought of losing her friendship, one of the few I had right now, made me feel awfully lonely. I'd just have to find a way to change the subject any time Lucian came up in conversation.

Pushing Celeste and Lucian out of my mind, I dodged the students still lingering in the hall on my way to homeroom. My first class couldn't begin soon enough.

2

As I expected, Lucian didn't show up at school that day. Surprisingly, I was able to focus on my classes even though I occasionally wondered if he'd been released on bail yet.

By the time I got home, I had more than enough homework to consume my afternoon and evening. With only a minute to spare, I stopped by the pasture fence and said a quick "hello" to Gypsy who approached as soon as she saw me. Her breath blew out in a fog from the cold air, her coat thick and ready for winter.

After I gave her a pat, she turned and trotted back to Cadence and Prince, her hooves crunching on the fallen leaves. My book bag hanging from one shoulder over my coat, I walked across the driveway to the house, my shoes grinding on the gravel. Becca hadn't returned from work yet and Gabriel was still in Boston, so I let myself in before heading straight up to my room where I spent the next several hours buried in homework.

Sometime after the sun went down, giving way to darkness outside my window, I heard Becca return home. Doors opened and shut, chairs scraped along the floor, and the dogs trotted across the house to go out and then back again when they returned.

I finished the essay I was working on and shut down my laptop, my grumbling stomach telling me it was time for dinner. Ready for a break, I left my books behind and rushed out of my room.

As soon as I stepped onto the top stair, I heard a knock at the front door, making me pause. Becca walked across the room wearing jeans and a purple sweater, her blonde hair reaching below her shoulders. She glanced up at me, her blue eyes meeting my gaze before she continued on her way to the door. The dogs circled her, whining when she reached for the handle.

Curious, I made my way down the stairs, stopping two steps from the bottom when Becca said a name I'd heard several times before.

"Everett. It's so nice to see you again. I heard you were back in town."

My heart accelerated at the mention of Lucian's father, and I dared to hope he'd share the latest news on Lucian. Raising my eyebrows, I waited for Becca to open the door wider, hoping to catch a glimpse of our guest.

"Becca, my dear. You look lovely as always," replied a smooth, deep voice.

"Thank you. You don't look like you've changed one bit. How long has it been? Almost a year?" she asked.

"Just about. The last time I spent more than one night in town was a year ago when I was back for the Winter Carnival."

"I hope you'll stay for the festivities again this year," Becca said.

"I'm not sure what my plans are right now. It all depends on how long it takes to clean up a few things," Everett said, his voice taking on a parental tone.

A pause pitched the house into silence, and I took that moment to step down to the floor, clearing my throat to get their attention.

Becca shot a nervous look my way before turning to the doorway. "I'm sorry. How rude of me not to invite you in." She pulled the door wide open, gesturing for Lucian's father to enter.

A tall, distinguished man with light brown hair and green eyes, Everett Dumante looked exactly as I remembered from the picture on

Cassie's dresser. Under his knee-length black overcoat, he wore a suit, his tie loosened around a stiff white collar.

When he stopped in the family room, his gaze settled on me while Becca shut the door. Then she rushed past him to stand between the two of us, clearly noticing his attention on me.

"Everett, this is Gracyn," Becca said. "She moved in before school started."

Everett flashed a soft smile, reaching out to shake my hand. "I heard. Gracyn, it's nice to meet you. Lucian speaks very highly of you."

"Thank you. Your son has become a friend of mine."

"I'm glad. I appreciate all you've done for him," Everett said quietly, sounding sincere.

"It was nothing, really," I insisted, feeling a little embarrassed.

Becca tossed a worried look at Everett. "About Lucian. How is he?"

Everett sighed. "He's out of jail, for now. I was at the courthouse today and posted bail for him. As I'm sure you can imagine, he's a bit shell-shocked. It seems I got back to town in the nick of time."

Becca nodded as Everett continued. "But I didn't come over here to discuss the case against my son. It's you I need to talk to. Lucian filled me in about several things, including your health. Becca, it seems you've tried to take on a few too many problems on your own."

Becca glanced at the floor, avoiding Everett's eyes. Deep concern lurked in his expression while he waited for her to explain.

With a long sigh, she raised her eyes to meet his, a forced smile on her face. "Can I get you a drink, Everett? A glass of wine or some tea?"

"Becca, stop stalling. You know this is no social visit."

"Fine," she relented, gesturing to the couch. "Have a seat. This is probably going to take a while."

Everett walked a few steps to the couch and sat down as Becca lowered herself onto the chair next to it. Not sure if I was welcome to join the conversation, I remained standing, my mood falling from the reminder of Becca's deteriorating health.

"Now tell me about your headaches," Everett said, his gaze focused on her.

She leaned her elbows on her knees, looking defeated. "They come and go. Some are worse than others."

"How long have you been dealing with them?"

"Long enough," Becca muttered.

"Have they been getting worse?"

"Yes," she said, exhaling. "But slowly. It hasn't happened overnight. And honestly, I don't want anyone making a big deal out of this. It's been a few weeks since I had one."

"Becca," Everett started, his voice stern like that of a parent about to launch into a lecture. "It *is* a big deal. You're far too important to the coven to not take this seriously."

"Well, last weekend when Celeste was missing, I used a lot of power and I was fine. I thought the use of my power was draining me and making me sick, but maybe not."

Everett didn't look convinced. "You've just brought up the other reason I'm here. Tell me what happened last weekend. Who's Marguerite?"

A look of shame washing over Becca's expression, she took a deep breath. "Marguerite is basically a big mistake." Becca recounted the events of the last week since Celeste's disappearance. Everything she said, I already knew, from the explanation that Marguerite was Becca's daughter to the way Lucian had helped us save Celeste. But Becca stopped before mentioning the book of evil spells, seeming reluctant to share it with Everett.

When she finished, he took her hands in his, searching her face for answers. "Becca, I know there's a lot more to this than you're telling me. What does this witch want? She had to have a reason to take Celeste."

I raised my eyebrows, surprised Lucian hadn't explained everything to his father. *You can't be serious,* a voice snuck into my mind. *Lucian's back under investigation. His problems must make Marguerite and her desire to get her hands on a bunch of evil spells seem frivolous. I can only imagine how overwhelmed he must feel after being arrested for the murder of someone he obviously loved.*

"Becca?" Everett asked, breaking me out of my thoughts. "Please, whatever it is, you need to tell me."

Taking a deep breath, she lifted her gaze, first glancing my way, then back at Everett. "Fine. I'll explain everything. My daughter, Marguerite, is after a book that was placed in my care several hundred years ago by one of the Salem witches before her hanging. The book is pure evil, and the spells it contains were used to cause disease outbreaks, floods, fires, and other natural disasters nearly a thousand years ago. Fortunately, one of the ancestors of the Salem witches managed to take possession of it and kept it from anyone else who might use it to harm others."

Everett watched her, his curious expression turning serious. A dark shadow racing across his eyes, he took in the situation at hand. "How do you know all this?"

"I'll show you," Becca said, standing up. Without another word, she left the room. Seconds later, she returned from the back hallway, a leather-bound book in her hands.

She took her seat in the chair, her eyes focused on the book. A tiny lock held it together, and she inserted a key, twisted it, and snapped the latch open. When she flipped the cover to the side, a dome formed above the pages, showing a small town. Becca placed her hands along both sides of the book and closed her eyes. "Sutton, England, 1210 A.D.," she said.

The village came to life with people hurrying in every direction and horses pulling wagons. The image mesmerizing me, I felt like I was watching a miniature movie. But the peace was shattered when fire erupted from a home, engulfing the thatched walls. As screams shot out through the town, several other buildings burst into flames. People scrambled outside, fleeing for safety. Many made it out in time, but not all. A man charged out of a house, flames shooting up from his clothing. He dropped to the ground and rolled, putting out the fire. When he stood up, he ran back to the house, tears streaming down his face as he called out a name. "Victoria! Victoria!" He circled the home, looking for a way in, but the inferno shot out at him every time he got close.

Oblivious to the commotion, a woman wearing a black gown walked through the town while people rushed by her, hopeless expressions on their pale faces. But the woman remained calm, her arms stretched out in front of her, an open book in them. She read the words, chanting in an unfamiliar language, a satisfied smile on her face.

"What is that?" Everett asked, the shocked look on his face mirroring how I felt.

Becca clamped the book shut, and the dome image disappeared. Then she opened her eyes. "Just one of the many examples of what the book can do. Or rather, the person who has it. I can show you more, but I'm going to warn you, it's not pretty."

"That's quite all right," Everett calmly replied. "I believe you. Where is the book now?"

"I don't have it," Becca told him. "Marguerite stole it from me two hundred years ago, so I put a spell on it and removed the words. They're locked in an amber stone that only I can touch." She paused, a thoughtful look crossing over her face. "Actually, that's not true. Celeste can also touch it, but I don't want Marguerite to know that. The stone will burn anyone else. Anyway, after I hid the words in the stone, I banished her to the crypt in the graveyard for eternity. And I put a protection spell on the cemetery."

"But how—"

"How did Marguerite break the spell holding her hostage?" Becca asked.

"Yes," Everett said.

I bit my lip, cringing at the memory of the night I let Marguerite out.

"It doesn't really matter how she got out," Becca stated. "She's back, and now I have to deal with her. But don't worry, she can't touch the stone and, if the spells aren't restored to the book, it's useless to her."

Everett took a deep breath, his shoulders rising and falling before he spoke. "Of course this is something I'm going to worry about. This behavior is unacceptable. We can't ignore her. She already threatened Celeste, so she obviously knows who to target."

"I know, Everett," Becca said with a long sigh. "But you have enough to deal with right now. Just worry about handling the case with Lucian, and I'll take care of Marguerite. She's my problem, not yours and certainly not the rest of the coven's."

"Becca, there's no way I'm going to let you handle this on your own. You're not alone in this town, and I'm not about to let you try to resolve something like this without any help from the rest of us. We might be a bit reclusive at times, but we're there for each other. I know you'd never let one of us deal with something like this on our own, so let us help you."

"Everett—"

"I'm not taking no for an answer," he insisted.

"You have enough going on. Don't you need some time to take care of things with Lucian?"

"A little diversion from that situation would probably be good for us," Everett admitted.

Before she could object again, a light tap sounded on the front door, breaking my attention away from them. I snapped my gaze to the door, thankful for the distraction from the book lying on the coffee table. "I'll get that," I said, signaling Becca and Everett to stay where they were.

I rushed across the room and whipped the door open. My breath caught in my throat at the sight of Lucian who stood on the front porch, his expression solemn, his hands buried in his coat pockets. His wrinkled black shirt hung over the waistband of his jeans, but the cross necklace that always stole my attention was missing.

"Lucian," I muttered, my heart thumping in my chest.

"Hello, Gracyn," he said, his tone flat. "I'm looking for my father. I've been waiting in the car, but I didn't expect him to take so long."

I stepped aside, and Lucian glanced into the room as Everett stood up. "Sorry, son, but I'm going to need a few more minutes. You're welcome to join us."

Lucian shot his father a stone-cold look. "I'll wait outside." Without a single glance my way, he turned and walked across the porch.

I didn't hesitate to follow Lucian outside. After shutting the door behind me, I wrapped my arms around my chest to ward off the cold air making its way through my sweater. A shiver raced up my spine, but I couldn't tell if it was from the bitter temperatures or Lucian's icy demeanor. He leaned on the railing, his back to me, the barn across the driveway beyond him hidden by the black cloak of night.

Without saying a word, I waited, hoping he'd turn his attention to me. Instead, he stared out into the abyss, seeming lost in thought. I wanted to reach out to him, to promise things would work out, but I couldn't, not when I wasn't sure.

After a few seconds, I cleared my throat and inched closer to him. Leaning my elbow on the railing, I gazed up at him. His mouth was flattened into a frown, his dilated pupils masking the color in his eyes. I held little hope I could break through his sullen mood, but I had to try.

"I've been worried about you," I said softly.

He let out a quick breath, his eyes not moving toward me. "Please don't. I'm the last person who should be on your mind."

"Are you kidding me? You're the only person on my mind right now," I said before I could stop the brutally honest words from tumbling out. If I was putting my heart out there, I didn't care. I'd say anything to get through to him and let him know how I felt.

"I'm sorry to hear that because I'm a lost cause. You have too much to risk by wasting your time with me."

"Really? What about when you came over here and we rode up to the rock? Or the day you took me to the pumpkin farm? Was I wasting my time then?"

"Those were better days. But unfortunately, they're over."

"They don't have to be. When this is resolved—"

Lucian whipped around to face me, his eyes locking with mine. "You don't get it, do you? Zoe came forward, told the authorities she lied about being with me when Cassie was killed. They might as well put the nail in my coffin. I'm as good as convicted."

"Did she lie? About being with you, that is?"

Lucian nodded, the defeat seeming to torment him. "Yes, Gracyn, she did. I was alone when Cassie died at the hands of a monster. If you must know, I was up on the rock painting that afternoon. I have no alibi, no evidence to prove I didn't kill my sister."

"They need more than that to convict you."

He sighed, appearing as though he didn't believe me. "Perhaps. But this is a small town, and they're looking for anything to put me away."

"So far, all I see is circumstantial evidence. Won't your father hire the best defense attorney he can find?"

"Of course. But—"

"No," I shot back. "Don't you dare give up this fight. I can tell you're ready to let them crucify you, and I don't know why. You can't accept anything other than the truth. What about the people who need you?"

"I'm not sure I understand."

"I mean your mother. How is she?"

"She's stable, for the time being. But if she doesn't check into a rehab program as soon as they release her from the hospital, I'm worried she'll overdose again. I'd like to fly out to Hawaii and spend some time with her, but I can't leave town while I'm out on bail."

"I'm glad to hear she's better. I'm sure it's hard on you to be so far away from her."

"Especially now that he's back." Lucian gave a swift nod to the door, indicating he meant his father, the bitterness in his tone unmistakable.

"I would think that's a good thing. He bailed you out, didn't he?"

Lucian nodded, the contempt never leaving his eyes.

"And he's in there talking to Becca about Marguerite," I said. "He wants to help Becca clean things up, but he's also worried about her headaches."

"We're all worried about that. If something happens to her now, we'll only have Celeste. Celeste is very young compared to Becca. It isn't fair to dump the weight of what three normally do on her shoulders, especially at a time like this with a diabolical witch running around. Becca and Celeste will be needed now more than ever until Marguerite is stopped."

"I understand. I just wish there was something I could do. I can't tell you how much I regret following the wolf into the woods the night of the dance. If I hadn't been so foolish, none of this would be happening."

"I hardly think you were foolish. She manipulated you to get what she wanted. And now she's causing chaos in more ways than one."

"What does that mean?" I asked with the sinking feeling there was something he wasn't telling me.

Shifting his eyes to gaze out into the darkness, Lucian inhaled deeply. "It's nothing, really. It would have happened eventually."

"What are you talking about? You're scaring me. Please, I don't want any more surprises."

He looked at me out of the corner of his eye before glancing away again. "Maggie, or Marguerite as we now know her, told Zoe about our day at the pumpkin farm. That's why Zoe broke up with me. And when she did, she told me I'd be sorry. Now I know she meant it, although I pretty much knew she'd run to her father and tell him we weren't together when Cassie was killed."

I sucked in a sharp breath, the guilt nearly choking me. First Celeste, now Lucian. The list of Marguerite's targets was growing. "Lucian," I started, not sure how to put my regret into words. "I had no idea. I'm so sorry. If I'd known all hell was going to break loose on the ones I care about, I never would have let Marguerite out. I would have fought the pain because all this isn't worth it."

"Gracyn," Lucian said, turning to me, his expression softening. "I don't blame you for any of this. Marguerite used you, and she would have gotten out of the crypt one way or another. As for Zoe, we weren't going to last much longer. I tried to keep it together with her, but it was getting old really fast. It was all an act with her, one I continued to pursue because I knew she'd turn on me the minute I broke up with her. If Marguerite hadn't meddled, we still would have broken up. It was just a matter of time."

"You can't be sure of that."

"I'm as sure of it as I am that the sun will rise tomorrow. You see, she knew."

"Knew what?"

"That my heart couldn't possibly belong to her when—" His voice faded away, and his eyes met mine, brimming with an unmistakable longing.

"When what?" I whispered, almost afraid of his answer.

At that moment, the door behind us opened, breaking the tension and stealing my one chance to get an answer. My hopes plunging, I pushed my question aside for now. Between Lucian's arrest and Marguerite's threats, there were far more important issues to deal with. Finding out why Lucian could no longer give his heart to Zoe would have to wait.

"Ready to go, son?" Everett asked, stepping out onto the porch.

"Yes," Lucian replied.

Everett turned to Becca who stood in the doorway. "I'm glad we had a chance to talk. You're a dear friend, Becca, and I'm not leaving town until Marguerite has been stopped. When will Gabriel be home?"

"Friday."

"Good. We'll meet again soon." Everett shifted his attention to me. "Gracyn, it was very nice to meet you. I wish it had been under better circumstances, but we'll get there one day," he told me with a warm smile.

"I hope so. It was nice to finally meet you as well," I said.

Everett acknowledged my words with a nod before placing a hand on Lucian's shoulder. "We'd best be going now."

Lucian drew in a deep breath and tossed one last look my way. Then he turned and marched down the steps without a word. Seconds later, he and his father drove away, the red taillights disappearing in the distance.

The silence returning, I spun around to face Becca. "I presume you and Lucian's father will be working on a plan to put Marguerite back in the crypt. Well, count me in. I'll help in any way I can," I said, determination in my voice.

After what Marguerite had done to Lucian, I was ready to make her pay.

3

The rest of my week dragged by. Lucian didn't return to school, and I didn't see him on the trails the one afternoon I managed to sneak in a ride before dashing up to my room for another long night of homework.

I expected Marguerite to show up at any moment, but she didn't return that week. Her absence left me feeling unsettled, as though I was constantly looking over my shoulder, waiting for her to jump out when I least expected it. I couldn't help wondering if Becca felt the same way. More than once, I heard her pacing the floors downstairs, as though frustrated with the wait. We hadn't spoken of Marguerite since Everett left the other night, but I suspected Becca was preoccupied with thoughts of her daughter, wondering when, not if, she would strike again.

Alex was the only light in my life that week. He met me in the hall at school every day and, when he suggested a quiet date for Saturday night, I eagerly accepted. My only other option would have been spending the evening alone, and that was the last thing I wanted with the heavy thoughts of Marguerite and Lucian weighing on me. Any time spent with Alex would provide a welcome distraction.

Saturday evening, after dressing in jeans, a burgundy sweater, and black boots, my hair straightened from the blow dryer, I rushed out of my room and down the stairs. The house was quiet, something I'd gotten used to over the last week. Ready to escape for the night, I went directly to the coat closet and grabbed my jacket. After putting it on, I headed out the front door. The sun had fallen below the treetops, casting hazy shades of purple across the twilight sky. A brisk wind blew, sweeping a few fallen leaves over the gravel driveway.

As I reached my car, Gabriel approached, rubbing his hands on his dusty jeans, his golden hair reminding me of a halo against the fading light. He had returned from Boston late the night before, but I hadn't seen or spoken to him all day.

"Hi, Gracyn," he said when he stopped, his blue eyes studying me. "Going out?"

"Yes," I replied, opening the car door. I was about to get in when Gabriel stepped closer.

"Really?" he asked, sounding curious, his eyebrows raised.

Nodding, I drew in a long sigh. "It is Saturday night," I said, not expecting the sarcasm that slipped into my voice.

"Of course. And I'm glad you're getting out, as long as you're being safe."

"And by being safe, you mean you want to make sure I'm not going out with Lucian," I said, meeting Gabriel's knowing gaze.

"Exactly," he stated.

"Well, you have nothing to worry about. I'm headed over to Alex's. He's waiting for me, so I've got to run. I didn't see Becca when I left, so will you tell her I'm not sure when I'll be home?"

"Of course. Have a nice night." Gabriel gave a quick wave before walking away.

I watched him head up the steps until he disappeared into the house, my mood souring from the reminder of his dislike for Lucian.

Shaking my head, I forced myself not to think about Lucian. I hadn't seen him since he'd left with his father several days ago, and the last thing I needed was to get carried away wondering how he was when I had a date with Alex tonight. Hoping I could stick to my plan, I hopped into my car and started the engine.

Ten minutes later, my GPS led me directly to Alex's red brick house that sat far back from the road, tucked into a wooded lot hidden from neighboring houses. Green shutters adorned every window on the front, and a ceramic birdbath stood among the bushes in the mulch beds. Lights burned from the inside, dark shadows stretching across the front lawn as dusk turned to night.

I parked in front of the garage and jumped out of the car. After tucking the keys in my pocket, I hurried down the sidewalk to the front door. The temperatures were falling fast, and I hugged my arms around my chest, only moving my arm away for a quick second to ring the bell.

Alex opened the door at once, greeting me with a dashing smile. "You made it. I hope you didn't have any problems finding the place."

"Not at all," I said. "Just like you told me, the GPS led me here without a single wrong turn." I stepped into the house while Alex shut the door behind me. After taking my jacket off, I folded it over my arms.

"Here. Let me hang that up for you," Alex offered, taking it from me before turning to the coat closet and grabbing a hanger. He hung up my jacket, closed the door, and leaned against it, his smile never wavering. "I hope you're hungry. The pizza got here a few minutes ago."

"Yes, I am. I spent most of the day on homework and didn't eat much. It's amazing how fast time flies when I have so much to do." I felt lame using homework as an excuse, but I couldn't tell him the truth—that worrying about Lucian and Marguerite had held my appetite hostage for days.

"I'm just glad you found some time to take a break and come over," Alex said, a teasing sparkle in his eyes.

"Of course," I answered, his playful expression making me feel a little self-conscious. "What's that look for? Do I have something in my teeth or something?"

"No. I was just realizing this is our first night staying in."

"And is that a good thing?"

"Yes," he declared, sliding an arm around my waist and pulling me against him. "I'll show you why." With a confident gleam in his eyes, he kissed me.

The moment his lips touched mine, I tensed up, unable to lose myself in his arms as I had in the past. I wanted to enjoy his kiss, to return the affection he showed me, but something held me back, nagging at me, as though I wasn't where I should be.

Before I could control my thoughts, an image of Lucian flashed through my mind, a complete betrayal to the night I had planned. *Great. You've done it again. You have one of the most desirable guys at school treating you like a queen, and all you can think about is dark, brooding Lucian. Lucian has more problems than ever right now. Do you honestly believe he's thinking about you tonight?*

No, I didn't expect Lucian to be pining over me when he was being looked at under a microscope by the police who seemed to want nothing more than to lock him up and throw away the key. But the words in my mind made me realize what was different tonight. Lucian might have the authorities breathing down his neck, but he was free from Zoe, making me wonder if I'd have a chance with him someday.

When Alex lifted his head, the mischievous look in his eyes told me he had no idea my thoughts were a million miles away. "As much as I'd love to continue this right now, I want you to get something to eat," he said. "Besides, we have all night for more of that."

Biting my lip, I took in his smile, a sudden uneasiness racing through me. I wasn't sure what he expected out of tonight, and I had to be careful to make sure things didn't go too far. But when my stomach grumbled, I decided my concerns weren't worth worrying about. "The pizza smells great. Lead the way."

Smiling, Alex gestured down the hall. "After you."

I nodded before walking ahead of him, glancing at the family photographs hanging on the light brown walls. Each framed portrait captured Alex with his parents over the years, some showing him as a young boy of elementary school age, his hair short, his frame thin and lanky. His parents shared his dark complexion and black hair, the family resemblance standing out in every picture. I had almost reached the end of the hall when I stopped to study a photograph of Alex at about three or four years old wearing a red sweater with a train on the front, a Christmas tree lit up in the background.

"Is this you?" I asked.

"Yes," he said with a groan. "I knew these pictures would be the death of my dating life."

"What? No, I think it's very endearing." I studied the little boy's joyful smile, but my mood fell when the pictures reminded me that my own family history was a question mark. The mother I thought was mine had adopted me and never told me. And Becca apparently knew who my birth mother was, but wouldn't tell me. A jealous streak shooting through me, I realized I'd never have what Alex had with his parents.

"What's wrong?" he asked gently, touching my shoulder from behind.

Taking a deep breath, I turned with a forced smile on my face. "Nothing. Sorry. I think all these family pictures reminded me of how far away my mom is, that's all." And now, I didn't even know who my birth mother was.

"Do you miss her?"

"Um, yes, of course," I said, faltering for words. "But I don't want to talk about her, okay? I'm sorry. Tonight is supposed to be fun, right?"

"Yes, it is," he said with confidence before softening his tone. "But you know you can always talk to me about anything, right?"

My eyes meeting his, I recognized the sincerity in their dark depths. "I know. And thank you. But let's eat. I'm starving. No more distractions." Without waiting for him to respond, I continued down the hall and into the kitchen.

Oak cabinets and stainless steel appliances lined the wall to the left, an island running parallel to them. Recessed lighting reflected in the speckled granite countertops, and a circular table sat in a nook surrounded by windows. White curtains pulled to the sides framed the view of a small backyard tucked between the house and the woods, at least what little of it could be seen in the fading light.

The table was set for two, and I took a seat before helping myself to a slice of veggie pizza from the box in the center.

Alex pulled a two-liter bottle of ginger ale out of the refrigerator, then sat down across from me. After placing the bottle to the side, he reached for the pizza.

"How was practice with the band last night?" I asked.

"Great. But it's probably one of our last sessions for a while since we don't have any more gigs lined up for the rest of the year." When I looked at him, a bit surprised by this, he smiled. "That's right. I'll have more time to spend with you now. And of course, you have to be my date at the Winter Carnival dance."

"I've heard that mentioned a few times. What is it?"

Alex swallowed the bite in his mouth. "Just a fun event to get everyone in the holiday mood. There will be activities all weekend, not like the Harvest Festival which is only one day. The town goes all out with decorations and holds a snow-sculpting contest. They even have horse-drawn sleigh rides. And then there's my personal favorite, the dance on Saturday night."

"Tell me about the contest."

Alex raised his eyebrows with a smile. "Why? Do you plan on entering?"

"Who, me? No, I doubt it. I'm only good at art on paper. But it might be interesting to check out what others make."

"It is. Some people get really elaborate, too. They make houses, churches, animals."

"Animals? Like what?"

"The most common are dogs, horses, maybe even a wolf. But I think the coolest sculpture I saw a few years ago was an ocean collage with fish, dolphins, starfish, and even an octopus."

I couldn't help laughing. "That sounds pretty crazy. I've never heard of such a thing before."

Alex laughed, reaching for his drink. "You also never lived in Sedgewick before, either."

"You have a very good point. But what if there isn't any snow?"

"There's always snow," Alex declared before taking another bite of pizza, his gaze meeting mine.

"Must be nice. Back in Maryland, it rarely snowed in December. The carnival sounds like a lot of fun. When is it?"

"Two weeks after Thanksgiving."

"And where is the dance held?"

"In the town hall next to the park. That will also be decorated like you won't believe with lights everywhere and Christmas trees in every corner."

"Sounds amazing."

"It is, you'll see. It's a black-tie extravaganza, so make sure you get a formal gown."

I smiled with a soft chuckle. "You make it sound like I'll be going to a ball."

"Yes, it's been called that before. But don't worry, it's really fun. Not stuffy like you'd imagine a ball might be."

"Well, I'm sure I'll have a great time if I'm with you," I said, my heart pitching at my own words when Lucian returned to the forefront of my thoughts.

"Of course you will," Alex said, not appearing to notice I wasn't as convinced as I tried to sound. "But now, back to serious business. How are you coming with your college applications?"

I groaned inwardly at the image of the unfinished paperwork sitting on my desk at home. I'd had every intention of submitting my applications a few weeks ago, but between Marguerite's threats and Lucian's arrest, I'd lost my focus. "It's going a little slow," I admitted.

"Maybe you can finish over Thanksgiving break. It's only three weeks away."

I forced myself to smile as though Alex had given me the perfect solution. "I hope so. Wow, I can't believe I've been here almost three months."

"That's right. You have. And you're still here," he joked, grinning from ear to ear. "Glad to see this town hasn't scared you away yet."

"Yet," I mused, my spirits slinking away once again at the thought of the supernatural world lurking in Sedgewick. Not wanting to talk about the town, I changed the subject. "What movie did you get for tonight?"

He rattled off the names of two recent action movies. "I'll watch either one. You pick."

"How about a double feature?" I suggested.

"Really? Because it'll be pretty late by the time we finish both of them."

"That's okay. I don't have a curfew. I can stay out as late as I want." I doubted Becca would be waiting up for me, especially since Gabriel had probably told her I was out with Alex for the night.

"Cool. Want to start now? We can finish eating in the family room."

"Sounds good to me," I said with a smile. "Let's go."

⌒   ⌒

"Gracyn, wake up."

I took a deep breath and forced my sleepy eyes to open. Yawning, the first thing I saw was Alex hovering above me. The room was dark, and shadows from the credits scrolling up the TV screen danced across the wall. "Did I fall asleep?" I asked, sitting up on the couch.

"Yes. I think your eyes were closed by the time you finished your last bite."

I glanced at the empty plate on the end table. "Sorry. I don't think I realized how tired I was. What time is it?"

"Eleven-thirty," Alex replied, tucking a stray lock of hair behind my ear. "Wow. That homework must have really worn you out."

"No, it's probably not from studying. I did some barn chores and then took Gypsy out for a ride this morning. That's more of a workout than it sounds like."

"As long as I didn't put you to sleep."

"Never," I said, flashing what I hoped was a convincing smile.

"Good. Because sometimes I can't figure you out."

I slid my legs off the couch while Alex backed up and took a seat on the coffee table in front of me. "I'm sorry," I said. "Don't take anything I do personally. I've just had a lot on my mind lately, especially this whole thing with Lucian."

"I wish you wouldn't let that bother you so much," Alex said, his tone falling flat.

I glanced away, wishing I hadn't mentioned Lucian. Looking back at Alex, I flashed an apologetic smile. "It's just heartbreaking to hear the rumors. I feel badly for him and his family."

"There's nothing you or anyone else can do," Alex said, his voice softening. "You'd be better off if you forgot about it. Let the authorities deal with him. The sooner they convict him, the better."

I nodded, trying not to let my emotions show. Alex's words were no different than what I'd heard all week, but they still hit me where it hurt, almost prompting tears to form in my eyes. At that moment, all I wanted was to go home. "Listen, if it's okay with you, I think I should take off now. I'm pretty tired."

Disappointment raced across Alex's face. "You're welcome to stay the night. That way you don't have to drive so late."

Shaking my head, I gently refused his offer. "Thanks, but I'd prefer to sleep in my own bed. I'll be fine."

"You sure?" Alex asked. "Because I meant you can take the guest room, in case you thought I meant something else."

I let out a soft laugh, meeting his concerned gaze and offering him a smile. "I figured that. And yes, I'm sure. It's only a ten-minute drive."

"Okay." Alex stood up, extending his hand down to me.

I took it and rose to my feet. We walked hand in hand through the dark house to the entry hall. Alex let go of me to open the coat closet and retrieve my jacket, then held it up behind me while I slid my arms into the sleeves.

"Thank you," I said, glancing back at him.

"You're welcome," he replied, stepping beside me and taking my hand again. "Come on. I'll walk you to your car."

Alex flipped on the outside lights before leading me out the front door. Stars dotted the black sky, and the cold night air cut through my clothes, the bitter chill waking me up. My eyes adjusted to the darkness while Alex led me down the sidewalk to the driveway, his arm draped over my shoulders.

When we reached my car, Alex stopped beside me as I fished my keys out of my pocket. I unlocked the car, the lights flashing in the darkness before I turned my attention toward him. "Thanks for tonight. I had a great time."

Alex inched closer. "Really? You only saw about five minutes of the first movie."

"Look at the bright side. You can always pick the movie."

"I guess I can't complain about that," he said, placing his hands on my shoulders. "Are you sure I can't convince you to stay? My parents are gone for the weekend, and that big house can get lonely. Besides, I make really good blueberry pancakes. Just don't tell anyone, okay?"

I couldn't help smiling at his invitation. "I won't, but I'm still going to pass tonight."

"Would it help if I begged? Because I'll do it, you know."

Meeting his gaze, I sighed. "I know it's late, but I'm a little weird about sleeping in my own bed," I explained, remembering the morning I'd woken up at Lucian's house in his sister's bed. In a flash, I shook the vision of her room out of my head. The last thing I needed was to think of Lucian when I was with Alex. I had already screwed up by mentioning Lucian a few minutes ago, something I hoped Alex would forget.

"Okay," he said, letting out a long breath. "I guess you should be going. But call me when you get home so I know you're safe."

"My house is about ten minutes away. I think I'll be fine," I lied, wondering if I should take Alex up on his offer to let me stay the night rather than head out alone on the road winding through the woods. As soon as the unsettled feeling slid over me, I pushed it away, refusing to let my fear of Marguerite and whoever killed Cassie take over my common sense.

"You may be right," Alex said. "But the deer are crazy this time of year. One jumped out in front of me when I was on my way home the other day, and they are really hard to see in the dark."

"I'll be very careful," I assured him before opening the door and sliding in behind the wheel. "Thank you for the pizza and movies."

Alex laughed softly. "I think you mean for the pizza and nap on my couch."

"You got me there. See you Monday?"

"Of course." He leaned down and placed a quick kiss on my lips. "Drive safely," he said before shutting the door and backing away.

The car pitched into darkness while I fumbled with my keys. As soon as I started the engine and flipped on the headlights, I glanced out the side window to see Alex waving from the sidewalk. I waved back, not sure if he noticed, then turned the car around.

Driving away from the house was like heading into a black hole. I could only see about twenty feet in front of the car in the headlight beams, so I kept my speed at a crawl until I reached the road where I stopped and looked both ways. Not a single car drove by in either direction.

I turned right and flipped on the radio, hoping some noise would help me stay awake until I got home. Music filled the car while I kept my attention focused on the road ahead. As the minutes passed, I tried to relax, but even the comfort provided by a familiar song didn't allow me to let my guard down. The curves cutting through the woods were sharp at times, and I worried that a deer would run out in front of me at any moment as Alex had warned. The last thing I wanted was to hit one and end up stranded on a lonely road at midnight.

I nodded my head to the music, singing along. As I put each mile behind me, I grew accustomed to the darkness and watched the double yellow lines in the center lit up by the headlights. Weary and ready to get home, I looked forward to climbing into bed.

I continued down the dark road, pushing the car a few miles above the speed limit. Just as I was starting to feel comfortable, I turned around a bend and a person walking in the middle of the road appeared in the headlights. My pulse accelerating from the surprise, I slammed on the brakes. The tires squealed and the car swerved into the opposite lane before returning to the other side and coming to a screeching halt.

My heart thumping nervously, I took several deep breaths and stared out the windshield, watching for any movement. But there was only a veil of black, the space around the car empty and void of any life.

What was that? I thought. *I saw someone. I know I did.* Then another thought struck me. What if I'd hit the person but hadn't felt the impact, and they were now lying in front of the car?

Apprehension settling over me, I remained in my seat, not sure what to do. I couldn't drive away, but I was too terrified to step out of the car onto the desolate road in the middle of the night. My imagination running rampant with images of slasher movies, I went from worrying that I could have hit the person to fearing whoever was out there. "Oh, no," I whispered, shifting into park, my nerves rattled. "This can't be happening. I should have stayed at Alex's. What was I thinking?"

Paralyzed with fright, I didn't know what to do. The car engine idled, the hum barely audible over the music still coming from the speakers. I swallowed hard, too afraid to move.

The stillness overwhelming me, I was painfully aware of being alone. I closed my eyes, praying this wouldn't end like a horror movie with my blood splattering the car.

When a knock on the window broke the silence, sheer panic shot through me, and I screamed. Bracing for the worst, my pulse hammering out of control, I willed myself to look up at the window. Ready or not, I was about to face whoever lurked on the other side.

4

Fear ripped through me as the image of a girl's body found in the woods ended up in my head. In spite of the unsettling image, I forced myself to turn toward the window, first looking down at the door handle. Relieved to find it locked, I glanced up, taking a deep breath to steady my nerves.

A figure loomed in the darkness, but all I could see was his waist and abdomen, his jeans, untucked gray shirt and brown coat giving me no indication of his identity. The notion that this could be Cassie's killer rolled into my thoughts. *Well, don't wait around to find out. All you wanted was to make sure you didn't hit the person. Since he's up and about, it's time to get out of here.*

Snapping my attention to the road ahead, I braced myself for a getaway. I was about to punch the accelerator when the stranger knocked again. "Gracyn. Ha! What're you doin' out here?"

My jaw dropping, I kept my foot on the brake and turned to see Mr. Wainwright leaning toward the car, peering in through the window. His thick hair was a disheveled mess, his bloodshot eyes dilated, and his scruff shaggier than it normally was in class. The thundering in my heart eased up, and I rolled down the window. Cold air rushed into the car, stinging my face, but it was the last thing on my mind. "Mr. Wainwright. You shouldn't be out here like this. What are you doing?"

"Taking a walk," he said, his words slurring together. "It's a nice night." He shifted his weight, pulling his arm back to his side, but lost his balance and fell to the pavement with a thud. "Ow! Damn it!" he grumbled. "Now that's gonna leave a mark."

I shook my head. Unbelievable. Mr. Wainwright, my History teacher, was drunk out of his mind. I unlocked the door and pushed it open, not wanting to move too fast and hit him since I couldn't see where he was. So I opened the door just wide enough to slip outside. "Mr. Wainwright?" I asked, finding him in a crumpled heap by the front tire.

I rushed to his side and knelt on the pavement. "Mr. Wainwright. Are you okay?"

He eased up onto his elbows, his movements shaky and wobbly. Instinctively, I reached out to steady him. "Come on. I'll help you up," I offered.

His bloodshot eyes rolling over me, he stared as if he'd never seen me before. "You're an angel. Thank you," he murmured.

Confused, I raised up a few inches to put some distance between us. "I'm hardly an angel. I'm just doing what any decent person would do."

"No. It's true. Ever since I saw you at the bar before school started, I knew there was something different about you."

I shuddered at his words, not sure what to think. He was my teacher, nothing more. And surely he didn't know what he was saying right now, so I brushed off his crazy rambling. His breath reeked of alcohol, and he could barely keep his eyes open. "Look, do you want a ride or do you want to stay here in the middle of the road and get hit by the next car that comes along?" I asked sharply even though it could be hours until someone else drove by.

He shook his head, seeming defeated. "Leave me. I have nowhere to go."

"Fine." I stood up, taking one look at my car before guilt took hold of me. I couldn't leave him here in the middle of the night on this lonely road. With my luck, another car would come along and hit him, and then I'd never forgive myself. "This is going to be fun," I muttered before kneeling down beside him again.

His eyes closed, he breathed slowly. Watching him, I remembered the night I drank too much tequila and how I'd lost the ability to know what was real around me. I only hoped I wouldn't have to carry him the way Alex had carried me. I'd never be able to get him in the car on my own, or would I? If there was ever a time to tap into my supernatural powers, now was it.

I touched his shoulder, trying to wake him up. "Mr. Wainwright. Please get up. I'll give you a ride home, but I need you to try to move."

He stirred, barely. "Come on," I begged. "I can't pick you up. You have to stand. Please at least try."

Just when I thought it was hopeless, he moved his arm. Lifting his shoulders off the ground, he opened his eyes and held his hand out to me. "I'll try anything for you," he slurred quietly.

Not sure what he meant, I brushed off his words since they made no sense at all. "Ready? Let's get you in the car," I said, grabbing his hand and pulling as hard as I could.

He rose to his feet and leaned against me, his legs shaky and unbalanced. With my elbow hooked around his waist and his arm over my shoulders, we stumbled a few feet to the back of the car. After flinging the door open, I helped him ease into the seat. "Think you'll be okay in there?" I asked as he slumped against the back.

He nodded with a drunken grin, his eyes half open. "I've been worse, you know."

"Oh. Okay, well, that's pretty bad because you're in horrible shape right now. And when you sober up, I think you should tell me what you were doing out here. What kind of guy wanders around these deserted roads at midnight?" I mused, not expecting an answer.

I started to back out of the car when he clamped onto my wrist, causing me to gasp, my heart nearly leaping out of my chest.

"A very lonely one," he stated clearly, as if completely sober.

When his hold on me loosened, I pulled my arm away. "Who did you expect to meet out here? Bambi? Next time, hit the clubs in Boston." Not giving him a chance to respond, I shut the door and returned to my seat behind the wheel.

Before driving off, I pulled my phone out of my pocket and dropped it in the cup holder. Unless Mr. Wainwright could direct me to his house, which was doubtful in his inebriated state, I'd need to call Becca. Otherwise, we'd have what I expected would be a very unwelcome houseguest for the night.

"So, where to?" I asked, glancing in the rearview mirror as I guided the car down the road.

"I don't care. Anywhere is fine," he murmured.

"Mr. Wainwright, that's not helping. You can't sleep in the back seat of my car all night."

"Then take me to the bar," he slurred. "Come have a drink with me."

"Never mind," I said, frustrated. "I'll figure out what to do." He must have passed out because I didn't hear another word out of him.

Instead of going home, I drove to town and pulled into a shopping center parking lot where I could keep an eye on Main Street. The light from an overhead streetlamp filtered in through the windows as I unfastened my seat belt. Twisting around, I wasn't surprised to see Mr. Wainwright's head tilted back. He was out cold.

"Great," I grumbled. "This is just what I need." Facing forward, I grabbed my phone and scrolled through my contacts. I considered calling Alex since he was probably still up, but I wasn't sure if he knew where Mr. Wainwright lived. Unfortunately, Becca was my best bet. She and Mr. Wainwright had a history and, even though I didn't know exactly what had happened between them, I suspected she knew where he lived.

Frowning, I stared at my phone, debating what to do, then settled for sending her a text. If she didn't respond within a few minutes, I'd try calling her. In a hurry, I typed a short message. *Need a little help. Call me ASAP. Don't worry. I'm OK.* After sending it, I watched the screen turn black. Now all I had to do was wait.

The seconds ticked by slowly, feeling like hours. I yawned several times, anxiously checking my watch, frustrated to see only a minute or two had elapsed. All I wanted was to get home and crawl into bed.

Driving an intoxicated teacher home was the last way I expected the night to end. I almost wished I had stayed at Alex's. Then I wouldn't be sitting in a deserted parking lot twiddling my thumbs while hoping Becca would read my text and call me.

Waiting in the silence, I scolded myself for feeling inconvenienced. If I hadn't come along when I had, there was no telling what might have happened to Mr. Wainwright. As messed up as he was, I didn't want him to be hit by a car and injured, or worse, killed.

My phone rang, breaking me out of my thoughts. Sighing with relief when I saw Becca's name flash across the screen, I answered her call on the first ring. "Thank God you're still awake," I gushed, letting out a long breath.

"Gracyn, what's going on?" Becca asked, sounding concerned.

"I'm fine," I assured her. "Really. I didn't mean to scare you."

"Then where are you?" she continued, cutting me off before I could tell her about my inebriated passenger.

"Oh, I might be sitting in the Sedgewick Plaza parking lot with my History teacher passed out in the back seat."

"Aidan?" Becca gasped.

"Who else?" I asked, annoyed once again that I was taking care of someone who should be able to fend for himself.

"Tell me what happened."

I relayed the events of the last twenty minutes, ending with the dilemma of what to do with him. "I can't dump him on a park bench," I stated as I seriously considered doing just that. But then I shook the notion out of my head. "I don't know where he lives. Can you help me get him home?"

"Yes. Sit tight. I'll be there in ten minutes. When I pull up, I'll flash my lights. Then follow me. I know where to go."

"Good. Thank you." I hung up the call and leaned back against the headrest, prepared to wait the longest ten minutes of my life.

It was hard to miss Becca when she arrived. Her SUV was the only vehicle I'd seen since pulling into town. When she flashed the lights, I drove out of the lot and followed her on Main Street.

The storefronts were dark, not a single soul out and about in the shadows cast across the sidewalks by streetlamps. It was approaching midnight, and yet I was wide awake, frustrated that I needed to drive an adult home, especially one who should know better than to drink too much.

On the other side of town, Becca pulled into an alley, drove a block, and turned again. We ended up in a gravel lot behind the row of shops lining Main Street. A few cars were parked next to the buildings, but the lot was void of any signs of life. I stopped next to Becca's SUV, leaving plenty of room to open the side door. As I hopped out, her door slammed shut and she rushed over to me.

She shook her head, her arms folded across her navy coat. Under it, she wore white flannel pants and tennis shoes, and I suspected she hadn't taken time to change out of her pajamas before leaving the house. "Gracyn, thanks for calling me. I can't believe he would be so stupid."

"He's pretty messed up. I've seen him drinking a few times, but he was never this out of it. If this isn't a good reason not to drink, I don't know what is. He could barely stand up in the road."

"Well, let me have a look at him."

I stepped away, gesturing to the back door. Becca looked grim as she opened it, sucking in a deep breath when she saw him. "Damn it, Aidan. What were you thinking?" She bent down and stretched into the car, mumbling at him for a few minutes.

I let her take her time, staring out into the darkness cloaking the parking lot. Only moonlight reached the alley, the buildings blocking the soft light from the streetlamps on the other side.

Finished with her lecture, Becca scooted out of the car. "This isn't going to be easy. I need your help. But at least I found these." She held up a set of keys.

"Is he still alive?" I asked sarcastically.

"Yes. Believe me, if alcohol was going to be the death of him, he'd already be six feet under."

I shook my head, part of me angry for the interruption into my night. But the other part of me felt sorry for him. Something was obviously tearing his heart apart, making him sabotage his life. It was sad, pathetic, and downright depressing. "How does this happen to someone? I mean, he seems like a pretty nice guy. A lot of girls at school have a crush on him. Not me, but I guess I'm a little weird."

"It's hard to tell. Life gets more difficult as you get older."

I raised my eyebrows, figuring she knew that better than anyone after living for several centuries.

"Well, let's get this over with," Becca said. "I'll try to wake him up long enough to get him on his feet. We'll both have to take a side, and hopefully he can walk for us."

"But if he doesn't?" I asked.

She flashed a coy smile. "Then I'll carry him. But I'm not about to make this easy for him. He needs to deal with the consequences." Without waiting for me to respond, she ducked back into the car.

After a minute of rustling, she pulled his legs out while he slumped against the back of the seat. He opened his eyes, a glazed look spreading over them when they settled on her. "Am I dreaming?" he slurred.

"No," Becca told him. "I assure you, this is very real. We're taking you home." She reached around his waist. "Out of the car. You're coming with me."

He flashed a crooked grin. "Just don't leave me this time."

"Aidan, we are not having that conversation again. Now, stand up."

Holding onto her arm, he lifted his shoulders and stumbled to his feet before wobbling. He almost fell to the ground again, but Becca caught him. She took a deep breath before straightening her shoulders, supporting his tall frame as though he were as light as a child. "Gracyn, here, take the keys," she said, extending them out to the side. "His apartment is at the top of the stairs. If you can unlock the door, I'll bring him up."

"Are you sure?" I asked hesitantly before taking the keys. "Because I can help you if you need me to."

She shook her head, a knowing look on her face. "I'll be fine. It's not the first time I've brought him home, I just hope it'll be the last."

I nodded, then sprinted up the steps without another word. At the top, I tried two keys until one slid into the hole and turned, unlocking the handle with a click. I held the door open as Becca breezed into the apartment with Mr. Wainwright stumbling next to her. Holding him by her side, she whisked him across the room until they disappeared into the back.

I shut the front door and turned on a light before rushing through the apartment to find Becca. By the time I stopped in the bedroom doorway, Becca was standing over the bed where Mr. Wainwright had landed in a crumpled heap. She took several deep breaths, as if a bit winded.

"Are you okay?" I asked her.

"Yes, I'm fine," she assured me with a swift glance my way before returning her attention to Mr. Wainwright. She moved to the foot of the bed and took off his shoes while I scanned the room. From what I could see in the dark, the only furniture was a bed, a dresser, and a nightstand. The hardwood floor was bare except for a pile of clothes heaped in a corner. A single window hung above the bed, hidden by a white curtain. The walls were plain, the dresser empty of pictures most people placed there. The room seemed just as lonely as Mr. Wainwright, suiting him in a sad way.

When I looked back at the bed, Becca had taken his coat off and pulled the comforter over him. "There," she said, turning to me. "That should do it."

"Is he going to be okay?" I asked.

"He might have a monster hangover tomorrow, but I'm sure he'll survive. He always does. Believe me, this isn't the first time he's had too much to drink, and I'm sure it won't be the last. Thanks for helping him tonight, even if it was a little awkward."

"I couldn't leave him in the middle of the road," I told her.

"I know. But you shouldn't have to put your drunk History teacher to bed, although stranger things have happened in this town." She shook her head with a somewhat amused grin, even as concern lingered in her eyes. "Well, come on. Let's go home."

I followed her back through the apartment to the front door. When Becca shut it behind her, I asked, "Will that lock without the key?"

She shrugged. "Doesn't really matter. No one's going to break in. He'll be fine," she said before brushing past me.

"That's good enough for me." Grateful our mission was complete, I hurried after Becca who was now halfway down the stairs.

When I reached the bottom, she was waiting for me. "I'm sorry you had to see that. Aidan's a good man and an excellent teacher. I hope you haven't lost all respect for him."

"Maybe some, but not all."

She frowned. "Listen, I'm serious. I need you to forgive him for this, okay? He's still your teacher, and I don't want this getting out."

I nodded sincerely. "That's not a problem. I won't tell anyone, not even Alex."

"Good."

"Under one condition," I added.

"What's that?" she asked with a deep sigh.

"Tell me why he's so depressed. He drinks because of you, doesn't he?" I didn't blame her for it, I just wanted to understand how a guy who could have so much to live for seemed to have given up all hope of happiness.

Becca's eyes glistened. "I wish I could deny it, but I can't. Tonight doesn't surprise me. Gabe and I went out to dinner, and Aidan happened to be at the restaurant. I can only imagine that's what set him off."

Frowning, I couldn't help feeling sorry for him. "At least there's an explanation for his drinking tonight. I know his reputation and all, but the last few times I saw him outside of school, he was actually sober," I said, although he probably hadn't been for long after leaving the haunted house. I clearly remembered him mentioning he was heading to The Witches' Brew for a drink, but I kept that detail to myself.

"I told him years ago we can never be together. He's human, and I'm not. It would never work. Other witches have tried having relationships with humans, and it always ends badly. I tried to encourage him to move away. To go to Boston or New York and start over. But he won't leave. He insists on carving out a sorry existence here even with the reminders of the time we spent together. In the end, I can't be responsible for him. He's made his choice."

"Is that what you want?" I asked. "For him to move away from here and out of your life?"

With a deep sigh, she wiped a few tears out of her eyes and glanced up the stairs at the door to his apartment. "If it would make him happy then, yes, of course. I have Gabe and a wonderful life. I only want the same for him."

I suspected there was a lot more she wasn't telling me, but it was late and I was tired. Now wasn't the time to dig any deeper.

Her eyes dry again, Becca looked at me. "Why don't you follow me home?"

I nodded, ready to put the last hour behind me, but before I could head to my car, Becca spoke again. "And Gracyn, if Gabe asks, this never happened."

5

I missed my mother. Even though I knew she wasn't my birth mother, I still thought of her as my mom. How could I not? She'd been there for me my whole life. I knew she loved me and I hoped she missed me, at least a little. I hadn't talked to her since Becca told me I was adopted and, in spite of everything that had happened since then, I wanted to hear her voice again.

As if she read my mind from across the Atlantic Ocean, she called at eight o'clock the next morning. My ringing phone woke me up, and I grumbled on my way across the room to the dresser, irritated at being dragged out of bed so few hours after climbing into it around one in the morning. When I saw *Mom* flash across the screen, my heart skipped a beat. I hadn't thought of what I'd say to her the next time we spoke, and now I had to think fast or not answer the call.

After a quick debate in my head, I realized I couldn't avoid her forever and decided to deal with it. Hoping this wouldn't be too awkward, I picked up the phone. "Hi, Mom," I said, making my way back to the bed. My gaze focused on the pillow, I longed to climb back under the covers. A faint pinging sound came from the window, a sign that rain was moving in. But the weather was the furthest thing from my mind as I plopped down on the bed, holding the phone to my ear.

"Gracyn, sweetie, I can't believe I caught you. I feel like it's been too long since we talked."

"Yes, it has," I agreed, sounding detached.

"Did I wake you up?"

"No," I lied.

"Well, you sound tired. Late night?"

"Yeah, sort of."

"Uh-oh. That doesn't sound good."

"I just fell asleep at a friend's house last night, so it was pretty late when I drove home. But I'm fine. I was going to get up eventually." Propping myself up against the pillows, I scanned my textbooks on the desk. A long day of homework awaited me, and the sooner I got started, the sooner I'd finish.

"Tell me how school's going. And have you discussed your Thanksgiving plans with Becca? I wish I could come back to the states, but I can't afford the time off right now. The travel alone will cost me a few days."

I hadn't even thought about seeing her for the holidays, so it was just as well that she couldn't make the trip. What would I say to her? At least over the phone I could pretend I didn't know her secret. But it would be harder in person. I imagined meeting her at the airport where the first words out of my mouth would be something along the lines of, "Hi, Mom. Oh wait, you're not really my mother."

Not wanting to discuss the holidays, I brushed it off. "That's okay. I'm sure you're busy with work. Besides, I'll be with Becca. She feels more like family every day."

I rolled my eyes, the tiny bit of sarcasm in my voice sending a twinge of guilt through me. Before my mother had a chance to comment, I launched into the subjects I knew were safe. The 'A' I had earned on a recent English paper. College applications almost ready to submit. Well, almost was a stretch, but I had to tell her something. I considered telling her about my Art class, but that would undoubtedly lead to Lucian, and I had no idea how I'd mention him. He was both a witch and a murder suspect. Either option wasn't a good way to introduce him.

A few times, I came close to asking her why she never told me I was adopted, but I couldn't get the words out. Nothing would upset her more than to think I wasn't happy. I couldn't do that, especially after all she'd done for me over the years.

So our conversation came and went pretty much as the rest of them had. She hung up seeming convinced I was doing well and with no clue about what was really going on. I felt horrible hiding so much from her, but I made a mental note to ask Becca again why I couldn't share anything with my mother. I should at least be able to tell her that I knew I was adopted.

I hid in my room for the rest of the day, drowning myself in English homework and Calculus problems. The rain picked up, the tear tracks on the window hiding the sky every time I looked up from my desk. I would have loved to take Gypsy out for a ride, but not in the cold, wet weather. At least this way I could finish my homework and possibly get ahead for the following week, because there was no telling what distractions the coming days would bring.

— ⌣

Monday morning at school, nothing surprised me more than when Lucian emerged from the crowd and stopped at my locker. The buzzing chatter in the hall fell away as jaws dropped and everyone looked at us. Ignoring the stares, I studied Lucian who stood in front of me, his dark clothes matching his reputation. Before I said a word, I noticed the cross dangling over his black shirt and remembered it had been missing last week when he and his father had dropped by.

Shifting my attention up, I smiled. "Hi," I said softly. "You're back."

"Yes," he said before glancing across the hall at the onlookers. At once, they turned to their friends, embarrassed that they'd been caught staring. Then Lucian looked back at me. "As long as I'm out on bail, no one can prevent me from being here, not even the police. I'm innocent until proven guilty."

I nodded, my mood souring for a brief moment at the idea of a murder trial ending with his conviction. But I brushed off that thought as quickly as it came. The important thing was that he'd returned to school, in spite of the rumors and whispers. "I'm glad you're here. Because you're right. You should be able to go on with your life until this circus is over."

Tilting his head, Lucian flashed a soft smile. "Is that what you think about all this?"

"Absolutely," I said. "I told you two weeks ago, and I'll tell you again. I know you couldn't hurt Cassie. I personally don't care what the rest of them say." I gestured to the students behind him in the hall. "Zoe's confession isn't going to be enough evidence to get a guilty verdict. It's purely circumstantial."

"I think you're the only person in this entire town who believes that."

"What about your father?"

He glanced down at the ground, a solemn look on his face. "I honestly don't know. He's been gone for so long, and then he came home to complete chaos. I know he wants to find Cassie's killer as badly as I do, but I also know he hasn't made up his mind about me, at least not yet."

"I'm sorry," I said, reaching for Lucian's hand. The moment I wrapped my fingers around his, giving him a gentle squeeze, I felt a pair of eyes on me. Looking past Lucian, I saw Alex across the hall, his dark eyes narrowed at us. Instantly, I dropped Lucian's hand, but it was too late. I tried to catch Alex's eye, but he spun around and disappeared down the hall before I had a split second to offer him a smile.

Let him go, a voice rolled out through my mind. *You know where you belong, and now Alex does, too. It's been a long time coming, so follow your heart.* After months of listening to my inner self telling me to resist my feelings for Lucian, I was caught off-guard by the words encouraging me to give in.

Glancing back at Lucian, I noticed a faraway look in his eyes. "Will you be at lunch today?" I asked.

"I'm not sure. It's hard enough being here for class. I might hit the library instead. You know, so I can get some time alone."

"Oh," I said, trying to hide my disappointment. "What about Art?"

He offered a slight smile. "I'll think about it."

"Good," I replied, my eyes locking with his.

"Well, I shouldn't monopolize your time any longer." He leaned toward me, lowering his voice. "It's bad enough one of us has a horrible reputation. You don't need to be seen with the likes of me."

I wanted to object, to tell him I couldn't care less what the world thought of me for being with him, but he whipped around and walked off. Within seconds, the crowd swallowed him up, and I was left alone.

I remained where I was, forgetting the books in my locker. The last few minutes replayed in my mind, my thoughts shifting from Lucian to Alex. The hurt and disappointment in his expression when he saw me touch Lucian's hand whipped a healthy dose of guilt through me. For months, I'd shielded Alex from my growing feelings for Lucian, but I suspected those days were over. I was convinced Alex had seen through me this morning, and I wasn't sure I'd be able to explain my way out this time.

─ ⁓

Aside from Alex avoiding me, my day went by just like any other until the bell rang at the end of History class.

I jumped up from my seat, slinging my backpack over my shoulder as Mr. Wainwright spoke over the rise of chattering voices. "Quiz tomorrow, guys. Make sure you do your reading tonight."

Groans erupted from the students filtering out of the room. I followed the mass of bodies, my sights set on the doorway when he called my name. "Gracyn. Do you have a minute?"

I planted my feet on the floor, feeling a shove against my back when a classmate bumped me from behind. "Sorry," I muttered as she skirted around me, tossing me an annoyed look. Turning, I walked a few steps against the crowd to Mr. Wainwright's desk.

He stood behind the chair, watching me until the room cleared. As soon as the last student left, he offered an apologetic smile. "Thanks for staying after class. I just wanted to say I'm sorry about Saturday night. I really wish you hadn't seen me like that."

I smiled softly. The man before me with his neatly brushed hair and white button-down shirt tucked into khakis pants looked nothing like the disheveled drunk he'd been Saturday night. "It's okay," I said.

"No, it's not," he insisted, taking a deep breath as he leaned against the desk. "I'm—" His gaze shifted down to the floor. "—embarrassed." When he looked up at me, he continued. "Last night is the first night I haven't had a drink in over eighteen years. And I have you to thank for that."

"Me? What did I do?"

"I don't want to be that drunk guy a nice girl like you ends up taking care of. Even if it was just by chance."

"Then don't be," I stated.

He smiled. "I wish it was that easy."

"Well, personally, I don't get it. I probably shouldn't tell you this, but I drank some shots of tequila a few weeks after school started. It was horrible. I thought I was going to die. Why would you do that to yourself over and over again?"

"You're right. You probably shouldn't have told me that," he said, dodging my question.

I felt my cheeks heating up. "Don't worry. I'm never doing it again."

"Good. Take it from me, you don't want to get started down that path."

"Does this mean you're going to give me the 'do as I say, not as I do' lecture?"

He grinned, shaking his head. "No. I'm sure you're a smart girl, and I don't have to say anything."

"No, you don't." I paused before changing the subject. "Do you remember getting to your apartment Saturday night?"

"Not really. It's all a big blur."

"Well, the only reason you got home was because of Becca."

Recognition crept into his eyes as if he remembered something. "I thought it was a dream. She really helped?"

"Yes. She had to. I didn't know where you live. Without her help, I would have had to leave you on a park bench. And considering it was about forty degrees and raining yesterday morning, that probably would have been miserable."

"Yes, it would have. So thank you. I really appreciate it."

"Well, I didn't do it alone. And it's a good thing Becca helped. There was no way I could have gotten you up the stairs to your apartment by myself." I wasn't sure if that was actually true, but it was believable.

"Can you please tell her I said thank you? And that I'll try to stop drinking?" He shook his head, bowing it in shame.

"Yes. I'll tell her. But she defended you."

He looked up, his eyebrows raised. "She did?"

"Yes. She wanted to make sure I didn't hold it against you, especially since you're my teacher."

As he smiled, I glanced at my watch, knowing I couldn't hang around much longer if I wanted to get to Art class on time.

"You need to go," he stated, noting my apprehension.

I nodded. "Yes, I don't want to be late. But I'm glad we talked. See you tomorrow, Mr. Wainwright." I started to turn away, but stopped when I remembered the one question I wanted to ask him. "What were you doing on that road, anyway?"

He looked up from the books he was stacking on his desk and paused, his expression thoughtful. After a few seconds, he sighed. "I honestly don't know."

"It was kind of far from town."

"Yeah?" he asked as though he didn't remember.

"Yes. At least several miles away."

"Hmm. I remember leaving the bar and wanting to get some fresh air."

"Seems kind of far to get some air." I quirked my eyebrows, not satisfied with his answer, but realized it wasn't my concern. What difference did it make why he'd been out there? *Because the woods around here are creepy. And what kind of guy goes wandering through them in the middle of the night?* a voice in my head piped up. *The kind of guy who could kill a young girl,* my alter ego answered before I had a chance to stop the debate in my mind.

I shuddered at that thought, frowning as I looked back at Mr. Wainwright. He looked harmless enough, and I knew Becca was convinced that only a witch could have killed Cassie, but anything was possible. He was in good enough shape that I supposed he could have driven a knife into her horse's heart.

"I thought you didn't want to be late," Mr. Wainwright said, breaking me out of my trance.

"Oh! Yes, thank you," I said before whipping around and running out the door. The crowd had thinned since most of the other students had already made it to their next class. Only a few kids lingered at their lockers, apparently determined to milk every last second between classes.

I took off down the hall, barely slowing to get around the corners. By the time I got to class, I was out of breath. I rushed into the room only to be hit with disappointment when I saw the empty bench by the wall. Ever since this morning when Lucian promised he'd be here, I'd looked forward to Art, especially after sitting alone last week.

The bell rang while I slowly made my way across the room and slumped into my chair, my mood darkening even though Art was my favorite class. I silently cursed myself for allowing Lucian's absence ruin it. Determined not to think about him, I reached for the supplies in my bag and hoped Ms. Friedman would assign an all-consuming project, one I could throw myself into until I forgot the green eyes haunting me.

— —

Not only was Lucian missing in Art class, but Alex was nowhere to be found after the bell rang. He usually walked me to my car, but not today— which didn't surprise me after he'd seen me with Lucian this morning. Part of me felt guilty for letting Alex see the emotions I'd worked hard to hide for months. He'd been good to me, there was no doubt about that. But every time we had a date, something went wrong. As much as I wanted to make it work, I suspected this morning had been a tipping point. I could have tried harder to find him, to apologize and explain once again how Lucian had become a friend, but I didn't have the energy to keep making excuses.

Instead of waiting at my locker in case Alex was looking for me, I headed out to my car in the cold, dodging puddles across the parking lot. As if in a trance, I slipped behind the wheel and drove off under the clear blue sky. After pulling up to the house, I parked in front of the porch and rushed inside to change. I didn't care how cold it was, at least the air was dry. I couldn't wait to get out to the barn and tack up Gypsy. The days were getting shorter, and even if I had five minutes of daylight left, I knew getting in the saddle would erase my troubles.

After bundling up in jeans, a heavy sweater, and a parka, I grabbed my hat, boots, and gloves and marched outside with the dogs. They scampered off in zigzags around the barn while I headed into the aisle, stopping to grab Gypsy's halter before leaving through the back doorway and approaching the pasture.

Gypsy jerked her head up when I reached the gate, letting out a nicker as she trotted over to me. I offered her a carrot and stroked the bridge of her nose while she chewed. "I think we need to move quickly," I said, noticing the sun hid behind a web of branches in its descent toward the western horizon. "This might be our last week to get out after school."

I slipped the halter over her ears and led her out of the pasture. After closing the gate, I continued on the way to the barn with Gypsy in tow when the crunch of tires in the driveway alerted me that someone had arrived. Assuming it was Becca coming home early, I halted Gypsy in the aisle. When I turned to her, my back to the front doorway, a familiar voice behind me made me jump.

"I thought I'd find you out here," Alex said.

I spun around, clutching the lead rope in my hands. "Alex. What are you doing here? I looked for you after class today, but I couldn't find you. I wasn't sure what happened." *Yes, you were,* a snarky voice drilled into my thoughts. *He was obviously upset with you, as he should be. Just like Maggie said weeks ago, how he's missed noticing your feelings for Lucian is a mystery that may never be solved.* Not at all comforted by my inner self, I forced myself to smile, hoping Alex's visit wouldn't be too awkward.

"I know," he said, remaining where he stood, his expression serious. "Sorry about that, but—"

"But what?" I asked softly when he didn't continue, nervous to hear his answer. I searched his face for a sign that it wasn't what I thought, but he wouldn't make eye contact with me.

"But I didn't know what to say to you," he said, sounding confused and hurt. "I think we need to talk."

My heart fell at his words. Not wanting to jump to any conclusions, I nodded. "Hold on just a minute." I turned around and secured the cross ties to Gypsy's halter. Then I hung the lead rope on a hook and approached Alex with a sinking suspicion that I wouldn't get out for a ride this afternoon since making things right with him was a far greater priority. "Okay. Can we head outside?" I don't know what possessed me, but I didn't want to hear this in the barn with Gypsy close.

"Sure. Lead the way," he said, gesturing to me.

With a nod, I walked ahead of him until we reached the back of his Jeep where I stopped and turned. "What's up?"

"I don't know how to say this, so I'm just going to come out with it. I don't think we should continue seeing each other."

And there it was, my fears confirmed. *Oh, please,* the sarcastic voice said, returning to my mind. *Don't act surprised. This has been coming for weeks. You've been using Alex as a crutch even though you've known all along your feelings for him are platonic. Don't play the victim here, because you know your heart is breaking over Lucian more than Alex.*

Fine, I retorted silently. *Perhaps you're right. But if I show no emotion, it will just hurt Alex more.* This called for a delicate balance of disappointment and regret. I didn't want to hurt him, and I hoped we'd remain friends because I couldn't afford to lose one of the few I had, although it probably wasn't fair of me to expect that.

"Oh," I said quietly, looking away from him and feeling a tear form in the corner of my eye. When I shifted my gaze back to him, he was watching me. "Dare I ask where this came from?"

"I think you know. Gracyn, I've tried, and I've been patient. I just don't think this is going anywhere."

"Does it have to go somewhere right now? We're only in high school."

Alex huffed with a painful smile. "I hoped it would go further than my girlfriend falling asleep on my couch at eight o'clock on a Saturday night."

"I'm sorry. I thought I apologized for that, but if I didn't, I'm apologizing now. I couldn't help it. And—"

"Gracyn, stop," he interrupted. "We both know it's over. It has been for a long time. I tried to win you over, to give you time, because I was hoping it would work out eventually, but it didn't. And let's face it, I'm not blind."

"What?"

"Please don't act surprised. You're so caught up in this whole mess with Lucian. I've tried to deny it and ignore the look on your face every time he's around, but this morning, seeing you with him, I realized it's him, not me. He's the one you want." Alex paused with a long sigh, watching me as though he had a lot more on his mind.

"Alex—" I began, but stopped when I realized I had no idea what to say. I wanted to tell him he was wrong, but couldn't because every word he'd just spoken was true.

"Don't try to explain. It's okay. I get it. He's the one with all the mystery, and that intrigues you. I'm not even mad. A little disappointed maybe, but it actually explains a lot. There's just one thing."

"What's that?"

"You deserve so much better than to fall for some guy who killed his sister. I mean, if you'd picked Derek, at least I wouldn't have to worry about you." In spite of the somber mood, Alex smiled. "I might have to kill him, but you'd be safe." Then he frowned again. "Lucian is really bad news, Gracyn. First it was Zoe, now you. I don't know what to think except that both of you have lost your minds."

"Please don't go there. I'm a big girl, and I can take care of myself," I said, knowing better than to try to convince him that Lucian was innocent.

Alex shook his head. "For your sake, I hope so. Just be careful, okay?"

"I will," I said.

"Good," he replied. "Well, I'd better go."

Nodding, I stepped away from the Jeep. I felt numb, as though I couldn't believe Alex was about to drive out of my life. Unlike the last time he'd broken up with me after my tequila binge, I knew he wouldn't be back. And surprisingly, part of me was ready to let him go.

Without another word, Alex hopped in behind the wheel and backed up as the headlights flashed on in the shadows. Then he drove away, leaving me alone in the cold.

6

I stood in the driveway, not sure what to do, when a familiar female voice cut through the silence. "It's about time. Good riddance if you ask me," Marguerite said.

With a gasp, I turned to see her emerge from the shadows in the woods. Her red hair hung in ringlets below her shoulders, providing the only color in the darkness. She wore all black, just like the night she'd held Celeste hostage as collateral in an attempt to force Becca to return the spells to the book.

I folded my arms across my chest as she walked toward me, her stride long and her shoulders square, a confident look in her icy blue eyes. "Where did you come from?" I asked. "And what's that supposed to mean?"

"The woods, obviously. And it means there was so much wrong about you and Alex parading around as a couple that I'm not even going to try to explain it. Anyone could see the two of you didn't belong together. I can't believe he lasted as long as he did with you."

"We might have lasted longer if you didn't stick your nose where it doesn't belong," I said, a little intimidated when she stopped inches away from me.

She smiled, appearing satisfied. "I did you a favor. Aren't you going to thank me?"

"For what?"

"For getting Lucian and Zoe to break up. I would've thought you'd be happy now that he's free to date someone else, like you."

I felt a frown settle on my lips. "Really? I wouldn't exactly describe him as free considering he's under investigation for something he didn't do."

"How can you be sure of that? I wouldn't jump to conclusions if I were you. I spent some time with Zoe, and the things she told me might make you think differently."

"What's that supposed to mean?"

A conniving grin formed on her face, her eyes narrowing. "Apparently, things weren't as great between Lucian and his sister as he may have made them out to be. According to Zoe, there was a little sibling rivalry going on there. Cassie was their father's favorite, bringing out a jealous streak in Lucian."

I glared at her, my eyes locking with hers and my blood running hot. "I don't believe that for a moment."

"Too bad. But let's face it, Cassie was the one with the white horse. She was practically angelic while her brother was the opposite with his black horse. He couldn't do anything right to please his father. Cassie, on the other hand, could do no wrong."

"No," I said, shaking my head. "You're just messing with me. He loved her."

"Hmm," Marguerite mused. "He sure has you wrapped around his finger. But I guess everyone needs someone to believe in them, even the bad guys."

My eyes narrowing, I took in her smug grin. "Who believes in you?"

She laughed, infuriating me even more. "Wouldn't you like to know? Well, I'm not about to spoil the surprise." She paused, glancing beyond me at the driveway. "But I didn't show up to make small talk. I'm on a mission. Where's Becca?"

I shrugged. "Probably still at work where she always is this time of day."

"Do you expect her home soon?"

"I don't know. If she has any errands to run, she could be late. I don't keep track of her every minute of the day."

"I suppose you don't." Marguerite took a deep breath, giving a roll of her shoulders. "But I have nowhere to be, so I'll wait. It's been too long. I'd like to have a word with my mother." Her attention shifting to the house, she brushed past me on her way to the front porch.

Frustrated, I launched into a jog to catch up with her, calling to the dogs on my way. They emerged from the shadows, Snow catching my eye at once while Scout blended into the darkness, his movements barely visible. With the dogs at my heels, I climbed the porch steps behind Marguerite, annoyed by her audacity as she let herself in the house. She stopped a few feet inside, causing me to nearly run into her after I shut the door. The dogs trotted through the living room, their nails clicking on the hardwood floor the only sound in the tense silence.

Before I had a chance to say anything, Marguerite walked across the room to the kitchen where she stopped behind the island. "Hmm," she said, scanning the counters. A second later, she reached for an open bottle of red wine. "Someone has good taste," she commented, pulling the cork out with a pop. "Now, where might I find a glass?" She opened a few cabinets until finding the stash of wine glasses, then turned as she reached for one. "Care to join me?"

I rolled my eyes at everything that was wrong with this entire situation. Who did she think she was, helping herself to Becca and Gabriel's things? And I most certainly did not want to drink wine or any other alcohol after the awful hangover I'd had a few months ago, not to mention watching what it was doing to Mr. Wainwright. "No. That's quite all right. But by all means, help yourself," I replied, sarcasm dripping from my voice.

She flashed me a smile before pouring the wine. Holding it up to her lips, she took a sip. Then she put the glass back on the counter and sighed. "At least someone in this house has good taste." Picking up the glass for another sip, she seemed completely at ease trespassing in someone else's home.

Realizing I wasn't getting rid of her anytime soon, I crossed the room and stopped on the other side of the island, facing Marguerite. "Don't you have any manners? You're basically stealing."

"I'm having a glass of wine. That's not stealing. The book on the other hand, well, yes, I guess I stole that. But it was worth it, or it will be once I get the script back."

"Don't you mean *if* you get the script back?"

Marguerite glared at me before her gaze drifted away. "I really love what Becca has done with this place. You should have seen it two hundred years ago, although I'm pretty sure it's been rebuilt since then. And the bedroom with the study off to the side, that's quite a nice feature."

Confused, I tilted my head. "How do you know about that?"

"I checked it out a few weeks ago when I stopped by. No one was here, so I took a look around. Don't worry, I didn't steal anything."

At once, I remembered the afternoon I returned home to find the door open. "That was you?"

"Yes," Marguerite admitted, her eyes locking with mine. "Don't tell me you didn't already suspect that. I had to stop by. I simply couldn't stay away. After all, Becca is my mother."

Another memory rushed to the forefront of my mind. The picture I'd seen in Becca's room of her holding an infant. Perhaps the baby in her arms was Marguerite. *That's not possible if Becca had her two hundred years ago,* I thought. *The picture is too modern. It had to have been taken somewhat recently. You'll probably have to wait to find out more about it, unless you want to tell Becca you were in her room.*

Frowning at my inner self, I returned my attention to Marguerite, wishing she would leave.

"No, that's not going to happen."

"What?" I asked, confused.

"I'm not leaving until Mommy dearest returns. I have unfinished business to tend to."

"How did you know what I was thinking?"

She flashed a coy smile. "Call it intuition. A hunch. I'm pretty good at picking up on your emotions."

I huffed, immensely frustrated. I was searching for a comeback when I remembered Gypsy was still standing in the aisle and the other horses hadn't been fed yet. Not sure if I should leave Marguerite here alone, I deliberated my next action, assuming she'd do whatever she wanted, whether or not I was in the house. "Great. Well, listen, as much as I'd love to continue this conversation about nothing, I need to bring the horses in. I'll be back."

Turning on my heels, I walked across the room and out onto the porch. Fuming at the feeling of being powerless to get Marguerite to leave, I rushed down the steps and across the driveway to the barn. Minutes later, I finished putting the horses in their stalls for the night and left them with enough hay to keep them busy for a few hours.

By the time I returned to the house, Marguerite was pouring herself another glass of wine. As I returned to the island, she drew in a long breath, seeming annoyed. "Any day now, Becca," she said, tapping her nails against the granite.

As if on cue, an engine rumbled in the driveway. "It's about time," Marguerite muttered, not moving from her spot at the island. Instead, she continued to sip the wine, her eyes glued to the front door as she waited for Becca.

Before I could run outside to warn Becca, she appeared in the doorway, her eyes taking in the scene. "Marguerite," she said calmly, a briefcase in her hand. A long wool coat covered her gray suit, her blonde hair spilling over the collar. "You're back."

"Of course. You didn't expect me to disappear forever, did you? You should know I'm not going anywhere until I get what I want."

Becca held her gaze steady, her eyes on her daughter. "Of course not. What kind of fool do you think I am?"

"Then why don't we get this over with? Just reverse your little spell and restore the script to the book, and I promise you'll never see me again."

With a loud sigh, Becca shut the door. She walked across the room, dropped her briefcase on the coffee table, and continued to the island. "If I wouldn't do it for you two weeks ago, what makes you think I'll do it now?"

Marguerite shrugged with a fake smile. "I figured I'd ask nicely before I have to resort to making threats. Or would you prefer someone to get hurt?"

Becca narrowed her eyes, focusing on Marguerite's wine. "By all means, help yourself to our house and all it has to offer," she said, gesturing to the glass.

"Don't mind if I do," Marguerite said. "But back to business. Why don't we settle this peacefully? I promise I'll get out of your hair if you do this one little thing for me. I'll take the book and move to Europe or Canada, so don't worry, you won't witness my destruction."

"I won't have your bloodshed on my conscience."

"You locked me in a crypt for two hundred years. You owe me."

"I owe you nothing. You know that book has power beyond anything we ever need. You crossed the line, Marguerite. I won't budge on this."

Marguerite glanced at me, then back at Becca. "This is your only chance to work this out."

"By working it out, you mean me giving in?" Becca asked.

"Of course," Marguerite answered, her voice sickeningly sweet. "If I walk out of here without getting what I want, I'll have to resort to desperate measures. Until I get it, no one will be safe."

"What's that supposed to mean?" Becca asked. "Your power is no match for me, let alone the other witches here who will fight with me."

"I wasn't planning on picking a fight. So what's it going to be?"

"I can't believe you have the nerve to ask me that. The answer is and has always been no. You were never good at accepting no, even as a child."

Marguerite smiled as though she knew something we didn't. "Fine. Have it your way." The glass of wine still in her hand, she walked around the island and halted beside Becca. "But I will apologize for nothing. Make no mistake. I'll get what I want, or I will destroy everything you hold dear," she declared, her gaze shifting to me.

Before Becca could respond, Marguerite shot across the room in a flash. She stopped beside the empty fireplace where she threw her glass into the pit, causing a fire to erupt. Then she disappeared out the door, her movement as fast as lightning. Within seconds, she was gone, the door banging the frame in her wake.

The fire sparked and crackled until the flames diminished, leaving only a few glowing embers in the fireplace. Shattered glass littered the floor, the tiny shards scattered in front of the hearth. Silence fell over the house, and I glanced at Becca, wondering what she thought about Marguerite's threats.

"How long was she here?" Becca asked.

"I don't know. Maybe twenty minutes or so. But what difference does it make? She's clearly not going to give up."

"I never expected her to," Becca said with a thoughtful sigh. "Believe me, I know exactly how stubborn she can be."

"So what can we do?"

"I'm not sure, but I'll think of something."

I frowned, not sure I liked Becca's non-answer. "Basically, that means you don't know," I said, frustrated.

"For now," Becca said. "But don't worry, I'll come up with a plan. I always do."

"Well, I don't like the way she looked at me when she made her threats. So if you could hurry up, it would be greatly appreciated," I said. "In the meantime, let me know if I can help. I've got a score to settle with her."

"Really?" Becca asked. "Care to elaborate?"

"It's not nearly as bad as her getting her hands on spells that could destroy people, but she managed to mess things up with Alex." *Indirectly,* I added to myself, knowing the chain of events started with Lucian and Zoe's break-up which Marguerite was responsible for. Whether or not she could be blamed for Alex dumping me, pinning my split with him on her at least made me feel better.

"Uh-oh," Becca said, a concerned look filling her eyes. "Want to talk about it?"

I shrugged, a twinge of guilt poking at my conscience when I realized I wasn't broken up over losing Alex. "No, not really. But just so you know, it's over with him."

"I'm sorry to hear that. I thought something like this happened a few months ago and then you two got back together. I don't want to pry, but is this anything like that?"

Shaking my head, I shifted my gaze away from her. "No," I let out with a deep breath. "It's really over this time. He won't be back."

Becca approached and stopped close enough to reach out and touch my shoulder. "I know you probably don't want to hear this, but considering he's not like us, it's for the best. The longer you date a human, the harder it is to break it off when you know you have to."

"Like you and Mr. Wainwright?"

She nodded, a faraway look sweeping across her face. "Yes, exactly."

I drew in a sharp breath, surprised she was admitting her feelings for him. But as quickly as her emotions appeared, they vanished when she walked across the room and hung her coat in the closet before turning back to me. "Are you hungry? I can make dinner. What are you in the mood for?"

"I'm not sure," I replied, realizing food was the furthest thing from my mind.

"Well, think fast. I'm going to change, and then we can start dinner."

"Okay," I said, sure it would be harder than it should be to decide what I'd like to have for dinner. My nerves were frazzled from the events of the last hour, mostly due to Marguerite's threats, but if I didn't want Becca to catch on, I needed to find my appetite soon. "Would you like me to clean up the mess by the fireplace?"

"That would be great. Thank you. I'll be back in a few minutes," Becca said.

As she headed down the hall leading to her room, I made my way to the utility closet to get a broom, hoping to sweep my thoughts of Marguerite away with the broken glass.

7

ecca didn't say much about Marguerite that night during dinner, but I suspected her visit weighed heavily on Becca's mind. Two things in particular bothered me—the doubt planted in my mind about Lucian's jealousy of Cassie and the way Marguerite looked at me when she promised to destroy everything Becca held dear.

When it came to Lucian, I refused to believe Marguerite. Not once had he ever shown any sign of jealousy toward his sister. I might not have been very good at reading people, but the grief and sorrow lurking in his eyes every time he mentioned Cassie was unmistakable. So I put those thoughts aside, leaving the concern that Marguerite would target me next. As unsettling as it was, I wouldn't let her threats consume me. I'd remain vigilant, but I wouldn't live in fear. I had to keep busy and study hard because once this was all over, I had a future to prepare for.

The next day at school I approached my locker alone, the hum of voices in the crowded hallway seeming louder without Alex to distract me. In spite of knowing my relationship with him had to end, I missed him. I'd grown to love seeing him each morning, and I had a feeling my days were about to get lonely and quiet without his company.

As I sorted the books in my locker, my parka hanging from the hook and my bag on the floor beside my feet, a pair of hands covered my eyes, sending my world into darkness.

"Guess who," whispered a familiar deep voice.

I couldn't resist smiling at the sound of Lucian's voice. Whipping around, I met his gaze, surprised by the casual grin on his face. "Hi. You're talking to me here at school two days in a row? To what do I owe this honor?"

"I would think you'd know."

Letting out a deep breath, I nodded. "Ah, Zoe. Guess that wasn't hard to figure out."

"That's right. She can't stop me from talking to you now."

I wanted to ask why she cared in the first place, but I refrained. If she had considered me competition for Lucian's affection, I was flattered. But now wasn't the time to fish for compliments or remind Lucian he should have been able to talk to anyone he wanted when he'd been dating her.

"Speaking of relationships, where's Alex?" Lucian asked. "He never lets you out of his sight in the morning."

"That's not true," I said, then realized it was. I glanced at Lucian, feeling a frown fall upon my face. "But it doesn't matter now. We broke up."

"Oh," Lucian said softly, watching me curiously. "I'm sorry to hear that. Are you okay with it? Or did you break it off with him?"

I shook my head. "No, to tell you the truth, it was his idea. He said we weren't getting anywhere, and you know what? He's right. Every chance we had at a real date was ruined. I honestly don't blame him. I know he tried, and maybe I did, too, just not as hard." I stopped talking when I noticed Lucian staring at me and wondered why I seemed compelled to explain the details.

"Sounds like it's over for good."

"Yes," I muttered. "This isn't like last time. I know better than to think he'll come back to me again."

"Is that what you want?" Lucian asked.

"I'm not sure. He was the first person I met when I moved here. He was a good friend, and I'm going to miss him. But as far as being boyfriend and girlfriend and having a future together is concerned, that was probably doomed from the start. Although I give him credit for putting up with me this long after my track record on our dates. Let's see, I either got drunk, had a massive headache, or fell asleep."

Lucian smiled, an amused look on his face. "Fell asleep?"

"Yes. That was Saturday night. Don't ask."

"Don't worry, I won't. That's a pretty big blow to a guy's ego. No wonder he broke up with you."

"Gee, thanks for the confirmation. I knew it had to end eventually, so in a way, it's just as well. I'll be fine, but it's going to take some getting used to," I said, not sure if I was trying to convince Lucian or myself.

"Good. But if I may make a request, let's not talk about him anymore. It kind of ruins my mood."

"Really?" I asked, quirking my eyebrows. "Why would you care?"

"Because I don't like the thought of you with another guy. Never did."

My heart skipped a beat at his confession, and I wondered once again if he had feelings for me. Not sure how to respond, I smiled. "You know, this is nice."

"What is?"

"Being able to talk to you in the middle of the hallway where anyone can see us."

"Yes, it is. In spite of everything going on, I can talk to anyone now."

I wanted to tell him he always could have, but I bit back the words.

"And I was going to ask if you'd like me to walk you to class," Lucian said. "If you don't mind being seen with me, that is."

"What? I don't care about that."

"Perhaps you should. I'm a disgrace, you know. People are talking about me now more than ever. Don't the stares and scrutiny bother you?"

I shook my head, frustrated by the truth in his statement. The general consensus seemed to be that Lucian was as guilty as sin. The entire town had already condemned him, regardless of the lack of concrete evidence. "No. I don't care what anyone thinks. Let them stare and let them talk. I'm just glad you're back at school and you're not letting them prevent you from going to class."

"I always knew I liked you for a reason. Thank you," Lucian said.

"You don't have to thank me. I'm only doing the right thing. The rest of them don't know you like I do."

My eyes locking with his, the other students became a blur around us. After a few seconds, I glanced away. "Just let me finish up here," I said, turning back to my locker. Reaching for my Calculus book, I felt a warm glow take over my heart. After all the time Lucian and I had spent together where no one could see us, we no longer had to hide, if that's what we'd been doing. Even if we only remained friends, I was ready for the world to know I would stand by him.

I finished packing up my book bag, slung it over my shoulder, and shut the locker door. Then I spun around to see Lucian waiting patiently for me, his eyes meeting mine right away. "Ready?" he asked.

"Yes. Let's go."

He gave a swift nod before reaching for my hand. The instant he touched me, a tingle ran up my arm and I looked down with a gasp. His gesture felt completely natural and was welcome, but I think it confused both of us.

Lucian must have taken my reaction as a sign his touch was unwanted because he let go of me. Without a word spoken between us, we set off into the crowd, walking side by side. The students opened up a path for us, the humming voices tapering off as everyone watched us.

"See," Lucian said smugly. "I told you they'd stare."

I glanced at the students, grateful when they returned to their conversations, resuming whatever they'd been doing before they gawked at us so rudely. "And I told you I don't care. Let them."

Smiling, I looked up at Lucian, meeting his gaze once again while he walked me to homeroom.

The last person I expected to see that day found me as I was getting in my car to go home after school.

"Gracyn! Wait up!" a voice called from behind me while I tossed my book bag in the back seat.

I shut the door and turned, surprised to see Derek jogging across the parking lot. The sun shone brightly in the clear sky, but the temperature was only in the forties. I wore my parka, gloves, and a knit hat, my red curls falling over my shoulders. Derek looked comfortable in a black leather jacket, his hands bare and his blond hair shining in the angled sunlight.

"Hi, Derek," I said when he stopped a few inches in front of me.

"Hey. I wanted to see how you're doing. Alex told me what happened."

"Oh," I muttered with a long sigh, my eyes shifting away from his gaze. When I looked back at him, I offered him a subtle smile. "I'm fine. Really. It's no big deal."

"Don't tell Alex that," Derek said. "He'd be crushed to know you're okay with this. Although you looked pretty cozy with Lucian all day."

So that was the real reason Derek found me. I had a feeling he wanted to know more about what was going on with me and Lucian than to offer his condolences and check up on me. "We're friends. I thought you knew that."

"But he's back under investigation. Don't you think it would be better to stay away from him?"

"Is that what you really wanted to talk to me about? Because it's kind of cold out here. I need to get home to take care of the horses and start my homework."

"No, sorry. I didn't mean it like that. I was worried about you because of Alex, that's all. And honestly, he still cares about you. I know he's avoiding you right now, but he's taking it harder than he's letting on."

I sighed, hoping the drama of our break-up wouldn't last much longer. "I hope that's not true. But let's face it, I think both Alex and I knew it was going to happen sooner or later. In fact, the longer we stayed together, the worse it would be. So it's for the best."

"I don't think he sees it that way."

"Maybe not yet, but I'm sure he will. Besides, now he can find a girl who might make it through a date without ruining it somehow."

"You're being way too hard on yourself. You've had a run of bad luck, that's all."

"Thanks, but I think there was more to it than that," I said.

"Perhaps you're right, but I'm not going to mention that to Alex. I told him I thought it was just bad luck, too. He really liked you, you know."

"Great. Now you're making me feel guilty."

Derek grinned. "Sorry. Do you want me to leave you alone?"

"Not necessarily."

"Okay. Do you want me to ask you out?"

"What?" I gasped, surprised that Derek would take advantage of his friend's loss.

"I was only kidding," Derek said. "I'm saving myself for Zoe. You should know that."

"Any luck with her?"

"Not yet, but that's because I'm biding my time. You know, giving her a few weeks to get over Lucian. I don't want to be her rebound guy."

"Why not? You might have a better chance."

"Ha, ha," Derek grumbled.

"What about Celeste? I thought you said she wasn't that bad."

He shrugged, looking away the minute I mentioned Celeste. "She was missing when I said that. I was worried about her, but now she's fine."

"So you only said that because she was gone? Sorry, I don't buy it."

Derek frowned. "Look, with her, it's complicated. You and I both know any relationship I have with a human can't last. I have an eternity to decide what to do about Celeste."

"Not if she finds someone else first."

"Like that's going to happen."

"You never know," I said. "Nothing surprises me anymore. I've learned to expect the unexpected, as cliché as that sounds."

"Well, I didn't come over here to discuss my love life."

"Why not? It's much more interesting than mine," I teased.

"Okay, I'll give you that. I was just worried about you and wanted to make sure you're okay. You're a friend, even though I teased you about going out when we first met. Now we know we have a lot in common."

"Yes," I said with a smile. "We do. And it's nice to have a friend. Thank you."

"You're welcome." Without any warning, Derek pulled me into a hug.

For the brief instant I remained in his arms, I looked across the parking lot and my smile faded. Lucian stood next to his Range Rover, his arms crossed, his eyes narrowed as he stared directly at us. I caught his gaze and smiled, hoping to melt his icy expression. Waving my fingers without moving my hand away from Derek's back, I held my gaze on Lucian steady.

To my surprise, his frown softened and he gave a swift nod my way before jumping in his truck and driving off. A warm glow settling over me, I knew it wouldn't be long before I'd see him again.

When Derek released me, we said our goodbyes before he headed across the parking lot. I hopped in my car, turned on the engine and backed out of the parking space. Then I began the drive home, ready to tackle the books for the night as long as I could keep Lucian out of my mind.

8

For the rest of the week, Lucian met me at my locker every morning. It was quite the change from starting my day off with Alex's smile, but Lucian made me forget what I'd had only a week ago. It seemed hard to believe that the guy who'd captured my attention behind the scenes, remaining untouchable at school, had turned to me when he needed a friend.

A part of me hoped Lucian would ask me out for the weekend, but when that didn't happen, I shamed myself for the disappointment settling over me. *He has far more important things on his mind than getting a date,* a voice of reason told me more than once on Friday. *Give the poor guy some time to get through this. If you were being investigated for murder, the last thing on your mind would be starting a new relationship.*

I left school Friday afternoon prepared to spend the weekend alone. Celeste had turned me down when I asked if she wanted to come over for pizza. She mumbled something about needing to get up early on Saturday for a riding lesson, but I suspected she was avoiding me because of all the time Lucian had spent hovering around me in the halls.

Saturday morning, I tried to jump into my homework after breakfast, but my heart wasn't in it. My eyes drifted to the overcast sky out the window, my thoughts on one person—Lucian. The laptop in front of me was propped open, the screen blank. I had an essay to write for Literature, but no words came to my mind. Instead, a voice in my head reminded me that I had all weekend for homework and I didn't need to start right away.

Determined to get out of the house for a while, I jumped up and threw on a pair of jeans and a black sweater. After brushing my hair and clipping it behind my ears, I ran down the stairs, grabbed my coat, and rushed outside. The cold air giving me a chill, I slipped my hands into a pair of gloves, my keys jingling. Without giving my plans any thought, I jumped into my car, not sure where to go.

I had no idea what I intended to do when I pulled up next to Lucian's Range Rover in his driveway. The stone mansion towered over the lawn, and all was still on the estate grounds. I hesitated after shutting off the engine, figuring Lucian would wonder what I was doing here. And I wasn't sure of that myself.

Refusing to let my doubts get the best of me, I hopped out of the car and shut the door. The brisk air nipping at my cheeks, I pulled my coat around my chest and hurried up the sidewalk until I reached the mahogany doors. I held my hand up, poised to knock, but paused, my heart quickening. Before I made another move, the door opened.

"Lucian," I gasped, noticing the long-stemmed white roses in his hand.

"Gracyn. This is quite a surprise," he said casually as he stepped outside and shut the door behind him, his black coat a sign he was on his way out.

"I'm sorry," I said awkwardly, feeling my face burn up, my cheeks surely turning as red as my hair. "I was all alone this morning, and I just...well, I needed to get out. But I see you have somewhere to go. I'll leave." Whipping around, I felt the sudden urge to run away as fast as I could. What was I thinking? Clearly Lucian had plans today that didn't involve me. A tear formed in my eye, and I choked back the lump growing in my throat. *Don't you dare come unglued,* I warned myself. *You showed up here unannounced. What did you expect? He obviously has something to do that doesn't involve you. Maybe you should stop dreaming about him and get a life.*

"Hey, wait a minute," Lucian called out, jogging around me and stopping in front of me. "Why are you leaving when you just got here?"

I halted, wishing he wasn't blocking the path to my car. I had never been so embarrassed. "Because," I said as if I didn't need to explain. When his curious eyes met mine, I gestured at the roses. "Those are beautiful. You obviously have plans, and I didn't mean to interrupt." I suspected a girl somewhere in town was waiting for him. For all I knew, the roses were for Zoe and they were getting back together. I thought he had moved on from her, possibly to me, but I must have been mistaken. It certainly wouldn't be the first time a guy I liked wasn't interested in me. With an exasperated sigh, I looked up into his eyes. "If you could move out of my way, I'll get going so you can leave. I'm sure someone special is waiting for you."

"Yes," he answered solemnly, not bothering to move an inch, his unwavering gaze seeming to see straight through me. "You're right. Someone special is waiting."

"Well, then, you shouldn't keep her waiting."

"Doesn't matter. She's not going anywhere."

Not understanding, I tilted my head, arching my eyebrows.

"Today is Cassie's birthday. She would have been fifteen." Lucian held his emotions in check, managing to keep his voice steady, but I sensed that his grief was taking a toll on him. "She didn't even get to see her thirteenth birthday. I've taken flowers to her grave every year on this day since she died."

My breath caught in my throat as I blinked back tears. "Oh," I let out with a long breath, mentally kicking myself for my unwarranted jealousy.

"Do you want to come with me?"

"Um, no, that's okay. I don't want to intrude."

"You're not. I wouldn't mind a little company. At least on the way to the cemetery. When we get there, I might need a minute alone." Tears welled up in his eyes, and one escaped, rolling down his face and over his five o'clock shadow until he wiped it with his free hand.

"Are you sure?"

"Gracyn, there's one thing you need to know about me. If I don't want you around, I'll tell you. I'm pretty up-front about that stuff. And I'm all alone today because my dad's in New York for business."

"He's working on a weekend?"

Lucian nodded. "Weekends, holidays, all hours of the night. He works nonstop."

"Doesn't he want to visit Cassie on her birthday?"

"I have no idea. He might be avoiding it because the reminder of losing her is too painful. He left yesterday, but he'll be back tonight. Although he said it was for business, I have a feeling it's more than that," Lucian added, his tone holding a layer of disgust.

I suspected there was a story behind his last comment, but I elected to leave it be. If he wanted to tell me what he meant by that, he would when he was ready.

Lucian gestured toward the driveway. "I don't know about you, but I'd rather not stand around here all day talking about my father. Shall we go?"

I nodded, then followed him to the Range Rover. He unlocked it with the remote, the lights blinking once. I jumped in on the passenger side, still a little unsure about going to the cemetery with him.

Lucian slid in behind the wheel. "Would you mind?" He handed the roses to me over the console.

I reached for the plastic covering the thorny stems. "Not at all."

"Thanks." He flashed an appreciative smile before turning on the engine. Throwing the gear into reverse, he backed around my car until we faced down the driveway. Then he eased the Range Rover forward. "So, what brought you over here today?" he asked.

"I don't know. It was a little too quiet at the house. Becca and Gabriel are out running errands, and I wasn't in the mood to take Gypsy for a ride in this weather. It's pretty cold today."

"I know. Look at that sky." Lucian nodded toward the heavens. "I think we'll see the first snow before the sun goes down."

"What?" I asked, my eyes opening wide. Snow in November? It couldn't be.

"Don't look so alarmed," Lucian said with an amused smile that faded as quickly as it appeared. "I thought you were ready for winter."

"I'm trying to be, but we'll see. I never liked driving in the snow."

"I keep forgetting you're from the south. Don't worry. They're pretty good about treating the roads up here. And if you get stuck or you want a ride somewhere, just let me know. I'll take you."

"Really?"

"Of course," he said as though I didn't need to ask. Then he looked straight ahead, his carefree demeanor disappearing when the frown returned to his face.

Silence stretched between us, and I fumbled with the roses in my lap, beginning to feel a bit awkward. Lucian turned onto the road leading toward town, but the scenery changed little. Gray clouds hovered low, skimming the bare branches at the top of the trees now ready for winter. When we got closer to town, houses dotted the landscape, the lawns faded to light brown, some with leaves piled in the corners.

Wanting to break the silence, I wasn't sure if I should ask him about Cassie or stay away from that subject. In the end, I remained quiet and kept my eyes glued to the window. No matter what was said, I felt as though I was intruding on a personal moment even though I knew Lucian wouldn't have invited me to come with him if he really didn't want me here.

Lucian drove through town to the other side and turned onto a back road leading into the country. A few minutes later, the woods on the left opened up into a small clearing. Nestled far back from the road was a white church, its steeple rising up in front of the trees in the background.

After turning into the empty parking lot off to the side, Lucian pulled up to the edge of a small cemetery situated between the pavement and the woods. Gravestones, some tall with square corners and others round at the top, were scattered across the yard. "We're here," he announced.

"Cassie's grave is here?"

"Yes."

"Oh," I said, confused. "I was wondering if all of the witches were buried up in the woods where the crypt is."

"No. Actually, very few are up there, and those that are died hundreds of years ago. Until you broke the spell protecting the boundaries, none of us could get past the fence."

More questions about the hidden graveyard and Marguerite crept into my mind, but I shoved them aside. Now wasn't the time to think about her. "Where are the rest buried?"

He shook his head. "Why the morbid curiosity?"

I shrugged, feeling my cheeks darken with color. "Sorry. Sometimes I ramble on about stupid stuff when I'm not sure what to say." I gazed out the windshield, wondering which tombstone marked Cassie's grave.

"It's okay. But to answer your question, some are buried in traditional cemeteries like this one, and some are buried at their homes."

"Oh." I recalled seeing a tall stone in the corner of Lucian's property along the edge of the forest. "I thought I saw a grave at your house near the woods. Is one of your ancestors buried there?"

"No. That's where we buried Cassie's horse. But we brought Cassie here. We wanted her to be near the church because she loved it so much."

"That makes sense."

"It was almost like bringing her home. This was one of her favorite places," Lucian said quietly, tears welling up in his eyes. "On Sunday mornings, she'd barge into my room and wake me up. If I even considered not going to church, she read me the riot act. She could be quite persistent."

"That still amazes me," I said softly. "You don't hear about kids loving church very often. I'll admit I never got into it. The extent of my church attendance has always been about once a year. Christmas Eve."

"I was never a big fan, either." He paused with a sigh. "It's time I go to her. Mind if I take those?" He nodded at the flowers in my lap.

"Of course not. Here," I replied, giving them to him. His fingers grazed mine, and I lifted my eyes to meet his when a tingle lit up my skin. Pulling my hand back into my lap, I sighed with a faint smile. "Take your time. I'll wait here."

"You sure?"

I nodded. "Yes. I have nothing to do today and nowhere to be. Now go."

His expression remained flat, as though he was fighting to hold back tears. "Thank you." He hopped out of the car, shut the door, and headed into the graveyard, his head bowed and the roses in his hands. After winding around several tombstones, he stopped in front of one in the middle and knelt before it, his shoulders hunched over. Wanting to give him some privacy, I leaned my head back and closed my eyes, prepared to let him take as much time as he needed.

After a while, I began to grow restless as the temperature inside the SUV dropped, sending a chill over me. I opened my eyes to discover a winter wonderland out the window. Snowflakes drifted down from the sky, a dusting already covering the Ranger Rover's hood and the pavement. Sitting up, I looked for Lucian and saw him in front of the stone exactly where he'd been minutes ago. Or was it hours? I had no idea of how much time had passed. His head hung low, one arm extended out to the top of the stone. The roses were propped up against it, the white petals bright next to the gray surface.

Gathering my courage, I slipped out of the SUV. The cold air hit me at once, but I was quickly distracted by the snow sprinkled like sugar on the stones and grass. Even the branches in the distance were outlined by white, the winter scenery reminding me of heaven.

My sights set on Lucian, my heart aching from the overwhelming sorrow he must be feeling, I walked across the cemetery until I reached him. Stopping behind him, I placed my hand on his shoulder. He didn't move, but I heard him sniff, his grief causing a lump to form in my throat.

Fighting back tears, I dropped to my knees beside him and wrapped an arm around his shoulders. Leaning toward him, I locked my gaze with his, the tears in his eyes telling me how hard this was for him. I paused, close enough to feel the warmth of his breath. "I'm so sorry," I whispered.

He sighed, his eyes never leaving mine. "It doesn't get any easier. In fact, when I think about all the time she lost, all the years she's been gone, it gets harder. She should be alive right now, growing into a young woman. But she'll never get that chance," he said, the sorrow in his voice shattering my heart into pieces.

"I know. But there's nothing you can do, nothing anyone can do."

He swallowed hard, nearly choking on his breath. "I hate this day. I really do. It's just another reminder that her death is final and she's never coming back."

I nodded, the snowflakes a blur when tears filled my eyes. "What can I do?"

"Stay with me, please."

"Of course. I'm here, and I'm not going anywhere."

He drew in a deep breath, shuddering as he exhaled. "You know what hurts the most?" he asked.

"No."

"I feel responsible for this."

"Lucian," I started. "You need to stop blaming yourself."

"But it's true. I should have been there for her. I should have protected her. I'm as guilty as whoever put her in the grave."

He raised a fist, about to pound it into the stone when I caught his wrist with speed and power I didn't know I had. Letting go of him, I raised my hand to touch his face, his unshaven jaw feeling like sandpaper. "I will never believe that," I declared, swiping a tear on his cheek with my thumb. All I wanted was to take the pain away for him, but I had no idea how.

"You believe in me. You stay with me and give me the benefit of the doubt. Why, I'll never know. But thank you. I don't know how I'd be able to get through this without you."

I swallowed, not sure what to say. He was inches away, his eyes watching me, his lips tormenting me. I wanted to feel them on mine, to wipe away the sorrow this day caused him, but I didn't want his kiss to be overshadowed by death.

Closing my eyes, I threw my arms around him and rested my chin on his shoulder. Taking a deep breath, I felt him lean into me and squeeze my chest as though holding on for dear life. He shuddered, choking back sobs with a few raspy sniffs.

After what seemed like forever, I backed out of his arms. "I'll give you a few more minutes, okay? But we should go soon. The snow is starting to pick up."

Nodding without a word, he turned his attention back to Cassie's tombstone. I stood up and walked through the snow-covered grass until I reached the parking lot where I rushed over to the Range Rover and slipped into the passenger seat.

A few minutes later, Lucian opened the door and got in behind the wheel. We rode home in silence, the somber mood wrapping around us. I was afraid if we tried to talk, we'd break out in tears. Instead, I studied the snow falling beyond the window, unable to appreciate the wintry beauty after watching Lucian grieve for his sister, a young girl taken from the world long before her time should have been up.

When we arrived back at Lucian's house, a blanket of snow covered the grass, bushes, and driveway. Lucian parked next to my car now hidden by a two-inch layer of powder on the roof, hood, and windshield. After he shut off the engine, we sat in silence for a moment, watching what looked like a blizzard outside.

After a few seconds, I took a deep breath and turned to Lucian. "I thought you said they treat the roads around here. Because they looked pretty white to me."

His expression softened, and I suspected he was fighting to push his sorrow away now that we were home. "It's only a few inches. You can drive through it. Unless—"

"Unless what?" I asked.

"Unless you'd like to come in for a while. I can make some hot chocolate. My father is gone for the day, and we'll have the house to ourselves."

Lucian's invitation warmed my heart even though guilt nagged me after visiting Cassie's grave. But if Cassie had really been as wonderful as Lucian said, she'd want him to find some happiness in his life after she was gone.

Feeling a soft smile take over my expression, I looked up at him. "I'd love to."

9

Lucian's house was dark but warm when we walked in after stomping the snow off our shoes on the doormat. As Lucian shut the door, I brushed a few flakes off my shoulders, relieved to be out of the cold. Before I had a chance to slip out of my coat, Diesel, Lucian's Doberman, trotted into the entry hall.

With a grin, Lucian opened the door again, the wintry air blasting inside. "Do you want to go out?" he asked.

Diesel took one look at the snow and whimpered before spinning around and retreating into the kitchen.

I couldn't help laughing. "What was that?" I asked. "I thought dogs love the snow."

"Not my wimpy dog," Lucian said. "He'll eventually make it outside when he has to, but he hates rain, snow, wind, and even heat on the rare occasion the mercury hits ninety up here. Talk about thin-skinned. He can barely survive if it isn't seventy-five degrees."

I shook my head, finding it hard to believe a dog as big and intimidating as Diesel was so particular. Maybe he wasn't as tough as he seemed. "I don't know if I'll ever be able to look at him the same way again."

"Trust me. I know what you mean," Lucian muttered, rolling his eyes with a sly smile that faded a moment later. "Would you like to take your coat off? You are going to stay for a while, aren't you?"

"Yes," I replied, pulling off my jacket and handing it to him. "Mind if I leave my shoes in here? I don't want to track snow into the house."

"No, of course not," Lucian said as he hung our coats in the closet before turning back to me. "In fact, I'll do the same."

After we kicked off our shoes, Lucian led me into the kitchen, flipping the light on when he passed through the doorway. The stainless steel appliances, dark brown cabinets, granite countertops, and round table reminded me of the last time I was here when we carved our pumpkins after returning from the farm about a month ago.

I took a seat at the island while Lucian filled a teapot with water, placed it on a burner, and turned the flame to a high setting. When he finished, he looked at me. "Hungry?"

"Not really." After watching him at his sister's grave, knowing another one of her birthdays had come and gone, the solemn mood had sent my appetite running for the hills.

"Me, neither," he said quietly. "The water will take a few minutes to heat up. Let me get everything ready." He turned and grabbed two coffee mugs from the cabinet. After dumping a spoonful of hot chocolate mix into each one, he left them next to the stove and circled the island. Sitting down next to me, he leaned an elbow on the counter. "I'm sorry about today."

"What? Lucian, no, you have nothing to be sorry for. This must be a very hard day for you."

"Yes, it is," he answered with a slight nod. "I keep hoping it'll get easier, but it never does. Her birthday is a reminder of where she'd be in life and what she'd be doing now. At fifteen, she'd be in high school, quite possibly starting to break a lot of hearts." He smiled, a faraway look drifting over his eyes. "And I, of course, would threaten any boy who tries to come near her."

"I'm sure you would."

His expression collapsed into a frown, the grief appearing once again in his eyes. "Listen to me talking about protecting her. Clearly, I failed miserably at that."

I shook my head, wishing he'd forgive himself for her death. He didn't seem able to let go of the guilt twisting around his soul. "Lucian," I started, reaching out to touch his hand. I waited until he looked up, meeting my gaze before I continued. "You can't keep doing this to yourself. How many times do I have to tell you her death wasn't your fault? This is really eating you up inside."

He pursed his lips, tears glistening in his eyes, then sucked in a deep breath. "Thank you. If we ever find out who put her in the grave, I might be able to get past it. But until then, I don't know if I can."

"You need closure. And you're not the only one. Everyone around here wants to see justice served."

He huffed, a frustrated look spreading over his expression. "Except they all think I did it and that it'll only be a matter of time before I'm locked up. I came back to town on her birthday for the last two years, but I snuck in quietly just long enough to leave flowers at her grave. I knew I couldn't face anyone around here, not even my father if he happened to be in town. It's hard enough that I feel guilty because I wasn't there to protect her, but knowing what everyone else thinks is like throwing salt in my wounds."

I squeezed his hand, my heart breaking at the sadness in his tone. "Don't worry about them. Someday, when the truth is revealed, they'll realize how wrong they were to jump to conclusions. I know you didn't do it, and one day, they'll know it, too."

"Thank you," Lucian said. "I still can't believe I found you and convinced you of this, but I'm glad you're here."

"You didn't have to convince me. I can see the truth, maybe because you've opened up to me, shown me something you've kept hidden from everyone else," I replied, my words ending in a whisper.

Our eyes locked on one another while silence fell over us. All I saw before me was a young man the world had given up on, who needed someone to believe in him. I wanted to be that person, to stand beside him when no one else would.

With a deep breath, I mustered a smile and pulled my hand away, ready to break the heavy mood and talk about something else. "Tell me about the Winter Carnival. Alex mentioned it last weekend. It sounds like fun."

Lucian's expression softened. "It is. I missed it for the last few years, but it's a huge town tradition. What exactly did Alex tell you?"

"He said there will be everything from a snow sculpting contest to a ball. But one thing he said made me wonder about something. Perhaps you can shed some insight."

"What's that?"

"Well, I don't know about up here, but from what I know about the weather, there's no guarantee it'll snow the same time every year. Alex said it always snows for the carnival, and that just seems a bit unlikely."

Lucian grinned. "Is that so?"

"Yes. So tell me how it works around here."

"If I said pure luck, would you believe me?"

I raised my eyebrows as the teapot began to whistle. Lucian jumped up, hurried around the island to the stove, and turned off the burner. He poured steaming water into the mugs, stirred each one for a minute, and turned to place them on the island. "Would you like some whipped cream?"

"Yes, please," I replied. "And don't be stingy. I like a lot of cream."

"Coming right up." He pulled a can out of the refrigerator and added a healthy dose on top of the hot chocolate in both mugs, causing the steam to disappear.

I reached for one and took a sip, the cool cream blending with chocolate for the perfect mix of warm and sweet on a cold winter day. My gaze drifted to the window, the horses grazing in the snow-covered pasture looking like they belonged on a Christmas card.

"So, luck, is it?" I asked as I put my drink down, returning the conversation to the Winter Carnival.

"I was going to say magic, but I wasn't sure you'd believe me."

"Months ago, I'd say never. But now, I think I believe in magic more than luck," I replied with a smile, meeting his eyes as though we shared a secret.

"Good. You're starting to get used to things around here."

"Yeah. Hard to believe, though. It's awfully strange to think of magic as being normal."

"But it is for you."

"At least I'm not the only one," I said thoughtfully, wrapping my hands around the mug again. "I know we have supernatural power and can work magic, but to be honest with you, I haven't seen anything too spectacular. It's definitely not like anything I've seen in movies or on TV."

He laughed. "Stick around. Maybe something will surprise you one of these days."

"You've surprised me," I said quietly.

He raised his eyebrows with a sigh. "Really? Right back at you."

I felt a blush spread through my cheeks, heating them up. Looking away, I searched for something else to say, but my mind came up empty.

Lucian must have noticed the awkward moment because he changed the subject. "Thanksgiving is coming up in a few weeks. Are you planning to stay here? Or are you going to see your mom?"

I shrugged, not sure how I felt about my mother these days. "I'll be here. I talked to her last weekend, which was strange because we haven't talked in over a month. She said she can't come back for the holidays. And oddly enough, I'm okay with that. I don't know what I would say if I saw her again, knowing she lied to me my whole life. It's easy to pretend I don't know I'm adopted on the phone, but seeing her in person might be a little difficult."

"I think she had a reason for never telling you."

"Maybe. But it's still a sore subject with me. I miss her, but I want to know the truth."

"About what?"

"My birth parents. I don't even know who they are. You wouldn't happen to know that, would you?"

He shook his head. "Sorry. None of us knew you existed until you moved here. You should probably ask Becca."

"I have, and she knows, but she won't tell me and I don't know why."

Lucian arched his eyebrows. "Hmm," he mused. "That is odd. Give her some time. If there's anyone around here to trust, it's Becca. I'm sure she'll tell you when the time is right."

"Gee, thanks. Take her side," I said with a groan, making a mental note to bring it up again with Becca the next chance I had. Wanting to talk about something else, I asked the first thing that came to mind. "Tell me about Europe and what you did over the last two years. You never talk about it."

He smiled, the faraway look in his eyes returning. "I know. It was hard to enjoy traveling over the last few years because it was merely an escape."

"There still had to have been something good about it." I paused, studying his reaction and wondering if I'd gone too far. "But it's okay if you don't want to talk about it," I added.

"No," he said. "It's not. And you're right, it was pretty amazing to wander around Europe for a few years. I may have felt lost in the world, but I got to experience some places many people will never see."

Lucian proceeded to regale me with tales of his adventures in Europe as I sipped my hot chocolate. He described the lights of London, rolling hills covered with rows of grape vines in Tuscany, and my personal favorite, the art museums in Paris. A few hours passed, the mood lifting, and I suspected Lucian's memories of his travels across the ocean distracted him from Cassie's birthday.

Around four o'clock, a rumbling sound interrupted our conversation. When I glanced at Lucian, he frowned. "Garage door. My father is home."

A moment later, Everett appeared in the kitchen wearing an overcoat, a plaid scarf tucked under the lapels. "This is a nice surprise. Hello, Gracyn."

Huffing, Lucian walked away from the island, carrying the mugs over to the sink.

I stood up, my attention focused on Everett. "Hi. It's nice to see you again."

"You, too, dear. I'm glad to see you're keeping Lucian company," he replied before a loud clank sounded against the counter.

Lucian whipped around, scowling at his father. "How are the roads?" he asked, his tone cold.

"They're fine," Everett said. "The snow stopped, and it looks like the sun's trying to come out."

"Really?" I asked, glancing out the window. The low clouds had lifted, and the falling snow had cleared. Sunlight sparkled on the blanket of white covering the ground, blades of grass breaking through the surface in places. Time had flown by, and I hadn't even noticed the change in the weather.

I shifted my attention back to Lucian, my mood sinking at the sight of his frown. Clearly, the afternoon was coming to an end. "Well, um, thank you for the hot chocolate," I said. "But if the roads are clear, I should probably get going. I'll see myself out."

Without waiting for a response, I brushed past Everett on my way to the entry hall. As I slipped into my boots, Lucian appeared, an apologetic smile fluttering over his lips. "I'll get your coat," he said. "It would be rude of me not to walk you out."

"Thank you," I said as he turned to the closet. After grabbing my parka, he held it out behind me while I slid my arms into the sleeves. He was so close, causing my pulse to quicken until I took a deep breath, forcing it to slow when I sensed Lucian backing away.

I swiped the base of my neck, pulling my hair out from under my collar. Then I headed for the door and opened it, slipping outside with Lucian behind me.

We trudged down the snow-covered sidewalk until we reached the driveway. Patches of pavement broke through the slush, the slightly increased temperature starting to melt what had fallen. The sun hovered above the horizon, casting shadows across the blanket of white hiding the ground.

When we got to my car, Lucian insisted on clearing off the windshield for me. As soon as he finished, I tossed the brush in the back seat and turned to him. "Aren't you cold? You didn't put your jacket on."

"A little. But you're worth it."

Smiling, I dodged his gaze for a moment. "You're just saying that."

"No," he said, waiting until I looked back at him to continue. "I mean it. I...I think you know that."

Tilting my head, I arched an eyebrow. "I honestly don't know what to think anymore. You're very confusing sometimes."

"I'm sorry. I have a lot on my mind right now. And you just broke up with Alex."

I took a deep breath, not wanting to think about Alex who I still missed, but only as a friend. "That was a long time coming. I don't think my heart was ever really in it."

"Good. I was hoping you weren't too hung up on him."

"You were?"

"Yes. But I've said too much. I should go in, and you need to get home before the melting snow starts to refreeze on the roads."

I nodded, a little disappointed when he turned to leave. Instead of getting into my car, I watched him, waiting. A second later, he stopped and spun around. "If I'm still around by the carnival, will you save me a dance?"

My heart swelled. "Yes," I said. "Of course."

He smiled. "Great. Well, see you next week." Then he was gone, rushing down the walkway to the house.

I felt my smile linger as I jumped in the car and started the engine. The Winter Carnival couldn't begin soon enough. Images of the town covered by a blanket of snow, sculptures of penguins and polar bears erected in the park, and a horse-drawn sleigh giving rides to eager children filled my mind on the way home. When the vision of Lucian kneeling before Cassie's grave snuck into my thoughts, I gave it a mental push. I wanted to end today by remembering Lucian's stories of Europe and the promise of the future, whether or not we'd actually have that dance at the ball.

As soon as I got home, I opened the door to find Gabriel pacing in front of a roaring fire in the hearth. He snapped his gaze toward me, the concern in his icy blue eyes washing away my good mood.

I halted without taking my coat off. "What's going on?"

"Where were you?" he asked, sounding a little miffed.

"Out. I didn't think I needed to check in. Becca told me when I first moved here she wasn't going to keep tabs on me."

"That was before we had a diabolical witch on the loose." Gabriel sighed, running his hands through his blond hair. "I'm sorry. I didn't mean to sound so upset. I was just worried."

"Well, I'm fine. I'll try to let Becca know where I am next time. Speaking of her, where is she?"

Gabriel nodded at the hallway leading to their bedroom. "She's not feeling well. She said her headache wasn't as bad as they've been, so she just took a migraine pill. I doubt she'll need anything stronger. She seems to be resting comfortably."

"I'd feel better if she didn't have to take anything at all."

"So would I." Gabriel paused, studying me. "Are you staying home for the rest of the night?"

I nodded. "Yes. I'll be here."

"Good. I need to take care of a few things, and I'm not sure when I'll be back. Can you check on Becca in a few hours? I'll bring the horses in before I leave."

"Okay. But the roads could get a little slick. It's pretty messy out there."

Gabriel smiled as though I didn't know what I was talking about. "I'll be careful. Thanks for sticking around. If Becca asks where I went, just tell her I'm not about to let Marguerite threaten my family. And I can't sit around here waiting for her to strike again." He crossed the room and grabbed his coat from the closet. After putting it on, he headed for the door. "Make sure you lock up behind me," he said.

Giving me no further explanation, he slipped outside. Confused and worried, I did as he instructed and clicked the deadbolt into place. I had a feeling it was going to be a long night spent worrying about Marguerite, even though I'd managed to forget her all afternoon.

10

The next day, Becca seemed to be feeling better and asked if I wanted to take a ride on the trails with her and Gabriel. In spite of the chilly temperatures, I accepted, eager to get outside and clear my head. I expected Becca and Gabriel to bring up Marguerite when we left, but to my relief, they struck up a conversation about the holidays and the Winter Carnival. Listening to their steady chitchat, I followed behind on Gypsy, enjoying the morning scenery. Yesterday's snow had melted, leaving the tree branches bare and the ground soft and muddy.

My attention shifted to Lucian's mansion when we passed the trail leading to his estate, and I wondered what was keeping him busy today. Was he painting? Working on homework? Spending time with his father? Knowing he tensed up every time his father appeared or was brought up in conversation, I doubted the latter. I considered calling Lucian when I got home, then decided against it. Showing up on his door step yesterday was enough of a surprise for the weekend.

I didn't have to wait as long as I expected to hear from him. That afternoon while I was working on a History assignment, my phone buzzed. I reached for it, surprised to see a text from an unknown number. Curious, I opened the message right away.

Hi, this is Lucian. How's your day going?

Pleasantly surprised, I felt a smile spread across my face. This was the first time Lucian had used my phone number since I'd given it to him about a month ago. Caught off-guard, I paused, then quickly typed a response, not wanting to keep him waiting on the other end. *A little boring, but productive.*

Then I'll let you get back to work. I don't want to interrupt.

That's okay. What are you up to?

At that moment, my phone rang, showing the caller ID as the same number as Lucian's texts. I answered it on the first ring. "Hello," I said.

"Hi," Lucian replied quietly. "I thought calling would be a little easier than texting."

"Yes, it is."

"Anyway, would you like to take a ride with me this afternoon?"

"What, no unannounced visit blaming your horse for bringing you over here?" I teased.

He laughed. "I think we're past the point of needing to be coy."

"I'm glad," I said. "But I hate to break it to you, I rode out with Becca and Gabriel this morning. If I'd known another invitation would come later in the day, I might have gotten my homework done earlier and waited."

"Maybe next time?" he asked.

"Definitely," I replied, hoping next time would happen soon.

"Good. Then it's a date. I'll just make sure to ask you in advance. Well, I'd better run if I'm going to get out for a ride."

"Okay. Thanks for calling."

"Sure. See you tomorrow?"

"Of course." After a quick goodbye, I hung up the phone and slapped my palm against my forehead with a deep breath. Rolling my eyes to myself, I heard the words "Thanks for calling" echo in my mind. What was that? It sounded so cold and formal, the complete opposite of how I felt when I was with Lucian.

There's nothing you can do about it now, I told myself. *So get back to work and try to be more relaxed when you see him tomorrow. If you see him tomorrow that is, because you never know around here.*

Wishing my inner self wasn't always right, I dove back into my homework, determined to finish before thoughts of Lucian carried me away.

— —

The next morning began like any other Monday. Becca's SUV was gone when I headed out to my car, although Gabriel's BMW still sat in front of the house since he wasn't returning to Boston until later in the week. Tossing my book bag in the back seat, I heard a whinny and looked up to see Gypsy trotting in the pasture along the fence, her head held high and a spring in her step. She practically floated over the ground, her hooves barely seeming to touch the ground.

I watched her for a moment, wondering what had caught her attention. When nothing materialized, I shrugged, figuring she had some excess energy to burn off in the cold weather. Without giving her another thought, I jumped in the driver's seat and started the engine. After turning on the heat, I backed up the car, then guided it down the driveway. My gloved hands on the steering wheel, I turned onto the road and began making my way toward town.

As the air flowing from the vents began to warm up, I drove down the familiar road while listening to a country song. The woods were dark, the rising sun's rays coming through the tallest branches at an angle. The scenery reminded me of the dead of winter, not a single leaf left on any tree, the shades of brown and black giving off a gloomy mood.

The route I took to school every day was only a few miles, and I'd memorized every bend in the road along the way. At the bottom of a hill, I anticipated the right hand curve coming up and moved my foot from the accelerator to the brake. But when I pressed it, the car didn't slow down.

Assuming I hadn't pushed hard enough, I let up on the brake and tried again, but nothing happened. The car continued rolling forward, picking up speed until it was going too fast to make the turn up ahead. My heart pounding with sudden fear, I slammed my foot against the brake one more time, praying it would work, but I found out the hard way prayers alone were no use. The tires continued spinning, propelling the car toward the sharp turn ahead.

Feeling hopeless, sheer panic blasting through me, I closed my eyes and let out a scream as the car skidded off the road and catapulted down an embankment into the woods. Gripping the steering wheel as hard as I could, I felt my fingernails digging into my palms through my gloves while I was bounced around in the seat. Within seconds, my car hit a tree, stopping abruptly with a loud crunch. The airbag went off, trapping me between the wheel and the seat.

Remaining where I was, I tried to catch my breath, my heart hammering out of control. "Holy crap. What just happening?" I muttered to myself, grateful to be in one piece. But as my pulse began to slow down and I realized I was still alive, reality set in. I couldn't believe I had lost control and wrecked my car. I'd never even had a fender bender, despite learning to drive around Washington, DC on some of the busiest roads in the country.

I cringed at the thought of examining the damage, but I didn't have a choice. After pushing the deflated airbag aside, I crawled out of the car. The leaves crackled under my feet, and a hissing sound came from the engine. I walked around the open door, drawing in a sharp breath at the sight of the front grill smashed up against a tree. The hood and right fender were destroyed, and steam rose from the crumpled metal.

The car was a mess, to say the least. Shaking my head, I reached into my coat pocket for my cell phone. I scrolled through my contacts, not sure who I should bother this morning. If I called Becca, she'd have to leave work to come get me. If I called Gabriel, he'd probably tell Becca right away, and then I'd feel guilty for interrupting her at work. I certainly couldn't call my mom in Russia. There was nothing she could do to help me.

I scanned the names in my call log, pausing when Alex's name passed. *Don't even think about it,* a voice in my head warned, prompting me to roll my eyes at myself. *Of course not. We're not even on speaking terms. Derek might be one to call, but I don't have his number.*

Passing up Alex who I probably didn't need in my list of contacts anymore, I continued searching everyone I knew until Lucian's name appeared. Only yesterday, I'd added his number my phone, and now I needed to use it. My finger hovering over the call icon, I wondered if I'd sound like a damsel in distress who conveniently needed him the day after she'd gotten his phone number.

So you're going to stand out here stranded? my alter ego asked in a sarcastic tone, chastising me for my silly insecurities. *Just call him. It was an accident, one you're going to have to get over. Unless you want to walk, he's probably your best bet.*

Feeling as though I had no other choice, I placed the call and put the phone up to my ear.

Lucian answered on the second ring. "Good morning," he said.

"Hi," I replied, not sure how to explain my predicament. "You wouldn't happen to be on your way to school, would you?"

"I am," he said slowly, sounding curious. "Why?"

"I...um...I need a little help."

"Uh-oh. That doesn't sound good. What's going on?"

After taking a deep breath, I explained with as little detail as I could manage that my car was smashed up against a tree.

He swore under his breath before responding. "Gracyn, you need to be more careful."

"I was careful," I insisted. "Can you please just get here soon? I'm stuck, and even though town isn't too far away, it's still a long walk."

"Sure. I'm on my way now. I should be there in a few minutes. And I'll call a tow truck. Just sit tight."

"Thank you," I said, wondering where he thought I could go. I hung up and walked around my car, studying the damage again, still not wanting to believe it. I couldn't imagine how much the repairs would cost, assuming the car wasn't totaled. After a few minutes spent looking at the mangled hood and fender, I decided I'd seen enough and walked up to the side of the road to wait for Lucian.

Before long, his black Range Rover appeared in the distance. Lucian slowed down and pulled to a stop on the shoulder of the road, then hopped out wearing jeans and a gray shirt under a dark coat. He rushed over to me and grabbed my hand, a concerned look on his face. "Are you okay? You're not hurt, are you?"

"No," I said, shaking my head. "The air bag went off, so I'm fine. But my car is in pretty bad shape. I don't know if it can be fixed."

"Your car is the least of my worries. It's you I care about," Lucian said, his eyes locking with mine.

"I thought we're strong and we heal fast," I said, thinking back to the night Becca and Gabriel told me I was a witch and that I wouldn't get sick often, if at all.

"We are, but our bodies are no match for the kind of catastrophic injuries a car accident can cause. Look at Cassie. She couldn't heal from a knife wound. We heal fast from bruises and scratches, and we don't get sick often, but unfortunately, we aren't invincible."

His mention of Cassie made me wish I hadn't brought it up, but there was still so much I didn't understand. I was beginning to get used to the idea that being a witch meant little in my life would be black and white any longer. I had many shades of gray to get used to.

"Oh," I said with a deflated sigh. "Well, I assure you, I'll be okay. My car, on the other hand, has seen better days."

"Let's take a look," he said, dropping my hand and leading the way down the embankment. He drew in a sharp breath when he stopped next to the front end. "Looks pretty bad. What exactly happened? A deer?"

"I wish," I said with a groan. "The brakes went out on me. I kept pushing, but nothing happened. The car picked up speed from the hill until it went off the road."

Lucian's expression fell into a serious frown. "When's the last time you had it serviced?"

"Before I left Maryland to drive up here. But it's not like I've put a lot of miles on it since I moved to Sedgewick."

"No, I'm sure you haven't. Well, I called the service station in town before I got here, and a tow truck is on the way. They'll check it out. You're sure it was the brakes?" Lucian asked as though he didn't believe me.

"Yes. I mean, I think so." I wished there was another explanation, such as a deer or getting distracted with the radio. But my memory was clear, and I remembered the exact moment the car picked up speed while

I held my foot down on the brake. "Look, maybe we shouldn't speculate on it. I'm just thankful I didn't get hurt."

"We'll find out what happened," Lucian stated. "We have to. You could have been killed. This is serious."

The tone in his voice sent a chill up my spine. "Okay. I'll leave that part to you because I need to focus on taking care of what's left here. Do you think my car can be fixed?"

Lucian raised his eyebrows, studying the smashed hood again. "I don't know, but it doesn't look good."

"Great," I muttered. "I don't have the money to buy a new car. My mom is going to kill me."

When Lucian tossed me a curious look, I explained, "I know she's across the ocean, but she's still not going to be happy. This will probably jack up my insurance rates."

"The purpose of having insurance is in case of accidents like this. And don't worry about it. If money can fix it, it's not a problem."

"Easy for you to say," I mumbled, thinking about my dwindling savings from the summer I'd spent lifeguarding. I'd never taken on a job during the school year, but maybe it was time to look for one.

At that moment, a rumbling sound came from the road. Lucian and I turned our attention toward the incline to see a red tow truck pull in behind the Range Rover, its orange lights flashing. Without another word, we scaled the hill and reached the shoulder as the burly, bearded driver wearing an oil-stained denim jacket climbed down from the cab.

"Thanks for getting here so quickly. Her car is down there," Lucian said, pointing at the wreckage. "Think you can get it up to the road?"

The tow truck driver raised his eyebrows when his gaze followed Lucian's gesture and landed on my mangled car. "Shouldn't be a problem. The real question is what are we going to do with it? Let me take a closer look." He scrambled down the hill. "Was somebody doing some stunt driving or what?" he called up to us.

We hurried back to my car where he let out a low whistle. "You sure did a number on this heap of metal. I can tow it back to my garage, but you're going to need a body shop after we repair any engine damage.

And even then, I don't know for sure, but your car may have gone its last mile."

"Great," I said with a groan, my worst fears confirmed.

"Can you do us a favor?" Lucian asked.

The driver looked at Lucian, a skeptical look on his face.

"She said her brakes went out. Can your guys take a look at them to confirm what happened?"

"What—" I started, about to protest when Lucian silenced me with a knowing look.

"Sure," the driver said. "We'll be able to tell if it really was the brakes. Although, brake failures are pretty rare these days in newer vehicles. This car doesn't look more than four or five years old. But we'll take a look at them. The insurance company's going to need a report, anyway." He turned to me. "You do have insurance, right Miss? Please tell me you do."

I nodded sullenly.

"Good," he said before climbing up the hill to his rig where he started preparing the chains. An occasional car passed by, the occupants staring curiously at the roadside scene.

Lucian and I walked back to the tow truck. "Anything more we can do?" Lucian asked the driver.

"Nope," he replied. "I've got it from here."

"Thank you," Lucian said. "What do we owe you for the tow and assessment?"

"About a hundred for this morning. Once I get it back to the shop, it's gonna take some time to tear it apart. I'll bill you for the labor."

"No problem." Lucian counted a few bills, then handed them to the driver. "Here you go. Thanks again for getting here so quickly." When he finished with the driver, Lucian turned his attention to me. "Come on, Gracyn. Get your things, and let's go." Without waiting for me, he headed for his Range Rover, leaving me reeling with frustration.

Taking a deep breath, I returned to my car, grabbed my book bag from the back seat, and raced up to the road to meet Lucian as he was getting in the SUV. "What's that all about?" I demanded.

"What do you mean?"

"Why do you care how the brakes failed? Or do you think I'm lying?"

"That's not it. Get in, and I'll explain," he said before shutting the door.

I hurried around to the other side and jumped in, pulling the door shut with more force than I intended to use. "Okay," I let out with a sigh. "What's going on?"

He turned to me, a serious look in his eyes. "In this town, nothing ever is what it seems. I'd like to know if the brakes are okay or if they were intentionally damaged. After what happened to Celeste and knowing Becca's long lost enemy is roaming around still trying to get what she wants, I'm not leaving anything to chance."

I opened my mouth, but no words came out as I realized he was right. It would be better to know exactly what had gone wrong with the brakes. As much as I hoped it had been mechanical failure, I had a sneaking suspicion a certain redhead was behind this and that I wouldn't feel safe until she was dealt with.

11

Lucian and I didn't speak on the way to school. The moment my car went off the road flashed through my thoughts about a dozen times, reminding me how lucky I was to walk away in one piece.

When we pulled into the school parking lot, Lucian found an empty space and turned off the engine. I started to open the door, but he grabbed my wrist, causing me to shift my attention to him, my other hand poised on the handle. "What?" I asked softly, searching his eyes for an answer.

"Wait. Before we go in, I want to talk to you here where we have some privacy." He paused, his expression stoic, giving nothing away.

"Okay. We can talk. What is it?"

He shook his head with a deep sigh, his eyes meeting mine. "I don't think I realized how much your accident rattled me when we were back there at the scene."

"I know," I agreed. "Now that I think about it, I'm just glad I walked away. I'm not even going to worry about my car right now. When I think about what could have happened if the airbag hadn't gone off, I realize I might not be sitting here right now."

"Exactly," he said. "Listen, Gracyn, I'm worried."

"About what? It's over, and I'm safe. I just want to go to class right now and forget all about this morning."

"You might be safe for today, but whoever did this meant business. It's not a good situation. I need you to be very careful from now on."

Narrowing my eyes, I tilted my head. "What are you trying to say?"

"Think about it. If you had your car serviced a few months ago and drove what, maybe a thousand miles since then, most of them on the way here, I doubt the brakes went out from wear and tear. And you heard the tow truck driver. Brake failure is pretty rare these days. Which means someone caused this." He ran his hands through his hair, his eyes drifting to the window before returning to me. "I already lost someone I care about. I'm not about to let that happen again."

"We don't know for sure that's what's going on here. I appreciate your theory, but it could have been a freak thing. Cars can break from time to time. A faulty wire or a worn out piece of metal. I'm sure the mechanic will have an explanation soon. And then you can stop worrying about me."

"No," he said, shaking his head. "I'll never stop worrying about you. Not after all I've been through." He released my wrist and clenched his hand into a fist. "And especially not until we find out who killed Cassie."

His words sent a shiver up my spine, the notion that Cassie's killer could have messed with my car rattling my nerves. Nodding, I looked away from his intense stare. "Yeah," I muttered, my gaze wandering to the red brick school in the distance. Students crossed the parking lot on their way to the entrance, their lives blissfully normal, something I'd never feel again. My mood sinking, I drew in a deep breath, trying to find something positive to hold onto. "Well, we can't hide in the car all day. I think I'll be safe enough at school. Perhaps we should go in now?"

"Sure," he replied before we jumped out of the Range Rover. With my book bag hanging from my shoulder, I fell into step beside Lucian as we approached the school. The other students in the parking lot and on the lawn fell quiet, their eyes following our every move. I forced myself to ignore them as I did every time they stared, but it still hurt. Just once,

I'd like to walk beside Lucian and not be the center of attention. My spirits plunging lower than they'd been after my accident, a reassuring voice entered my mind. *They're just curious because Lucian drove you to school. Ignore them. This, too, shall pass just like their stares in the hallway that faded last week.*

Hoping the voice of reason in my thoughts was right, I focused on the school ahead. As soon as we entered through the front door, Lucian and I parted ways to go to our lockers in the short time we had left before the bell would ring. While I was at mine, Celeste ran by. Her eyes were locked on me, a cold look in them, and she didn't stop. Shaking my head, I turned back to my locker, but I couldn't help wondering what that was all about.

I found Celeste after homeroom and called her name, but she ignored me and ran off through the crowd. Without hesitating, I rushed after her, dodging the students in my way until I caught up to her. "Celeste!" I called from a few feet behind her, but she didn't slow down. I pushed myself to go faster and finally got close enough to grab her hand. "Celeste!"

She stopped and whipped around. "What?"

"Hey, why the cold-shoulder treatment?" I asked.

"I was just leaving you alone so you could spend more time with Lucian. He sure seems to have wrapped you around his finger."

"Celeste, please don't go there again. I—"

"No," Celeste said firmly, interrupting me. "All I know is that he broke up with Zoe and was arrested for murder, and now you can't seem to stay away from him. What's going on with you? Have you lost your mind?"

"I don't believe he did it for a minute."

"But—" Celeste lowered her voice. "She was just a child. Please, you need to see what you're doing. Everyone is talking about what a fool you are. It's killing me that he's thrown the wool over your eyes. One day you're going to see what a huge mistake you're making. You don't want to take a risk like this, one that could have deadly consequences."

I took a deep breath, ready to spill every detail making me believe Lucian was innocent. But one look at the conviction in her brown eyes told me to hold off. "He helped us get you back a few weeks ago," I reminded her. "Don't forget that." Without another word, I spun around and walked away, wondering if I'd just lost one of the few friends I had.

— ◠ —

My day proved to be far less exciting than the morning drive to school, at least until I walked into the Art classroom where Lucian was waiting for me. As soon as I approached the desk we shared and took my seat, he spoke. "There was nothing wrong with your brakes."

"What?" I gasped, dropping my book bag to the floor. "That's impossible."

"I talked to the mechanic, and he said the brakes were in good shape. The pads were like new, and all the lines were intact. They couldn't find a single thing wrong, and they blamed your accident on driver error. They seem to think you hit the accelerator instead of the brakes."

"I assure you, I didn't. I know what happened."

"And I believe you."

"You do?" I asked. "Then what do you think is going on?"

He took a deep breath, a frown flattening his mouth. "Magic. This was the work of a witch, and I'm pretty sure I can guess who's behind it. Where has Marguerite been hiding out? Have you seen her lately?"

"No. The last time I saw her was a week ago," I said with a sigh, my gaze shifting to the front of the room where Ms. Friedman sat behind the desk waiting for the bell to ring. "She showed up at the house last Monday afternoon." I hadn't forgotten a single moment of her visit, including Alex's departure right before she appeared.

Looking back at Lucian, I studied his reaction, remembering Marguerite's threat to destroy what Becca held dear before she disappeared out the door.

"We need to find her," Lucian stated. "This insanity has to stop. First she messes with Celeste, and now you. It's unacceptable. What's Becca doing to stop her?"

"I don't know what Becca can do right now. I'm sure she'd put an end to Marguerite if she could. She's the one who banished her to the crypt, even though Marguerite is her daughter. If she hasn't done it again, maybe she can't."

"You might be right, but this whole thing is messed up. There has to be something else we can do."

I choked out a tense smile. "Don't look at me. I'm new to all this. I wouldn't know how to cast a spell if it hit me in the face."

"We'll have to work on changing that," Lucian replied. "Maybe once Becca finds out Marguerite sabotaged your car, she'll try harder to come up with a solution. Perhaps we should all get together this evening."

"No," I objected. "No we. I'll talk to her, I promise." I paused before muttering under my breath, "As long as she's not resting from another headache."

Lucian drew in a long breath at my comment. "Well, this situation keeps getting better and better. She's still sick?"

"From time to time."

He shook his head, leaning his forehead on his hands. "We're all doomed. I'm going to end up going to trial for something I didn't do, Becca's going to meet her end soon, leaving us with one of the purest of hearts, not the three we should have, and Marguerite will get her way or else destroy the rest of us."

"When you put it that way, maybe I should pack up and move to Russia."

"Maybe you should," he said, his eyes meeting mine. Then a small smile peeked out on his face. "I'm only kidding. You're not going any-where. And you brought up an excellent point a minute ago. I think it's time you learn how to use magic. How much has Becca taught you?"

"Virtually nothing."

"Then forget her. I'm going to teach you. You need to understand your power so you can use it if you need it. Because I'm afraid you'll need it soon."

"I've asked you how many times to do this, and you're just now agree-ing to it?"

He shrugged. "We don't use our power unless we need to. Under normal circumstances, it wouldn't be necessary. Are you free today after school?"

"I suppose," I said, not particularly eager to learn something I only needed to protect myself from an evil witch.

"Good. We'll leave straight from here as soon as class is over."

Before I could answer him, the bell rang and Lucian shifted his attention to the front of the room. Wondering what exactly he planned to teach me later today, I waited for Ms. Friedman to begin her lecture for the period, even though I knew concentrating on art for the next hour would be hopeless.

— —

We had just left the school parking lot when Lucian got an unexpected call. "Yes," he said coolly, holding the phone up to his ear with his right hand, his left one on the steering wheel. Reflections of tree branches from overhead flickered across the windshield as we drove along the road winding through the woods.

"I see," he said, his tone dropping. "I kind of had something planned for this afternoon." He paused, and I heard the muffled tone of a man's voice coming from the phone. "Okay, yes, it can be postponed. I'll be there as soon as I take Gracyn home." Without saying goodbye, he hung up and dropped the phone in the cup holder between the seats.

"What is it?" I asked, curious to know what had soured his mood.

"That was my father. Apparently, we had some visitors at the house today, and they'll be returning tomorrow. I need to go home."

"Really? Who was it?"

"The police. They had a search warrant and spent the entire day making a mess of our second floor, including Cassie's room. And tomorrow they're coming back to search the downstairs. I need to get home and help my father put things back in order. But I won't leave you until Becca gets home. We may have to postpone your first training session until the weekend."

"Okay," I said, caught between feeling disappointed because Lucian couldn't start teaching me how to use magic and sick to my stomach at the thought of his house torn apart by the police in their search for evidence I didn't believe existed. "The weekend will be fine."

"Good. And I'm sorry. The timing of all this really sucks. It might be hard for me to focus sometimes, so let me apologize in advance."

"Lucian, you have nothing to apologize for," I said sincerely.

"Yes, I do. I can't be who I want to be and do what I want to do right now. I feel trapped and, until the case is dropped or a verdict is reached, it's hard for me to think about anything else," he explained, his eyes locked on the road ahead. A mailbox came into view around a bend, and he slowed the Range Rover before turning into Becca and Gabriel's driveway.

Within seconds, he pulled up to the house beside Becca's SUV. "Good," he said, shifting into park and shutting off the engine. "You won't be alone. I'd like to see Becca before I go."

We hopped out of the truck as Becca and Gabriel appeared on the front porch. "Gracyn!" she let out with relief, rushing down the steps to greet me while Gabriel lingered behind the railing, his narrowed eyes locked on Lucian. "I heard about what happened to your car a half hour ago. I tried to call you, but you didn't answer, so I ran home."

"Sorry," I said, remembering I hadn't wanted to reach for my phone when I heard it buzzing in my book bag as Lucian and I were walking out after Art class.

"Why didn't you call me this morning?" Becca asked.

"I...I didn't want to bother you while you were at work," I replied, feeling lame.

"What? Don't ever worry about that again. You totaled your car. I wish you had at least sent me a text after it happened."

"I thought you said you wouldn't be looking over my shoulder."

"Yes, but for God's sake, you could have been hurt. I was shocked I had to find out from a friend who heard about it at the garage today. Next time, don't worry about bothering me. If it's something this important, I want to know about it. I'm here to help you when things go wrong like this."

"Good," Lucian said, speaking up for the first time since we'd arrived. "Now perhaps you'll get serious about handling Marguerite." When Becca shot him a confused look, he explained that my brakes had failed, but when the mechanic tested them, they appeared to be working just fine.

"Damn it," she swore under her breath. "Marguerite has outdone herself now. She ought to know better than to go after Gracyn, especially since Gracyn is the only reason she got out of the crypt."

"Great way for her to thank me," I commented.

Becca glanced at me. "Well, that's my daughter. She'll use anyone to get her way, and then she'll turn on them in a heartbeat. I tried to raise her right, but the harder I worked to instill morals and values in her, the more she defied me."

While Becca spoke, Gabriel headed down the steps and stopped behind her, placing a hand on her shoulder. "I'm sure you did your best," he told her.

She nodded, her gaze shifting to Lucian. "Lucian, thank you for giving Gracyn a ride to school and home today. We really appreciate it."

"You're welcome," he said. "But what about Marguerite? I think we've got a big problem here."

"Yes," Becca let out on a long sigh. "If I know her as well as I think I do, she's going to get more brazen with her threats. This is only the beginning."

"Great," Lucian said, a bit of sarcasm in his voice. When Becca looked at him, her eyebrows raised, he continued in a nicer tone. "Perhaps it's time to come up with a plan."

I looked at him, confused. "Good idea. Do you have one?" I asked.

"Not at all," he replied.

"Becca?" I asked, hoping she'd suddenly have the answer.

"If I knew how to get rid of her, I would have done it by now."

"If you want my advice," Lucian began. "It's time Gracyn learns how to use her magic. If Marguerite threatens her, she'll only be able to fight fire with fire. I'm happy to do what I can there."

"Lucian, you have your own demons to deal with right now," Gabriel said, his voice cool, as though he still didn't trust Lucian in spite of all he'd done to help us over the last few weeks.

"You think?" Lucian retorted before softening his tone, ignoring the implied accusation in Gabriel's comment. "I could use a distraction. I may not have been able to save Cassie, but I'm not about to let someone else in this coven be threatened."

Becca paused thoughtfully, then frowned. "You're right. Gracyn needs to learn more about her power. If you can take care of that, I'll reach out to the others. There has to be something we can do. But if not—"

When her voice trailed off, Lucian and I locked eyes. "Then what?" he asked, sliding his gaze toward Becca.

"Then I need to make sure I protect the book. Whatever happens, I have to secure the script," Becca replied.

"I thought you already did that," I said.

"I'm sure you've figured out by now no spell is locked in place. There's always a way to break it. I'm going to put a back-up plan in place."

"Good," Lucian said. "But why haven't you done this sooner?"

"Because it's not as easy as it might seem. You see, I need another witch to help with this. Celeste is the only one who can protect the script should anything happen to me," Becca explained. "I think it's time I filled her in on what she'll need to do if I don't make it out of this alive."

12

After Lucian headed home to help his father clean up the mess from the police search, Becca called Celeste and asked her to drop what she was doing and come over right away. Becca only explained it was urgent once, and I gathered from listening to her end of the conversation it was enough for Celeste to comply.

As soon as Becca hung up and placed her phone on the island, she looked at me. "We have about fifteen minutes before Celeste gets here. Is there anything more I should know about what happened today?"

I glanced down at the counter, not sure what to say. When I looked up, Becca was watching me as though she expected an immediate answer. The seconds ticking by, Gabriel approached and stood beside her, his gaze on me. "No," I said. "Lucian told you everything. That's all I know."

Her expression softened. "This whole thing really worries me. Marguerite has a bad temper, especially when she doesn't get what she wants. There's no telling what she'll try next." Becca shook her head with a sigh, then changed the subject. "You seem to be spending a lot of time with Lucian. Mind if I ask what's going on there?"

"Yes, Gracyn," Gabriel chimed in. "We've been over this before. I wish we knew why you keep showing up with him after we've warned you time and time again to stay away from him."

I shot Gabriel a look of contempt before shifting my attention back to Becca. "He's a friend. And believe me, I could use one of those since Alex and I broke up."

"I don't suppose that has anything to do with the time you're spending with Lucian now, does it?" Becca asked.

Looking away from her, I found it impossible to lie. "Maybe. I've been a little lonely without Alex to talk to. And Lucian's been really nice to me."

Becca tilted her head, her eyebrows arched. "I've noticed. I'm glad he was able to give you a ride today and I realize he helped us a few weeks ago with Marguerite, but doesn't he frighten you?"

"That's kind of a dumb question," I told her point-blank. "I wouldn't be spending time with him if he did. He's been nothing but wonderful to me. I don't care what circumstantial evidence the authorities have, I'm not buying it. Zoe ratted him out because she was mad about something Lucian did with me. That's all. Other than Zoe's confession of not being with him when Cassie died, there's no evidence he killed her, at least none that I know of. And no one will convince me he did it without cold, hard proof. I trust him, probably more than I trust anyone else around here."

Becca reached across the counter and put her hand on mine. "You always try to see the good in people, don't you?"

"I guess so," I replied, my voice softening after my outburst.

Becca met my gaze, her eyes shining with concern and compassion, not the judgment I expected to see. "For everyone's sake, I hope you're right."

"Now you, too?" Gabriel asked, directing his question at Becca. "Are you crazy, giving him the benefit of the doubt? He's as guilty as sin. There's no way he's getting away with it this time."

"Gabriel," Becca said firmly. "We don't know that."

Just when I thought they were about to launch into an argument, the tension mounting between them, I heard a car pull up to the house. Becca rushed around the island and headed to the door while I hung back, not sure how Celeste would react to my presence. Before the bell rang, Becca pulled the door open and Celeste stepped into view, her long hair falling over one shoulder in a braid and her jeans dusty.

"Celeste," Becca said warmly. "Thank you for coming." She embraced Celeste in a hug before gesturing toward the family room. "Please, come on in."

"Of course," Celeste replied, stepping into the house. Becca shut the door with a click while Celeste stopped and turned. "I have to admit, I was a bit surprised by your call. What's going on?"

Becca's smile faded, a look of concern sweeping over her blue eyes. "We have a little trouble in town. I don't suppose you remember the witch who kidnapped you a few weeks ago, do you?"

Celeste shook her head, a blank look her eyes. "Not really. I don't remember much of anything about those few days, except waking up in the graveyard."

"That's what I was afraid of. I'll explain everything. Please, make yourself comfortable." Becca led Celeste to the couch where she sat down. "Can I get you something to drink?" Becca asked.

"No, thank you," Celeste said, her posture stiff. "I'd rather just cut to the chase and find out why I'm here."

"Very well, then. I'll be right back."

When Becca disappeared down the hallway to her bedroom, I approached the couch. "Hi," I said, feeling a little hesitant since the last time I'd spoken to Celeste at school ended on a sour note.

She nodded, barely glancing my way. Instead, she sat stone still as though she was in trouble for something. Not sure what to do, I took a seat at the other end of the couch as silence fell over the room.

Becca returned a few seconds later, the amber stone in her hand. She approached us and sat down in the end chair while Gabriel took a seat in the one across from her. Holding the rock out, she twirled it around, the light from the end table lamp reflecting on its smooth sides.

"What is that?" Celeste asked.

"It's a very special stone," Becca answered. "Inside are the words to a book that was stolen from me a few centuries ago. As soon as I realized the book was missing, I cast a spell to remove the script and lock it in here."

Celeste's eyes opened wide, her attention fixated on the rock. "It must have been some book," she commented.

"It still is. The spells contained on its pages can give the user enormous power. The destruction it could cause is indescribable. Until recently, the witch who stole it was locked away, but she managed to escape and now she'll stop at nothing to get me to reverse the spell, thus giving her access to the script in the book."

"Why are you telling me this?" Celeste asked, seeming confused.

"Because there are certain conditions under which this spell can be undone. One of them is my death."

Celeste drew in a sharp breath, shaking her head in protest. "Becca, no," she gushed. "You can't die. You can't leave us. We need you. If you die, then I'm the only one left, and I can't take on that responsibility now. It's too soon."

Becca smiled calmly. "I certainly don't want to leave you now, but there are things beyond my control. I may die soon, I may not, but eventually, it will happen. You and I are the only two purest of hearts left. When I'm gone, you'll have to take over."

Celeste glanced at Becca, her expression alarmed. "I know that's always been in my future, but I'm not ready for it right now."

"Ready or not, it will happen someday. And we'll work on preparing you. For now, listen to me carefully. If something happens to me, you need to find this stone and cast the spell again, returning the script to the safety of this rock." She handed the amber stone to Celeste. "You're the only one other than me who can touch it."

The rock resting on her open palm, Celeste looked up at Becca, surprise registering in her brown eyes. "Really?"

"Yes. It's protected in case the wrong person gets their hands on it."

Gabriel stood up, a smile on his face. "Here. I'll give it a try just for laughs." He reached down, moving his finger into place just above it, then hesitated. After a moment, he touched it, instantly jumping back. "Ow! Yes, it's protected, all right."

Becca rolled her eyes. "Okay, Gabe, enough antics. You barely made contact with it." She paused, returning her attention to Celeste. "Anyone other than you or me will be shocked if they touch it, and it will burn them if they hold it for more than a few seconds."

"How will I know the spell to use?" Celeste asked.

"I'll teach you. You'll need to be prepared."

Celeste nodded, but didn't appear confident. "Fine. But is that really the answer? Can't we do more? I mean, if you're saying this witch was locked away for a good reason, wouldn't it be better to put her back where she can't hurt anyone?"

"If it was that simple, I would have done it weeks ago," Becca said.

"Where is she? Maybe if we all put our strength together, we can banish her," Celeste insisted.

"It was hard enough when I did it two hundred years ago," Becca explained. "It took the strength of six experienced and powerful witches to cast that spell."

"Celeste is right," Gabriel said. "If you did it once, you should be able to do it again."

Becca sighed. "I've considered it, believe me. But our coven is relatively young. Our powers grow as we age, so I'm not sure we'd have the collective strength to do it. And I don't want to put that kind of pressure on the others. Besides, there are ingredients required. Back then, Marguerite was living in my home. It was easy to get a strand of her hair and a drop of blood from her horse. She's hiding now."

"Then we need to lure her out," I stated. "If she wants the words, then let's promise to give them to her."

"She'd see through that in a heartbeat," Becca said. "I believe she'll wait until she's ready to strike. She's probably watching our every move, calculating the right time. And she's close, we know that. We think she sabotaged Gracyn's car today." When Celeste looked at me, Becca told her about my accident on the way to school this morning.

"That's horrible. Are you okay?" Celeste asked, turning to me.

"Yes," I replied. "I'm fine. Just a little shaken up."

"Okay, good," she said with a sigh. "Becca, this is really serious. Shouldn't the rest of the coven hear this?"

"I'll let them know when the time is right. For now, the script is safe in the stone. I'm still here, so I'll watch over it. But if anything happens to me, you'll need to find it and reinstate the spell."

"But if your death reverses the spell and I replace it, then would my death break it as well?"

Becca nodded. "Yes. You catch on fast."

"Wow," Celeste said, her voice low, fear in her expression. "No matter how you look at this, it's bad."

"I know," Becca replied. "I'm reliving my worst nightmare from two hundred years ago."

"Where did the book come from, anyway?" Celeste asked.

"Medieval England. It ended up in the hands of a Salem witch before she was executed in the trials. She gave it to me to keep it safe, and yet it was still compromised. I fixed things two hundred years ago, but I never expected Marguerite to come back." Becca paused until Celeste met her gaze, holding it. "Listen, everything that has been said here today must stay between us. Do not tell a single soul what I've told you, not even your parents. Do you understand?"

Celeste nodded as if in a trance, her brown eyes soft and sincere. "Yes."

"Good. Now come with me," Becca said as she stood up. "I want to show you where to find the stone should something happen to me."

Celeste followed Becca into the back hallway while I waited with Gabriel. Silence took over, the mood heavy. "Well," I finally said. "Never a dull moment around here."

"Used to be dull all the time," Gabriel mused. When I glanced at him, he raised his eyebrows. "Until you showed up."

I sucked in a deep breath, nearly choking on it. I had no idea what that was supposed to mean and was about to ask when he smiled. "Sorry. I couldn't resist a little teasing right now, you know, to lighten the mood."

I shook my head. "Oh, I thought you were serious."

"No, why would I be?" he asked before getting up. "Guess I'll head out to bring the horses in. Unless you want to do it?"

"Um, no, I'd like to say goodbye to Celeste."

"Suit yourself," Gabriel said before grabbing his jacket from the coat closet and leaving out the front door.

When Celeste and Becca returned to the family room, I stood up. "Are you done?" I asked.

"Yes," Becca said. "Celeste knows exactly what to do." She turned to Celeste, taking her hand. "You can do this if you have to. Do not be afraid. You have far more strength and power than you give yourself credit for."

Celeste nodded weakly, seeming unsure. "Okay. I'll try to remember that."

Becca gave her a hug, then released her. When Celeste headed for the door, not bothering to say goodbye, I ran after her. Out on the porch, I called to her before she started down the steps to the driveway. "Celeste?"

With a deep breath, her shoulders rising and falling, she stopped and turned.

"Can we please be friends?" I asked. "I don't know what happened earlier today, but I miss talking to you."

She studied me, a concerned look in her eyes. "I'm worried about you."

"You shouldn't be."

"But I am because you're always with Lucian. I'm not angry at you for it, I'm scared."

Shaking my head, I remained quiet, hoping she'd explain.

"You're my friend and I don't want to lose you. I know you weren't here when Cassie died and you never knew her, but it's hard for me to get close to you when I'm afraid you'll end up just like her." She let out a deep breath. "Wow, I can't believe I just got that off my chest."

"I'm glad you explained it to me," I said. "But I'm not going anywhere. I feel perfectly safe when I'm with Lucian."

The fear in her eyes deepened. "And that's why I'm worried. Your trust could get you killed because he could do it again. So be careful and watch your back, okay?"

I swallowed nervously, the conviction in her voice sending a chill over me. "I'm always careful," I whispered.

"Good," was all she said before rushing down the steps. Seconds later, she jumped in her car and drove off, leaving me to wonder exactly how we had just left our friendship.

13

Lucian arrived at seven o'clock the next morning to give me a ride to school. When I heard the Range Rover in the driveway, I ran out the door, my book bag hanging from my shoulder. The cold morning breeze stinging my cheeks, I hurried to the passenger side and jumped in, grateful for the warmth. "Good morning," I said. "Thanks for the ride."

"No problem. How'd it go with Celeste?"

I shrugged, fastening my seat belt as he backed up and drove down the driveway. Shadows danced over the windshield from the rising sun peeking through the tree branches. "As good as can be expected, I guess," I said, leaving out the small detail that she was still scared of him. "Becca handled most of it, and she spent some time alone with Celeste. I guess we just have to trust the two of them to take care of this."

Lucian slowed the SUV when we approached the road, then looked both ways and pulled out, heading in the direction of town. "You sound skeptical."

"Why wouldn't I be? I feel like I should be doing more. Marguerite is my problem. I'm the one who caused all this chaos by releasing her, so I should fix it."

"You're being too hard on yourself. You were manipulated, and you didn't know what was happening."

I wanted to agree with him, but part of me wouldn't allow it. No matter how many times I heard that it wasn't my fault, I couldn't throw up my hands and relinquish the responsibility. I wouldn't find peace until Marguerite was no longer a threat to me or anyone else. "Unfortunately, knowing that doesn't make this any better. I'm probably going to worry about everyone, especially Becca, until this is over."

A frown settled over Lucian's face. "I know. She's very important to the coven. Even though things have been peaceful as long as I've been alive, I know the purest of hearts have always looked over everyone. There have always been at least three of them. Cassie actually made four of them until one died when she was a baby. Becca's the oldest, and she's always been an anchor to the coven. I can't imagine things without her."

"Me, neither," I muttered, not wanting to think about losing her. I paused, watching the woods out the window, my thoughts heavy. "Maybe we shouldn't talk about her anymore. What happened when you got home yesterday?"

He bit his lip, a look of frustration spreading over his eyes. "The cops made a total mess of the upstairs. I was up 'til midnight putting things back in order."

"What about your father?"

"He helped a little, but he spent most of the night in the office working, as usual."

"Do you know what he thinks about all this?"

Lucian shook his head. "Not sure, to be honest. We don't talk much." There it was again, the tension between him and his father.

"Maybe you should now that he's home. He's your family."

"I know, but we're not close. We never have been."

"It's not too late to change that," I said softly, hoping to see his anger fade.

"He may be all I have right now, but I don't have to like him. Every time I look at him, I just see what he did to my mother. He pushed her away and broke her heart, and it's nearly destroying her. She didn't deserve to be cast aside like a second-class citizen."

"Is that what happened?"

Lucian glanced my way, his eyes full of contempt. "He has a girlfriend, Gracyn."

"What? Oh, I didn't know that." Lucian's animosity toward his father suddenly made sense. "Does your mom know about her?"

"I don't know," he said. "I certainly haven't told her. That's the last thing she needs right now."

"Have you asked him about her? His girlfriend, I mean."

"Of course. I've even met her. He said he never felt like that about anyone before. He swore he tried with my mom, but it was different, cold, almost like an arranged marriage. Then he was on a business trip in New York a few years ago and met someone who swept him off his feet, so he says."

"But he's still married to your mom?"

"That's just a technicality. They haven't spoken in years."

"It sounds complicated."

"Trust me, it is."

Silence filling the SUV, I didn't know what else to say. Settling back in my seat, I focused on the road ahead, my mood plunging into a hazy realm between unsettled and downright depressed. As much as I wanted to help Lucian find some comfort in his parents' situation, I suspected nothing I said would make him feel better about it. So I refrained from pressing the issue. Perhaps I'd see more of his relationship with his father in the coming weeks, but until then, I had plenty to do, starting with learning how to deal with a witch who might strike when we least expected it.

—◦—

Lucian began my training Saturday morning. It was the weekend before Thanksgiving, and the air was frigid. High clouds hid the sun when I stepped out onto the porch to find Lucian leaning against the railing.

"Ready?" he asked, the silver cross dangling over his black shirt catching my attention in the overcast light.

"I suppose," I said, still not sure what to expect. I slipped on a pair of gloves, grateful for the sweater I wore under my jacket and the knit hat covering my head. My hair hung loose over my shoulders, keeping my neck warm.

"What's wrong? A little too early for you?" he asked.

"You could say that," I replied, noticing the smile on his face and gleam in his eyes. "It's only eight-thirty. Couldn't it have waited until maybe ten?" I'd had no idea he wanted to start this early until he called an hour ago to tell me to get ready.

"I find I have the most energy in the morning."

I raised my eyebrows. "How much energy will this require?"

"You'll see," he replied with a grin. "Come on. Let's go."

He gestured for me to lead the way. I took one step and stopped when I saw Shade waiting in the driveway. "We're not driving?"

"No. And I took the liberty of tacking up Gypsy for you while I was waiting." As if on cue, she walked out of the barn, the reins looped over her neck and the saddle secured to her back.

"Where are we going?" I asked, heading down the steps and across the driveway until I reached Gypsy's side.

"Up to the rock. This isn't something we can do in a gym," Lucian replied before climbing onto Shade's back. "Get on. Time's wasting."

Knowing I had no other choice, I led Gypsy to the mounting block and hopped on. As soon as my feet found the stirrups, I gathered the reins, hoping I was ready for whatever Lucian had in store for me. After I gave him a quick nod, he nudged Shade into a walk and headed for the trail leading into the woods. Gypsy and I followed, the quiet broken by the horses' hooves plodding on the ground.

We rode at a walk until we reached the open field Lucian and I had galloped across several weeks ago. "Let's pick up the pace," Lucian said. "We need to move a little faster. I have a lot to show you today."

"All right," I replied, prepared to grab Gypsy's mane when Lucian pushed Shade into a steady trot. Sighing with relief since it was far too early in the morning for a gallop, I posted to the rhythm, sitting up straight and pushing my heels down every time I rose out of the saddle. The cold air whipped against my face, but before long, I grew hot under my heavy sweater and jacket.

About fifteen minutes later, we reached the top of the hill where the rocky cliff jutted up to the sky. "Please tell me we're not climbing up there today," I said as the horses halted.

"Not right now. We need a place where we won't be disturbed, and this seemed like the best option." Lucian hopped off Shade and approached Gypsy. "Okay. Let's get started."

I dismounted and turned, surprised to find Lucian inches away. I stopped and glanced up at him, his stare unsettling me once again. My breath got stuck in my throat, his gaze rendering me speechless. His broad shoulders filled out his jacket, blocking my view of the field even though everything around him was a hazy blur. Trying to resist the pull he had on me, I waited for him to speak.

"Ready?" he asked, his voice quiet, like he'd lost his focus for a few seconds.

I nodded without a word, thankful when Lucian backed away, breaking the awkward moment.

"Good," he said with a smile. "Now try to find me."

Confused, I started to laugh when he vanished just like that. There was no blurred movement of him running into the woods, not even a flash. In an instant, the world around me became still and silent.

"What in the world?" I gasped, spinning around and looking for him. But all I saw were the horses grazing in the corner of the otherwise empty field, the trees reaching for the sky in the background. "Lucian! Where are you? What's happening?"

"Over here." His voice came from the side, but when I snapped my attention in that direction, he wasn't there.

Shaking my head, I scanned the entire area, but all that caught my eye was a blue jay flying overhead. It landed on a nearby branch, watching me from its perch.

With a frustrated huff, I spun around, feeling helpless. I wasn't sure whether to be amazed or frightened. When I looked back at the bird, two hands covered my eyes. "Miss me?" Lucian said from behind me.

My heart nearly dropped into my stomach. Whipping around, I backed away from him, noting the smug grin on his face. "How did you do that?" I asked.

"Magic."

"And is this part of my training, or are you just messing around?"

"A little bit of both."

"Okay," I rolled out slowly. "So are you going to tell me how you disappeared into thin air?"

"I didn't really disappear. All I did was cloak myself so you couldn't see me, but I was still here. You need to learn that one. It could help you some day."

"Oh, fun," I said sarcastically, finding it hard to believe I was actually contemplating learning how to make myself invisible. "How does it work? Do I have to know a spell or something?"

"No. It's way too soon to work on spells. Spells aren't something we do often, anyway. Everything I'm about to show you today comes from your inner energy. You just have to want to make it happen. Feel it inside you." His eyes locked with mine, the intensity in them unnerving me.

Forcing myself to focus, I nodded, remembering the first time I'd felt that energy flow through me, causing me to break a grown man's hand. "Like when I defended myself against Sam's stepfather?"

"Exactly. The problem now is that you have to learn to protect yourself from another witch, not a human. So you need to learn to cloak yourself. It could be one of your best defenses."

"Okay. I'll try. But what else are you planning to teach me?"

"Maybe something like this," he said, stepping back and raising his hand. He stared at his palm and a spark appeared, growing into a ball of fire. When it reached the size of a baseball, he threw it across the field, hitting a tree branch. It split away from the trunk with a loud cracking sound and fell to the ground.

I watched in amazement, though not nearly as shocked as I'd been when I first learned magic was real. To my dismay, things like this were starting to feel normal. "Impressive," I said. "Celeste turns feathers into doves, and you can make fire out of air. Maybe I can take some strands from Gypsy's tail and create a new herd of horses."

Lucian smiled, choking out a laugh. "What did Celeste do?"

When I described the night she filled my bedroom with doves, he shook his head. "I never thought she had it in her."

"What do you mean?"

"I don't mean her power. Everyone knows she's going to be the most powerful witch in the coven one day. I mean breaking the rules. We're not supposed to play with magic. It's not a toy. She's got a little more spunk than I've given her credit for. Good for her."

"Then what are we doing here? Are we playing with magic?"

"Not at all. You need to know how to tap into your energy in case you need it. Using magic for survival isn't against the rules. If Marguerite tries anything else, you have to be ready to defend yourself. And I aim to ensure it's a fair fight."

"Fair? Something tells me that's not possible. She's two hundred years old and knew what she was her whole life. I just found out a few months ago."

"That's no reason for you to roll over and let her win. But if this is making you nervous, there's another option."

"What's that?" I asked, not sure I was going to like his answer.

"I become your personal bodyguard and never leave your side. Which house should we pick, mine or yours? Probably mine since it's a little bigger, and I'm guessing Becca and Gabriel wouldn't be too happy if I moved in."

Rolling my eyes, I groaned. "Okay. I get it. Let's keep going with the lesson."

He paused, grinning from ear to ear. "Actually, I kind of like the alternative. What do you say?" Before I could respond, his smile collapsed into a scowl. "Unfortunately, I don't know how much longer I'll be around to protect you. So we have to move on and make sure you know how to defend yourself. No more small talk. Let's get back to work. Your turn. I want you to concentrate on cloaking yourself."

I stood where I was, feeling a bit silly while he watched and waited, seeming to expect something to happen. Shrugging, I took a deep breath. "How? I don't even know where to begin."

"Close your eyes and channel your energy. Focus on the invisible. You can do it, I know you can. You have just as much power as any of us, or you never would have hurt your friend's stepfather the way you did."

Realizing I had to try, I let my eyelids fall shut. Darkness claimed my world, making every sound around me seem louder. Birds chirped from the woods, and I heard a squirrel's feet scraping against the bark of a tree as it scampered up into the branches. Somewhere in the distance, light footsteps trudged through the leaves, like those belonging to a deer making its way through the forest.

I imagined hiding from Lucian, and a warm glow swept through my veins. As the heat inside me grew, taking over, I whipped my eyes open.

Lucian looked around as though he couldn't see me. "Good job. Now where are you, my star student?"

Amazed, I watched him walk in circles, his hands out in front of him. When he got too close to me, I jumped out of the way, wondering if he'd hear my footsteps in the grass, but he didn't seem to notice.

For a few minutes, we played a game of cat and mouse. Lucian continued to wander, searching the area, but I evaded his hands every time he came near. Finally, when his back was to me, I spoke up. "How do I come back?"

He spun around. "Just will it to happen."

"It's that easy?"

"Should be."

"Okay." I blinked my eyes, concentrating on making myself visible again. When I looked at Lucian, his eyes met mine, and I knew he could see me again. I smiled, proud of myself for doing what would have seemed impossible a few months ago. "That wasn't hard."

"No, it's not. And if you want to hide something other than yourself, all you have to do is touch it and channel the same energy."

"Really? What about another person?"

Lucian nodded. "It'll also work on Gypsy as long as you're touching her. But it's one of the oldest tricks in the books, so you can bet Marguerite will be expecting it. Now let's work on some other skills."

For the next few hours, Lucian showed me things I never expected I could do. He taught me how to create a ball of fire in my hands, make a log from a stick, and move things with my mind. Some of the tasks were easier than others, but I felt like I was finally learning how to use my power. The only thing that bothered me was knowing I'd probably need these skills to defend myself against Marguerite.

We were practicing the fire trick when the ball I threw never made it to the woods. I hurled it at the trees in the distance, but it stopped in mid-air halfway across the field. Confused, I turned to Lucian, about to ask him what was happening when a familiar laugh cackled over the breeze. Spinning around, I drew in a sharp breath at the sight of Marguerite. The fireball had been reduced to a pile of ashes in her hands, the gray flakes sifting through her fingers and falling to the ground.

"What's this? A lesson in magic, I presume?" she asked sarcastically, approaching us. A chestnut horse followed her, its red coat standing out against her black clothes.

"What do you want?" Lucian demanded.

"Just to give you both a little advice. Your session here is nice, it really is. But she'll never be strong enough to defeat me. You're a fool if you think otherwise."

Swallowing hard, I forced myself to stand tall, refusing to let her chip away at my confidence.

Marguerite stopped a few feet in front of us, her blue eyes narrowed and a smug grin on her face. "But keep working on it, by all means. I love a good challenge."

"Stay away from her. I have half a mind to take you out right now," Lucian said. "After what you did to Celeste, the others are waiting for you. No one's going to say a word if I rid the world of a wretched mess like you."

"Go ahead and try," she said with confidence. "You're no match for me."

Lucian scowled, but stayed where he was. "Why don't you just leave us alone?"

"I have no desire to deal with you. It isn't even Gracyn I want. But if Becca won't do what I ask, then she leaves me no choice. I know she'll give in if it means saving Gracyn."

"And the car? The brakes? That was you, wasn't it?"

Marguerite smiled. "Perhaps."

"She could have been killed. What were you thinking?"

"I wasn't going to let that happen. I was there, watching the whole time. Because let's face it, if she dies, then my leverage is gone. I just wanted to rattle some nerves. Seems to have worked." Marguerite stepped closer to Lucian, her eyes on him. "Listen up. If you care about this little half-breed here, you'll convince Becca to reverse her spell on the book and restore the script. Once the words are back on those pages, I'll leave all of you alone."

"And if I don't?" Lucian asked.

Marguerite stepped back, her hands on her hips. "You will. You just need a little convincing. Maybe this will change your mind." She raised her arm and flicked her wrist, causing an invisible force to send him flying backward through the air before he slammed into a tree.

I watched in shock as he crumpled to the ground. Turning to Marguerite, I drew in a deep breath, but never had a chance to speak.

"Consider that another warning," she said. "Now go home and report all of this to Becca. Make sure you tell her I'm not giving up until I get what I want. And understand one thing. The longer she holds out on me, the more pain I'll cause."

Then she whipped around, jumped on her horse, and galloped away.

14

I rushed to Lucian's side and dropped to my knees beside him. Shade trotted over, stretching his neck down and nudging Lucian with his muzzle, a concerned look in his soft brown eyes. "Lucian!" I said.

Lucian opened his eyes, a dazed look in them while he raised a hand to the bridge of Shade's nose. "What happened?" he asked as he sat up.

"Marguerite just slammed you into a tree," I replied, glancing behind him at a huge crack in the trunk. "It must have been a pretty hard impact. You splintered it."

Lucian turned to look at the damage, a look of pain on his face. "Ow. Yes, now I remember. She doesn't know who she's messing with. Where is she?"

"I have no idea. She took off a minute ago."

"Well then, her punishment will have to wait." Lucian started to stand, wincing as he got to his feet.

"Are you okay?" I asked, rising beside him and placing my hand on his arm.

"Yeah, I'll be fine. I think she hurt my pride more than anything. I wish you hadn't seen that."

"Why? We're all in this together."

"Because I'm supposed to be the tough guy. You know, invincible. I should be saving you, not the other way around."

Tilting my head, I folded my arms across my chest, feeling a smile roll onto my lips when I couldn't keep a straight face. "And why is that? Because I'm a girl and you're a guy?"

"Something like that," he said with a shrug. "Guys can be very insecure, you know. We need to be heroes. Otherwise, we don't know what you ladies see in us."

I paused, wondering if that meant his feelings for me extended beyond friendship. As much as I wanted to ask him, I chickened out, knowing this wasn't the right time to launch my questions about our relationship. Instead, something Marguerite said slipped into my mind. "Marguerite called me a half-breed. Do you have any idea what that's all about?"

Lucian's mouth twisted in confusion. "Yes, she did. It implies you're only half witch, meaning one of your parents is like us and one is human. But I'm sorry, I have no idea where she got that idea."

"Hmm," I mused with a huff. "Guess it's time to start pushing Becca to ante up."

"She still hasn't told you who your parents are?"

"Nope," I said with a frown, frustrated with Becca's refusal to tell me what she knew about them. To think Marguerite knew who my parents were infuriated me. "It's starting to get really old. Every time I bring it up with her, she conveniently changes the subject. And now I'm going to have a complex."

"Why?"

"Because if I really am only half witch, I must be in a class all by myself. I'm not like you, and I'm not human. How many other half-breeds are part of the coven?"

Lucian shrugged, his expression softening. "None, sorry. But I wouldn't let it bother you. As far as I can tell, you're as powerful as any of the rest of us. Look at what you did here today. You picked up on everything I showed you as if it came naturally to you."

"I tried."

"Well, you did fine. But now Marguerite knows what we're up to. She's not going to be easy to get rid of. Damn! As if I don't have enough to deal with right now."

"I'm sorry," I said.

"It's not your fault." Lucian paused, glancing at the horses grazing about twenty feet away. "Ready to call it a day?"

"Sure," I said, disappointed with the idea of heading home. I wished he'd suggest we get together later, perhaps for dinner.

You seem to keep forgetting he's under investigation for murder right now, a voice in my head scolded. *Give the guy a break. He probably won't be ready to get involved with anyone until that's behind him. Let him have some space and time.* My spirits fell even though I knew I needed to be patient. The cops were breathing down his neck, watching his every move. Dating was probably the furthest thing from his mind.

"Are you coming?" Lucian asked, his voice breaking me out of my thoughts.

Shifting my attention to him, I jogged across the field, approaching him as he held his hand out to me. "I'll give you a leg up," he offered.

I stopped and flashed an appreciative smile. "Thank you," I said softly.

But he made no move. Instead, he raised his hand and moved my hair behind my shoulder. His fingers grazed my jaw, sending a wave of electricity through me. My breath hitched, my heart fluttering. "What?" I asked quietly.

"I'm starting to like my alternative plan a little better," he whispered.

His eyes held my gaze, mesmerizing me. "And what was that again?" I asked, incapable of remembering anything at this moment.

"You know, spending every waking minute together."

"Really?" I asked, my earlier insecurities disappearing. "Wouldn't that be a bit much?"

"No, never. Although you might get sick of me."

"No, I wouldn't," I said a little too quickly.

"You never know. I can be a little moody at times."

"No," I gushed, mocking him with surprise.

"Yes, it's true. And I don't want to bring you down." He paused, then looked away from me, his expression falling into another frown. "Come on. I'll help you get on so we can head home."

I nodded without saying a word and turned around to face the saddle. Lucian bent down and wrapped his hand around my calf, causing my heart to skip again. I took a deep breath, jumping on three and landing in the saddle. When Lucian let go of me and walked over to Shade, I picked up the reins and slid my feet into the stirrups, glad to have some distance between us. Perhaps it was better he hadn't suggested we do something later. I had a feeling I'd have enough trouble getting him off my mind after this morning. A date with him would probably make my head spin and cause me to lose all sense of reality, something I barely seemed able to hold onto these days.

— ❧ —

The rest of my day was a complete bust. I tried to study, but couldn't stop thinking about the morning. Whether it was the memory of moving things with my mind, the image of Lucian flying through the air before slamming into a tree, or Marguerite's claim that I was a half-breed, I wasn't sure. All of the events from the day tumbled through my head, taking over my thoughts until I closed my History book, giving up on the chapter I was reading.

I wanted to talk to Becca, but she and Gabriel had gone to the store to get the few ingredients they didn't have for Thanksgiving. So instead of pushing her for answers about my parents as I'd planned, I set up my easel and worked on a painting since it was the only thing that seemed to help me relax.

By the time I ventured downstairs after the sun went down, the house had been decorated for the upcoming holiday. A fall wreath of red, yellow, and gold leaves hung on the front door, and orange candles were centered on the coffee table. Becca was in the kitchen, humming as she manned a pot of spaghetti on the stove.

"There you are," she said when I approached the island and sat down. The dogs snoozed on their beds by the table, not batting an eye at my entrance.

"Yes. I'm here," I replied.

"Are you staying in tonight?"

"It looks that way," I muttered, my mood souring at the idea of being on my own for another Saturday night.

"You don't sound too happy about that. Do you miss Alex?"

"A little," I lied, realizing I'd been too consumed with Lucian to spend any time missing Alex.

"Not to change the subject, but I wanted to ask if you've talked to your mom about your accident."

I frowned, still finding it hard to believe my car was gone. I also had no idea if or when I'd get a replacement. "Yes and no. I told her about it in an email and, of course, she asked right away if I was hurt."

"You told her you're fine, right?"

"Yes. It only took about six emails because she didn't seem to believe the first five. But we haven't talked about getting a new car."

"Why not?"

"I don't feel right asking her for something like that. Besides, Lucian's been giving me a ride to and from school, so I haven't really needed a replacement yet."

Becca raised her eyebrows, but refrained from mentioning Lucian. "Listen," she started. "About a new car. Gabe and I would like to help you with that. I feel somewhat responsible for this mess, so maybe some weekend, we can go to a few dealerships and see what they have. We should probably look for something with four-wheel drive, since you'll need it up here. If you can use the insurance money as a down payment, we'll cover the rest."

"Becca, that's very generous of you, but I don't know if I can accept it."

"Why not? We're family."

"Yeah," I grumbled. "So you say. But I'm still not clear on that. Care to elaborate?"

"Gracyn, please, let's not dredge this up again."

"Why not? It's not going away until you tell me the truth. Why won't you tell me who my parents are? You have to know my curiosity is killing me."

Becca took a deep breath, her eyes shifting, avoiding my gaze. "I'm sorry, I'm just not sure if you're ready."

"If I'm ready, or if you're ready?" I clarified. "Or perhaps it has something to do with the fact that I'm what's known as a half-breed. Half witch, half human."

"What?" she gasped, the color draining from her cheeks. "Where did you hear that?"

"Marguerite mentioned it this morning. Is it true?"

"You saw Marguerite again?"

"Yes," I replied. "She dropped in on me and Lucian while he was teaching me how to use my power in case I need to defend myself against her. But that's not important right now. I'm not going to stop asking you who my parents are until you tell me."

"It's complicated," she said, her voice low.

"Yeah, you've mentioned that before. Here's the thing. I don't care. Just blurt it out. Why all the secrecy?"

When Becca didn't respond, I drew in a frustrated sigh. "Because it's true, isn't it? I am a half-breed."

She looked up, a guilty glaze in her eyes.

"Great," I said. "That's just great. What does this mean? Am I going to be looked down upon? Is that why you don't want me to know? So the other witches don't shun me or something?"

"No, it's nothing like that. No one will really care as long as you abide by our code to never use your power for selfish reasons and that you keep our secrets safe and away from humans."

"Am I less powerful because of it?"

"That doesn't appear to be the case. When you were born, we wondered about that. But ever since you cursed your friend's stepfather, not to mention broke his hand, I'm pretty sure you're just as powerful as you'd be if both of your parents were witches. Besides, it's not really important. You're a beautiful young woman who's also strong and generous. You should be proud."

"It would be easier to know who I am if I knew who my parents were," I said, starting to give up any hope of finding out tonight. Once again, Becca didn't seem ready to indulge me.

"I know, but—" Her words were cut off when Gabriel walked in through the front door. He took off his coat and hung it up in the closet before approaching the island.

"Hmm," he said, going straight for the bottle of red wine on the counter and pouring a glass. "Smells good. Did you make meatballs, too?" he asked, lifting the lid off the pot of tomato sauce.

"Of course," Becca replied before launching into a conversation with him.

Disappointment struck me, but it was no worse than it always was when I tried to get answers out of Becca with no success.

She can't hide the truth forever, a voice slid into my head.

Maybe not, but it looks like she's going to try, I added, my hopes sinking. One of these days, I had to push harder, demand an answer, as long as it didn't come to anything confrontational. She'd eventually realize how much she was hurting me by keeping my parents a secret and, until then, I had to be patient.

15

The next week was Thanksgiving, giving me a much needed break from school. I had plenty of homework to catch up on, not to mention a pile of college applications on my desk to finish. Beyond that, I hoped to work on my painting. The vision of Shade and Gypsy in the field up at the rock the other morning had inspired me. Their contrasting colors of pure black and red sprinkled with white were a perfect combination to recreate on canvas.

Thanksgiving was quiet, much like it had been with my mom in the past. Becca and Gabriel worked in the kitchen, preparing a feast for the three of us. When I offered to help, they shooed me away, telling me they had everything under control and that I should enjoy myself until it was time to eat.

After spending several hours up in my room engrossed in a book, I wandered downstairs at four o'clock. "Hmm," I said, taking in the aroma of roast turkey as I headed for the kitchen where Becca was peeling potatoes. "That smells delicious."

She looked up at me. "We should be ready to eat in about an hour. You came down at the perfect time. Would you mind setting the table?"

"Of course not." I immediately went to work, putting out plates, silverware, and glasses. But it only took a few minutes before I finished. "Now what?"

"Um," Becca quirked her eyebrows and glanced around. "Would you go out and see if Gabriel needs any help in the barn? He left about a half hour ago to put the horses away so we wouldn't have to do it after dinner."

"Sure," I said before heading straight for the coat closet to grab my jacket and gloves. I hurried outside, down the porch steps, and across the driveway, the sun hovering above the treetops nearly blinding me and the cold stinging my face.

As I rushed ahead to the barn, the dogs wandered about, their noses glued to the ground. I entered the barn to find it dark and empty with no sign of Gabriel. Piles of manure mixed with soiled wood shavings littered the stalls, making me wonder what Gabriel had been doing all this time.

Curious, I left through the back doorway and approached the pasture where Gypsy and Cadence nibbled at what little grass remained. They snorted, not seeming to care that their dark bay companion was missing.

"That's odd," I muttered before whistling to Gypsy. As soon as she trotted over, I opened the gate to let her through and shut it behind her. She followed me back to the barn where I snatched her halter from a hook and slipped it over her ears. Wasting no time to tack up, I led her out to the driveway and climbed onto her back from the mounting block.

"Let's see if we can find Gabriel and Prince," I whispered, nudging her sides with my calves. She picked up a brisk walk, her hooves clattering against the gravel with every step.

We set off into the woods on the trail, but after a few minutes, Gypsy turned and headed through the forest, leaving the path behind. The light grew dim, the branches shielding what was left of the sun as it dropped to the horizon. We hadn't gone very far when I saw Gabriel's dark bay horse standing between two trees in the distance, his brown coat blending into the woods. He stood alone, his head hung low, his ears flickering every few seconds.

I halted Gypsy about fifty feet from Prince and listened carefully, picking up on hushed whispering. My eyes flew wide open, and I scanned the surrounding area in the direction of the voices, my heart accelerating when I saw Gabriel. But my attention was pulled away from him when a flash of red moved through the forest, disappearing like lightning. Then he turned, looking in my direction.

Without a second to spare, I channeled my energy in a swift blow, concentrating on cloaking myself and Gypsy. Holding my breath, I watched Gabriel approach Prince as though nothing was out of order. My attempt to hide must have worked, and I let out a sigh of relief. Not wanting to linger any longer, I spun Gypsy around and pushed her into a canter, hoping to return home before Gabriel.

I ducked down close to Gypsy's mane, dodging the branches while she charged through the woods. My heart pounding, images of the red flash I'd just seen sent my mind whirling with suspicion. Marguerite was in the vicinity again, and I couldn't be sure when or where she'd show up next, but I felt certain it would be soon.

Before long, Gabriel wandered into my thoughts, the idea of him with her rolling a shiver up my spine. When I started to speculate on what he'd been doing in the woods, I tried to tell myself there had to be a reasonable explanation. But I couldn't get rid of the nagging feeling that something wasn't right.

Back at the barn, I returned Gypsy to the pasture, hung her halter on the hook beside her stall, and grabbed the wheelbarrow and pitchfork. By the time Gabriel showed up, I was ankle-deep in manure and dirty shavings.

"Gracyn," he said when he led Prince into the barn. "You don't have to do that. I told Becca I'd take care of the chores out here."

"I don't mind," I said, pausing to study him from where I stood in the center of Gypsy's stall. My gaze meeting his, I wanted to ask where he'd been, but at the same time, I didn't want him to suspect I knew anything. Pushing my doubts aside, I flashed what I hoped was a convincing smile to convey that everything was fine. "Becca said dinner will be ready soon. If we work together, we can finish out here faster."

He hesitated, his stare unsettling me. "Sure. That sounds like a good plan. I'll get to work as soon as I untack." Instead of turning to his horse, Gabriel stood in the aisle, watching me with a thoughtful look in his blue eyes.

"Great," I said quickly before shoving the pitchfork tines under another pile. Out of the corner of my eye, I saw him shift his attention to Prince, relieved the awkward moment was over. The last thing I wanted was to make small talk, especially after finding him off the trail.

How I managed to get through the next twenty minutes working in the barn with Gabriel, I'd never know. The image of him in the woods when he was supposed to be taking care of the horses and the flash of red replayed over and over in my mind. As the minutes ticked by, I grew more convinced he was up to no good. I resisted the urge to run to Becca and share what I'd seen with her, telling myself the red blur could have been a figment of my imagination. After all, Marguerite had become a thorn in my side since her last few appearances, especially when she'd slammed Lucian into a tree. And I wasn't sure how Becca would react if I led her to believe I didn't trust Gabriel.

Dinner that evening was anything but enjoyable. I filled my plate with turkey, mashed potatoes, and dressing, but my appetite had vanished the moment I'd found Gabriel off the trail. Throughout the meal, I listened to Becca and Gabriel talk about the upcoming carnival, biting my tongue every time the image of Gabriel sneaking around in the woods returned to my thoughts, tempting me to mention it. Instead, I forced down most of what was on my plate before excusing myself and retreating to my room.

Once upstairs, I went to my desk and gazed out the window, the twilight hour marked by the sky's hazy shade of purple. My thoughts shifting from Gabriel to Lucian, I wondered how his Thanksgiving was going. I'd kept my phone by my side all day and had yet to hear from him.

Feeling frustrated with too much pent-up energy, I sighed, not ready for another long night. Then an idea formed in my mind. I jumped up and ran downstairs where Becca and Gabriel were relaxing on the couch as a fire crackled in the hearth.

"Becca, can I borrow your car?" I asked.

She glanced at me, seeming surprised. "I suppose," she replied before getting up and joining me in the kitchen where I peeled back the plastic wrap covering a half-eaten apple pie. "May I ask where you're going?"

"I thought I'd take some dessert to a friend. Is that okay?" I asked, cutting a piece and sliding it onto a small plate.

"Sure. How long do you think you'll be out?"

"Maybe an hour or two. He's not expecting me, but I can't sit up in my room all night. I'll go crazy."

"And who might this friend be?"

I raised my eyebrows, surprised she had to ask.

"Lucian?"

When I nodded, she frowned, and I wondered if she was going to say no.

"I figured as much," she said. "Okay, I'll get my keys." She disappeared into the hallway leading to the master bedroom before returning with them jingling in her hand. "Tell Everett I said hello," she said with a small smile as she gave them to me.

"I will if I see him. Thanks."

Becca returned to the couch while I covered the piece of pie with plastic wrap, grabbed my jacket and gloves, and rushed out the door before either she or Gabriel could object. They seemed to have let up on the time I spent with Lucian since he'd brought me home after my car accident. I wasn't sure my reprieve from their lectures would last forever, but I was enjoying the break for now.

A few minutes later, I pulled into Lucian's driveway and parked beside his Range Rover. Lights lit up the mansion, making it seem warm and inviting, unlike the cold, dark feeling that had shrouded the estate on many of my previous visits.

With the plate in my hands, I approached the mahogany doors and rang the bell. Waiting in the cold, I exhaled slowly, watching my breath form a fog in front of me. Seconds later, Lucian's father opened the door, his blue jeans and light brown shirt a casual change from the suits he'd worn in the past.

"Gracyn," he said, a smile lighting up his handsome face. "This is quite a surprise. Please, come in." He gestured toward the entry hall.

I stepped inside, turning to him as he shut the door, the scent of turkey filling the house. "I'm sorry to show up unannounced, but I thought I'd bring Lucian a piece of apple pie. I wasn't sure if he was alone today. I hope you had a nice Thanksgiving."

"We did, thank you. It was very relaxing."

I smiled, not having a chance to reply when a woman's voice came from the kitchen. "Everett?"

I glanced at the hallway as a tall woman appeared in the doorway. She leaned against the frame, her long black curls hiding her shoulders and her smooth dark skin nearly flawless. Appearing to be in her thirties, she wore a burgundy sweater with jeans, her look simple, yet elegant and confident.

"Gracyn, this is a friend of mine from New York." Everett beamed when his eyes fell on her. "Samira, I'd like you to meet Gracyn. She lives next door and is a friend of Lucian's."

"Hello," she said, a slight accent in her voice.

"Hi," I replied, assuming she was the girlfriend Lucian had mentioned last week. Then I shifted my attention back to his father. "Is Lucian here?"

Everett tossed a swift nod in the direction of the stairs. "He's been hiding all day. Perhaps you can convince him to come down for something to eat. I'll take you to him. Samira, I'll be right back."

Samira nodded with a soft smile, her gaze landing on me one last time before she returned to the kitchen.

I followed Everett up the stairs, and he led me down the hall until we stopped at the third door. After knocking twice, he cracked it open. I peeked inside to see a bed made up with a navy comforter surrounded by walls painted light gray. But the room was empty.

"He must be in the studio. This way." Everett continued down the hall to the far end where he halted in front of another closed door. He knocked again, this time louder.

Music spilled from the room when Everett pushed the door open to reveal a large open space. No furniture covered the vast expanse of hardwood floor, and paintings of all sizes leaned against the walls. Two windows were centered on the wall facing the door, the black night as smooth as velvet rolling out beyond the panes.

Lucian stood in the corner at the far end of the room, his back to us as he faced an easel, completely lost in his work while he swept a brush across the canvas.

"Lucian," Everett said in a firm yet gentle tone. When Lucian turned, a scowl on his face, his father continued. "You have company."

Lucian met his father's stare before looking at me, his eyes softening a little.

"Thank you," I said to Everett.

He nodded. "I'll leave you two alone, but if you convince him to join us downstairs, there are plenty of leftovers for both of you."

"That's very generous, but I already ate. I'm not really hungry."

"Well, he didn't, so maybe you can break him away from his work long enough to grab a bite."

"I'll try," I told him.

Everett flashed one last smile before leaving me alone with Lucian in the studio.

I slowly walked across the room, my gaze drawn to the paintings lining the walls, some leaning in stacks of two and three. Several easels had been set up, and a long table against the back wall was cluttered with jars of paint, brushes, and other supplies. It was an artist's haven, a place to draw and create with no distractions.

After setting the dessert plate on the edge of the table, I approached Lucian who continued working, his back to me. The painting of a beautiful woman with long auburn hair and soft brown eyes wearing a blue gown took my breath away. "Wow. That's beautiful. What's your inspiration for this?" I asked when I stopped beside him.

"My mother," he said, his eyes focused on the woman looking back at him from the canvas.

"If that's what she really looks like, she's gorgeous."

"That's how she used to look, before he hurt her," Lucian muttered, his frown hard.

I reached up and touched his shoulder, but he didn't move, not even to glance my way. "You really care about her, don't you?"

"Yes," he said, dipping his brush in a jar of paint and working on the ruffled skirt to her dress. "Too bad I can't say the same for my father."

"Look, I'm sure it's hard to accept your parents' situation, but you're going to have to."

Lucian dropped the brush onto the easel ledge and whipped around, his eyes cold. "Did you meet his girlfriend? He had the audacity to bring her here for the weekend. If I could leave town, I'd be on a plane right now."

"Yes, I met her. She seems nice."

Lucian swallowed, narrowing his eyes. "Sure, she's nice if you like black magic."

"What?"

He nodded, sparks flying from his eyes. "You heard me. She's from Ethiopia. An African witch. That's all we need around here."

"Have you talked to your father about that?"

"Of course. But he says he's in love with her and that I should accept her."

"Look, I don't know your father very well, but he came back to town when you needed him. Maybe you can give him the benefit of the doubt."

"Why? It'll just make him think I've accepted his fling. And I'll never approve of his behavior."

"Is that what it is?" I asked, doubt creeping into my voice. The way his father had looked at Samira led me to believe there was something special between them.

"I don't know. He says he's in love with her in a way he's never been in love before. But how do I know that? Does that mean he just used my mother to get children? And now his daughter is dead and his son is under investigation for her murder. Maybe he wants me to end up in jail. Then he'd be rid of his entire family, setting him free to ride off into the sunset with that stranger."

"Or maybe he wanted her to spend the holiday here so you could get to know her."

"He's dreaming if he thinks that'll happen."

Realizing this conversation was going nowhere, I looked around the room, studying the paintings. "Are all of these yours?" I asked, gesturing to them.

He shook his head. "No, not all. My mother also loved to paint. Some of them are hers."

"Really? You never mentioned that."

"I know. I don't like to talk about her much. It's too hard when I know she's going through a tough time."

"I understand. But would you mind showing me some of her work? I'd love to see something she painted."

Nodding, Lucian walked across the room to a stack of paintings leaning against the wall. He shuffled through them until he paused and slipped one out to the side. The image of a little boy sitting in front of a Christmas tree captivated me. He wore a suit, his hair combed neatly and his young eyes angled downward to the baby in his arms, a pink blanket wrapped around her.

I felt the bitter sting of tears in my eyes, but blinked them back, refusing to let my emotions get the best of me. "This is stunning. Is that you?"

Lucian nodded. "With Cassie. That was about two months after she was born. I remember it was the happiest I'd ever seen my mother. She loved Cassie, perhaps because my father treasured her. Maybe my mother knew she had done something to make him happy."

"It's a shame to see it hidden away in this room. You should get it framed and hang it up. It doesn't do it justice to be collecting dust in here."

"I thought about it, but I like keeping her paintings in here where I don't have to share them. Besides, I don't want to put it where my father can see it. He doesn't deserve to have this memory after what he did."

The bitterness in Lucian's voice struck a chord in my heart. I reached for his hand, and his eyes locked with mine. He stepped toward me until we were so close that I could feel the heat from his chest. He threaded his fingers through mine, closing them as he raised our linked hands up between our hearts.

"I want you to know I will never do that to you," he said quietly, his words barely audible over the music.

I nodded, a bit surprised by his promise since our relationship had never gone beyond that of friends. "But—"

"Shh," he said, holding a finger up to my lips with his free hand. "I know what you're thinking, and it will happen when the time is right. It's just not now. I need you to be patient. We have to wait."

"Wait for what?" I asked, confused and frustrated. He was teasing me, tempting me with something he didn't seem ready to give. Part of me wanted to give up on him. Stop hoping there would be more and move on. But I couldn't. He'd gotten under my skin, and I had to be patient as he asked. The investigation wasn't over and, until he was cleared, I couldn't expect anything more than friendship from him. "I'm sorry," I said, shaking my head, embarrassed by my question. Pulling away from him, I glanced back at the table. "I brought you a piece of apple pie in case you're hungry."

"Thank you. That was very thoughtful."

"Your father said you haven't eaten dinner yet. Maybe you can have the pie after you get some leftovers."

"Please tell him I'm not hungry."

When my eyes met his, a renewed sadness swept over me. I wished Lucian could come to terms with his father's decisions, but I didn't press him. "If that's what you want. But I'll leave the pie in case you change your mind."

He nodded, a small smile forming on his lips before they flattened into another frown.

Silence stretched between us, the music taking over the moment. I took a deep breath. "I should be going. See you soon?"

"Yes," he said before returning to his painting, not bothering to offer to walk me out.

My heart heavy, I grabbed the pie and left the room. As I shut the door, I hoped he would find some peace, not only tonight but also in the future. He couldn't change his parents' situation, but perhaps one day he would accept it and not let it stand in the way of his own happiness.

16

I hurried downstairs to the foyer and headed straight for the kitchen where I found Everett and Samira sitting at the island, coffee mugs and empty dessert plates on the counter. The table was spotless, and even though the food had been put away, the scent of turkey and seasonings hung in the air. I stopped in the doorway, smiling shyly when Everett and Samira turned their attention to me.

"Leaving so soon?" he asked.

"Yes. Lucian's really caught up in his work this evening. I just wanted to drop this off in case he decides to come down for dinner later." Remaining in the doorway, I held out the plate.

Samira stood up and walked over to me before taking the dessert. "I'll take care of that," she said.

My eyes meeting hers, I nodded. "Thank you. Well, have a nice night." As I turned and headed into the entry hall, I heard footsteps behind me.

"I'll walk you out," Everett said, beating me to the door. Not wasting a minute to get a jacket, he stepped outside with me and shut the door. The cold air took my breath away, the lights glowing in the darkness.

We followed the sidewalk until we reached the driveway and stopped. I was about to get in Becca's SUV when he spoke.

"I'm glad you came by," he said. "I haven't been able to get through to Lucian since I returned. You seem to be the only person he trusts right now."

I sighed, not sure how to respond.

Everett watched me, a forced smile on his face. "I only want to help him, but I know he blames me for his mother's depression." He shook his head, then continued. "I did everything I could think of to save our marriage, but sometimes your heart takes you where you least expect it to. His mother is a wonderful woman, and I loved her. In a way, I still do. But I was never in love with her. When Lucian and his sister were young, I felt our marriage slipping away and I didn't know what to do. I felt like I'd been backed into a corner. Then I met Samira on a business trip in New York, and everything changed."

"Why are you telling me this?"

"Because I need you to know it's not something I planned. I finally found the one, but the circumstances made it complicated. Perhaps if I can get you to understand, you can help Lucian understand, too."

"But you're still married—"

"Not willingly," he said, interrupting me. "I filed for divorce almost two years ago. It's not final until Genevieve signs the papers, but in my mind, it's a done deal."

"Have you told him?"

Lucian's father bit down on his lip, his eyes shifting to the ground. "I keep meaning to, but with the investigation open again, I know he has enough to deal with right now. He doesn't need this on top of all everything else."

"I think you should tell him," I said. "He's not that fragile. Maybe it'll give him some peace of mind where his mother's concerned. Please. Now that I know, I'll feel like I'm hiding something."

Everett took a deep breath, pursing his lips. "I'll think about it, okay?"

"Please do," I said as Samira appeared, her arms wrapped around her chest.

"Everything okay out here?" she asked.

Everett turned around. "Yes, we're fine. I'll just be another minute."

"Okay," she said, her gaze lingering on us for a moment before she returned to the house.

"Samira seems very nice," I told him as soon as I was sure she couldn't hear me. "Lucian said she's from Africa, and he mentioned black magic. What's that all about?"

"Black magic is nothing to fear, as much as my son might want to believe otherwise because he's not happy about Samira being in my life. Her powers are very strong, and she can do many things we can't."

"Like what?" I asked, curious but not surprised to learn a different kind of magic existed. Nothing about the supernatural world shocked me anymore.

Everett smiled, shaking his head. "I don't think there's enough time to go into all that. Besides, it's cold out here. You should probably be heading home."

Disappointment falling over me, I pulled Becca's keys out of my pocket. "Yes, I guess you're right. Thank you for walking me out."

"You're welcome, Gracyn. Drive safely," he said.

After offering him an appreciative smile, I hopped in the SUV and drove off into the darkness.

— —

The next morning, I wandered downstairs still wearing my pajamas to find Becca and Gabriel sipping coffee at the table. A skillet of scrambled eggs and hash browns sat on the stove, a glass lid covering them.

"Good morning," Gabriel said with a smile, his eyes catching mine before I snapped my gaze away and went straight to the counter. "We saved some breakfast for you."

"Thanks," I muttered as the image of him in the woods yesterday flashed through my mind, bringing my suspicions back in spades. I poured coffee into a mug, splashed some creamer in it, and leaned against the counter, not wanting to join him and Becca at the table.

"Up late?" he asked.

"Something like that," I murmured before taking a sip.

Becca stood up from the table, an empty plate in her hands. "How soon can you get dressed?" she asked on her way to the sink.

"Why?" I asked while she loaded the dishwasher.

"I think we should go to the mall today," she explained as she closed the door.

I raised my eyebrows, surprised by her plans. "Are you serious? This is the biggest shopping day of the year. It'll be packed."

"I know," Becca replied. "But I have the day off, and you, my dear, need a dress for the carnival. It's only two weeks away, and I'm guessing you don't have a formal gown."

"No," I admitted. "You're right about that."

"Then how 'bout it? I think I'm going to get a new dress, too. I've worn all my other ones to this event at least twice."

"Okay," I agreed after a moment of deliberation, hoping the crowded mall would take my mind off Gabriel's mystery ride in the woods yesterday and Lucian's sullen mood.

"Great," Becca said with a smile, seeming oblivious to my troubles. "I have the perfect store in mind. It'll be fun, even more so than picking out your Homecoming dress."

I sighed, not sure I agreed with her. Dress shopping had never been my cup of tea, but I had a feeling I didn't have a choice in the matter.

Fifteen minutes later, after getting dressed in jeans and a sweater, I sat in Becca's SUV as we made our way to the mall in the next town.

"I hope this doesn't take all day," I said.

"What's that?" she asked, glancing at me before looking back at the road twisting through the woods.

"Finding a dress. I have no idea what I'm looking for."

"You'll know it when you see it. And this store is amazing, I promise."

As much as I wanted to keep up the small talk about our shopping trip, my inner self didn't allow me to pass up this moment. "Becca, I need to tell you something," I blurted out. *You'd better be right about this,* a skeptical voice in my head warned. *Because if you're wrong about Gabriel, she may never forgive you. So be careful choosing your words. Don't speculate on what he was doing yesterday. Just stick to the facts.*

Her eyes slid my way, her expression falling. "Oh, no. This doesn't sound good. You're not pregnant, are you?"

"What?" I let out with a loud gasp. "No, definitely not."

She smiled with a laugh. "I didn't think so."

"Then why did you ask?"

"Because you sounded too serious and I wanted to lighten the mood. Okay, so if that's not it, what do you need to tell me?"

I drew in a deep breath, summoning my courage and hoping she'd believe me. "Yesterday when you sent me out to the barn to get Gabriel, he wasn't there. I found him and Prince in the woods."

She raised her eyebrows, her smile fading fast. "So he took a quick ride. What's wrong with that?"

"Nothing, I guess. But he told you he was going to clean the stalls and feed the horses. Instead, he was way off the trail. The worst part is that I may have seen Marguerite out there. I wish I could be sure, but it happened really fast. Although I'd know the color of her hair anywhere."

No emotion registered on Becca's face. She remained quiet, her eyes focused on the road.

"Did you hear me?" I asked.

"Yes," she said, her voice clipped. "I heard you."

"And? Do you believe me?"

With a deep sigh, Becca shifted her eyes to the side with a reassuring look. "Of course, I do. I just can't believe I never anticipated this. First Celeste, then you, and now Gabriel. She really won't give up. Did either one of them see you?"

"I don't think so. Lucian taught me how to cloak myself, so I tried it and it seemed to work, even on Gypsy."

She shook her head. "I'd be willing to bet you weren't fast enough for Marguerite. If she was out there, I'm sure she saw you and expects you to tell me."

"So what should we do?"

Becca shrugged. "I don't know. I'm going to have to give it some thought. Thank you for coming to me with this, though. The more I know about what she's up to, the better I can be prepared for her next move."

"Are you going to mention it to Gabriel?"

"No," Becca stated. When I glanced at her, she continued. "There's a lot you don't know about Gabriel. Confronting him wouldn't be a good idea."

"Really? Why?" I practically held my breath, waiting for her response.

"Because Gabe has always been one of the weaker witches in the coven. He had a rough childhood because of it. We always needed to look out for him, to make sure he stayed in line. He's far more susceptible to temptation than the rest of us."

"And yet you married him?"

"Yes," Becca replied with a smile. "Don't get me wrong. He's not all bad. But I'll start from the beginning. He grew up around here in the fifties, so he's a lot younger than me. His bloodline was weak when it came to supernatural power, although his family had their good points as well."

"I don't understand."

"Our powers come in different levels. No witch is as powerful as the next one. It's like any skill. Gabe's family was known for needing help with their garden and sometimes, we had to get them out of trouble. They knew they were weaker than the rest of us, and they tried to compensate for it. When Gabe was eighteen, his mother was killed during a spell gone wrong."

I cringed, not sure I wanted to know more, but my morbid curiosity slipped out. "I'm afraid to ask what happened."

"Her husband, Gabe's father, tried to use more power than he had to increase their harvest when he set the barn on fire. She was trapped inside, and both she and her horse died. He managed to escape, but couldn't handle the guilt and grief that followed. A week later, he took his own life."

"Oh," I let out on a long sigh, almost wishing I hadn't asked. "That must have been very hard on Gabriel."

"It was. But after twenty years of not coping with it, he pulled himself together and found something he was good at."

"Which was?"

"School, academics. He might not be very powerful in the supernatural sense, but Gabe is extremely smart. He studied hard and was accepted to Harvard. He excelled in his classes and put all his effort into his career. He's one of the most respected doctors at the hospital. And he loves working in the ER. I don't know how he deals with that much blood, but he thrives on the challenge of stitching up stab wounds, setting broken bones, and everything else he has to do. I believe it saved him from his past."

"Wow. I had no idea."

"Of course you didn't. Please don't tell him you know any of this."

"I won't. But what does it have to do with Marguerite?"

"It just concerns me because like I mentioned, the weaker witches are more susceptible to temptation. And while I can't be sure of her motives, I wouldn't put it past her to use him against me."

"What a mess," I said, frustrated by the thought that things were only getting worse.

Becca looked at me and flashed a smile. "We'll get through this. I took care of her once before."

"You seem awfully confident. I'd feel better if you could use the same spell that worked last time and throw her back in the crypt."

"I would, too. But it's complicated. The power needed to put her away again is enormous."

"Yes, you've mentioned that," I said with a sigh. "It just feels like we're waiting for her to make the first move. I'm not sure I can handle any more of her games. What if she stops playing around and someone gets hurt, or worse, killed?"

"I don't know," Becca muttered. "But I can't give in to her threats. She won't stop until she gets what she wants, and I'm not going to hand her the keys to destruction. We'll beat her at this, it just might take a little time."

"Time," I muttered. "It seems like that's what it always takes."

"Trust me, I know what you mean. After four hundred years, you'll get used to it."

I shook my head. Months ago, this conversation would have seemed absurd, but now, I didn't bat an eye. "That's right. I have hundreds of years to go. As long as Marguerite doesn't get me first."

"She won't," Becca declared. When I looked at her, my eyebrows raised, she continued. "I won't let her if it's the last thing I do. Mark my words, we'll stop her soon."

"Good," I replied, impressed by her confidence. "I just wish you knew how."

"When it comes to magic, sometimes it's hard to be prepared with a spell, but we'll fight her when the time comes."

Her words did little to comfort me. I didn't know how she could sound so sure things would be fine in the long run without a concrete plan. Perhaps she was putting up a brave front to make me feel better. Whatever the case, I was ready to talk about something else, even dresses.

"So, on to nicer subjects. I hope you're ready to pick out a dress for me because I suck at shopping," I said.

"I'm sure that's not true." Becca paused, a soft smile forming on her face when she glanced my way. "Cheer up, Gracyn. You look like you're being punished."

"Yeah? Well, thinking about getting a dress just reminds me that I'll be alone at the ball."

"Do you miss Alex?"

I felt a twisted expression tug at my face. "Not as much as I probably should. I think between Marguerite and Lucian's investigation, I've been too distracted to miss him. You haven't said much about Lucian lately, by the way. Am I to presume you trust him now?"

A thoughtful look crossed over her eyes, and she sighed. "I doubt he's going to try anything while the police are breathing down his neck."

"What's that supposed to mean?" I asked with a huff. "Do you still think he could have hurt his own sister?"

"I've told you many times, I don't know. I'm not going to pass any judgment without solid evidence, but I also won't write him off as a suspect. And now, since Zoe admitted lying about being with him that day, I'm afraid to say, it doesn't look good for him."

"Do you think he'll be convicted? They need more proof than the lack of an alibi, don't they?"

"I'm sure they do. But I can't help wondering if something peculiar happened that day. Maybe Cassie's horse snuck up on him, startling him, and he reacted in a way he couldn't take back. Maybe it was an accident."

I didn't like that thought at all. "How could someone accidentally kill a horse?"

"I don't know, but anything's possible," Becca muttered.

I wanted to say more to defend Lucian but held my tongue, sure nothing I said would change Becca's mind. Instead, I dropped it. "Mind if I turn on the radio?"

"Of course not," she replied.

Without another word, I turned the knob on the dashboard and found a radio station playing holiday music. As the lyrics to *Silent Night* filled the car, I slumped against the seat and watched the woods outside the window.

The scenery became a blur while a storm raged on in my mind, tormenting me with thoughts of Lucian. My mood sinking, I realized I was heading out to buy a dress for a ball I'd be attending alone because the only guy I wanted to be my date was suspected of murder.

17

Preparations for the Winter Carnival began the next week. Within days, holiday decorations were strewn all over town. Red bows were tied to lamp posts, lights twinkled from trees lining the sidewalk, and a twenty-foot tall Christmas tree stood in the town park. Glass ornaments sparkled from its boughs, and a gold star at the top pointed to the heavens with its center tip. Store window displays were sprinkled with fake snow, and wreaths hung from the doors of every business along Main Street.

Despite the cold weather, the skies remained clear, the snow failing to make an appearance. Each passing day seemed more frigid as Arctic air became anchored in place over the area. When Lucian picked me up in the mornings, heat blasted out of the vents and the seat warmer was on high. I didn't miss the chore of scraping ice off my windshield, not to mention getting in a freezing car. As much as I hated to admit it, there were advantages to not having my own vehicle.

By the end of the week, my homework piled up again and I forgot about the upcoming carnival even with my new gown hanging in the closet. Friday morning began like the rest, with me rushing out the door bundled up in a coat, hat, and gloves, my book bag hanging from my shoulder and tall boots keeping my legs warm. As usual, Lucian was waiting in the driveway while I locked up. Then I ran down the steps and hopped into his Range Rover, dropping my bag by my feet.

"Good morning," I said, pulling the door shut and flashing a smile.

"Hello," he replied as he turned the SUV around and we headed down the driveway. "Ready for the weekend?"

"Always," I replied.

"I think we should get together."

"Really?" I asked, caught off-guard at his suggestion.

"Yes. Things have been a little too quiet lately. We should practice the skills I taught you two weeks ago. I want to make sure you haven't forgotten anything."

"Oh," I said quietly, disappointed he meant work, not pleasure. "Okay, sure. Just tell me when and where."

"Tomorrow morning. I'll pick you up. This time we're going somewhere new. I don't want to risk Marguerite finding us again. It defeats the purpose if she knows you're preparing for her to strike."

"Yeah," I said wistfully, watching the trees pass by. The thought of Marguerite put me in a bad mood, and I hoped she wouldn't crash our next training session. This week had been particularly quiet, making me wonder when she'd show up next. "What time should I be ready?"

"Eight o'clock sharp."

"Why do you insist on starting so early on a Saturday?"

He shrugged. "I'll take any excuse to get out of the house as long as my father and his friend are still there. With any luck, I'll be gone before they get up."

"They're still in town? How much longer are they staying?"

"At least another week. The carnival is next weekend, and my father has made it quite clear she'll be his date for the ball. He said it's time he stopped hiding his relationship with her, even if some of the others might frown upon it."

"Why would he hide her? Aside from the fact that he was, or is still married?"

Lucian slid his eyes my way, a disdainful look in them. "She's from the other side of magic. Some in the coven fear black magic, and they may not be very receptive to her."

I sighed. "Maybe they need to give her a chance."

"What's that supposed to mean?"

"Just that you shouldn't judge a book by its cover. How much do you really know about her? Besides, your father told me black magic is only dangerous if a witch uses it in a destructive way."

"Well, all I care about is the fact that my father chose to start a relationship with someone new after casting my mother aside like a worn out pair of shoes."

"I know, but I hate to see you holding it against Samira. She seems nice."

"Whose side are you on?"

I pursed my lips together, wondering if I'd said too much. "I'm sorry. I don't want to get in the middle, but it about killed me to see you upstairs alone on Thanksgiving. It was like walking into a home with two completely separate families. And he is your father. Right now, he's the only family you have, at least in town. Maybe you two should talk."

Lucian shook his head. "Not until he takes the trash out."

I sighed, noting the bitterness in his voice. Without knowing his father had filed for divorce, Lucian would probably never see things any differently. I wanted to convince him to give Samira a chance, but I had a feeling any attempt I made would be wasted. "Okay," I said. "I'll be ready at eight tomorrow if you want to start early." I paused, glancing up at the blue sky before changing the subject. "Where's the snow? The carnival is about a week away. I thought the town would be buried by now."

"Don't worry. It'll happen, and when it does, you might appreciate days like today."

"I just wish it wasn't so cold. At least the snow makes it pretty."

"Be patient," he said, a smile crossing over his lips. "You'll see it soon enough."

"Why do I get the feeling you're not telling me something?"

"Because here in Sedgewick, there's always a surprise lurking around the corner. You never know what's going to happen."

"You've got that right," I grumbled, leaning back in my seat. *At least you don't have to wait too long,* I reminded myself. *The carnival will be here before you know it.* Thoughts of the town event reminded me about the ball, lowering my spirits. I watched the web of branches in the woods fly by, the silvery gown I'd bought last weekend flashing through my mind. It now hung under a plastic cover in my closet, not to be worn until the carnival. Under other circumstances, I might have been excited about the ball, but knowing I'd be going alone sent my mood into a black hole for the rest of the day.

— —

Lucian arrived at exactly eight o'clock the next morning to pick me up. I said a quick goodbye to Becca before rushing out the door and jumping in the SUV. Still a little tired, I greeted him, then fell quiet as he drove through town.

When we left the business district and began making our way into the countryside, my curiosity stepped up a notch. "Are you going to tell me where today's adventure will be held?" I asked, watching as the distance increased between the houses spread out on large lots surrounded by woods. The lawns were dull brown, and evergreen garlands wrapped around mailbox posts.

"No. We'll be there in ten minutes, so don't worry. You'll find out soon enough."

"Why am I not surprised you're making me wait?" I muttered, wanting to push for more details, but giving up because he was right. Ten minutes wasn't long at all.

We rode in silence until Lucian turned onto another back road. After passing an old country store and some farms, he slowed down and pulled into a gravel driveway. The SUV bumped over ruts and through potholes until we reached the parking lot of a drive-in movie theater at the end. A huge white screen loomed in the distance, and speakers perched on posts at the front corner of every parking space. In the back, a small concession stand had been boarded up, the plywood sprayed with graffiti.

"I feel like I just traveled back in time," I said as Lucian shut off the engine. "I didn't know these still existed."

"Have you ever been to a drive-in?" he asked.

"No," I replied with a smile, amused by his question.

"They can be fun."

"And you know this from experience?" I asked, astounded.

He flashed a smile, chuckling. "Yes, believe it or not, I've been here once, but it was many years ago."

"Really?"

"Yes," he said, his expression softening, a thoughtful look on his face. "I brought Cassie to see a kid's movie a few years before she died."

I swallowed, noticing the painful glaze in his eyes. Wanting to lighten the mood, I didn't press him for any details. "Is this place still open?" I asked.

He nodded. "In the summer. I think they operate from May through September. It's the only drive-in within a hundred mile radius."

"Interesting. I still can't believe there's one around."

"Want to come here sometime? I mean, next summer."

"Are you serious?" I asked, surprised by his question.

He shrugged. "Maybe. It could be fun. But first, we have a few things to take care of." He paused, placing his hand on the door handle. "Well, come on. Let's get started. I think there's a pretty good chance Marguerite won't find us here."

"That would be nice," I replied before hopping out of the Range Rover. After shutting the door, I met Lucian on the other side. "Okay. What's on the agenda for this morning? More of the same?"

"Hmm," he mused. "Why don't we start with a warm up?"

I shrugged. "Sure. What did you have in mind?"

"Just see if you can keep up," he said with a grin before sprinting away. Within seconds, he disappeared.

Huffing, I scanned the surrounding area until I saw him across the lot, leaning against a speaker post. I shook my head and launched into a jog to catch up to him. "No fair," I complained when I reached him. "You didn't prepare me for your lightning speed."

"And you didn't even attempt to keep up. How do you think you'll outrun Marguerite if you don't try?"

"I'm not sure outrunning her is going to be my best defense."

"Whether it is or isn't, you need to be ready to run if you have to. You can't rely on one defense. How you handle her depends on how she comes after you."

I cringed, not wanting her to target me at all. "What if she doesn't? What if all her threats end up being empty? You know, to throw us off?"

"It doesn't matter. These are still good skills for you to know. Now, let's try again. Ready?"

I nodded. "Ready as I'll ever be," I muttered. On my last word, Lucian took off across the lot, this time weaving around the speakers like a barrel-racing horse. I followed him as fast as my legs would go, swerving around the posts while my surroundings blurred. By the time I stopped beside Lucian on the other side of the lot, I nearly fell forward from the momentum. He caught my arms, keeping me on my feet.

"Much better," he said. "See, you have more in you than you thought."

"That was kind of weird. I barely saw anything because I was going so fast."

"You'll get used to it."

"I'm not sure about that. You're not going to make me do laps now, are you?"

Lucian smiled in a way that made me wish I hadn't asked. "No. I have something else in mind. Are you afraid of heights?"

"Not really. But that doesn't mean I can promise you I'll be ready for whatever you're planning next."

"Ever see a cat jump up to something really high, like a fence?"

"Yes," I answered with a groan, not sure I liked where this was going.

"Good. Now it's our turn. Just stay here and watch me. Once I'm at the top, you try it."

"At the top?" I asked, my jaw dropping. "What—"

Before I could complete my question. Lucian took off, running across the lot and heading straight for the screen. When he was about twenty feet out, he jumped into the air, landing on top of it.

I blinked a few times, not sure I believed what I was seeing. The screen had to be at least thirty feet high.

"Gracyn!" Lucian called. "Your turn. Come on up! The view is amazing."

"Oh, no," I said, shaking my head, the cool air nipping at my cheeks. The longer I stood in one place, the colder I got. But I wasn't ready to leap up to the top of a movie screen just to get warm. "I can't do that."

"Sure you can. All you have to do is focus." Lucian stood in the center, his silhouette dark against the blue sky behind him.

"Yeah, right. Focus and then jump thirty feet into the air," I said in disbelief. "Not going to happen."

Lucian stepped off the screen and landed on the ground below, not even bending his knees on impact. He jogged over to me, a smirk on his face. "Man, that felt good. I love getting outside for a workout. It's helping me burn off some energy."

I laughed, shaking my head. "I'm glad you're enjoying yourself. You don't even look out of breath."

"That's because I'm not. Now, come with me. We'll jump together."

"No way," I said, staring at his outstretched hand like it was out to bite me. "I can't. I mean it."

"You only think you can't." Lucian stepped closer to me, his body heat warming me up. "Do you trust me?"

I looked up at him, meeting his eyes, and my resolve began to crumble. This wasn't fair. I didn't think I could resist him. "Yes, I suppose so."

"You don't sound convinced. Do you honestly think I'd ask you to do something I didn't think you could handle?"

"Probably not," I answered.

He laughed. "You have so little faith in me. I'm crushed. But think about it this way, do you want to have the confidence to handle Marguerite, or do you want to let her walk all over you? I have a feeling she thinks you're weak, that you can't do many of the things the rest of us can."

I frowned, the thought of her smug smile sending a mad rush of fury through my veins. I couldn't let her have the upper hand. Perhaps Lucian was right and I should try to jump. "And maybe she thinks a half-breed can't be as strong as she is. She's going to be very wrong."

"Does that mean you're ready to give it a shot?"

With a determined sigh, I set my sights on the movie screen. "Yes." I put my hand in his, and together we ran toward the screen.

"Jump!" Lucian yelled when we were about twenty feet away.

Squeezing my eyes shut, I pushed off the ground with all my might. I opened them a moment later and found myself on top of the screen which turned out to be a cement wall about a foot wide, giving me just enough space to feel comfortable. My heart pounding, adrenaline pulsing through my veins, I let out my breath. "Wow, what a rush!"

"See? You have to start trusting me, but more than that, you have to start believing in yourself. You have all this power which you've always had. You just never knew how to use it."

I nodded, feeling a smile spread across my lips. "Thank you for helping me and showing me these things. I just wish—" My voice fell away as thoughts of Marguerite's threats filled my mind.

"I know," he said, his eyes meeting mine as though he sensed what was running through my head.

Letting go of his hand, I turned and sat down, my legs dangling over the edge. I couldn't believe I was sitting on a wall several stories high with nothing to prevent me from falling, and yet I wasn't afraid.

Lucian followed suit, leaning his hands to the sides of him. We looked out over the parking lot and concession building. Beyond them rolled tree-covered hills under a clear blue sky, the morning sun inching its way up on the eastern side.

"This won't last forever," he said. "We'll get through it somehow."

"I hope so," I said, wishing I could share his confidence. "But it seems like Marguerite should be thanking me since I was the one who freed her."

"Yeah, ungrateful bitch," he said, causing us both to chuckle in the face of danger. "I think she already forgot that part."

"I wish I could change what happened that night," I said quietly. "Do we have the power to go back in time?"

"No," Lucian said. "That's one we can't do. Sorry."

"But we can scale tall buildings," I said, my tone uplifted.

Lucian turned to look at me, catching my eye. "Exactly."

In that instant, I wanted to capture the feeling of being away from the world, similar to the afternoon Lucian had taken me up to the rock. It seemed like we were the only two people in existence. I felt safe, which was ironic considering my legs were hanging over the edge nearly thirty feet high.

A few minutes later, Lucian broke the silence. "Ready to get down?"

His question jolted me back to reality. "Down?" I asked, feeling like a deer caught in the headlights.

"Unless you want to stay up here forever."

"No," I said. "But you held my hand on the way up, so you're holding it on the way down."

Lucian stood up and reached for me. "Deal," he said as I clamped my fingers around his and rose to my feet. "Ready?"

I closed my eyes, hesitating. "Yes," I gritted out, feeling my heart leap when we jumped out into the air.

The way down was effortless and, after a split second in the air, my feet touched the ground. The impact was no harder than what jumping off a few steps felt like. Opening my eyes, I smiled. "That wasn't so bad," I commented.

"You didn't think I brought you here to torture you, did you?" Lucian asked.

"No. I just can't believe what I can do."

"And now you have many ways to defend yourself. If I hadn't shown you these things, you'd still be able to do them, you just wouldn't know how."

"So, what's next? Can we fly? Or do we need broomsticks for that?"

He laughed. "No, that's another one we can't do. We'll practice what you learned a few weeks ago."

"Okay. Good. No more surprises."

"That's right. If you're ready, why don't you get started?" He gestured to me, letting out a hearty laugh when I made myself invisible.

We spent the next two hours working on all I'd learned so far. As we hoped, Marguerite didn't make an appearance, much to our relief. By the time Lucian drove me home at noon, I was exhausted and went straight to the kitchen for lunch. Then I retreated up to my room, prepared to spend another long Saturday afternoon and evening alone.

18

Excitement began building Monday at school. On more than one occasion, I overheard students speculating about a snow day, but I pushed their musings aside, sure they were nothing more than wishful thinking. Instead, I trudged through the week, my days seeming to run together. Lucian picked me up every morning and gave me a ride home in the afternoon. We talked at school, spending time together in between classes and at lunch. At least his return to school was old news, and no one paid any attention to us.

By Thursday evening, no snow had fallen. Without giving the weather a second thought, I climbed into bed, focused on school the next day rather than the upcoming weekend carnival scheduled to begin the following evening.

It felt like I'd just fallen asleep when I heard Becca's voice. "Gracyn," she said, giving my shoulders a gentle nudge. "Wake up. It's time."

Tired, I cracked an eyelid open. Her blonde hair hovered above me, falling over her shoulders, while her blue eyes sparkled with mischief. "What?" I muttered.

"Come on. We need your help."

"Help with what? And what time is it?"

"It's almost two in the morning. And we need your help with a little... um...decorating."

Taking a deep breath, I propped myself up on my elbows, my curiosity getting the best of me. "Decorating?"

"Yes. So get up, get dressed, and meet me and Gabe downstairs in five minutes. And wear warm clothes. We'll be outside."

She started to leave, but stopped when I spoke. "Oh, no," I said, waiting for her to turn around before I continued. "Not until you tell me what's going on. It's the middle of the night in case you haven't noticed."

She smiled. "Of course, I know that. We can't do this any other time. We have to make sure the town is sound asleep. This is witch business and you, my dear, can help us. You've asked me about your powers, and now you'll get to use them. But if we don't hurry, we're going to be late. We're meeting the rest of the coven at the town park."

"That's all you're going to give me?" I griped.

"Yes, for now. But don't worry, you'll find out in fifteen minutes." With that, she whipped around and flipped the wall switch to turn on the dresser lamp before leaving my room.

Squinting in the light, I sat up and twisted my legs around the edge of the bed. Knowing I had no choice but to do as she asked, I stretched with a big yawn and resolved to get through this, whatever it was.

After changing into jeans and a heavy sweater and pulling my curls into a ponytail, I rushed downstairs to find Becca and Gabriel waiting for me. "I'm coming," I told them, heading straight for the coat closet to get my jacket and boots.

As soon as I put them on, I followed Becca and Gabriel outside. The cold air stung my cheeks, and I pulled a hat on over my hair. There might not have been any snow, but it sure seemed cold enough for it. After climbing into the back seat of Becca's SUV, I remained quiet for the few minutes it took to get to town.

When we pulled onto Main Street, not a single light burned inside the store windows or out on the sidewalk. Becca parked behind about a dozen cars lined up beside the curb, and the three of us jumped out.

We hurried across the street and through the gate to the park. Benches were scattered along the perimeter, the huge Christmas tree taking center stage. My eyes slowly adjusting to the shadows, I followed Becca and Gabriel to the crowd gathered around the tree. I recognized many of them—Celeste and Derek, their parents, Lucian's father, and several others I remembered from Celeste's house the night she'd been missing. With a frown, I noticed Lucian wasn't here right away, reminding me he wasn't welcome.

Everyone was smiling, the mood seeming cheerful. After greetings were exchanged, Becca approached Everett and hugged him. "It's so good to have you back," she whispered before taking her place beside him. Gabriel stood next to her, and I fell into place on his other side, watching and waiting.

"Everyone ready?" Becca asked.

The others responded by nodding. "Yes," several of them confirmed in a whisper.

"Okay. You all know what to do. Join hands and let's get to work."

Gabriel took my left hand while Derek clamped onto my right one. They lifted my arms to the heavens, and I felt warmth rush through me.

"Focus, everyone," Becca said. "Let our energy work its magic."

After a few minutes passed, heat coursed through my veins, making me wish I could break away from Derek and Gabriel long enough to shed my jacket. A breeze blew, pushing a stray leaf along the ground. I glanced at the others, surprised by the intensity in their eyes, then looked up at the sky. Thick hazy clouds churned high above, swirling as they dropped, coming closer to the ground.

"Perfect," Becca said. "It's working. I want this year to be our best yet. So everyone, give it all you've got." She paused, sliding her eyes my way. "Gracyn, let the energy flow through you and focus on it. Anything you can add will help."

Confused, I took shallow breaths while scanning the rest of the coven before lifting my gaze back up to the sky. Within seconds, tiny specs began to form, filling the air. At first, they resembled dust particles, but they grew larger and started coming down faster. The snow started light and gentle, but quickly gained momentum, transforming the park into a winter wonderland.

Minutes later, a blanket of powder covered the ground, hiding the grass and sidewalks. The flakes kept falling, dropping a veil of white over the Christmas tree in the center of the circle. The sky took on a rosy glow, the darkness lit up by reflections on the snow.

I wasn't sure how long we stood there, our hands locked together as the storm intensified. I felt snowflakes hit my face, melting on contact. The energy swept through my veins, keeping me warm. The snow was mesmerizing, the winter scene seeming like nothing short of a miracle.

By the time Becca released everyone, I was wide awake. "We did it," she said, a smile on her face. "This is going to be one of our best years. Great job everyone."

When Gabriel and Derek let go of me, I pulled my arms back to my sides and the warmth inside me began to fade.

Derek flashed a smile my way, catching my eye. "Pretty cool, huh?" he said.

"Yes," I agreed with a nod.

"And the best part is no school tomorrow."

"What?" I asked, not sure I believed him.

"That's right," he said. "School is always canceled the Friday before the carnival. Gives us a chance to sleep in after a little midnight exercise. Well, I've got to run. See you this weekend."

"All right. See you," I said before he turned and jogged away. I glanced at the dispersing crowd, wanting to say hello to Celeste, but she had already left the park through the gate and was crossing the street with her parents.

Knowing I wouldn't have a chance to say hello to her, I followed Becca and Gabriel. "How long will it snow?" I asked as we walked back to the SUV parked on the street.

"All night," Becca replied with a gleam in her eyes. She glanced at Gabriel, their eyes locking like they shared a secret.

Noticing their stolen moment made me cringe, the memory of seeing him in the woods on Thanksgiving returning to my thoughts. But

I had done my duty and told Becca, so it was up to her to deal with him. Shifting my thoughts back to the snow still coming down like a blizzard, I brushed the flakes off my shoulders and arms.

"This is really amazing," I said.

Becca smiled, appearing satisfied. "We've worked our magic for the carnival for years. It seems to get easier every time."

"The people in town don't question why it always snows for this event?" I asked.

"No," Gabriel chimed in. "I think they enjoy it too much to wonder how it happens."

"I thought we had to keep our powers hidden," I said.

Gabriel nodded. "We do, but this is the one exception we make. It's a treat for us to share a little magic every now and then."

"Well," I began as I stopped at the SUV back door and turned to admire the newly fallen blanket of snow covering everything in sight from the Christmas tree in the park to the street and sidewalks. "I can't argue with you. It looks magical out here." Ready to return home, I opened the door and slipped into the back seat. I couldn't wait to climb back into bed, although I wasn't sure I'd be able to sleep after helping a coven of witches start a snowstorm.

— ❦ —

The next morning when the alarm woke me up, I grabbed my phone and confirmed school was canceled for the day, just as Derek had promised. Grateful for the reprieve from another early morning, I fell back to sleep for a few hours before getting up around nine o'clock. Still sleepy, I went straight to the window and pushed the curtain aside, drawing in a sharp breath at the wintry landscape. A thick blanket of snow covered the driveway, barn, and branches while more came down. Smiling at the memory of helping the others start the storm, I turned away and headed to the dresser to grab some clothes. I hadn't even opened a drawer when something thumped against my window.

"What was that?" I muttered, running to my desk and pushing the curtain aside. Outside, Shade stood in the driveway, his black coat speckled with snowflakes. Beside him, Lucian looked up at me and waved.

Without a moment of deliberation, I threw on a pair of jeans and a sweater, then ran a hand through my hair, frustrated with my unkempt curls. Knowing I didn't have much time, I pulled them into a ponytail before rushing out the door. As soon as I descended the stairs, I held my breath, hoping Becca and Gabriel weren't up yet to ask me where I was going. Finding the coast clear, I grabbed my jacket, boots, and hat from the closet and escaped out into the winter wonderland.

"To what do I owe this surprise?" I asked Lucian as I approached, finding it a little hard to walk in the deep snow burying my ankles with each step.

"I know I should have called or texted first, but I couldn't help myself. The snow is amazing, don't you think?" He lifted a hand, his eyes focused on the flakes landing on his black sleeve.

"Yes, it is. And I don't mind that you didn't call first. I kind of miss your surprise visits."

"Then I'll try not to disappoint you in the future."

I smiled, noting the warmth in his voice. "I also missed you last night."

"So, you were abducted in the middle of the night by witches, I take it."

Laughing, I nodded. "Yes. But that's not all. I helped them create this." I swept my hand out, gesturing to the snow.

"Good. You're learning."

I caught his gaze and felt my smile fade. "I would have liked last night better if you'd been there."

The carefree look in his eyes disappeared. "I wasn't welcome. I think you know that by now."

I gave a subtle nod, wishing I hadn't mentioned it. After he'd been chased away by Celeste's father the night he tried to help find her right before Halloween, I couldn't imagine what the coven would have done last night had he shown up. Hopefully his name would be cleared soon, allowing him to participate in the future.

"What are you doing here?" I asked, changing the subject.

"I wanted to ask you to take a ride with me. I love riding in the snow. It's beautiful. What do you say?"

I didn't waste any time making my decision. "I'd love to."

"Great," he said with a smile before a serious look crossed his face. "Would you like some help getting Gypsy ready?"

"No. I've got it. I'm a lot faster at tacking up than I was a few months ago." Without another glance his way, I ran into the barn and saddled Gypsy as fast as I could. After buckling the last bridle strap, I threw the reins over her neck and led her outside.

Gypsy took one step into the deep snow and stretched her neck down, swiping her muzzle across the surface. When she lifted her head, the snow sticking to her nose looked like sugar. I laughed. "You like this stuff, too, huh?" I muttered.

She tossed her head in the air, then pawed at the ground.

"Good. Let's go. The boys are waiting for us." I moved her up a few steps until she stood next to the snow-covered mounting block. Without bothering to brush off the steps, I climbed to the top and swung my leg over the saddle. As soon as I was seated, I picked up the reins, slid my feet into the stirrups, and nudged her sides with my heels.

Gypsy launched into a trot, her movement smooth as though she floated across the driveway, her hooves barely making a sound in the snow. Clouds of powder billowed around her neck, and falling snowflakes stung my cheeks. Feeling as though I didn't have a care in the world, I smiled, the magical winter scene captivating me.

When we caught up to Lucian and Shade who waited at the trail entrance, Lucian smiled with a nod before sending Shade into a canter. Off we went, flying through the forest, the horses kicking up the snow.

Grabbing Gypsy's mane, I barely felt the cold. The reins slipped through my fingers an inch, and I released my feel of the bit in her mouth, allowing her to charge full speed ahead. The forest was quiet and still, the snowflakes rushing down from the gray sky the only movement across the land, the horses' hoof beats silenced by the thick blanket covering the ground.

Adrenaline whipped through my veins as we continued deeper into the woods. When we reached the open meadow, Shade opened up his stride, taking the lead. I squeezed Gypsy into a gallop until she reached his side. He slowed to a steady canter, and we practically floated across the field to the woods on the other side where the horses slowed to a walk.

Breathing heavily, Gypsy snorted and tossed her head, launching the snowflakes that landed on her mane into the air. I dropped the reins, letting the buckle rest on her withers and giving her a chance to stretch her neck.

"That was a good workout for them," Lucian said, relaxing his grip on the reins as Shade shook his head, his long mane rippling against his neck. "Wasn't it awesome?"

"Yes," I answered. "It felt like she was floating, like her feet never even touched the ground. And it's so beautiful out here. I've never seen anything like it."

"You'd better get used to it, because it's going to look like this for three months, if not longer."

"Really? It won't melt soon?"

"No. The Arctic air usually gets trapped in place over Sedgewick for the winter."

I shot him a curious look, my eyebrows raised. "And who might be responsible for that?"

"All right. You've got me. Yes, we have a hand in it because it's good for the next harvest. By keeping the ground frozen all winter, the bugs die off and the soil is more fertile in the spring."

"Oh," I said. "But in the meantime, we have at least three months of feeling like we're at the North Pole."

"Exactly. I hope you're good at staying busy inside."

"Between homework and painting, I think I can manage." I paused, my thoughts shifting to a more immediate event. "But I don't really want to think about the next three months. I'm more interested in the next three days." I glanced at him, not sure how to ask the question burning in my mind. "What are your plans? For the weekend, I mean."

He looked ahead, his eyes void of emotion. "I'll be around."

"Meaning?"

"I'll probably be holed up in the studio, painting."

"What about the carnival?"

He turned to me, a knowing look in his eyes. "You can't possibly think I could come. I probably wouldn't be allowed in through the door. I'm surprised they let me to return to school, although they really can't keep me away. The carnival is a whole different story. I'd never blend into the crowd. You and I both know it would just end up being a very bad situation."

"Oh," I answered, my hopes of seeing him over the weekend going up in smoke. "I guess you're right."

"But you're going, aren't you?"

I shrugged. "I think I have to."

"Don't sound so excited about it."

I smiled, letting out a loud huff. "Hard to get excited when I know I'll be alone."

"Did you get a gown for Saturday night?"

"Yes," I said. "But only because Becca took me shopping and insisted I buy one. I don't know why I'm going, though."

"Because you should. This town is your home now, and you need to participate in these things."

"It just...it won't be much fun, that's all." Taking a deep breath, I looked away from him. There was so much I wanted to tell him, starting with the fact that I didn't care what anyone else thought, I still wanted him to come to the ball. And if that was impossible, then I'd trade my fancy new dress for jeans and a sweater to spend the evening with him hidden away at his house. *Good luck with that,* a sarcastic voice trilled through my head. *You haven't even been on a date together. You can't invite yourself over for an evening.*

With a frown, I groaned inwardly at my thoughts, knowing I had to be patient.

Lucian halted Shade, and Gypsy stopped beside them. "It won't be like this forever," he said, his gaze meeting mine. "You have many years ahead of you here, so you should get to know the town and enjoy these activities."

I nodded, not feeling any better.

"We should probably head back now. I don't want Becca and Gabriel to wake up, find you missing, and start to worry," he said before pivoting Shade around in a one hundred and eighty degree turn.

Twisting in the saddle, I watched them stick to the path the horses had made in the snow. With a heavy heart, I spun Gypsy around and cued her to follow, a little disappointed our ride would be over soon, especially when it looked like I wouldn't see Lucian again for the rest of the weekend.

19

The next evening, I went through the motions of getting ready for the ball, but my heart wasn't in it. I had no idea why I was putting so much effort into a dance when I'd probably spend it watching everyone else have a good time. *You're going for Becca,* I reminded myself. *And Lucian was right. This is your home now. You need to participate in town events. Besides, around here, you never know what's going to happen. Would you rather stay home while the entire town is gathered in one place? Why not just walk outside and call for Marguerite to come and get you?*

Frustrated, I emerged from the bathroom wearing my robe, a towel wrapped around my neck under my wet hair. I went straight to the closet to admire the floor-length strapless dress made of gray ruffles sprinkled with silver sparkles, hoping it would inspire a little excitement. But all it did was send my spirits crashing to the ground. Refusing to believe the night would be a total waste of my time, I returned to the bathroom to dry my hair.

I had just finished with the blow dryer when a knock sounded on my bedroom door. "Come in," I said, letting out a low whistle as Becca appeared in the doorway wearing a long blue gown. Her hair was piled up high in loose curls, a few wispy strands falling beside her ears. A silver necklace sparkled around her neck, the matching earrings pulling out the color in her dress.

"How are you coming?" she asked.

"I'm almost ready. I just need to get dressed." I took off my robe, snatched my dress from the hanger, and stepped into it. After pulling it up over my strapless bra, I zipped it as far as I could reach before turning to Becca. "Could you give me a hand?"

"Sure," she said, coming to my rescue and zipping the back to the top. "Now, let's do something with your hair. Have a seat." She gestured to the bed.

"What do you have in mind?" I asked, plunking down on the edge.

"Something elegant. So relax and let me take care of this for you." I felt her pull my hair back before she lifted it off my shoulders. I wished I could see what she was doing in the mirror, but it was on the other side of the room. "Excited for tonight?" she asked as she worked.

"Not really," I replied with a disenchanted sigh.

"I know the timing for the ball is pretty bad for you. Have you spoken to Alex since—"

"Since he dumped me?" I finished for her. "No, not one word."

"I'm sure he'll be there. Maybe you can talk to him."

I knew that wouldn't cheer me up because he wasn't the one I wanted to see tonight, or any night for that matter. "No. I doubt that's going to happen. There's a good reason Alex broke up with me. It was over. We were friends, and I miss that friendship, but he wanted more than I could give."

Becca continued working with my hair, and I felt the slight tug of hair clips being inserted. "When you put it that way, I guess he's not going to cheer you up tonight."

"Not at all. Maybe we shouldn't talk about boys right now. I'm more worried about what Marguerite will do the next time she shows up," I said, not intending to put a damper on the evening. But if thinking about Marguerite was the only way to get thoughts of the depressing ball out of my head, I'd take it.

"There now, we can't be thinking such awful things tonight. I don't want you worrying about her. I'll be there, as well as the rest of the coven. She's not going to try anything right under our noses."

"I wish I could believe that. I think she's waiting until you least expect her to strike, and that's exactly when she will. So we shouldn't let our guard down."

"Perhaps you're right," Becca said quietly. "I'll make sure I keep an eye out for her tonight. In the meantime, your hair is done." She pulled her hands away from me. "Go check it out in the mirror."

Curious, I rose and shuffled around the bed to my dresser. Facing the mirror, I drew in a sharp breath at the girl looking back at me. My strawberry blonde hair had been swept up, rhinestone clips securing it in place. A few loose curls hung beside my ears, and my shoulders were bare, exposing my collarbone above the dress neckline. "Wow," I said. "This is amazing. How did you do this?"

Becca grinned. "I'll admit I've never been great at hair and working with my hands. So I tapped into a little magic. What good is being a witch if I can't have a little fun every once in a while?"

"Really? That's how you did this?"

She nodded. "I did my own the same way. I just closed my eyes and imagined what I wanted. The energy guided my hands."

"That's the craziest thing I've ever heard. But if that's how you did it, it works for me. I love it."

"Good. I have something else for you that didn't come from magic." She opened the clutch she'd placed on my bed and pulled out a velvet box. "You need something flashy to finish off your look."

"Thank you, but you don't have to do that."

"Nonsense. I want you to borrow this set tonight. It will go perfect with your dress," she said before opening the box and holding up a teardrop necklace. "Turn around."

As soon as I complied, she clasped the chain around my neck. When I turned to face her, she handed me the matching earrings. "Put these on and meet us downstairs. It's time to go." She smiled at me, pride and satisfaction in her expression. Then she crossed the room and disappeared into the hallway, leaving me alone.

I went back to the dresser, slipped the earrings on, and studied my reflection, wishing I had someone special waiting for me. But I didn't and, somehow, I had to get through the night. Holding my head up high, I reached for the small silver purse containing my phone and keys before rushing out the door.

— ◦ —

We arrived in town around seven o'clock, long after the sun had gone down. The streetlights lit up Main Street, their yellow glow reflecting off the blanket of white covering the ground. Narrow paths on the sidewalks and street had been cleared for pedestrians, but traffic wasn't allowed near the park due to the festivities.

Gabriel pulled into the lot a few blocks away from the town hall and found one of the last empty spaces. We hopped out of the SUV, and I followed Becca and Gabriel into town, thankful Becca had talked me into wearing white boots under my long gown. Satin gloves reached my elbows, keeping my forearms warm, and a wrap covered my shoulders, but did little to shield me from the cold.

I hurried behind Becca and Gabriel, catching glimpses of snow sculptures scattered along the sidewalk. Hoof prints and sleigh tracks marked the section of the road that hadn't been cleared, evidence of the fun-filled day I'd missed by staying home.

As we approached the town hall, music floated out the door every time it opened. A steady stream of people all dressed up, the men in tuxedos and the women in long shimmering gowns, made their way down the sidewalk to the ball. Not paying attention to anyone in front or behind us, I followed Becca and Gabriel through the double doors with a handful of other guests.

At once, the muffled music intensified, drowning out the chatter. Warm at last, I slid the wrap off my shoulders as I stepped to the side near the wall, taking in the huge room. Evergreen garland stretched across the mantle of a massive stone fireplace on one side while a Christmas tree rose up to the cathedral ceiling in the opposite corner. Red and white lights lit up the branches, and smaller Christmas trees speckled with more lights had been scattered around the perimeter. A bar had been set up against the back wall across from the stage where a band played holiday music.

I scooted along the side of the room, staying out of the crowd's way. When Gabriel started to pull Becca out onto the dance floor, she stopped and turned to me. "Will you be okay alone for a while?" she asked, her necklace glittering in the lights.

"Of course," I assured her, wishing I believed that.

"Okay," she said, not picking up on my lie before she and Gabriel disappeared into the crowd, leaving me on my own.

Leaning against the wall, I scanned the ballroom, looking for a familiar face. The only one to catch my eye right away was Alex who held a blonde girl in his arms, twirling her about while the music played. He watched her with a smile, his eyes lighting up when she whispered in his ear. I sighed, happy for him in spite of the spark of jealousy shooting through me at the sight of them sharing a magical night of romance. My envy didn't stem from missing Alex, but rather from my desire to be with someone special, something I knew wouldn't happen tonight.

Not sure what to do, I headed for the bar in the back of the room and hopped up on an empty stool in the corner. Two bartenders wearing crisp white shirts filled wine glasses and opened beer bottles, handing beverages to the patrons lined up in the center. In no hurry to get a drink, I gazed out at the dance floor, amazed at the beautiful gowns and polished tuxedos everyone wore.

A few seconds later, Everett and Samira walked in through the front door. His black and white tuxedo was pressed, his light brown hair neatly brushed. On his arm, Samira outshined every other woman in the room. Her burgundy dress hugged her trim figure while diamonds glittered around her neck. Her black hair had been swept up, showing off strong but elegant shoulders.

When all eyes shifted to them, a hush fell over the crowd. Everett and Samira paused, their heads held high and proud. Everett cast a disapproving look around, but it faded when Becca emerged from the crowd and greeted him with a hug. Then she shifted her attention to Samira, offering her hand to the woman. At that moment, voices started up again, as though Everett and his date were suddenly old news.

I watched them disappear into the crowd, then looked back at the door, hoping Lucian would walk in behind his father. But next up was an older couple, their hair nearly as white as the snow outside. Disappointed, although not surprised, I turned to face the bar again, realizing this night was turning out exactly as I'd expected.

"Are you alone?" a male voice asked from behind me, making me jump.

I snapped my attention to the side where Mr. Wainwright leaned his elbows on the counter, raising a finger to one of the bartenders when he looked over. "I'll be right with you," the bartender said as he twisted a corkscrew into a bottle of wine.

Mr. Wainwright nodded, then turned to me. "Well?"

I took a deep breath, wishing I could say no. But I couldn't lie. "Yes," I let out on a long breath, my tone indicating I wasn't happy about it.

He smiled warmly. "That makes two of us."

"Can I ask why you came if you knew you'd be alone?"

He shrugged with a frown. "Habit, I suppose. This is an annual tradition, and it's nice to have a drink somewhere other than The Witches' Brew for a change."

"What about not having a drink at all? I thought you were swearing off alcohol after I found you stumbling down a lonely road in the middle of the night."

"I did, for a week."

"Then what happened?"

"Reality set in. I needed a pick-me-up from the harsh reminder that no matter what I do, the woman I love will never come back to me."

My heart ached for him, and I wished he wouldn't give up. "Maybe someone else is out there for you, you just haven't found her yet."

"No way," he said with a shake of his head. "At least not in this town. And how could I leave all this." He gestured to the crowd, his eyes locking on someone.

I followed his gaze to see Becca dancing in Gabriel's arms, a bright smile on her face. "It's not the town keeping you here, it's Becca, isn't it?" I asked, shifting my attention back to Mr. Wainwright.

He nodded and turned to face the bar again. "Very good. You get a gold star for the night."

Before I could respond, the bartender approached. "What can I get for you, sir?"

"Bourbon and Coke," Mr. Wainwright answered. "Better make it a double. I'll need it tonight."

I rolled my eyes, not sure why it mattered to me if he drank his sorrows away. "Mr. Wainwright, with all due respect, perhaps you should go easy on the booze tonight. It's a ball, and I don't think you want anyone to have to carry you home."

He smiled. "Thank you for your concern, but I live two blocks from here. I'll be fine. Besides, if I'm not and I fall on the way back to my apartment, I'll land in the snow."

"It's pretty cold out there. You'd freeze."

"So be it. I'd rather freeze to death than die of a broken heart."

The bartender returned and placed Mr. Wainwright's drink on a cocktail napkin. "Thank you," he said. "Just start a tab for me, would you? I'm going to be here a while."

I frowned, wishing I didn't care that my History teacher was drowning himself in alcohol. Turning away from him, I scanned the crowd again and noticed Celeste lingering against the wall across the room. She looked amazing in a dark green dress that shimmered in the lights, her hair pulled to one side and hanging in curls over her shoulder.

"Excuse me," I murmured to Mr. Wainwright. "I'm going to say hi to Celeste."

Before he could respond, I jumped up and headed in her direction. But when I passed a window, something white flew by outside, reminding me of the doves Celeste had created in my room a few months ago.

My curiosity piqued, I ran out the door and around to the back of the building, hoping to find it.

I trudged through the snow, holding my dress up, once again thankful for the tall white boots Becca insisted I wear tonight. Music hummed inside the building, sounding muted through the windows. Tuning it out, I stopped behind the town hall, my heart taking off at the sight of Lucian standing in the center of the yard. Wearing a tuxedo that stood out against the snow, he held his arm out while a speckled white owl landed on him as though summoned.

"Thank you," he said. "You've been very helpful."

The owl let out a low hoot before spreading its wings and launching off his forearm, disappearing into the night.

Lucian lowered his hand, his eyes glued to mine. Smiling softly, he walked toward me, his gaze never leaving me. I stood in the snow, my pulse thumping out of control and pure happiness warming me.

He stopped inches away from me, causing my breath to hitch. "You look amazing," he said.

Feeling a blush heat up my cheeks, I smiled. "You're here," I whispered as though I didn't believe it. "I was hoping I'd see you."

"I told you to save a dance for me. But since I'm not about to cause a commotion by going inside, I had to find a way to get you out here. My plan worked like a charm." He paused, holding his hand out to me. "May I have this dance?"

Without hesitating, I reached for him, feeling the heat of his touch through my glove. "Yes," I said, mesmerized by the gleam in his green eyes.

He pulled me against him, wrapping both arms around my shoulders, the warmth of his body sending a flush through me. Then he started to move with me in his arms, his steps timed perfectly to the rhythm of the muffled music. My pulse quickening again, I realized we were alone under the stars glittering in the black sky.

He led the dance, at first moving me from side to side and back and forth, then twirling me around until I landed against his chest. Sliding my arms over his shoulders, I pulled him closer, breathing in the scent of his aftershave. Dancing with Lucian made me feel like I was floating on air, as though caught up in a dream. I closed my eyes, wanting nothing more than for this moment to last forever.

Lucian spun me around again, and I landed with my back next to his chest. He wrapped his hands around my waist, lighting a fire in my stomach and making my blood run hot. I felt him kiss my neck, his breath tickling my skin, electricity trailing in its wake. I trembled, wanting to feel more of him, to touch him, to lose myself in his arms. I started to turn, but he tightened his hold on me, locking my back against him.

Then he raised a hand to my ribcage, his lips moving up to my ear. "Close your eyes," he whispered.

Holding my breath, not sure what he was doing, I complied, his touch becoming far more intense as soon as my world went black.

"Are they closed?" he asked.

"Yes," I murmured with a slight nod.

"Good. Keep them closed. Now, ready?"

I nodded again. In an instant, he whipped me around, twirling me in circles as we crossed the field. When we came to an abrupt halt, his arms locked my back against his chest. "Okay. You can open them."

My eyelids fluttered open just enough for me to realize we were no longer in the courtyard behind the town hall. Instead, we stood on the rock overlooking the town. Snow covered the landscape as far as the eye could see, the moonlight casting a hazy glow across the sky. "What?" I gasped. "How did you do this?"

He whipped me around in his arms until I faced him. Smiling, he ducked his head closer to me, his eyes locking with mine. "You know how. Magic."

It must have been some kind of illusion because I could still hear music playing in the background. But we were completely alone at the top of the mountain where no one could see us. Nothing had ever felt so right.

We began to dance again, whirling around and kicking up the snow at our feet. The scenery blurred in the background, the cold air completely forgotten. All I could see was Lucian, his finely chiseled features and light brown hair perfectly clear. His mouth was set in a concentrated look, his eyes intense, filled with desire.

I wasn't sure how long we danced on the rock, but I could have stayed there in his arms all night. We made our way across the top, stopping at the edge when the music ended. Lucian dipped me backward, circling my waist with his arm. Hovering over the side of a cliff with only him to hold me, I drew in a sharp breath. Trusting him to keep me safe and the sheer exhilaration of submitting to his control pitched my heart into a frenzy.

"Are you afraid?" he asked, dangling me over the edge a little longer.

"No," I stated. "I'm not."

In a flash, he lifted me up to him, stepping back until my feet were planted on the rock a safe distance from the drop-off. "Good. Because you never should be," he said quietly.

He pulled me close to him, his hands running down my back and then up until they reached my shoulders. I slid my arms around him, watching him, waiting for more and hoping this moment would never end.

Lucian ran his fingers along my collarbone and up to my jaw where he swiped his thumb over my bottom lip. A tingle raced through me, and I swallowed, ready to feel more of him. In slow motion, he leaned toward me, stopping when his lips hovered above mine, so close, yet not touching. "I've waited too long for this," he whispered before kissing me.

I closed my eyes, letting his lips work their magic on me. At first, they were as light as a feather, almost hesitant, as though he doubted my feelings for him. I leaned against his chest, sifting my fingers through his hair, hoping he'd realize there was nowhere I'd rather be than here in his arms. His lips started to move against mine, pressing harder, sparking a passion deeper than anything I'd ever known. He opened his mouth, flicking my tongue with his, setting my blood on fire.

His kiss deepened while his hands moved down my back, one of them slipping over to my side and roaming down to my hip, electricity following the path of his touch. With each passing second, we clung to each other under the star-filled sky, alone high above the snow-covered rolling hills. His kiss intensified, becoming urgent, an unsatisfied hunger forming between us.

Wanting this moment to last forever, I was ready to give in to the feelings I'd been holding back for too long. But my hopes were crushed when Lucian abruptly lifted his head and pulled away. "No," he said, looking down at me, his eyes pleading me to forgive him. "This was a mistake." He dropped his arms to his sides and backed up.

"Lucian," I said, overwhelmed by the urge to burst into tears. "I don't understand."

"I know. There's no way you would. I'm sorry, but I have to go." Then he spun around and took off. In the blink of an eye, he was gone, his footprints in the snow the only evidence he'd been here.

The muffled music in the background snapped me out of my trance, and I found myself back in the courtyard behind the town hall. I stood in the snow, feeling a cold breeze sweep across my skin. Tiny snowflakes drifted down from the clouds that had moved in, hiding the stars. Ignoring the flakes pinging my bare shoulders, I glanced in the direction Lucian had gone and waited, hoping he'd return.

But after a few minutes passed, I realized he wasn't coming back.

20

Tears stung my eyes as I stood alone in the courtyard, the snow-flakes hitting my shoulders and melting on contact. The white landscape no longer appeared heavenly to me. Black thoughts plunged my mood into despair. Barely able to breathe, I felt like I'd been stood up at the altar, except this seemed worse. As far as I knew, I was the only person who believed in Lucian. I thought we had a connection, a bond from all the time we'd spent together. But I must have been wrong.

Gathering my composure, I swallowed the lump in my throat while a tear rolled down my cheek. I took my glove off to avoid smudging it with makeup and wiped my face. Crushed by Lucian's rejection, I trembled, my heart shattered into a million pieces.

Time standing still, I had no idea what to do next. Going back to the ball would be torture. I couldn't bear to see the smiles and watch people dancing in the arms of a loved one when I'd just been deserted. Instead, I waited for my tears to dry, burying my emotions deep inside until I grew numb.

Holding my head up high and taking a deep breath, I was about to return to the ball when Marguerite appeared in front of me, her red curls spilling over her black leather jacket. "I think the party's in there," she said, gesturing to the town hall.

"What are you doing here?" I demanded, my voice tense.

Her icy blue eyes locking on me, she smiled. "Just checking on my insurance. Are you having a good time out here in the snow all alone?" she asked, her sarcastic tone grating on my nerves.

"I'm not going to bother answering that because I'm sure you don't care," I replied before rushing past her. But she grabbed my wrist, pulling me to a stop beside her.

"You're right. I don't," she said flippantly before her voice took on a sinister tone. "I'm here to leave a message with you. Tell Becca she's running out of time. I want the script restored to the book now. I'm tired of her delay."

"And if she doesn't do it?"

"Then you'll be the one banished in the crypt at the graveyard. Think you'd like to spend a few centuries on a cold cement floor?"

I shuddered at the memory of the dark stone building, wishing once again I could go back in time and leave the wolf in chains. "That won't happen," I declared, surprised by my confident tone.

She snickered, releasing my wrist. "Don't sound too sure of that. You never know around here."

Before I could say another word, she disappeared across the yard, leaving a cold wind in her wake. I shivered, convinced tonight couldn't get any worse. My mood falling to an all-time low, I set my sights on returning to the ball, no matter how hard it would be to see the happy couples.

But I never made it back inside. Derek approached as I was about to open the door, stopping me. "Hi, Gracyn," he said with a smile, his blond hair seeming lighter than usual against his black tuxedo.

"Hey, Derek," I replied, glad to see a familiar face.

His expression softened the instant our eyes met. "Uh-oh. What happened? You look like someone just died."

I let out a heavy sigh. "It's been a rough night."

"But it's still early."

"Maybe for you. Are you just now getting here?"

"Yes. I'm fashionably late. But I wouldn't miss it for anything, even if I don't have a date," he said, his last words ending on a low note.

"You and me both," I muttered. "I don't suppose you'd mind giving me a ride home, would you?"

"What?" he asked, not seeming to believe me. "You've got to be kidding. Oh, wait a minute. I know what's going on. Alex is in there with his date, isn't he? I'm sorry you had to find out tonight."

"First of all, no, I'm not kidding. And secondly, it's not about Alex. I'm glad he has someone to share tonight with. I have no hard feelings toward him. He deserves some happiness since I ruined just about every date we had."

"Then what's going on with you? Wait, don't tell me. Let me guess. You're going to turn into a servant girl covered in cinders at—" He paused, glancing at his watch, then raised his eyebrows. "—nine o'clock."

"Something like that," I said. "My carriage already turned into a pumpkin."

He smiled, shaking his head. "Gracyn—"

"Please," I begged, catching his eye and hoping he'd oblige me. "I'll do anything."

"Fine," he relented. "Maybe on the way home, you can tell me why you look like doom and gloom."

"If that's what it takes to get a ride," I said.

"Okay. Come on. Let's go before you freeze out here." Derek wrapped an arm around my shoulders in a brotherly gesture and led me to his car parked in the farthest corner of the town lot two blocks away.

"Great spot," I said when he unlocked the doors with the remote, the lights flashing in the darkness.

"I know. Guess that's what I get for being late to the party," he said, opening the door for me.

I slid into the seat, grateful to find the car still warm.

As soon as Derek hopped in behind the wheel, he turned on the engine and headlights then gave the wipers a quick flash to clear the dusting of snow off the windshield. He pulled out onto the street, and we began making our way toward the outskirts of town when he broke the silence. "Okay, spill it. If Alex isn't the reason for your dark mood, why are you running away tonight?"

"I'm not running away," I tried to insist, but lacked conviction. "Well, maybe I am."

"I don't get it. You look stunning tonight, and everyone likes you. I'd be your date if you'd give me a chance."

I huffed, suspecting Derek was only saying that to make me feel better. "Thanks. That's very sweet of you, but I could never do that to Celeste. It was just hard to be alone surrounded by all the happy couples, which is why I needed to take a break outside." I paused, hating the lies coming out of my mouth. But I didn't know what else to say. I couldn't tell Derek about dancing with Lucian and having the most exciting kiss ever before the sting of rejection crushed me. Just remembering the moment Lucian walked away brought tears back to my eyes.

Taking a deep breath to compose myself, I continued with a safer topic. "The only person I talked to earlier was Mr. Wainwright. At least he was sober, although I doubt he still is." The thought of the drink he had ordered lingering in my mind, I wondered if I could use one. A shot of alcohol might erase the pain and torment caused by the guy who had stolen my heart over the last few months, only to break it the first chance he got.

Sure, go for it, a snarky voice in my head rolled out. *Just don't forget the nausea and headaches that will follow. I doubt Lucian will cure your hangover with his miracle tea again. He pretty much told you he wouldn't.*

Derek let out a soft chuckle. "It wouldn't be the same to have a town function without Mr. Wainwright drowning his sorrows in alcohol," he mused. "But seriously, I'd hang out with you, even if you won't let me be your date. I'd even dance with you, if you begged me to."

The twinkle in his eyes made me smile. "Beg?" I repeated.

"Yes, you'll have to beg after all the times you turned me down."

"I'd rather see you dance with Celeste. She still likes you, you know."

Derek's smile faded instantly. "Yes, of course I know that."

"And she looked amazing in there. You should see her."

"That doesn't surprise me. I've seen her dressed up. She cleans up nicely."

"Then what are you waiting for? Maybe when you get back to the ball, you can give her a chance."

"I'm not sure," he said under his breath.

"Would you do it for me?"

"Wait a minute. How is it I'm doing you a favor by driving you home, and yet you're asking me for another one?" he teased.

"Because this favor isn't for me, it's for Celeste. All she wants is a chance. After the night I've had, it would make me happy to know someone else's dream might come true."

"What do you mean, the night you've had? I thought you were just a little down because you're alone?"

I pursed my lips together and stared out at the falling snow streaking through the headlights. "Maybe it's a little more than that," I said quietly.

"I'm not surprised. But I'm guessing you don't want to talk about it," he said as he reached our driveway and turned onto the gravel, guiding the car through the woods until the house emerged at the end.

"Yes," I answered in a whisper when he pulled up to the front porch. Holding myself together, I turned to him. "Thank you for the ride. You're a good friend."

He nodded, his blue eyes soft and concerned. "Yeah, a lot of good it's doing me," he quipped before his voice settled into a serious tone. "But really, Gracyn, I want you to know you can tell me anything, even if it's something you don't want Alex to know. I can keep a secret, especially for you."

"Thanks. You're really great, you know that?"

He blushed, looking away as I put my gloved hand on his and squeezed. When he returned his gaze to me, I smiled. "Now go make a girl's night. You don't want another heart to break, do you?"

Hoping Derek would give Celeste a chance, I slipped out of the car. He waited until I climbed up the porch steps and waved before turning around and driving away.

Alone, I unlocked the door and entered the dark house, disappointed the distraction Derek had provided was gone. As I shut the door and twisted the deadbolt into place, I heard the dogs' heavy breathing from where they slept on their beds, but their presence did nothing to comfort me. Without turning on a single light, I headed straight for the stairs, ready to get out of my gown and forget all about this lousy night.

— —

As soon as I changed into a pair of flannel pajamas, I went to my desk and shoved the curtains aside. Outside, the light snow continued to fall, but I knew it wouldn't accumulate much. It looked pretty though, lighting up the darkness with tiny white dots.

Without any warning, Lucian's face appeared in the reflection, his expression hard as he turned away. I lifted my hand to touch the window, watching the image disappear instantly, as though he would never return to my thoughts, my dreams, my life.

Tears forming in my eyes, I held them back as best as I could and slipped into bed. I pulled the comforter up to my chin, wanting to forget the painful memory of his rejection. But I had a feeling it would be a long time before I recovered from the moment he pulled away and walked off, leaving me alone in the snow outside the town hall.

Sleep came easier than I expected. I thought I'd toss and turn for hours, but I was exhausted from the emotional whiplash of the night and quickly drifted off.

Sometime later, I opened my eyes to find myself in the woods under a summer sky. A breeze rippled through the leaves overhead. Birds chirped and squirrels scampered about, collecting acorns and chasing each other across the branches. Curious, I began walking along the trail leading to Lucian's estate.

At first, I savored the summer warmth, grateful for a change from the winter weather. I looked up at the sky, basking in a ray of light that snuck between the leaves. Holding my arms out to my sides, I spun around like a child, a smile on my face.

When a piercing scream shot through the air, I broke out of my trance and slammed to a halt, pausing to catch my balance. Without another second to spare, I ran into the woods and up the hill leading to the graveyard. I didn't even think about where I was going. Something pulled me, and my legs kept moving, taking me farther away from the safety of the trail. At the top, the forest was shrouded in heavy fog, the white mist hiding the tallest branches and making it difficult to see.

I slowed down, tempted to turn back, but powerless to do so. Staring into the thick cloud in front of me, I continued walking ahead with the invisible force pulling me. I couldn't see a thing until I emerged into the clearing outside the graveyard fence. There I stopped at the sight of Lucian in a white T-shirt and jeans, his back to me.

My heart skipping a beat, I watched him kneel beside a white horse lying on a bed of leaves. Its flanks moved slightly, the look in its glassy eye one of defeat and hopelessness.

Lucian looked around, his eyes searching the surroundings, his gaze passing over me as though I wasn't even there. He bent his head and reached for the handle of a silver dagger sticking out of the horse's chest. With a swift movement, he pulled it out, spilling blood onto the ground as the horse took its final breath.

I felt like a knife had been staked into my heart. Barely breathing, I shuddered when Lucian stood up, the bloody weapon in his hands. Tears rolled over his five o'clock shadow, and a red mark stained his shirt. He looked down at the horse, then at the knife in his hands. Staring at it, he dropped it before falling to his knees again.

"No!" he cried, stroking her lifeless head and neck. "No, no, no!" He collapsed on top of her, his sobs filling the silence, wrenching my soul.

The scene in the woods ended at that moment, but I didn't wake up from my dream. Instead, I found myself in Cassie's bedroom corner standing between the nightstand and the wall when Lucian rushed in through the doorway, a folded black cloth in his arms. He looked over his shoulder before stopping in the center of the room.

He glanced at the church painting on the wall next to the window, then his gaze skimmed the bed, the windows, and finally, the dresser. His head bowed, his shoulders hunched over, he approached it and placed the cloth on the surface in front of the mirror. He unwrapped the material to expose the bloody knife he had pulled out of Cassie's horse. He hesitated, staring at it for a few seconds before folding the cloth over it and opening the bottom left-hand drawer. A frown on his face, he placed the covered knife in the drawer and shut it. Then he chanted something in a language I didn't recognize before leaving the room.

As soon as the door clicked shut, my eyes flew open. Sucking in a deep breath, I found myself back in bed, sweat sticking my pajamas to my skin. My heart thumped out of control while the images from my dream rolled through my head like a movie stuck on replay.

The visions left me reeling with suspicion that what I'd seen had really happened. Not wanting to believe it, I could only think of one way to prove my mind was playing tricks on me. I had to get over to Lucian's estate and check Cassie's dresser drawer as soon as the sun came up.

21

I waited until daylight broke to make a mad dash to the barn. Sunlight streamed through the snow-covered branches when I stepped outside dressed in jeans and a heavy sweater under my parka. In my rush, I'd only taken the time to pull my hair into a ponytail before running out the door, careful to be quiet and not wake up Becca and Gabriel. The last thing I needed was them asking questions about my night.

Without a car, I had no choice but to tack up Gypsy. A few minutes later, I led her out of the barn, flipped the reins over her neck, and climbed into the saddle. Urgency whipping through me, I kicked her sides as soon as my feet found the stirrups. Sensing my hurry, she took off at a gallop, her stride churning up the snow, causing a cloud to surround us.

I grabbed her mane as she charged through the woods, heading down the path. The cold air burned my throat and stung my cheeks, but I pushed the discomfort aside, instead focusing on one thing—finding out the truth.

When we reached the trail leading to Lucian's estate, Gypsy slowed enough to make the turn, then raced down the hill between the fences, each stride taking me closer to the answers, or so I hoped. The horses in the field pawed their way through the snow, nibbling what little grass they found and paying us no attention.

Gypsy galloped past the barn and around the side of the house to the front where she slid to a stop by the sidewalk. I dismounted and approached the door, but hesitated when I got close enough to knock. My pulse quickening, I choked back the doubts running rampant in my thoughts. What was I thinking? Just because I had an incriminating dream didn't mean I had any right to enter someone else's property uninvited. Shaking my head, I started to turn back when the vision of Lucian standing over Cassie's horse with a bloody knife in his hands whipped through my mind again, as real and vivid as the sights around me.

You have to do this, a voice in my head declared. *If you don't get up there and see for yourself that there's nothing in the drawer, your dream will haunt you forever and you'll regret not taking the chance to find out the truth.*

I took a deep breath, wondering why the police hadn't found the knife by now if it was here. Something told me not to believe humans would've had any chance of finding it. Mustering every ounce of courage, I banished my doubts and ran back to the door, about to knock when it cracked open on its own.

Dropping my hand, I pushed the door and peered into the dark entry hall. "Lucian?" I called softly, getting no response other than silence.

My heart ramming into my chest with every beat, I stepped inside and shut the door. I looked up to the railing at the top of the stairs, pausing for a moment, waiting for someone to appear.

Nails tapped on the floor from the doorway leading to the kitchen, and I turned, clutching my heart when I saw Diesel. He watched me, his expression curious while I waited for him to growl or attack. I started to back up, sure the Doberman would come after me any second. My eyes never leaving him, I did a double-take when he approached, his head down and stubby tail wagging. He nudged my hand in a greeting, and I pulled it back when he licked me.

"Okay," I muttered, confused. "Now we're friends, I guess. Where's Lucian?" The only time Diesel had acted aggressively toward me was the afternoon I'd stopped by when Lucian was out, so I drew the conclusion that he must be home.

I froze, expecting Lucian to appear, but the only movement was Diesel spinning around and trotting back into the kitchen without giving me an ounce of trouble. When silence returned, I closed my eyes. *Please forgive me,* rang through my mind before I dashed up the stairs.

At the top, I hurried while making my footsteps as light as I could, not wanting to be heard. I found Cassie's room right away and darted inside, coming to an abrupt halt at the sight of the light purple walls and comforter I remembered from the morning I'd woken up in her bed after passing out in the graveyard. The pictures of her on the dresser drew my attention at once, causing me to lose sight of my mission for a moment.

The drawer, a voice reminded me. Snapping out of my trance, I crossed the room and knelt down, but stopped, not sure if I was ready for this. Closing my eyes, I tugged on the bottom left-hand drawer. Holding my breath, I opened my eyes and my heart nearly fell into my stomach when I saw the black cloth.

Biting my lip to keep the tears at bay, I reached into the drawer and unfolded the cloth to expose a silver dagger, the tip dark brown from what appeared to be dried blood.

Drawing in a sharp breath, I rocked back on my heels. "No!" I cried, moisture filling my eyes. "No," I repeated, shaking uncontrollably. "It can't be. No, no, no! This has to be another stupid, weird dream!"

"It isn't a dream," Lucian said from the doorway. I looked up, my blood cold with fear. Dressed in all black, Cassie's cross hanging around his neck, he lingered several feet away from me.

"You...you have the knife," I stuttered, still in shock.

"Yes," he confirmed, stepping into the room, his eyes steady on me, showing no emotion. Not anger, not sadness, not even betrayal at finding me here. It was as though he'd been expecting me.

"And it's been here all this time?"

"Yes," he repeated.

"But that doesn't make sense. The police searched your house. Why didn't they find it?"

"I put a cloaking spell on it. They couldn't see it. Neither can my father or anyone else, except you."

I glanced at the knife in the drawer, then returned my stare to Lucian as I stood up. "Why me?"

"Because of last night," Lucian replied before walking toward me.

I backed up until my shoulders hit the wall, feeling trapped, suddenly afraid of him in a way I'd never been. "What? I don't understand."

"There's an old legend in our coven that says when two witches are soul mates and truly meant to be together, they form an unbreakable bond. This bond connects their thoughts, makes them immune to the magic of the other one. I never believed it because I don't know anyone it's happened to." He paused, stepping closer to me. "But last night, our kiss triggered it. I saw things I never expected to see."

"Like what?"

His face twisted in anger, his eyes glaring. "I saw you in your friend's stepfather's car during the storm. I saw him put his hand on you, and I've never felt so helpless and angry in my entire life. If he lived around here, his funeral arrangements would be underway at this moment."

The memory of Sam's stepfather whisked across my thoughts. "That's over and done with. I don't want to talk about it. But—" I glanced at the dagger in the open drawer before looking up again, meeting Lucian's gaze. "You have the knife that killed Cassie. Did you...did you kill her?" I asked, unable to stop the words from pouring out.

Tears formed in Lucian's eyes, and his lip quivered. A sad glaze washed over his expression before disappearing. "If you're asking me that, then you must doubt me. I don't know how to answer you in a way you'll believe me."

"But—"

"No!" he exclaimed, raising his voice with such conviction that I jumped. "Just stop right there! You always said you believed in me, but I see that's changed."

"What else would I think?" I asked, my voice barely a whisper. "You've had the murder weapon all this time."

Lucian took a deep breath, his anger and frustration subsiding. "I was up on the rock that day, painting, when I heard her scream. I couldn't just keep working and ignore it, so I jumped on Shade and took off to find her. But instead, we found Angel with a knife in her heart. I searched the area for any trace of who had done it, but I saw no one. So I did the first thing that came to me without thinking things through. I pulled the knife out, hoping I could heal her."

"Can we do that?"

"Apparently not. I tried everything I could think of, put every ounce of my energy into magic, and yet she died as I watched. I'll never forget the last breath she took." Lucian paused, closing his eyes as if shutting out the awful memory of that day. When he opened them, he continued. "By the time my senses came back, I realized my fingerprints were all over the knife."

"But the killer's fingerprints would also be on it."

"There's no way to be sure of that. If the killer had worn gloves, then only my prints would be on it."

I shifted my eyes back to the knife, doubts racing through my mind. I wished Lucian had told me this before, but he hadn't and now I had to decide what to believe. Conflicting emotions twisted inside me. I wanted to trust him, but knowing he'd kept the murder weapon hidden for years made me doubt his innocence.

"So you never told anyone," I mused, shaking my head.

"No," he admitted. "Gracyn, you have to believe me. I didn't kill my sister."

My eyes filled with tears again. "I don't know what to believe anymore," I whispered.

"Then believe this," he said before kissing me.

My eyes fell shut and I leaned into him, responding to his touch. Desire pulsed through my veins, sending my head into a spin. Everything became a blur at that moment, including right versus wrong. Without another thought wasted on the knife, I wrapped my arms around his shoulders, pulling him to me. He stepped closer, his chest nearly crushing me. Heat tore through me when his tongue touched mine, at first light and teasing, then urgent, as though a kiss wasn't enough.

He slipped his arms around my waist and lifted me off the ground before carrying me to the bed where he lowered me onto the comforter and stretched out on top, his weight locking me in place.

Pure joy consumed me. After he had pushed me away the night before, I'd been so sure I'd never see him again. But now, knowing he still wanted me, I almost cried with relief. I wanted him, too, so badly that my thoughts became a foggy mess. All I could think about was being here with him, as though nothing else existed. I ran my hands up his arms to his shoulders before sliding them down his back to the waistband of his jeans.

He touched my jaw, then trailed his fingers down my neck and cupped his hand under my hair, lighting my skin on fire. Nothing had ever felt so right.

But Lucian's touch and the heat pulsing through my veins weren't enough to keep me away from reality for long. A moment later, my eyes opened and the first thing I saw was the picture of Cassie on her horse propped up on the dresser. The vision of Lucian holding the knife returned to me, taking my breath away as shock hit me again and the world came to a screeching halt.

My muscles tensing up, I looked at Lucian, suddenly very afraid.

"Get off of me," I whispered with as much force as I could muster. Scrambling beneath him, I pushed at his chest, adrenaline coursing through my blood. Something had broken inside me, like I was seeing him for the first time.

"Gracyn, please," he said.

"No. Just get away, now."

"No, Gracyn," he said, grabbing my arms and pinning me below him. "You have to listen to me. I can explain."

"You already tried, and I...I don't know what to think. I need some time to figure this out."

"What do I have to do to convince you I didn't do it?"

"You can't," I said, staring up at him. "You're trying too hard, like the guilt inside you is eating you up. You have her necklace and yet, you hid the knife for years. None of this makes sense."

Lucian let go of me and sat up, defeat crossing over his expression. "You're right. How could the murder of a twelve-year-old girl make sense any at all?"

Seizing the moment, I jumped out from under him. As soon as I was on my feet beside the bed, I looked at him. "You've had plenty of chances to tell me the truth. Why didn't you?"

"Gracyn, all you need to know is that I didn't do it. I swear with every ounce of my heart, I didn't kill my sister."

"You should have called the authorities the minute you found her horse. You should have turned the knife over to them."

"How do you expect humans to believe a girl died when her horse was the real victim? And how would it look if I was at the scene of the crime minutes after it happened? There's no way could we have gotten there that quickly if I was human and Shade was just a regular horse."

"It's the truth. All anyone cares about is the truth."

"And the truth is the only blood an analysis will find on that knife is equine blood, not human blood. There was no way I could release it to the authorities. The entire coven would be at risk."

"So you elected to lie instead?"

He looked down, shame registering in his eyes. "I didn't know what else to do."

"Why not bring the knife to the coven? Tell them and ask for their help?"

When he hung his head again, refusing to look at me, the answer stared me right in the face. "Why would you do that if you were guilty?" I asked, my words adding a thick layer of tension to the room. "That's why you ran away from me last night, isn't it? You knew I would find out."

"Yes," he said quietly.

Tears of betrayal stung my eyes when I realized what this meant. Without another word, I ran out of the room, down the stairs, and out into the snow where Gypsy waited to take me home.

22

As soon as Gypsy slid to a stop in the driveway back at home, I jumped off into the snow, leaving her with the reins looped over her neck, and raced into the house. Slamming the door behind me, I stopped and leaned against it, trying to catch my breath. Then I looked up to see Becca behind the island, stirring eggs in a pan on the stove.

"There you are," she said, not seeming to notice my panic. "I didn't know where you disappeared to last night, but I brought your wrap and purse home. You left them on a bar stool."

"Becca," I said, letting out a deep breath as I ran across the room to the kitchen. "I need to talk to you."

"What's going on?" she asked, a concerned look in her eyes. She dropped the spoon on the counter and approached me, not bothering to turn the burner off.

I drew in several quick breaths, feeling like I was hyperventilating. My heart pounding out of control, my thoughts were a complete blur except for the clear image of the blood-stained dagger hidden within the folds of the black cloth.

"I...I saw it. The knife, the one that killed Cassie, I mean her horse. He has it. He's had it all along," I made out in short gasps.

Becca's face paled, fear buried in her expression. She placed a hand on my upper arm, her gaze meeting mine. "Are you sure? Slow down and tell me everything."

I took a deep breath, filling my lungs with air while I prayed for the courage to tell her exactly what had happened even though a part of me didn't want to. My allegiance to Lucian had run so deep for so long that I felt like I was betraying him. *If he killed his sister, you owe him nothing,* a voice rang out in my head. *He'll get what's coming. And if he didn't do it like he said he didn't, the truth will be revealed in time. But for now, you can't hide the fact that you know he kept the murder weapon hidden for over two years.*

Lifting my gaze, I saw Becca watching me, waiting for me to speak. I began slowly, starting with a brief recollection of what happened outside the town hall last night in the courtyard. I glossed over Lucian's kiss, my chest tightening when I remembered his lips on mine. But I couldn't let it weaken my sense of right and wrong, so I went on to describe my dream and how it led me to the dagger in Lucian's room.

When I stopped talking, I studied her, surprised by her calm reaction. "It's unbelievable, isn't it?" I asked. "I feel like I stepped into a nightmare. I never saw this coming."

"Of course, you didn't," Becca said softly, sounding thoughtful.

"What do we do now?" I asked. "I left the knife where it was. Maybe I should have taken it, but I wasn't sure. I'm so confused. I don't know what to do."

"I'm sure you don't. This is a huge shock. I have to say, in spite of the rumors and all the people who had already convicted Lucian in their minds, I never wanted to believe he did it."

"I know," I said, starting to think a little more clearly since I'd gotten everything off my chest. "But there's so much going on right now, I don't know what to think. Is it true what he said? That when two witches are meant for each other, they can see each other's thoughts, feel their emotions, and know what happened to them in the past? He also said we're immune to each other's magic now."

"Yes, at least that's what the legend has always foretold," Becca said.

"You don't sound very convinced," I replied.

"I'm not sure what I believe. Until now, it's only been a prophecy that was never confirmed. In all my years, I don't know anyone who has experienced it."

"Great," I said with a groan. "I'm a half-breed witch responsible for releasing Marguerite who has her sights set on an evil book of spells that will enable her to wreak havoc on the world and, now, I'm the only one to have fallen into this weird love trap. I'm cursed. That has to be it." I shook my head, frowning as Becca watched me, her eyebrows raised. "I'm sorry. I'm a terrible person. A girl was brutally murdered and I may have uncovered the most important clue that could lead us to find out who did it, but all I can think about is myself."

Becca offered a reassuring smile. "You've been thrown into this more abruptly than anyone I know. I'm sure it's a lot to absorb right now."

"Every time I think things can't get any worse, they do. But if I'm connected to Lucian, why did my visions only show what happened after the horse was stabbed? Will I see where Lucian was at the time of the murder?"

"I wish I could answer that," Becca said. "But I don't know how the bond between you two works. For now, we can only go with what you saw. And we need to figure out what to do about Lucian."

My heart heavy with a mixture of fear and sorrow, I pursed my lips, waiting for her to continue. When she didn't, I broke the silence. "What do you mean? Should I have taken the knife? I can't believe I left it over there. He could have moved it by now."

Becca shook her head. "I doubt that. I'm sure he knows it'll only be a matter of time before you find it again. There is one thing I could try, if I can get ahold of the knife."

"What?"

"A tracing spell, one that would let me see into its past." She paused, appearing worried.

"What's wrong?"

"Tracing spells are complicated. I used one a few months ago on that awful doll, but it took a lot of power and seemed to make my headaches worse. The truth is, I don't know if I should even attempt it right now."

I shuddered, not sure if the possibility that Lucian had killed Cassie frightened me more than the thought of losing Becca. If this spell put her at risk, it wasn't worth it. "Can anyone else do it?" I asked.

"Probably not," Becca said. "Celeste is the next one in line, but she's still very young. I doubt she'll be powerful enough to conjure up the past."

"What if several witches combine their power?" I asked.

"That can be tricky. Let me give it some thought. In the meantime, we can't keep this to ourselves."

I drew in a sharp breath. "What do you mean? Do you think we should turn the knife over to the police?"

"No," she said, shaking her head. "That would be too dangerous. We have to keep the authorities out of this. But we have to tell Everett. He deserves to know everything. Cassie was his little girl, and Lucian is his son. Perhaps this matter will be better left to him."

I nodded, relieved she wanted to tell someone. I felt like I would explode if I had to keep my knowledge of the knife's whereabouts to myself.

"Well, you're already dressed. Just let me turn off the stove and we'll go."

"Right now?"

"Yes," she confirmed. "We might as well get it over with."

"What about Gabriel?" I asked, wondering if she planned to get him up for this.

"He's not here. A colleague of his went into labor last night, so he was asked to cover her shifts for the next week. He hated to miss the last day of the carnival, but he didn't want to say no to the hospital."

"Oh," I said, realizing I'd been too distracted to notice his car was gone this morning.

As Becca turned back to the stove and shut off the burner, the unattended eggs now fried to a crisp, doubt snaked through me. In spite of what I'd seen and what I knew had to be done, I felt like I was about to betray Lucian in the worst way possible. If he was telling the truth and he hadn't killed Cassie, I hoped it would be proven soon.

After untacking Gypsy and turning her out in the pasture with Cadence and Prince, I jumped into the passenger seat of Becca's SUV where she waited for me with the engine running, the heat turned up high. In silence, we made our way down the road to Lucian's estate. The pavement was clear, the blacktop visible between walls of snow nearly three feet high on the sides. A thick white blanket covered the forest floor and outlined the branches, but the winter beauty did nothing to lift my mood. Numb from the anticipation of confronting Lucian, I felt like we were on the way to a funeral.

When we arrived at the Dumante estate, Becca and I rushed up to the front door. I hung back while she knocked, tempted to hide in the car even though I knew I couldn't. I had to be strong and get through this.

Lucian's father opened the door dressed in jeans and a gray shirt, his hair neatly brushed and curiosity brimming in his eyes. "Becca," he said. "This is quite a surprise. I thought we'd see you in town a little later for the last of the festival."

"Everett, we need to talk," she said quietly. "It's serious."

His expression hardened, and he stepped outside, shutting the door behind him. "What's going on?"

Becca nodded at me. "I think Gracyn should tell you."

I hesitated, barely able to find my voice. Taking a deep breath, I launched into my recollection of the morning in as little detail as I could manage. While I spoke, Everett appeared to grow more disturbed, a sad look of betrayal falling over his eyes.

"I'm so sorry to be the one to tell you this," I said when I concluded my monologue. "But I couldn't not tell anyone. I just didn't know what to do."

"You did the right thing," he stated.

"Everett," Becca said. "We want you to know we're not going to the police or anyone else with this information. We're leaving it with you."

"Thank you," he said. "I guess I should find my son. He has some explaining to do." When I started to turn, intending to run back to the car, Everett stopped me. "No, Gracyn. Please stay. I want you and Becca to come inside. We all need to confront him together."

My nerves a complete wreck, I followed Becca and Everett into the house, the warmth doing nothing to calm my fears. How could I look Lucian in the eye after ratting him out? *This can hardly be compared to tattling*, I told myself. *A girl is dead. Justice must be served, no matter what the cost. The truth is all anyone wants. Cassie's father is entitled to an explanation from Lucian after he hid the murder weapon for over two years.*

While Becca and I waited in the foyer, Everett charged up the stairs and ran down the hall.

"Lucian!" Everett's voice boomed through the house. "Lucian! I want a word with you, now!" A minute later, he hurried back down the stairs. "He's not up there. Come with me."

He led us into the kitchen where Samira stood behind the stove, a sizzling sound filling the room. She looked up immediately, her expression worried. "What is it?" she asked.

"We have a problem. It's Lucian. I have to find him," Everett told her, urgency in his voice.

She turned off the stove, wiped her hands on a towel, and ran around the island to our side. Without another word, Everett led us down the hallway to a family room lit only by a fire raging in the stone hearth. Dark cherry wainscoting covered the walls, and a grid of matching woodwork crisscrossed the ceiling. Lucian sat in a corner chair, his eyes fixated on the crackling flames. He didn't even look up when we stormed into the room. Instead, he remained perfectly still, the knife resting on his lap, the dark cloth that had concealed it for years under it.

"Hello, father," he said, his voice calm, his gaze never leaving the fire.

"Lucian!" Everett gasped, stopping beside the coffee table and looking at his son, a mixture of disbelief and disappointment on his face. His expression fell, his eyes taking in the dagger. He held his arm out to the side, keeping the rest of us at bay, indicating he planned to handle this. "What have you done?"

Lucian lifted his eyes from the fire to meet his father's stare. "Ah, you're just like the rest of them. I knew it would only be a matter of time before the pitchforks came out."

"You didn't answer me."

"I shouldn't have to because I did nothing."

The room grew quiet, the fire hissing in the background. I watched the scene unfold, my heart breaking in so many places, I wasn't sure I'd ever be able to put it back together.

"But you have the knife that killed your sister," Everett stated.

"That I do," Lucian admitted, standing up with it in his outstretched arms.

"And you didn't even try to hide it this morning," Everett said, his voice sinking.

"Why would I? What's the point?" Lucian's eyes slid toward me for a moment before reverting back to his father. "Gracyn would find it now, no matter what I do with it. So I guess the game is over. Here." He crossed the room to stand in front of his father. "Take it."

Everett hesitated, his eyes drawn to the silver blade, the tip darkened with dried blood.

"Take it!" Lucian hollered, making me jump. "You know you want it. Then you all can crucify me. I know it's over. There's no way I can convince you I didn't kill Cassie." A tear rolled down his face, tugging at my heart.

I stepped up, not sure what I believed anymore. "We just want the truth," I said quietly.

"You might," Lucian said, glancing at me before returning his stare to his father. "But everyone else just wants to see me behind bars. Forget about finding evidence beyond a doubt. Forget that I never did anything but love my sister. Hell, I took better care of her than our own parents, but no one seems to remember the things I did for her. They're looking for someone to blame, and I fit the bill."

Lucian shoved the knife at his father one more time. "Aren't you going to take it? What are you afraid of?"

"Son," Everett said, his voice calm and cool. "We need the knife. It may be the only way to find out what really happened that day." Moisture forming in his eyes, he took the dagger, then swallowed, keeping his composure. "Gracyn's right. All anyone wants is the truth. And the fact that you hid this for over two years is going to make you look guilty."

"Knife or no knife, that's all anyone thinks," Lucian said, his head hung low.

"Why did you hide it?" Everett asked.

"I didn't know what else to do. I struggled for a long time trying to decide what to do with it. Right after I found it, I couldn't eat or sleep, at least not until I put the cloaking spell on it and tucked it away where no one would find it. But I never expected Gracyn to break through my spell," he said, his eyes sliding my way.

As soon as my gaze met his, I looked down, the pain and betrayal buried deep in his expression whipping another dose of guilt through me.

"I'm glad she found it," Everett said. "There are ways to use it to try to see into the past."

Lucian shook his head. "You know as well as I do tracing spells are tricky. Very few witches are powerful enough to do it, and even if they are, it isn't always accurate. So why don't you just tell the rest of the coven what you found. I'm sure they'll find a way to punish me for my sins."

"Lucian," Everett began.

"No, father. Whatever you have to say to me doesn't matter anymore. You and I both know it's over. You've come back here, with your girl-friend, no less. Once I've been banished for eternity or burned at the stake, whichever punishment the coven decides is appropriate, you can forget about your old life and the family you had and start over with Samira. I'm sure that's all you want at this point."

Before Everett could respond, Lucian raced around the furniture and disappeared down the hallway. Then a door slammed, making all of us flinch. Without hesitating, I ran out of the room to the entry hall, through the front doorway, and around the side of the house. Coming to an abrupt halt in the deep snow, I watched Lucian ride Shade out of the barn at a gallop, a white cloud surrounding them as the stallion charged up the hill and into the forest.

A lump growing in my throat, I stood where I was for a moment. I had done this. This was all my fault. He would be condemned now, perhaps not by a court of law, but by the witches of Sedgewick. Justice would be served, whatever that meant by coven standards. But if he was innocent...

Do you really think that's possible? He hid the murder weapon for two years. He pulled it out of Cassie's mare as she took her last breath. It didn't take hours for that knife to kill her, it took minutes. How did he get to her so quickly while the real killer disappeared? Or had he been with her all along?

I didn't want to believe the damning words in my mind, but it was hard to ignore the evidence.

By the time I returned to the family room, Everett was sitting on the couch, running his hands through his hair. Samira sat beside him, her arm draped over his shoulders. The dagger rested on the coffee table, still on the black cloth. Becca stood beside the table, watching them and saying nothing, the tension in the room thick and foreboding.

Everyone looked up at me when I entered the room. "He's gone," I told them quietly, meeting Everett's stare. "He took off on Shade." I felt guilty, wishing I hadn't been the one to unleash the secrets that sent him running. Perhaps it had been better when the knife had been cloaked, leaving a trail of mystery.

Everett stood up and approached me, placing a hand on my shoulder, tears in his eyes. "I don't want you to ever regret telling us about the knife. You did the right thing."

"I wish I could be sure of that," I said, still hoping the evidence was leading us in the wrong direction. "What now?"

"I'm going to keep it for the time being. I haven't decided who to tell or what to do, but I need you and Becca to keep this to yourselves. If there's anything I believe, it's that my son wouldn't lie. If he swears he didn't hurt his sister, I believe him."

Glancing at Becca, I nodded while she silently agreed with a subtle movement of her head. "Everett," she began. "Gracyn and I will honor your request. But I want to help. Perhaps I can try a tracing spell on it."

"That's wonderful of you to offer, but I have another plan." Everett's attention shifted to Samira who stood up, her long dark curls falling halfway to her waist, her cream-colored sweater appearing almost white against her dark skin. "Samira."

She nodded, her black eyes studying Becca. "I can do it," she said. "Our magic runs deep, and it's powerful."

"Thank you," Becca said. "But I should help. Everett, I need to try."

"No," he objected, much to my relief. I didn't want Becca expending any energy that could drain her. "Your health is too important to risk. Samira is young and strong, much stronger than any of us."

"But—" Becca began.

"Sorry, Becca. My mind is made up," Everett declared.

"Okay," Becca relented before turning to Samira with a subtle smile. "Thank you for offering to help. When this is over, we'll get to know each other better."

Samira nodded, gratitude in her soft expression. "That would be nice. I've heard much about all of you, and I'll look forward to it."

Everett turned to me. "Gracyn," he said, his green eyes reminding me of Lucian.

"Yes?" I asked.

"Will you go find my son?"

I drew in a sharp breath, not sure I heard him correctly.

"He may not be perfect, but he's my flesh and blood. There's no way I can believe he hurt his sister. And he's right. He spent far more time with her than either her mother or I did. We need to get him back here, show him we'll stand by him until we know the truth. Can you do that?"

"Yes," I replied, a tiny bit of hope returning. If Lucian's father believed in him, then perhaps I could, too.

"Good." He paused, taking a deep breath before continuing. "I can't imagine what went through his mind when he found Angel that day. Lucian and Cassie were always running off into the woods, often going their separate ways. I can believe she was by herself when she met her fate. And it doesn't surprise me in the least that Lucian was the first one to find her. I want him to come home because I need to tell him I believe him. Will you find him for me?"

Debating what to do, I glanced at Becca and Samira, noticing their gazes on me. "You really think I can convince him to come back?"

"I do." Everett let out a small smile. "Ever since I got back to town last month, I've seen something different in him. It's like he found a new purpose in life. This is the first time in years I've seen a light in him, and I believe that light is you."

"What about the knife?" I asked.

"Let me worry about that. I'll do what's right for Cassie. All I want is the truth. If you have any more visions from that day, if you happen to see where Lucian was at the time she was killed, you need to let me know right away."

I nodded. "Of course. But I don't think those visions are going to stand up as evidence in court."

"This is never going to court," Everett said with more conviction in his voice than I would have thought possible. "I will personally see to that. My family has been torn apart for years, and I'm not about to stand for it any longer. So please bring him home. In the meantime, I'll have Samira get started with the knife."

"Okay," I said, hoping I'd be able to convince Lucian we hadn't sealed his fate with a guilty verdict. I was still surprised his father had backed off, giving Lucian the benefit of the doubt. And if Everett could do it, then I had no excuse but to continue believing in Lucian until something other than circumstantial evidence came to light.

"Good. Thank you, Gracyn. Please make sure he comes home before dark."

"I'll try," I said, sensing the urgency in his voice.

"Trying isn't good enough. You must do this. I'm afraid for him right now. I don't want this morning to be the last straw that makes him decide to jump off a cliff. I already buried one of my children, and I'm not about to go through that again."

Feeling my throat constrict, I swallowed the lump forming at the thought of Lucian running away for eternity. In that instant, the life or death threat sunk in and I felt tears brimming in my eyes. "I understand. And I think I know where he went." I paused, looking at Becca. "Can you take me home? I need to get Gypsy. I hope she's ready for another workout."

23

Back at the house, it felt like déjà vu when I tacked up Gypsy for a second time that day. Becca helped, putting on the bridle while I secured the girth to the saddle. When we finished, I led Gypsy back through the snow, following the path she'd made to the mounting block hours ago. Becca stood beside Gypsy's head as I climbed onto her back and gathered up the reins.

"Be careful," Becca said, looking up at me.

"I'll be fine," I assured her, worried only about Lucian. My heart was still breaking over the morning's events. Everett's warning that Lucian might give up and take his own life hit me hard. I couldn't let that happen, especially after I'd been the one to find the knife and turn it over to his father.

As soon as Becca stepped out of the way, Gypsy took off for the woods, kicking up a cloud of powder. We galloped down the path, passing the trail that led to Lucian's estate within seconds. I ducked down next to her mane, the snow-covered branches whipping by in a white blur. I didn't even feel the cold air nipping at my cheeks. All I could think about was finding Lucian before it was too late.

When we raced out into the meadow, Gypsy opened her stride, charging ahead as fast as she could go. The snow barely slowed her down, her movement feeling smooth, as though she was swimming. Minutes later, we reached the top of the hill to find Shade standing knee-deep in a snow drift, his ebony coat glistening with sweat in spite of the frigid air.

I halted Gypsy beside him and dismounted, ignoring the icy chill wrapping around my ankles when snow fell into my boots. Shoving my hands into my jacket pockets, I scanned the area for Lucian, not surprised he was nowhere in sight. Looking up at the rock, I frowned. I'd barely been able to climb to the top when the edges weren't covered in a slippery layer of snow.

Then I smiled, remembering the day at the drive-in and realizing I didn't need to climb up the side at all. Closing my eyes, I channeled my energy and pushed off the ground with as much force as I could muster. My landing on the rock came fast, and I bent my knees on impact.

I opened my eyes to see Lucian standing at the edge of the rock, looking out across the land. His head was bowed, his hands buried in his coat pockets. Beyond him rolled the sleepy, snow-covered town complete with a church steeple and cozy houses, smoke rising from their chimneys. But the peaceful setting didn't come with an easy life, at least not for Lucian.

"Lucian," I said quietly, hesitant to approach him.

"You didn't surprise me. I heard you arrive," he said without turning around.

"What are you doing?" I asked, worried one wrong word out of my mouth could send him over the edge.

He laughed, sounding sarcastic and not at all amused. "I'm contemplating the meaning of life," he said, his words cutting through the wintry silence like a knife. "I'm meditating, thinking, wondering what all of this means. What are you doing? Seems like a long way to ride just to talk to a guy you now think of as a monster."

"Lucian, please, don't."

He whipped around, his bloodshot eyes settling on me. "Don't what? Don't feel sorry for myself? Don't give up? Don't let the bitterness consume me, even when the only person I thought I could trust, the only person I thought believed in me, sold me out?"

Tears clouded my vision as his words punched a hole in my chest. Taking a deep breath, I refused to let my emotions snatch the last few shreds of composure I had left. "Look, I admit, when I first saw the visions and found the knife in Cassie's room, I panicked. That was the last thing I expected."

"Where are you going with this?"

"I had to tell someone. You can't blame me for that. Hiding the only piece of evidence isn't the answer. I have to believe the truth will be revealed sooner or later."

"And what do you think the truth is?"

"Honestly, I don't know. I believe what I saw in those visions, but I didn't see everything, including who killed Cassie's horse. So whether or not you believe me, I'm not convinced you hurt them."

A faint glimmer of appreciation crossed Lucian's face, but he didn't say a word.

"Neither is your father."

Lucian raised his eyebrows, seeming surprised.

"He sent me out here to find you and bring you home."

"Really? Why? What's he worried about? He has the house to himself now."

"I don't think he cares about that. He's concerned you'll hurt yourself. That you'll give up fighting for the truth and jump off a cliff. No matter what you think or how you feel about him, he cares about you."

Lucian narrowed his eyes suspiciously. "He has a funny way of showing it. Tell me, has he summoned the others to share this new evidence with them yet?"

"No. And he's not going to. None of us are."

"Maybe not now, but give it a day or two. He'll give in to the guilt, knowing it has to be done. Look, I'm sure you came here to try to do the right thing, but there's no hope. No good can come of this at all. You and I both know that eventually, I'll go down. And you know what, fine. So be it. Maybe I deserve to be punished because I wasn't there to protect her. And I'll never forgive myself for that. I might as well be guilty."

"Lucian, please, stop," I begged as he approached me.

He halted in front of me, his eyes stone-cold and his expression hard. "I didn't save her. I failed in the most miserable way. And in the blink of an eye, she was gone. I couldn't take it back and rewind the day. Believe me, if I could, I would have. So listen, do yourself a favor. I told you a few weeks ago to stay away from me. You can do so much better."

"But I don't want that. I want to help you get through this. And after it's over, I want to get to know the real you, not this angry, frustrated guy whose guilt is eating him alive. I know there's more to you than you let on."

He sighed, meeting my gaze. "I'm sorry if I gave you any false hope, but you're wasting your time with me. I'm a lost cause. You should go back to Alex. He was a nice guy, and he treated you well. That's what you deserve, not some washed-up soul tormented by a painful past."

"No," I said, shaking my head. "I'm not giving up on you." The more he tried to push me away, the more I was determined to stay by his side. "Besides, what do you think Cassie would say if she knew you were torturing yourself over something you didn't do? I may have never known her, but from everything you've told me, I'm sure she'd want you to move on and live your life. That she'd want you to enjoy the possibilities and look forward, not keep looking back every day."

"Maybe," he muttered. "But that day has yet to arrive."

Before I could say another word, he brushed past me on his way to the side of the rock where the horses waited below. Then he jumped, disappearing at once. I rushed to the edge in time to see him ride away on Shade, a cloud of snow in their wake, the hoof beats not making a sound on the soft blanket of powder.

Left alone, I stood still, frustrated by his cool demeanor. But I quickly realized he had every right to feel beaten down when the evidence incriminated him, especially if he was innocent. I only hoped Samira would be able to see into the dagger's past and clear him of this crime once and for all.

Ready to return home, I looked down and contemplated my jump to the ground. The rock was about half as high as the drive-in movie screen wall, so I expected an easy landing. Closing my eyes and taking a deep breath, I leaped away from the edge.

I felt like I was suspended in the air on the way down before my feet touched the ground. The snow provided a soft cushion when I landed, and I headed toward Gypsy only to come to an abrupt halt when a voice cut through the air behind me.

"Hello, Gracyn," Marguerite said, causing me to whip around. She marched through the snow until she stood before me, a sly grin on her face.

"What do you want now?" I asked with a long sigh, tired of her showing up when my world was turning upside down. "You threatened me last night, remember? Isn't there someone else you can terrorize today?"

"No. You're too easy to rattle. So, where's your boyfriend? I can't believe he left you alone again."

I cringed at her reference to Lucian as my boyfriend. At this point, I wasn't sure what he was to me. "He had to take care of something."

"Good. Then he won't be returning."

"No, probably not," I let out with a disenchanted sigh, my tone sarcastic. "So can you stop beating around the bush and just come out with it?"

"You know what I want. The book, the script, the spells. I want more power than any other witch can even dream of."

"Why? What do you possibly stand to gain?"

"Anything I want," she said. "Money, travel, adventure. Oh, and let's not forget playing God. I thought I'd start with a storm, maybe in a huge city. It'll be fun to ruffle some feathers."

"Sending storms through a city could hurt and kill people, not just ruffle a few feathers."

"Is that so?" She shrugged, smiling like the devil. "Oh, you know what? You should join me. I bet if we put our power together with the book, we could cause double the trouble."

"Are you serious?" I asked, not sure I heard her correctly. "I have absolutely no interest in becoming your partner in crime. What would ever make you think I'd enjoy that?"

"Oh right, you're too straight-laced and boring. And you are a half-breed, so you may not even be able to contribute much power."

My dark mood plunged to a new low at her mention of my ancestry again. "If you know so much about me, why don't you tell me what you mean by half-breed?"

"You know, one of your parents is a witch and one is human."

"I know that. I meant, do you know who they are?"

She shrugged. "I might know who one of them is. And I might also know who the other one is. So I guess my answer is yes."

"Then will you tell me?"

"Sorry, it's not my place. I'm sure you'll find out soon enough, when Becca decides to ante up. I still can't believe she's kept it a secret this long, but she's always been a bit odd if you ask me."

"She's your mother," I reminded her.

"Yes, I know," Marguerite said, wrinkling her nose. "Hard to believe sometimes."

"Is this why you found me today? To torture me about knowing who my parents are, but not tell me? If so, I think I've had enough."

"No, actually, it was to give you one last warning. Tell Becca I'm not going away. I've been far too patient, but I'll give her a few more days. After that, there's no telling what I might do."

"Fine," I said, huffing. "I'll give her the message."

"Good. And I know you will because you've always been the girl who does what she's told. Make sure you also tell her I'll kill her if I have to, since that's all I need to do to break her spell."

"How did you know that?" I gasped.

"I know everything," she said confidently. "You'd best never forget that."

Without thinking about my actions, I grabbed Marguerite's wrist. "If you kill her, I'll find you."

She laughed. "And do what, silly girl? You can't hold a candle to my power." With a flick of her wrist, she tossed me up in the air.

I landed in a heap several feet away from her, the snow providing a soft cushion over the frozen ground. At once, I jumped to my feet, my frustration growing.

"Well, this has been fun, as it always is." She whistled to her chestnut mare who raced across the field and slid to a stop next to her. "But I'm afraid I must be going. I have some planning to do." She swung up onto the mare's back and looked down at me. "Goodbye, Gracyn. Just think, the next time we meet may be our last."

Before I could say another word, Marguerite whipped her horse around and galloped across the field. Then they disappeared into the woods, leaving me alone with Gypsy.

24

After two hard workouts that day, I let Gypsy walk the entire way home. My mind was a whirlwind, thoughts of Lucian and Marguerite competing for center stage. Every time Lucian's green eyes appeared in my head, sadness took over, my heart breaking from his situation. And when the notion that he should have told me about the knife sooner showed up my thoughts, I gave it a hard mental push. He couldn't take back the past, and it wouldn't have done any good. Looking back, I was glad I'd gotten to know him without that information. I never would have given him the benefit of the doubt from the beginning if I'd known he'd hidden the murder weapon.

Marguerite, on the other hand, fueled my anger and frustration. Why she kept popping up at the most inconvenient times was beyond me. Hadn't last night behind the town hall been enough? Once again today, she tortured me with her grating sarcasm and bold threats. But so much time had passed since Halloween that I wasn't even sure she planned to carry them out. She kept talking big like she was capable of hurting someone, but I was beginning to wonder if she'd follow through. Doubts settling over me, I realized I'd better be careful. Perhaps she was waiting until we let our guard down to strike.

As soon as Gypsy and I reached the snow-covered driveway, I dismounted and pulled the reins over her head. I started to lead her toward the barn when Becca ran out of the house and met me in the driveway. "Good," she said, hugging a cardigan sweater around her. "You're back. Did you find him?"

"Yes. He was exactly where I expected he'd be."

"And?"

I shrugged, not at all happy that I hadn't been able to make things right with Lucian. "We talked, and then he took off. I can only assume he went home. I didn't have the energy to follow him and find out. I might try texting him later, after he has a chance to cool off."

"Yes, you should. And I'll check in with Everett to ask if he's seen him."

"Thanks. Can you let me know when you do? I want to make sure Lucian's okay."

"Of course."

I knew I needed to untack Gypsy, but I hesitated, a burning question on the tip of my tongue. "Becca, I'm a little confused."

"About what?"

"Everything. I don't know what to believe about Lucian. I was so convinced he didn't hurt Cassie, and now this. I'm not sure what to think."

"You need to go with what feels right."

"Perhaps, but what about you?"

"What do you mean?"

"I would have thought you'd want to turn the knife over to the authorities, and if not the authorities, at least the others. I'm a little surprised you're leaving the matter to Lucian's father."

Becca pursed her lips, a thoughtful look in her eyes. After a few seconds, she sighed. "If this had happened a day ago, I might have. But I can't do that now, because of you."

"Me?" I asked, confused.

"Yes. As you know, you're connected to Lucian now. You two are soul mates, and you have an unbreakable bond, a psychic connection. But the legend also warns that this love is so powerful, so all-consuming, should two soul mates not be able to stay together for whatever reason, they'll die of a broken heart. I can't risk anything that would lead to Lucian's incarceration, at least not until there's concrete evidence he killed Cassie. It's very possible he's telling the truth, that he pulled the knife out of Angel's heart in a moment of panic. So I can't jump to any conclusions."

My jaw dropping open, I placed a hand on Gypsy's withers in front of the saddle. "Well, this just gets better every day."

"I'm sorry to be the bearer of bad news, but your feelings for Lucian are so strong that, if something happens to him, you might not be able to overcome losing him."

I nodded, a part of me not surprised by this. I'd never felt so drawn to someone, like a magnet pulled me to him against my will. I was powerless to resist him, and now it made sense. I'd always promised myself to never let a guy turn my world upside down, yet that's exactly what was happening.

"Okay," I said. "I guess it's better that you've warned me about this. Thank you for telling me."

She smiled, her eyes meeting mine. "You've had a lot to deal with lately. I'll do whatever I can to make it easier. But right now, it's cold. I'm going to run inside and send Everett a text. Hopefully he's seen Lucian by now."

"All right. I'll be in as soon as I untack Gypsy and put her out."

As Becca headed for the door, I led Gypsy to the barn. Five minutes later, I returned to the house and retreated up to my room. After dropping my coat on the back of the desk chair and yanking off my boots, I curled up on the bed. Never before had I felt so defeated. I kept seeing the knife in Lucian's arms, the despair in his eyes. And when I let my guard down, I felt his kiss again. That moment outside the town hall less than twenty-four hours ago had been magical. I wanted to remember every second of it, and at the same time, forget it had happened. Because as Becca warned, I couldn't bear the thought of never feeling that way again.

Things were too quiet the rest of the day. I sent a text to Lucian to check on him, but he never responded. Becca was able to get through to Everett and reported that Lucian had returned home. As much as I felt like I needed to talk to him again, at least this news gave me some peace of mind.

Becca insisted I carry on with the homework I'd normally do on a Sunday afternoon, but I spent more time pacing the floors than focused on my textbooks. I finally received a text from Lucian around ten o'clock, telling me I'd need to find another ride to school because he'd be staying home for a few days.

The next morning, Becca dropped me off at school on her way to work. After she pulled away from the curb, I walked up to the front doors and pushed my way in with the crowd, painfully aware of Lucian's absence. For weeks, he had driven me to school and kept me company in between classes and at lunch. Even though I felt alone today, the real thing bothering me was not knowing how he was coping with yesterday's turmoil. I could only wonder if Samira had been able to unlock the knife's past with a spell, and my curiosity was killing me. Trying to push it aside, I reminded myself I should just focus on my classes for the day.

I wandered through the crowded hallway until I reached my locker and hung up my coat. Before I began sorting through my books, I heard a familiar voice. "Hi, Gracyn," Celeste said, leaning against the locker next to mine.

My jaw dropped at the sight of her bright smile. Gone were the black clothes and clunky boots, dark circles under her eyes, defeated expression on her face, and messy hair that always looked like it needed to be brushed. Instead, she wore jeans, tall brown boots, and a cream-colored sweater with a V-neckline. A horseshoe pendant dangled from a silver chain around her neck, and her soft curls looked like they'd been sculpted with a hair dryer, not a single strand out of place.

"Celeste?"

"What? Don't you like it?"

"No, I mean, yes. You look great."

"Thanks."

When she didn't elaborate, I continued. "Care to tell me what's going on?"

"Saturday night, that's what. The ball was amazing." The dreamy look in her eyes told me everything I needed to know. "He danced with me. I mean, me, Celeste Hamilton, the girl everyone has labeled a freak, with Derek Woodson, the cool, popular guy in a band. I don't know what came over him, but I'm not going to question his motives. I just want to enjoy the memory."

I smiled, grateful one thing seemed to be right for a change. "I'm so happy for you," I said before putting a mock frown on my face. "Wait a minute. You didn't put a spell on him, did you? Because that doesn't count."

She laughed. "No. I thought about it years ago, but spells to make someone like you never work. They always go wrong in the most horrible ways. So no, he asked me to dance all on his own."

"Then what happened?"

Celeste's expression fell for a minute, and I suddenly wished I hadn't asked her. She shrugged, her face appearing brighter. "Nothing, really. I know he probably only asked me because for once in his life, he didn't have some bombshell on his arm. Lacey didn't even show up, and Zoe already replaced Lucian with a football player. But I don't care. If he asked me because they were all taken, that's fine. I'll take him any way I can get him." She paused, then added, "Except out of pity. Even I have more self-respect than to let him feel sorry for me."

"Celeste," I said firmly. "Why would anyone feel sorry for you? You're a beautiful young woman. Perhaps Derek has finally come to his senses. You know, he is a boy, and they mature much more slowly than girls. He's probably just growing up."

"Well, it's about time," she said with a sigh before glancing at her watch. "The bell's going to ring any minute. I'll see you later, okay?"

"Definitely," I replied, still surprised she was talking to me again, but I assumed I had Derek to thank for that.

As soon as she disappeared into the crowd, I finished organizing my books and took off for homeroom. Before I got very far, I noticed Derek at his locker. He had just shut the door and turned when I approached. I wrapped my arms around him, planting a kiss on his cheek. When I stepped back, he turned a bright shade of red.

"What was that for?" he asked. "I need to know so I can do whatever I did to deserve it again."

I laughed. "Thank you."

"For?"

"Oh, please. As if you don't know. I just saw Celeste. You probably made her entire year Saturday night. Have you seen her today?"

"No, not yet. Why? Is she going to ambush me or something?"

"Not quite. But you may not recognize her. She looks great, and I think you had a little something to do with that."

"All I did was dance with her," he said in a low, almost fearful voice. "And it was only one time."

Shaking my head, I grinned while his face became a darker shade of red. "But it meant a lot to her."

"Oh, great," he groaned. "Thanks a lot, Pierce. Now I'm going to have to go into hiding again. Maybe I can get a place in the Witness Protection Program."

"Haven't you considered giving her a chance?"

"Considered it? Maybe. But I'm not ready for her yet. I still have a huge field to play before I settle down."

I raised my eyebrows. "Really? And where was that field Saturday night?" I asked, unable to stop the words from coming out.

He scowled, but laughter shone in his eyes. "Fine. Saturday night, I was on my own. But that doesn't mean anything. I still have college right around the corner."

"I thought you weren't going to college. Whatever happened to all that stuff about heading up to Vermont and becoming a ski-bum?"

He shrugged. "I really don't like you very much right now."

I smiled, grabbing his hand and squeezing it. "And I like you even more. You did a good thing, Derek. Deep down, you're a nice guy. It wouldn't hurt you to show that off a little more."

Without giving him a chance to object, I let go of him and turned around before heading to homeroom. I had to give him some credit. If I couldn't have my happy weekend, at least meddling enough to make Celeste's dream come true lifted my spirits and helped me forget my heartache over Lucian. It might not last forever, but I'd take that break, even just for a few minutes.

25

On spite of the chaos from the weekend, my day was slow and steady. I dove back into my classes, trying to pretend everything was normal, although it would have been a lot easier to concentrate if Lucian returned to school. But he never did. I called him that night only to get his voice mail, then sent him a text asking how he was and if he'd be around the rest of the week. When he responded, his message provided little comfort. *I'll be staying home for a while. Hope u can find a ride to school.*

I frowned at his text before throwing the phone on my bed and looking out the window at the black night. There was so much I wanted to tell him, but I didn't want to intrude on a sensitive family matter. His father was now in charge of the knife and would decide what to do next.

I managed to rope Derek into giving me a ride to school and home for the next few days. I was starting to enjoy his company, even if he seemed a little irritated every time I mentioned Celeste. But until he stopped smiling when she came up in conversation, I decided to talk about her as much as I could. Maybe he needed a little push to realize she had a lot of qualities he might actually be attracted to.

The week dragged on with no sign of Lucian each day. I began to feel numb, my mood falling further into a pit of despair. Classes and homework couldn't take my mind off him. The cold air didn't even register when I walked across the school parking lot each morning with Derek chatting beside me. In spite of his company, I felt lonely. He was a casual friend, not someone I'd grown attached to over the last few months.

Lucian, on the other hand, had allowed me to see into his soul, and his sudden absence from school chipped away at me. I couldn't stop wondering what he was doing to stay busy and not go crazy, to the point that my classes became a blur. I began to believe the legend, or curse as it seemed to feel like, was true and I'd never get over him. Whether or not that was the case, I never stopped believing his absence was only temporary. Once Cassie's murder was solved, things would change for Lucian. *If* her murder was ever solved...

Wednesday afternoon, I decided it was time to pay Lucian a visit. If he wouldn't pick up the phone when I called, hopefully he'd answer the door when I rang the bell. As soon as I got home and Derek's car disappeared down the driveway, I ran out to the barn and threw a saddle on Gypsy. Then we trotted along the snowy path until we reached the trail leading to Lucian's estate where we turned and continued on our way between the fences to the house.

I guided Gypsy around to the front of the mansion and halted her in the empty driveway. Frowning, I wondered if no one was home before realizing the cars could be in the garage. After dismounting, I left the reins over her neck and approached the door. I hesitated, then knocked, cringing at the nerves sweeping through me. I wasn't sure how I'd be received, but I wasn't leaving until I had a chance to let Lucian know he was missed.

A few seconds later, he opened the door, his black shirt hanging untucked over his jeans, the cross necklace dangling against his chest. My gaze was instantly drawn to the reminder of Cassie before I looked up, meeting the green eyes that haunted me far more than I cared to admit.

"Hi," I said quietly.

"Well, this is a surprise," he said, pulling the door wide open. "Come in."

I nodded and stepped into the entry hall, glancing at Diesel who watched us from the kitchen entrance while Lucian closed the door. As the lock clicked into place, I turned to him, relieved he wasn't keeping me at a distance.

"Thank you. I wanted to stop by and see how you're doing. I've missed you at school."

He sighed, folding his arms over his chest before his frown broke into a subtle smile. "I've missed you, too," he said, his words warming my heart.

"Where is everyone?"

"You mean my father and his...friend?"

"Yes."

"Out. Thank God. Every time they're here, I just lock myself in the studio upstairs. It's much better when they're gone." He paused, then relaxed and uncrossed his arms. "I'm sorry. I'm being rude. I should offer you something to eat or drink. Are you hungry?"

I took a deep breath, picking up the scent of tea. "A little."

"Good. Come on back," he said, leading me into the kitchen.

After hanging my jacket on the back of a chair, I hopped up on a stool at the island as he poured two cups of tea from the pot on the stove. He handed one to me, then put a plate of apple slices and grapes in the center of the counter and placed a few napkins beside it.

"Thank you," I said, helping myself. After a few bites, I lost interest in the food. "You know," I began cautiously. "I was hoping you'd call me back over the last few days."

"I wasn't sure what to say."

"Some people start with hello," I said softly, meeting his gaze.

He choked out a smile before his serious look returned. "I guess you're right. Maybe I'm overthinking this. It's just—"

"Just what?"

"I hate the way things ended between us last weekend. And I hate everything that's going on right now. Sometimes I wish you hadn't moved here, at least not yet."

"Why?" I asked, not sure how to interpret his comment.

"Because I don't want you to see me like this. I've been suspected of killing my own sister from the first day we met. I wish I could start over with you when this is all over. If it ever ends, that is. And I never want you to be afraid of me like you were when you ran away Sunday morning."

"I'm not," I assured him.

"Are you sure?" His question was simple, and yet so complicated at the same time.

I swallowed, averting my gaze from his. I took a deep breath before sipping the tea again, buying some time to find the right words. "Yes," I finally said, looking back up at him.

"It took you long enough to answer."

"I'm sorry. What do you want me to say? The last week, no, the last few months have been insane. I feel like I've been thrown into a raging river without a life preserver. I may be a good swimmer, but I don't know if I'm strong enough to keep fighting the current forever."

"I can understand that," he said.

I offered a faint smile. "So are we good now?"

"Why do you ask?"

"Because I feel horrible for telling Becca and your father about the knife. But when I look back on that morning—"

Lucian reached across the island and put a finger up to my lips. "Say no more. What's done is done, and I'm not blaming anyone for anything, at least not until we find out who killed Cassie. In fact, I don't want to admit this, but I think it's better that my father has the knife now. Keeping it a secret for so long was starting to weigh on me. I felt like I was going to snap."

"I hope it will somehow help us find out who killed her. In the meantime, dare I ask if you'll be coming back to school? You're still allowed to be there, at least until your trial."

"There isn't going to be a trial," he stated.

"Really?" I asked, my heart skipping a beat.

He nodded, not seeming as happy as I would have expected. "The DA's office hasn't publicly released this, but the police have no evidence. They have no choice but to drop the charges, again. I expect the news will break any day."

"That must be a huge relief," I said while an image of the knife flashed through my thoughts, reminding me the case could be reopened one day.

"They'll never get their hands on the knife," Lucian said, as if reading my mind. "It could reveal our secrets to humans. If my father decides to let anyone know we have it, he'll turn to the coven."

"Oh," I said, my voice flat. "So even if the authorities never get their hands on it, it's still not over?"

"No, not at all."

I took another sip of tea, wanting to ask if Samira had attempted to unlock the dagger's past, but I held my tongue. I didn't know how much Lucian knew about her offer to help and, given his animosity toward her, I didn't want to bring her up. Instead, I changed the subject. "Without school to keep you busy, what have you been doing over the last few days?"

He shrugged. "Painting, mostly. And when I get bored or start to feel cooped up, I take Shade out for a ride."

"That's it?"

"No, not completely. I've also been catching up on my reading. I used to love books, and I let that get away from me when I decided to go back to school this year. Sometimes I wonder what I was thinking when I did that."

"I'm sure you just wanted to get your diploma like everyone else." When he raised his eyebrows, I continued. "And I think it's well worth it. Just don't stay away too long. You don't want to get too far behind."

"I don't think it matters because I've pretty much given up on graduating. It won't do me much good, anyway."

"Yes, it will. Don't throw in the towel yet. You've worked hard these past few months, and you deserve the opportunity to finish just as much as anyone else. No one should take your education away from you. Besides, once Cassie's murder is solved and all this chaos is in the past, you don't want to have to start over again next year, do you?"

"I can always test out. You know, get my GED."

"Why would you do that when you can finish the year?" I stopped when the stubborn look on his face told me I wasn't going to change his mind. "Okay, fine, I won't keep bugging you about it. But wouldn't you rather get out of the house during the day, even if you just go to school to get a diploma that doesn't matter to you, than stay cooped up day and night, aside from riding your horse? Maybe that's one of the things your mother was trying to escape when she left."

"No," Lucian said, frowning. "I think she would have stayed if my father hadn't pushed her away."

"I'm sorry. I shouldn't have brought her up. I just meant maybe you need a purpose, something to work toward."

"My father was her purpose," Lucian muttered quietly, a thoughtful look in his eyes. "And he dropped her the first chance he had. Now he's shacking up with the African queen as though the mother of his children never existed."

I had so much to say to that, but held back, sure Lucian's anguish stemmed from his father's role in breaking his mother's heart, leaving a trail of drug abuse to follow. "No one can be someone's purpose. Your father can no sooner be her purpose than I can be yours. Perhaps she needed more than that, she just never figured out what it was."

"I don't know about that, but I blame him," Lucian said, his tone bitter.

"Have you talked to him about her lately?"

"No, of course not. We barely talk at all since I can't stand the sight of him. Being in the same room with him makes me sick to my stomach."

In that instant, I saw a boy lost without his mother. My heart going out to him, I reached over and placed my hand on his. "Well, I've talked to him." When Lucian looked at me, seeming surprised, I continued. "He told me he filed for divorce a long time ago. Your mother won't sign the papers, but in his mind, it's a done deal. He moved on."

"Why hasn't he told me that?"

"Maybe he tried, but you didn't give him a chance."

"Or maybe he knows I'll hate him more for it."

"He's letting her go, something he probably should have done a long time ago."

Lucian shifted his gaze to me, the sorrow buried deep in his eyes tugging at my heart. "Maybe he needed to leave her for himself, but I doubt that's what she wanted."

"Well, from what he told me, all I know is that it's complicated. He said he still cares about her. But he also explained he was never in love with her."

"He doesn't have to be in love with her. Love can grow. It happens all the time. But he met someone else—"

"Someone he fell in love with," I added softly. "How did you feel when you were dating Zoe but spending time with me? Remember the afternoon up on the rock and the day at the pumpkin farm?"

Lucian looked away and, for the first time, he seemed to understand what his father had gone through. "Trapped. Like I couldn't get out from under her thumb when I really wanted you."

"But you had time, and things ended up where they are now. Maybe that's how your father felt. He's in love with Samira. And from what I've seen, she's good for him. You shouldn't judge her until you get to know her."

Lucian frowned even though the stony look in his eyes softened. "Maybe," he said before catching himself. "But not now. It's too soon. I'll have to think about it."

I smiled with a nod, sure that was as much of a concession I'd get from him today. "Good. And it's okay if you take your time, as long as you eventually get there."

I grabbed another apple slice and took a bite. For the rest of the afternoon, I filled him in on everything he'd missed at school over the last few days, starting with Celeste's new stylish look, a result of Derek showing her the slightest bit of interest at the ball. When I finished, Lucian studied me, a curious look in his eyes.

"What?" I asked.

"After all you went through last weekend, you still took the opportunity to try to make something good happen to someone else. Not many people would think of others at a time like that."

I shrugged, a little embarrassed. "I couldn't resist. The timing was perfect. I'd do it all over again if I had to." I paused before changing the subject and asking Lucian about his plans for Christmas. We chatted for another half hour until I noticed the twilight shadows out the window and realized I'd lost track of time.

"Oh, wow," I said, glancing at the clock. "It's getting late. I should go. Poor Gypsy has been waiting outside since I got here."

Lucian smiled. "If she knows you're having a good time, she'll wait forever."

"I know. But I still feel a little guilty. She's probably hungry by now. I should get her home." I stood up and slipped my jacket on as Lucian circled the island.

"I'll walk you out," he said.

Taking my hand, he led me to the front door and out into the shadows where Gypsy stood ankle-deep in the snow. When we stopped beside her, he smiled. "Thank you for riding over this afternoon. It's been nice to have some company today."

"You're welcome. Will you come to school tomorrow? Please. At least it's Thursday and you'll only have two more days until the weekend. Then you can get caught up for next week."

He huffed, and I thought he was going to say no, but to my delight, he caved. "You really are serious about academics, aren't you? Well, even though I don't share your enthusiasm, all right. I'll pick you up in the morning. I'm not sure I liked Derek taking you to school, anyway. I don't want him making a move on my girl."

"He already did about five times a few months ago, even in front of Alex," I said with a laugh. "I think he finally got the hint. Besides, he knows the only one I want to see him with is Celeste. I haven't exactly been shy about that."

"Just in case, I better make sure you know who you belong with." Lucian slid his arm around my waist, pulling me toward him and kissing me. He lingered for a moment, sending my heart into a flutter before backing away, a teasing gleam in his eyes. "I've been wanting to do that all afternoon."

"You shouldn't have waited."

"I wasn't sure how you'd react."

"Well, now you know, so don't be shy." My comment earned me another kiss before he stepped back.

"You'd better go before I drag you inside and Gypsy ends up spending the night out here in the cold."

I felt a blush spread across my face and averted my gaze, not sure what to say. He hadn't been so bold in the past, at least not in words. When I looked up, I caught him staring at me. "What?" I asked.

"Didn't you hear me?"

"Yes, I heard you. Can you give me a leg up?"

"Of course," he said.

I turned to Gypsy, raising my hands up to the saddle, and bent my left leg. Lucian grabbed my calf and counted to three before launching me into the air. As soon as I settled into the saddle, I slid my feet into the stirrups and picked up the reins. "Thank you. I'll see you tomorrow?"

"Yes. I'll be waiting in the driveway first thing in the morning."

"Good." After meeting his eyes one last time, my heart glowing from his affection, I nudged Gypsy into a trot and headed around the side of the house, the sound of the shutting door the last thing I heard before pushing her into a canter.

We charged up the hill in between the fences, the snow-covered pastures flying by in a blur before Gypsy turned into the woods and headed home. My smile lingered, anticipation of seeing Lucian in the morning and getting back to a normal routine making me feel as though there was a light at the end of the dark tunnel.

At that moment, I didn't think anything could bring me down. Taking the chance on visiting Lucian had definitely been the right thing to do. But about halfway home, the memory of my afternoon with him vanished when a gust of wind kicked up the snow. Within seconds, Gypsy and I were engulfed in white-out conditions. I squinted, trying to see through the snowflakes whipping sideways, but it was impossible to make out the trees a few feet away.

Gypsy planted her feet, halting as the blizzard circled us like a tornado. She whinnied, the fear in her cry sending an icy blast of panic through me.

Spinning around, Gypsy pawed at the ground, snorting angrily. She tossed her head, her reddish mane barely visible in the dense cloud of snow swallowing us up. I couldn't see a thing, let alone tell which direction was which and how to get home.

My heart pounding, pure fear taking hold of me, I grabbed Gypsy's mane, hoping she'd get us out of the woods safely. Instead of charging through the storm, she raised her head, her ears pointed forward. Without any warning, she began backing up as a wave of solid white rolled toward us. She stood up on her hind feet, her hooves striking at the snow about to topple us.

I tried to hold on, but lost my balance and fell to the ground. The snow felt soft when I landed, wrapping around my neck and wrists, sending a shiver through me.

Catching my breath, I stood up and looked for Gypsy, but saw no sign of her. I spun in a circle, the blizzard closing in on me. My pulse quickened as fear lodged itself in my throat. Feeling trapped, I froze, not sure what to do. I was about to run straight through the blowing snow when the blurry shape of a person emerged. The figure came closer and, just when I recognized Marguerite's long red curls, my world went black.

26

I woke up in the snow, the blizzard continuing its reign over the woods when a familiar voice rang out above the howling wind. "Gracyn," Lucian said, kneeling beside me. "What happened?"

Not sure I knew the answer, I opened my eyes, trying to focus on his face behind the blowing snow. Shade lingered behind Lucian, his dark shape outlined in the dense cloud as he stomped his hoof, churning up the powder.

"I don't know," I managed to say as I sat up, my voice a whisper. "Everything was fine one minute, and the next thing I knew, this storm came out of nowhere. Gypsy went into a panic and reared up when a huge wall of snow came toward us. I fell and must have passed out." I looked around, overcome with worry when I didn't see her. "Where is she?"

Lucian glanced about before shifting his attention back to me. "I don't know. I didn't see any sign of her when I got here." An alarmed look crossing over his expression, he slid an arm around my shoulders. "Let me help you up. We need to get out of here."

I nodded before getting to my feet and allowing him to take my hand. Without another word spoken over the whipping wind, we approached Shade. Lucian hoisted himself onto the horse's bare back, then reached down and pulled me up in front of him. Wrapping his arms around my chest, he nudged Shade into a canter.

I felt secure, riding in front of Lucian with his hold on me so firm I barely moved. The snow hitting me in the face stung, and I turned my head, my hair shielding my cheek. I closed my eyes, hoping Shade would take us home. Whether he took us back to Lucian's house or mine, I didn't care. Anything was better than staying out in the blizzard.

I barely had a few seconds to feel safe before my throat tightened and it felt like a rope was squeezing my neck. I whipped my eyes open and instinctively raised a hand to touch the area that hurt. My skin burning, I swallowed back my growing fear, worried something was very wrong.

My thoughts shifted to Gypsy at once. She wouldn't have left me in the snow, so if she wasn't around when Lucian found me, surely something had happened to her. There was no other logical explanation, unless she had taken off to try to find help and became disoriented. The idea of her lost and alone sent a chill through me, although it didn't seem likely. Horses had a sixth sense, not to mention Gypsy had a supernatural power. I refused to believe a snow storm could cause her to lose her way.

By the time we emerged from the woods, my neck started to feel a little better, but the storm raged on in full force. Snowflakes shot out of the sky, blowing in the raging wind and hiding the barn and house behind a dense cloud. My curls whipping in front of my eyes, I pushed them away as Lucian halted Shade next to the porch steps. As far as I could tell from what little I saw beyond the blizzard conditions blurring everything in sight, the driveway was empty.

After dismounting, Lucian helped me down and ushered me into the house. As soon as he shut the door, the howling wind was reduced to a muted hum outside the windows. "Your jeans are soaking wet," he said, turning to me.

I stood in the family room, shivering and still in shock. Looking down, I saw wet patches where the snow had melted. "Yes. I'm freezing."

"You should get you up to your room. You need to change."

As cold as I was, I found it impossible to care about my clothes when Gypsy was missing. "No. I can change later. Can we check the barn to see if Gypsy made it home? I'm really worried about her." I paused, feeling something squeeze my wrists. "What in the world?" I asked, looking down to see rope burns on my skin.

I held up my hands, the air getting stuck in my lungs. "Lucian, what is this?"

He picked up my wrists, studying them, a deeply worried look in his eyes. Shaking his head with a frown, he looked back at me. "I'm not sure. But you're right. We need to find Gypsy. I'll check the barn. Wait here."

In a flash, he disappeared out the front door, the loud bang when it slammed shut making me flinch. I ran to the window and looked outside, but all I could see was the blowing snow. Turning around, I took off my jacket and waited, resisting the urge to run after him.

A few minutes later, he returned and twisted the deadbolt into place when he closed the door before approaching me.

"Anything?" I asked, holding onto a sliver of hope that he'd found Gypsy.

"No, sorry," he replied. "I put Shade in her stall since I'm not about to leave. I hope you don't mind."

"Not at all," I said before another thought came to mind. "Oh, no. I need to bring the other horses in."

"I took care of them. They have hay and water. Now let me see your wrists again."

"Why? What are you thinking?" I asked, dropping my jacket on the couch and holding my hands up again.

"I suspect," he started with a long, deep breath. "Someone's hurting Gypsy. That's why you have these rope burns. They're coming from her."

"Marguerite," I whispered, the memory of her red hair standing out in the blizzard right before I blacked out coming to mind.

"Marguerite?" Lucian asked, anger burning in his eyes.

"Yes," I answered. "I think I saw her in the woods before I passed out."

"Why does that not surprise me?" he muttered. "She must have Gypsy, and she's using her to torture you."

"What? No!" I cried, tears blurring my vision. The thought of Marguerite hurting Gypsy to torment me ripped my heart to shreds. "That's crazy. Why would she do such a thing?"

"Because she's an evil witch with no conscience," Lucian said.

"Well, it's absurd. We can't let her get away with it. We have to find them!"

"Gracyn, that's impossible. It's a blizzard out there. The best thing we can do right now for both you and Gypsy is treat these burns to help them heal. And you still need to get out of those damp clothes. You must be miserable."

I nodded, wiping at my tears. "Yes, I am because that bitch has my horse. I don't care how wet or cold I am, I want to get Gypsy back." I paused, determined to remain strong. "Wait a minute. How did you find me?"

"I knew something was wrong a few minutes after you left. I was kicking myself for not riding home with you, so I took off on Shade."

"Was it our bond?"

"Yes," he said, nodding with a soft smile. "I think you're stuck with me."

"I could get used to that," I replied shyly before my thoughts reverted back to Gypsy. "But I'm also stuck with Gypsy. She's a huge part of my life. I can't just leave her out there for Marguerite to torture."

"I know you'd do anything to help her," Lucian said, his voice calm. "But first, you have to take care of yourself. Let's get upstairs room where you can change."

Nodding, I walked toward the steps, aware of Lucian's presence behind me. He followed me up to my room which, under other circumstances, would have made me very nervous. But this afternoon, all I could think about was getting Gypsy back home safely.

I was about to open my closet when I felt something squeezing around my neck, choking me. Coughing, I spun around, confused. Lucian stood before me, a shocked look in his eyes as he gently touched my upper arm. "What is it?" I asked. "Why are you looking at me like that?"

Not waiting for his answer, I ripped away from him and ran to the mirror, gasping when I saw red marks around my neck. I lifted my hand to touch the tender flesh, flinching at the pain.

"This is insane!" I cried, whipping around, sure fear shone in my eyes. "We have to stop her."

"Yes, we do," Lucian said, approaching me. He took my hand in his, holding his gaze steady on me. "But first we have to remain calm. Heading out into a snowstorm will get us nowhere. We have to wait."

"Great. I didn't even know we were expecting a storm today. I hope it doesn't last all night," I grumbled, frustrated. "I wonder when Becca will get home. I'm sure she won't be happy to find out I'm being tortured by her evil daughter." I shook my head, wondering if life would ever return to normal. The longer I stayed in Sedgewick, the worse things seemed to get. Would it ever end? In four months, I went from being an average high school girl with my sights set on an Ivy League college to finding out I was a witch, no, make that a half-witch, and falling for the only guy in town suspected of murdering his sister. As if that wasn't bad enough, now I was a pawn in Marguerite's scheme to blackmail Becca into giving her a book of evil spells.

"Becca may not be able to make it home in this storm," Lucian said. "It's pretty bad out there."

I sighed, even more worried. "I don't know if I can handle this," I said.

Lucian met my gaze, a frown flattening his lips. "You can, and you will. You're stronger than you give yourself credit for. Besides, I'm not going to let anything happen to you. I didn't protect Cassie when she needed it, and I can never change that. But you're here now, and I'm not about to watch another person I care about be harmed. I will protect you at all costs. I'll do whatever it takes, even if it means not leaving your side for another second until Marguerite is put away for good."

"Do you promise?"

"With all my heart," he said before placing a soft kiss on my lips. "Now, you need to change into something dry, and I'm going to see what you've got in the bathroom for your wounds. We should put an antibiotic ointment on them, just in case."

Trying to stay calm, I watched him walk across the room and head into the bathroom. Turning to my dresser, I pulled a gray sweatshirt and flannel pants out of a drawer. When Lucian returned with a tube of first aid ointment, I held up the clothes on my way across the room. "I'm just going to change," I said.

After slipping into the bathroom, I shut the door, discarded my damp clothes, and put on the dry pants and sweatshirt.

As soon as I returned to the room, Lucian gestured toward the bed. Without a word, I sat down beside him, turning to face him as he twisted the cap off the tube and squeezed some ointment onto a tissue. "Will this hurt?" I asked.

"I doubt it," he said before dabbing it on my neck, the medicine feeling moist but not causing me any pain.

While he worked, I let out a strained smile. "Thank you for helping me."

"You're welcome."

"Will that stuff really work? I thought we heal pretty fast."

"We do, but it doesn't hurt to be safe. I don't know if this is really necessary, but I'd rather give it a shot than risk you ending up with an infection."

"Makes sense," I muttered as a growl erupted in the pit of my stomach and sharp hunger pains poked at me. "Ow," I said, wincing.

"What now?" he asked, pulling his hand away from my neck.

"She's hungry. I guess Marguerite's going to starve her, too." Anxiety spreading through me, I looked at Lucian. "We have to find her."

"You've said that several times. We will," he said with a confidence that surprised me.

"How? And when? I mean, we're just sitting up here and she's out there, somewhere."

"Exactly. But Gracyn, I've already told you we won't find her tonight."

"I know. I just wish we could try."

He shook his head, moving his attention to my wrists. They weren't as red as my neck had appeared in the mirror, but he applied the ointment to them anyway. "Well, it's impossible. Besides, even if it stops snowing, it'll be pitch black. And going up against a witch like Marguerite isn't like finding a human. She can use her power to make sure we don't find her. I have a feeling she'll only be found when she's ready."

I glanced at the window, the howling wind rattling my weary nerves. I knew better than to protest. Lucian was right. "Okay. But I'm probably going to end up pacing the floors all night. And the minute the sun comes up, even if the snow hasn't stopped, we're searching for her."

"We'll see," he said as he finished dabbing the ointment on my rope burns. He screwed the cap into place before standing up and placing the tube on my desk.

When he turned back to me, I looked up at him. "I'm scared," I said with a deep breath. "I keep hoping life will get back to normal, but it never does. Will the chaos ever end?"

"Probably not," he replied with a faint smile before sitting down next to me. "But things should get better. These last few months aren't a good example of our life around here. Once we finish with Marguerite, which will hopefully be soon, we can move on, and then you might actually find life around here to be a little boring."

"Will you still be here?"

He averted his eyes away from me for a minute before meeting my gaze again. "I wish I could tell you yes, but I don't know. Why?"

"Because if you are, then I hardly think it's going to be boring."

"Oh, I don't know. I'm not that exciting. All I do is paint in my spare time. And I tend to take on the role of the brooding guy who's always looking for something in life."

"I don't see you that way."

"Perhaps that's because you're what I've been looking for. I'll never forget the first time I saw you," he said. "Remember that?"

I nodded. "Yes. The party before school started."

"I thought I'd waltz in and sweep Zoe off her feet. Instead, I had to fight for one date with her, all while you were sitting with Alex on the bench. I remember wondering who you were and where you'd come from. Believe me, it took a lot of effort to convince Zoe she was the one I wanted when that mysterious redhead was watching, her eyes calling out to me."

"Really? Is that how it happened? Because I seem to remember you shooting me a look that made me think you hated me."

"I'm sorry. I know I did that to you a lot because I didn't know how to deal with my feelings. I had to convince Zoe she was the only one I wanted, and finding you came as a very unexpected surprise."

"A good one, I hope."

"Yes, it will be, although it feels like it's taking forever. Ever since school began, I knew it would end with Zoe. I was just afraid of the fallout," he said, his voice lowering to a whisper.

"But they're dropping the charges."

"I know and, of course, I'm relieved. But it was hard to go through the scrutiny all over again, not to mention have the police search our house. Talk about feeling violated. Just when I was hoping people would forget, the whispers and rumors got worse."

I nodded, sensing the frustration in his voice. Lifting my hand to touch his shoulder, I sighed. "I wish I could take that all away for you. I feel somewhat responsible since she broke up with you because of me."

"Don't ever feel like that. This mess started long before you got here."

"What can I do?"

"Nothing. But for now, let's not talk about it."

"Got it," I replied, shifting my gaze to the window, my thoughts returning to Gypsy. I stood up and approached the desk, then leaned over it and lifted my hand to touch the glass. The snow whipped by in a white blur, the wind singing a sinister tune. With a deep breath, I spun around and looked at Lucian. "I'm worried. I've never felt so trapped and so helpless. I want to get out there and bring her home. Tonight is going to feel like an eternity."

Lucian rose to his feet and stepped toward me, taking my hand. "I know. I don't know what we can do, either."

"But we have supernatural strength. Can't we put our power together and make something happen to find her?"

He shook his head, defeat in his eyes. "I'm sorry. We're strong, but we have limitations. If Becca was here, maybe she'd be able to help, but it's just us. We have to wait it out."

I huffed, giving my head a shake. Tears threatened to fill my eyes, but I held them back, wanting to be strong in front of Lucian. He pulled me to him, wrapping an arm around my waist and rubbing my shoulder with his other hand. Leaning against him, I closed my eyes, his solid chest warm and comforting.

After a moment, I looked up, meeting his gaze. Without a word spoken, his lips found mine, causing my heart to jump into a nervous flutter. The world faded away, and my worries became a distant memory. At first, he was soft and gentle, but within minutes, a passion ignited between us, consuming me. His mouth pressed against mine and I kissed him back, my senses thrown into a whirlwind. His tongue slid across my lips, causing a desire stronger than anything I'd ever felt to erupt in my veins.

Lucian ran his fingers along my jaw and under my hair, leaving a trail of chills in his wake. His other hand slid down my side until he reached my waist and slipped under my shirt. His palm touched my stomach, lighting my skin on fire, the heat pitching my heart into a frenzy. Breathless, I wrapped my arms around his shoulders, pulling him closer. Locked together, we stumbled a few feet to the bed where he lowered me onto the comforter. My rope burns no longer hurting, all that seemed to exist was Lucian's touch and the weight of his body pinning me to the bed.

Lost in his arms, I quickly forgot the rest of the world. The room became a blur in the background, and the only thing I clearly sensed were his hands on my skin, touching my abdomen before gliding up higher to the bottom edge of my bra. I held my breath, waiting for him to keep going, but he moved his hand back down to my waist, filling me with mixed emotions of disappointment and relief.

I didn't want this moment to end. His kisses and touch seemed to erase the chaos surrounding us, at least for a few minutes. But before long, thoughts of Gypsy snuck back into my mind, my conscience eating away at me. I couldn't betray her by forgetting she was in danger just because the guy I had wanted for so long made a move on me. If he was worth it, he'd wait until she was safe before we went any further.

Guilt cutting me to the core, I broke away from Lucian and looked up at him through a haze. "I'm sorry. We can't. I mean, we shouldn't do this. Not now," I whispered.

"You're right," he said, his voice low. "I'm sorry." Lucian sat up and scooted to the edge of the bed where he stood up.

"It's okay," I insisted, raising my shoulders and leaning against the headboard. "I just can't let myself go right now while Gypsy's gone."

"I get it, trust me. If Shade ever went missing, I think I'd be worried out of my mind, too." He paused with a sigh, a thoughtful look crossing over his expression. "Let's head downstairs and see what there is to make for dinner. We should eat to keep up our strength. I have a feeling we'll need it soon."

Nodding, I stood and followed him out of the bedroom. The wind howling in the distance, Gypsy filled my thoughts, and I prayed we'd get her back soon. Nervous and unsettled, my stomach lurched at the thought of food even though I knew Lucian was right. The best thing I could to do while trapped inside with a blizzard raging through the night was eat and preserve my energy for the fight to get Gypsy back.

27

After a hearty dinner of roast chicken and vegetables, Lucian and I paced the floors for hours, discussing a plan of attack for the next day. As expected, Becca didn't return home, and every time I looked outside, the snow was still falling, the flakes almost the size of quarters. As the night wore on, I grew more worried about Gypsy even though I didn't feel the ropes around my wrists and neck again. Just before midnight, Lucian insisted I get some rest and took the couch while I headed up to my bedroom.

I wasn't sure I'd get any sleep, but I must have dozed off because when I woke up, the red neon numbers on the alarm clock read six forty-five. Before I could think of anything else, the blizzard and Gypsy's disappearance came to mind.

Blinking a few times, I sat up in the shadows, wondering how she'd fared overnight. But I barely had a moment to worry about her before I heard a familiar voice.

"Good," Lucian said. "You're awake."

"Yes," I replied, my gaze shifting to where he stood in the corner across the room, his black clothes blending into the shadows.

Lucian stepped away from the wall, his hands behind him. "The sun will be up soon," he said, the flat tone in his voice making him nearly impossible to read. "So get up. It's time to go."

I slid out from under the covers, my attention focused on him. He seemed different, like something had changed since last night when he'd applied the ointment to my wounds before we made dinner. Looking down, I noticed the angry rope burns around my wrists had faded, the red marks faint and no longer painful. Relieved, I stood up and turned to him, my thoughts shifting back to Gypsy. If I was healing, she must be, too. "Okay. Are we heading out to look for Gypsy?"

"Yes. So get dressed and meet me downstairs. We'll grab a quick bite to eat before we leave."

"Got it," I replied.

Lucian left the room, shutting the door behind him. Ten minutes later, dressed in jeans and a heavy sweater, I rushed down the stairs to find him in the kitchen whipping up a batch of scrambled eggs while bacon sizzled in a separate pan.

"Smells good," I said, approaching the island. "But I don't know if I can eat this morning. I just want to get out there and start looking for Gypsy. I'll feel much better once we find her."

"I figured you'd say that, but I'm not letting you out of here without a good breakfast." He reached for a plate on the counter and filled it with a healthy helping of eggs and three slices of bacon. "Here you go. The faster you eat, the sooner we can leave."

I took the plate from him, knowing any objection I voiced would be wasted. Even though my stomach did flip-flops in anticipation of searching for Gypsy, I forced myself to eat. Lucian joined me with his plate, and little was spoken while we polished off our food.

As soon as we finished, we left the dishes on the table and grabbed our jackets. I followed Lucian outside and down the porch steps, the cold smacking me in the face. Chilled by the frosty morning air, I zipped up my parka before putting my gloves on. The snow had stopped falling, leaving another six inches covering the tire tracks in the empty driveway.

"What's the plan?" I asked when we stopped at the bottom of the steps.

"We'll ride out on Shade. Maybe we can find her hoof prints in the snow."

"I don't know," I said. "The storm left a lot of new snow. Their tracks are probably hidden by now."

"It's worth a shot," Lucian replied, his gaze shifting to the barn. He whistled, and Shade emerged from the doorway, the reins hanging from his neck. "Come on." Lucian held his hand out to me, and I reached for it. He led me to Shade and hoisted me onto the horse's back before jumping on behind me and locking his arms around my chest. Then he kicked the stallion into a gallop, and we took off into the woods. The trees passed, the cold wind stinging my face. I drew in a sharp breath, turning my head to place one cheek against Lucian, the other side taking the brunt of the wintry air.

Lucian guided Shade up to the rock at the top of the hill where he yanked the horse to a stop. "Marguerite!" he called.

I glanced at him over my shoulder. "What are you doing?" I asked, confused. "Do you really think Marguerite is going to answer you? I doubt she's just going to appear and hand Gypsy over to us."

"I have another plan," he said quietly.

Raising my eyebrows, I met his knowing gaze. He offered a smile so subtle I barely noticed it before his expression hardened and he tore his eyes away from mine. "Marguerite!" he yelled. "I know you can hear me. Now come on out. We made a deal."

I gasped, my chest tightening. "What are you talking about?" I muttered, shocked by his words.

"Marguerite!" Lucian hollered again, ignoring me.

A few seconds later, she appeared between two trees in the distance. Calm and confident, she walked across the snowy field in her tall black boots, her steps high with a purpose.

She stopped a few feet in front of Shade and tilted her head to the side, her hair falling over one shoulder and her blue eyes settling on us. A satisfied smile crossing her lips, she took a deep breath. "Well, I never expected you to follow through on your end. You brought her."

"Of course I did. I told you I would."

"And I told you I'd believe it when I saw it." She paused, lifting her eyes to me. "Well, let's have her. I can't exactly take her from where she is now."

"I know that," he scoffed before dismounting and pulling me down to the ground. He grabbed my arm, dragging me to Marguerite.

When we reached her, she sighed thoughtfully. "Why are you giving her to me? I forgot to ask you that when you made your generous offer."

"Does it really matter?"

"Yes, it does. Even though I love this turn of events, I need to know what's behind your motives. Are you setting me up? Because things that appear too good to be true generally are."

Lucian groaned and shoved me toward Marguerite. "Take her. She knows too much."

Marguerite grabbed me when Lucian let go, her nails digging though my sleeve, making my arm feel numb. "Really?" she asked, her eyebrows arched. "Do tell."

"About my sister. Gracyn found something that could put me away for the rest of my life. So take her. I need to get rid of her."

My heart nearly leaped out of my chest, and a lump formed in my throat, choking me. Was he admitting to killing Cassie? After all this time, the emotions, the grief, the memories of her, he'd been lying all along? The notion that I'd been played for a fool struck me like a knife being wedged into my heart.

Marguerite smiled, seeming amused by what sounded like a confession from Lucian. "Well, I never would have expected it, Lucian. You and I, we're not so different after all. I'm impressed."

"I'm nothing like you. Accidents happen. It doesn't mean I wanted it. But what's done is done, and I can't change it. So here, take Gracyn and do what you want with her. If you could silence her, it would be greatly appreciated. Unless you just put her out of her misery first. I guess that's the only way to guarantee I'll stay out of jail."

Marguerite shrugged. "We'll see. I have to keep her alive, for now. But if I get what I want from Becca, then maybe."

"Good. Just remember who did you a favor," Lucian said.

She laughed. "This is quite a surprise. I never would have guessed you'd turn her over to me. And I hadn't planned on taking her, because if I had, I would have done it yesterday when I grabbed Gypsy. But I like your idea better. Now Becca will really have something to worry about. I have to say, Lucian, you're way more fun than I expected. Maybe we should get together when this is all over. I could use a partner in crime once I get the book. What do you say? You and me, conquering the world together?"

She tossed him a seductive smile. I swallowed the bile rising into my throat and ripped my arm out of her grasp, surprised when I broke free. Without turning to see her reaction, I charged away from both of them, running toward the woods and not looking back.

I almost made it to the tree line when I slammed against an invisible shield and fell into the snow. The wind was knocked out of me, and I struggled to catch my breath as I rose to my feet. Spinning around to see Lucian and Marguerite heading my way, I backed up until my shoulders touched the wall.

Marguerite stopped in front of me and shook her head. "Really, Gracyn? Don't even try to escape. Because if you do, I still have Gypsy." Marguerite's voice lowered. "Poor Gypsy. She hasn't eaten all night, and if only she wouldn't fight the ropes so hard, she wouldn't bleed as much."

"What have you done with her?" I hissed.

"Save your breath. You're coming with me, and the two of you will be reunited in hell. Well, it isn't really hell, but it's under my control, so it might as well be." She waved her arm, and my wrists snapped together as though a rope was being tied around them. As soon as they were bound, she yanked on them, causing me to stumble toward her.

"There," she said. "Much better. I didn't need to drag you by the arm the whole way and risk breaking a nail." Marguerite turned and looked at Lucian. "You've been very helpful. Don't forget my offer. I know I won't." She raised a hand to his shoulder, trailing her fingers down his arm.

He watched her, his eyes cold. I wished I could read what was going through his mind, but I had no idea. All I knew was that he'd sold me out. As much as I didn't want to go with Marguerite as her captive pawn, I suddenly didn't care. What good would it do to escape with a broken heart?

"I'll think about it," Lucian said. "But don't get your hopes up."

She flashed him another smile. "I love a good challenge," she said before pulling on the invisible rope secured around my wrists. Within seconds, we set off into the woods, leaving Lucian far behind in the meadow.

28

The snowy landscape was a white blur as Marguerite pulled me through the woods. Barely able to catch my breath, I couldn't believe this was happening. What had Lucian done? I refused to believe all the time we'd spent together had been a ruse, but I knew I couldn't trust him any longer. He'd turned on me, thrown me to the wolves when I needed him the most.

The thought of Lucian made me sick to my stomach. As I ran behind Marguerite in an attempt to keep up rather than be dragged through the snow, I couldn't let go of feeling I'd been betrayed by the one person I thought cared about me.

Pushing my thoughts aside, I vowed to stay strong. I wouldn't let Lucian crush my determination when I needed it the most. I had to get out of this mess with Marguerite, and I'd never accomplish that blinded by tears.

When Marguerite slowed down, an abandoned barn came into view. The planks were weathered and rotting, the windows caked with dust. The rising sunlight lit up the snow covering the ground and the roof, and a trail of hoof prints led to the entrance. Marguerite followed their path and dragged me inside before the door slammed shut and a familiar nicker rang out. Gypsy.

Breathing in the musty smell of moldy hay and dust, I scanned the barn in the dim light coming from an oil lantern hanging from a hook. On one side of the aisle were broken walls, the space beyond them littered with discarded wood and hay bales blackened from decay. Stalls were still standing on the other side, the doors bent and hanging from the hinges as though one blow would take them down. One stall was closed, the topline of a reddish mane barely visible on the other side.

"Gypsy!" I gasped, starting to run for her when a yank on the invisible rope binding my wrists together jerked me back.

"Oh, no," Marguerite said. "You don't need to get any closer to her."

I turned, glaring at Marguerite who stood a few feet away from me. A smug smile crossed her face as she studied me the way a lion watched a lamb, waiting for the right moment to strike.

"Fine. But since you have me, why don't you let her go?"

She chuckled and shook her head, her hair swaying. "Not a chance." She paused before her voice softened, much to my surprise. "I have to say, I'm truly shocked at Lucian. I mean, how much time did he spend teaching you to defend yourself against me? Then, in a shocking turn of events, he delivers you to me. How ironic. Some boyfriend."

I felt the sting of tears return to my eyes, and I blinked them back, feeling foolish and ashamed. Her words sliced through me because she was right. "What's your point?" I muttered.

"Just that you should stop clinging to the hope that there's some tiny bit of good left in him. Forget it. He showed his true colors this morning. Although I'm impressed. I love the bad boys. I meant what I offered him. Could be fun, especially now that I know what he's capable of."

"Is there a reason you have to remind me of what I already know? I just want to forget about him, so can we please talk about something else? Anything at all."

She smiled again and stepped closer to me. "My, aren't you a bit feisty today? But that's no surprise. So am I. We can't be too different, you know, since we're cut from the same cloth."

"What's that supposed to mean?" I gritted out, tired of her game.

"If you haven't figured it out by now, you're not as smart as you look," Marguerite said before losing interest in me as she held up a hand and studied her fingers, her face falling into a frown. "Damn, I broke a nail."

I rolled my eyes with a loud huff.

She looked up, tilting her head before approaching me. Then she picked up my hand, studying it until I whipped it away from her. Marguerite glanced up, catching my eye. "We are so different," she said in a long breath. "Haven't you ever heard of a manicure? It's one of the most amazing modern luxuries I've discovered."

"I don't have time for something like that."

"Oh, yes, you have to study and get good grades." She threw her head back and laughed. "Like it's going to do you any good, dear Gracyn."

"I think it's none of your business what I choose to do with my life."

"You're right about that. I just don't understand why you want to work. But then again, some people have no sense of adventure. Now, I wonder what I should do first once I get the spells restored to the book. Hmm, that's going to be a tough decision."

"How can you be so confident you're going to get them back?"

"I keep forgetting how much you still don't know. It's really quite simple. When Becca finds out you're gone and I have you, she'll do anything in return for your safety. My plan to use Celeste didn't work, but now the stakes are higher. You and Gypsy will get me what I want, or I'll have to do something I may regret." She paused, a smile forming on her face as she shook her head. "No, I wouldn't regret hurting you, or even killing you. Nothing would be harsh enough if Becca doesn't give me what I want. At least Lucian shouldn't get in my way again like he did on Halloween. Since he just gave you to me, I'm guessing he's washed his hands of you."

"You don't need to keep reminding me of that," I said, my teeth clenched while a pang of heartache whipped through me at the memory of Lucian handing me to her.

"I know, but it's so much fun. You should see the look on your face. I can tell you're consumed by this twisted grief of losing him. Well, let me tell you something, you probably never had him to begin with."

"Do you have a point in torturing me, or are you just doing it for entertainment?"

She shrugged. "I'm not sure, although I have to find a way to pass the time. Midnight tonight seems so far off, but I want Becca to worry for a while. After what she did to me, banishing me in a crypt for centuries, eighteen hours is nothing."

"I get it. You don't like her."

"That's right. In fact, I despise her. She's everything I learned to hate—pure, simple, all about just taking what you need to survive. It's so antiquated. What good is having so much power if you're never going to use it?"

"She does use it, just in ways you'll never appreciate."

"True. Because who can appreciate a meager existence living in the same small town for centuries on end, growing the same fruits and vegetables year after year? Boring. And then what did she do? She fell in love with a human. She's a disgrace to our kind. But back to business. Once I get what I need, I'll be done with her."

"You really disgust me. She's your mother. I don't even know who mine is. I'd give anything to know who my parents are, and you're ready to sell one of yours out. You can't even see that she's a kind, respectable soul who tried to turn you into a decent person."

"And she failed," Marguerite said in a condescending tone before her eyes narrowed, her voice lowering. "Don't worry. This will all be over in less than twenty-four hours, and then you can go back to life as usual. You'll have centuries to find out who your parents are, well, at least your one witch parent. And if Becca doesn't tell you, then come find me. I'll be happy to tell you, but only after I get what I want."

"Then I won't count on you because I don't think Becca's going to give in to your demands."

"She will, or I'll take the one thing she holds most dear. You." Marguerite sighed, her eyes roaming around the barn before settling on the stall behind me. "Well, I've had enough of the small talk, although it's one of the first real conversations we've ever had. But I have a date, so I need to run."

"A date?" I asked, wondering why I was surprised. Nothing Marguerite said or did should have shocked me at this point.

"Yes. Believe it or not, I may be a few hundred years old, but I still like to have fun." She pursed her lips in thought. "But before I go, I need to take care of you. What's your preference? The stall or the aisle floor?"

"You're seriously asking me that?"

"Yes."

"I don't care. Pick one. It makes no difference to me."

"Then you'll stay right where you are."

I raised my eyebrows.

"I know what you're thinking and no, I won't be staying to watch you for the next several hours." She held her hand up, chanting a few words in a whisper. "There. That'll hold you until I get back."

"What—" I raised my hands, the invisible rope around them now gone, and felt a wall in front of me.

Marguerite laughed. "You're surrounded on all sides, including above and below you. You won't go anywhere while I'm out. And don't try any funny business. All those tricks your so-called boyfriend taught you aren't going to work on me. I'm a lot stronger than you'll ever be, and my magic will beat you every time."

Before I could say a word, she turned on her heels and disappeared in a flash, her red hair the last I saw of her. Alone in the silence, I was about to sit down when Gypsy nickered from the stall. I turned and met her gaze, her sad eyes cutting through me like a knife.

"Hi, girl," I whispered. "We're going to get out of here, I promise. I don't know how, but we are. I just need some time to think this over."

I started to approach the stall, wanting to reach out and stroke her neck, but the invisible wall stopped me. Trapped, I dropped to the cold, dusty floor. Leaning against the shield, I pulled my knees up to my chest and rested my forehead on them. This was going to be the longest day of my life.

━━ ⌒

I dozed off at some point, exhausted after standing up to Marguerite had taken every ounce of my energy. I craved the reprieve sleep brought, but it didn't last long. My dreams found me, taking me to the rock overlooking the town. Under the warm summer sun beating down from a blue sky, I stood at the back, watching Lucian at his easel, painting a woman who wasn't there. On the canvas, she stood at the edge of a cliff, her white dress blowing in the wind and her brown hair swaying against her back. Beyond her, the painted town mirrored the landscape Lucian looked out over, thick forests covering the mountains, houses dotting the rolling hills, and a church steeple rising from a clearing in the valley.

A few birds darted across the sky, but Lucian ignored them, his attention locked on his masterpiece. I watched his brush strokes, surprised when he painted the woman's foot hovering off the edge, as though she was about to jump. Sorrow overwhelmed me, the emotions from the woman ready to give up on life numbing me.

Then a scream ripped through the air. Lucian's paintbrush fell to the ground with a clattering sound when it landed on the rock. He whipped around from the canvas, his face ghastly white and his attention focused on the woods behind him. He didn't see me, but how could he when it was only a dream?

In a flash, he ran across the rock and jumped. I turned, looked down, and watched him leap onto Shade before pushing the stallion into a full gallop. They charged into the woods, the thundering hoof beats becoming softer until they faded in the distance.

With a gasp, I woke up in the dark, dusty barn and took a deep breath as the dream replayed over and over again in my head. I knew at once I'd seen what really happened the day Cassie was killed. Lucian had been telling the truth all this time. He was innocent, that much I knew. If only I could prove it.

29

Wide awake, I stood up only to remember I was locked in an invisible cage. I folded my arms across my chest, my heart pumping furiously in the wake of my dream. As comforting as it was to know Lucian hadn't killed his sister, it prompted more questions to tumble into my thoughts. Hours ago, he'd acted as though he was guilty as sin, handing me off to Marguerite to get rid of me because he claimed I knew too much. Now, knowing what I knew, his actions made no sense.

My confidence crumbled when another theory surfaced in my mind. Perhaps he just wanted to get rid of me because he wasn't as attracted to me as I was to him. Maybe he was worried my feelings for him would lead me to do something crazy.

Well, I'd show him I didn't need a man in my life to be happy. I had a lot going for me—good grades and a stack of applications to Ivy League schools on my desk to finish. There went my plan to lift my spirits. I hadn't submitted a single application amidst the chaos of the last few months. Then and there, standing in the dusty barn locked in a magical holding cell, I decided if I ever made it home, those applications were going out the very next day. No more procrastinating. It was time to move forward. The sooner I got into college, the sooner I could make plans for the future and prove I didn't need Lucian, Alex, or any other guy to complete my life.

I shook my head, determined to get my affairs in order as soon as this mess was over. *If* it ever ended. Feeling like a caged animal, I started to pace but ran into the invisible wall after two steps. I stopped, shifting my weight from one leg to another until I grew tired and slid back down, knowing I'd be better off not wasting energy by standing.

Sitting on the cold ground, I waited for Marguerite to return. The seconds felt like hours, and my resolve to stay alert fell by the wayside. I wasn't sure when, but I drifted off to sleep again. The next time I opened my eyes, the barn was hazy. The lantern flame had died down to a flicker, and all was silent. Gypsy barely stirred on the other side of the wall, although I knew she was there, tired and hungry, but not ready to give up.

Sometime later, muffled footsteps echoed through the barn, and I caught sight of a shadowy figure in the aisle. I thought I saw Lucian, but everything was blurry, like I was caught between a dream and reality. He approached and knelt before me, reaching out to touch my cheek and trailing his fingers down the side of my face. Then I felt him kiss my forehead.

Shocked, I looked up, but he was gone, as if he'd vanished into thin air. It must have been a dream, the hazy vision coming in and out of focus, confusing me, my mind playing tricks on me. He'd never come back, not after delivering me to Marguerite. Frustrated, I vowed never to think of him again.

I was about to doze off again when Marguerite appeared and stooped down before me, a vicious smile on her face.

"Good. You're still here," she said, her tone sarcastic.

"Where did you think I'd be?" I gritted out, my hammering heart jolting me awake.

She laughed. "Did you have a nice nap? I put a spell on you to make you sleep, just as an extra precaution so I could be sure you wouldn't get into trouble while I was gone. It looks like it worked."

I huffed, realizing why the world looked so foggy.

A hand reached down beside Marguerite. "Haven't you done enough to the poor girl? She's probably exhausted."

I drew in a sharp breath at the sound of Gabriel's voice. A chill trailing up my spine, I looked up to see his golden hair in the dim light, his clothes as dark as the shadows behind him. "What...what are you doing here?" I asked. "I thought you went back to Boston."

He shrugged with a sinister smile. "Of course you did. You and Becca are so gullible. You believe everything. You both made it so easy for me to plan everything out with Marguerite. And you were most helpful in bringing her back."

"Something I'd rather forget altogether," I muttered. "That wasn't exactly one of my best moments."

"Perhaps for you," Gabriel said, kneeling in front of me. "But your mistake was my advantage. I was convinced when you moved back that your presence would awaken Marguerite. I was right, although you took long enough."

Narrowing my eyes, I tilted my head, not following him. But I didn't say a word because Gabriel continued. "You're related to Marguerite, and only a blood relative could set her free. Believe me, if I could have done it myself, I would have. I tried a few years ago, but that backfired on me. So I had to wait. Talk about feeling like time was standing still."

"How am I related to her?" If Marguerite wouldn't tell me, maybe I could get an answer from Gabriel.

"That's a long story I don't have time for. Sorry, Gracyn." He paused, studying me. "Well, stay here like a good little pet for now. I've got a book to dig up."

Done with me, Gabriel and Marguerite stood up. "I told you she'd be easy," Gabriel said, wrapping an arm around Marguerite's shoulders. "I still can't believe Lucian handed her over to you."

"Well, it's only the beginning. We still don't have what we want," Marguerite said.

"We'll get it," Gabriel declared. "Trust me. You just have to be patient."

She slid her arms up around his shoulders and pulled him toward her. "You know patience is not one of my virtues," she said before kissing him on the mouth.

A sick feeling took over my stomach, and I looked away, disgusted by them. Was there no one left to be trusted? First Lucian, now Gabriel?

My thoughts were broken by Marguerite's sultry voice. "You know where to go?"

"Yes," Gabriel replied. "You've only reminded me five times this morning. You'll have the book in your hands today." I heard him plant one last kiss on her lips before he ran off. Within seconds, hoof beats thundered into the barn. They stopped, then started again as it sounded like the horse galloped out of the barn and into the snow.

By the time I dared to look around, Marguerite had disappeared. Left alone again, I bit my lip and stood up, determined not to let her spell make me fall asleep again. I would wait until Gabriel or Marguerite returned, and hopefully by then, I'd have a plan to escape. Even though I knew that probably wouldn't happen, my wishful thinking put me in a better mood, at least for a little while.

— ~

As the hours crept by, I had no concept of the time. Whether it was still day or night had fallen, I had no idea. The windows were either boarded up or stained with dust and dirt, not letting any sunlight through the panes. Birds found a way into the barn, their wings fluttering as they flew up to the rafters, their chirping breaking the silence from high above. The wind howled outside, beating against the walls. The barn seemed to be falling apart, and I imagined a strong gust could take out some of the rotting boards at any moment. Snow drifted in through the door at the end of the aisle, evidence that winter still controlled the land.

Growing restless, I stood up again, my stomach growling. Cold and hungry, I looked at Gypsy, hoping she'd provide me some comfort, but her head hung low, a defeated expression in her eyes.

"Hey, girl," I said softly. She took a deep breath, her ears flickering my way. "We'll get out of here, right?" I asked, knowing she couldn't answer me.

"Of course, you will," Marguerite said from behind me.

I whirled around, relieved to find her alone. "I wasn't talking to you," I muttered, my voice low and distrustful.

"I don't care," she replied flippantly before letting out a sigh. "Well, this day couldn't be any more boring. Why did I give Becca until midnight? What was I thinking? She's probably been pacing all day, wondering where you are. I wish I could be there to see the anxious look on her face, but it's better for me to stay out of sight for now. After all, I want her to wait and worry."

"Just like you did with Celeste? Can't you be a little more original rather than repeating your own tactics?"

"But it's so much fun to watch my victims squirm," she said in a sugary voice, a feigned look of innocence on her face. "Well, I'm bored, so whatever shall we do?" She paused, thinking for a minute before her face lit up. "I know. Let's play truth or dare."

"What?" I grumbled, shaking my head. "How do you even know that game, anyway?"

"Are you kidding? It's been around as long as I have. We used to play it growing up, but times have certainly changed. Back then, the most anyone would dare you to do was hold hands with a boy. Now anything goes. Okay, I'm going first. I pick truth. Tell me Gracyn, what's it like to fall in love with someone who throws you away the first chance he gets?"

I crossed my arms over my chest in defiance. "I'm not playing your stupid game."

She huffed. "Come on. Don't be such a spoilsport. One game. Please? For me."

"Why would I want to do anything for you? I don't even like you."

"But if you answer the question, then you get to ask me anything. Or dare me to do something."

"Fine. It sucks. There, you got your answer and now it's my turn. What are you doing with Gabriel?"

Marguerite flashed a Cheshire Cat smile. "Hmm," she said, narrowing her eyes. "Why do you care?"

"Because, in case you haven't noticed, he's married," I gritted out. "To Becca, your mother," I added, feeling like I was on a trashy talk show.

"I know that, but he doesn't love her. He never did. How could he when she was obviously never in love with him? She loves someone else, so I did him a favor."

I shook my head, wishing I could take back the question. "Fine. Do what you want. I guess it takes two to tango. It didn't look like you dragged him here. Well, you got what you wanted, and we played your stupid little game. I think we're even now."

"We'll never be even," she insisted a little too strongly.

"Fine," I replied in a clipped voice, rolling my eyes at her dramatic antics. "So, I guess I'm stuck here until midnight."

"Or longer. We'll see."

"Great. You wouldn't happen to have anything to eat around here? I'm starving."

"No," she said, her tone flat. "Besides, I'm not feeding you. That would give you strength, and I need you to stay weak, remember?"

"No, I don't remember that, but somehow, it doesn't surprise me." I paused, stifling a yawn as I sat down, wishing she'd go away. Instead, she stooped to my level. "Can't you leave me alone?" I asked. "I just want some peace and quiet."

"Sure, no problem. But before I go, I want you to know one thing."

"What's that?"

"If you decide life around here isn't exciting enough, you're welcome to join us once we have the spells restored to the book."

"No thanks. I don't even know why you'd suggest that. I already told you I don't want to run off with you and help you cause misery and suffering."

She shrugged. "Hmm. You're right. I'm not sure what got into me. It must be some kind of family loyalty I didn't know I had."

"About that. Would you mind explaining how we're related?"

"Yes, I would," she said. "Now, I'm going out. I can't stay cooped up in here until midnight. It feels like a prison." She paused, then laughed. "Oh wait, for you, it is a prison."

"Thanks to you."

"I know." Without another word, Marguerite stood up and whistled. Her chestnut mare blasted in through the open back door, cantered down the aisle, and slid to a halt beside her. Marguerite jumped onto the horse's back in a single movement, then gave her a swift kick before they galloped out of the barn.

30

With night approaching, I grew hungrier by the minute. Dusk brought colder temperatures, sending a chill over me even though I wore my parka and gloves. I dropped back to the ground and pulled my knees up to my chest, wrapping my arms around them. Trying to ignore my growling stomach, I focused on not shivering, knowing it would expend energy I couldn't afford to waste.

The longer I waited, the more I realized Gabriel and Marguerite had to be defeated. My blood ran hot now that I knew they had teamed up. After what must have been several hours, I stood up and stared straight ahead. Holding my hands up, I touched the invisible wall. Then I pulled my arms back to my sides and closed my eyes. Praying for the strength to break the shield, I curled my hand into a fist and swung at the air in front of me with as much force as I could muster. But when my knuckles slammed into the shield, I felt like I'd hit a brick wall, my knit gloves too thin to cushion the blow.

"Ow!" I muttered, wincing. I clasped my fists together, pressing them to my chest while I waited for the pain to subside. Feeling defeated, I gave up hope that anything else would work. Marguerite had won, at least for now.

Once again, I sank to the ground and waited. I tried to doze off, but my hunger kept me awake. My senses seemed heightened as I listened for any sound indicating Gabriel and Marguerite were back, but all I heard was the occasional squeak of a mouse, making me squirm while I watched the floor around me for any sign of rodents. To my relief, none appeared.

Forever seemed to come and go before footsteps on the dirt aisle caught my attention. Snapping my gaze up, I peered through the shadows barely visible from the dying flame of the oil lantern. To my surprise, Lucian rushed toward me, his black overcoat falling to his knees and a look of worry in his eyes.

Shocked, I drew in a deep breath, afraid I was seeing things. I blinked, but Lucian was still there, coming closer, a purpose in his steps and his eyes locked on me. My rebellious heart skipped a beat, betraying me after he'd callously tossed me to Marguerite hours ago. Not sure what he wanted or how he'd found me, I remained on the ground, wondering if he'd accepted Marguerite's offer to join her.

He stopped in front of me and knelt down, reaching out to touch my arm. I flinched, refusing to look him in the eye. "What are you doing here?" I asked.

"I've come to get you and Gypsy."

"What?" I asked in disbelief. "You sent me here. You gave me to Marguerite! Why do you care what happens to me?"

"Because you're the only one for me. When I told you I would protect you at all costs, I meant it."

I shook my head, frustrated that his words contradicted his actions. "I don't understand," I told him, shifting my gaze up to meet his.

"I know. And I'm sorry. I can explain everything, just not now. There isn't time. Becca's right behind me. She'll be here any minute."

"She will? Why? If Marguerite finds her, there's no telling what she'll do to get those spells."

"I know, but Becca insisted. I'm not sure what her plan is, but I've only been focused on getting you back," he said. "How do you feel? Can you stand up?"

"It doesn't matter if I do. I'm trapped. Marguerite set up an invisible shield around me, and I can't get out. You might be able to penetrate it, but I'm stuck."

"That does present a problem." He sighed before standing up and glancing at Gypsy. "Guess I'll start with Gypsy," he said before opening the stall door and slipping inside.

I rose to my feet and watched him over the top board as he bent down. "What are you doing?"

"Untangling the ropes around her legs. At least I can free one of you."

A commotion at the end of the aisle snapped my attention away from Lucian and Gypsy. Marguerite rode into the barn, halted her chestnut mare in front of me, and dismounted. "It's almost show time," she said, a look of anticipation on her face. "I can't wait to see the look on Becca's face. She's probably been so worried about you."

"You don't have to wait," Becca announced, stepping around the back corner. "I'm here, so let's get this over with."

The color drained from Marguerite's face as she turned. "How did you find us? I put a cloaking spell on this place."

"Guess it didn't work. You must be losing your touch," Becca said, heading down the aisle toward Marguerite, her long white coat standing out in the shadows. "But you'll be happy to know I brought what you want." She whipped her hand out of her pocket, revealing the amber stone.

Marguerite's shocked expression transformed to one of delight. "Good. At least you learned from your mistakes. You should have handed it over to me last time, then we wouldn't be in this mess now, would we?"

Leaving her horse's side, Marguerite approached Becca and reached out to the stone, hesitating when her fingers were less than an inch away. Raising her gaze to Becca, Marguerite pulled her hand back to her side. "Remove the spell," she demanded.

"Not until you let Gracyn go."

"Oh, no," Marguerite said. "I did what you asked last time, and you never held up your end of the bargain."

"Yes, I did," Becca replied calmly. "You wanted the stone, and I gave it to you."

"Only to let it burn me," Marguerite hissed. "Now I know better. So let me repeat myself. Remove the spell and restore the script to the book, or your precious Gracyn will pay the ultimate price. And when I'm done with her, I'm going to be your worst nightmare. Because I know your death will break the spell. Even I didn't want to resort to killing you, but you may leave me no choice."

Surprise registered in Becca's eyes for a split second before her composure returned. "You wouldn't dare try," she said. "I'm older and stronger."

"Is that so?" Marguerite asked, stepping closer to Becca. "Perhaps you're forgetting your headaches. I'm not sure you'll be stronger when one of them strikes again."

"If you know my weakness and how to get to me, then why the charade of taking Gracyn? Seems a bit elaborate."

"Because it's fun to watch you squirm. And for the record, I didn't take Gracyn. Her boyfriend gave her to me."

Before Becca had time to respond, the sliding door at the front rolled opened and Gabriel walked in, his hair and clothes disheveled. "Marguerite, I'm back. Man, you sure buried this thing deep. The ground was frozen solid, but I managed to break through it," he said on his way down the aisle, a large leather-bound book in his arms. As soon as his eyes fell on Becca, he stopped, his complexion turning pale.

"Becca," he whispered.

"Hello, Gabriel," she said in a hushed voice, as though she'd been expecting him.

Silence fell over the barn while Becca and Gabriel locked eyes. But Marguerite didn't appear amused. "Oh, please," she said with a groan. "Don't act so shocked. Your marriage is over, in case either one of you didn't notice. Becca, your husband has been cheating on you with me, but I have a feeling you won't care. Everyone knows you never loved him because your heart belongs to a human. Now that we've got those details out of the way, let's get down to business."

Ignoring their blank stares, Marguerite stepped up to Gabriel and grabbed the book from him, an elated smile spreading across her face. She closed her eyes and took a deep breath, inhaling the book's earthy scent. "It feels good to have it back," she said, brushing dirt off the edges. Holding it up, she turned around, facing Becca again.

"The words, Becca. Reverse the spell. Now," she ordered.

When Becca hesitated, Marguerite shot an arm out to the side, her palm facing up toward me. In an instant, I was launched off my feet and slammed into the shield surrounding me. Pain ripping through my back, I fell into a heap on the floor.

"I mean it," Marguerite said, her voice louder. "I'm not giving up. Last time, you got lucky. I'm not so sure you will tonight."

Becca eyed the book, then moved her gaze to the stone in her hand.

"No!" I cried, sitting up and ignoring the bruised feeling spreading through my shoulders. "Don't do it, Becca. Please, I can handle whatever she wants to do to me. Just don't give in, please!"

Shaking her head, Becca glanced my way. "I won't let her hurt you, not now, when you have so much to live for." She looked at Marguerite, the defiance in her expression gone. "Fine. You win." Holding the amber stone out in front of her, Becca chanted something in an unfamiliar language. Her voice was soft at first, growing louder as she continued. The stone took on an energy, its soft glow bursting into flames until sparks shot out from it. After the fireworks rained down to the dusty ground, the stone went dark.

Silence returning, Becca bowed her head. "It's done. You got your wish," she said quietly, her voice full of defeat.

I shook my head, fighting emotions of fear and disappointment. I didn't want this, but Becca had made her decision.

Marguerite opened the book, a satisfied look in her eyes when she saw the words written on the pages. She took a deep breath, closing her eyes and running her hands over the pages like she couldn't believe it.

"Finally," she murmured. "I have it. I'll be the most powerful witch in the world. I've waited an eternity for this."

Opening her eyes, she glanced at me. "Gracyn, you're free to go."

I lifted my arm, relieved to find the invisible shield gone.

"And Gabriel," Marguerite continued, her attention shifting to him. "You shall come with me. Are you ready?"

He shot Becca a look of contempt while sliding an arm around Marguerite's shoulders. "I've been ready for years," he said before kissing her on the lips, passionately, brazenly, as though proving a point.

Pulling back from Marguerite, he cast a disdainful look Becca's way. "Too bad you brushed me off as being weak. Your lack of confidence in me made you sloppy. I found your journal and read all about how you threw Marguerite, your only daughter at the time, into the crypt. I figured if I could find the book of spells, I'd finally rise above all of you. I'm tired of being mediocre, and the book will help me become more powerful than anyone in this pathetic coven."

"Gabriel—" Becca started before he interrupted her.

"Save your breath. I'm leaving, so you can go back to your human boyfriend. With your headaches getting worse, it's likely you won't outlive him."

"You're messing with the wrong witch," Becca told him. "You may think she loves you, but she's just using you to get what she wants. As soon as she gets bored with you, she'll find someone new. Isn't that right, Marguerite? How many men did you drive to their graves after breaking their hearts? Five? Six? Oh wait, no, it was more like twenty."

"I don't care," Gabriel said. "I'll take my chances. Anything is better than living in your shadow."

"Gabe," Becca began. "You know that's not how it was. I looked up to you and respected you for your work as a doctor. You've done many great and wonderful things. You've saved countless lives, and you should be proud of that."

Darkness flashed over Gabriel's expression. "Yes, perhaps I have. But it's never done me much good around here," he muttered before shifting his attention to Marguerite, a renewed look of confidence in his eyes. "We're wasting valuable time with these two. We got what we wanted, so let's get out of here."

Marguerite's eyes locked with his, satisfaction in her expression as she ran her fingers around the edge of the book. "We will have anything our hearts desire," she told him. "Money, power, everything."

"Where are we going first?" he asked.

"I'm not sure," she said. "I'm still getting used to the idea that we finally have the book." She flipped through the pages, her eyes closing again.

"You won't get away with this," Becca said.

Marguerite's eyes flew open, and she laughed. "Really? What are you going to do about it? For as powerful as you are, or could be, you're a sorry excuse for a witch. With you and your little coven, it's all about living a simple life, growing just enough food to carry you through the winter. Don't you get bored? Don't you want to see new places and have some excitement in your life? What am I saying? Of course not, because that would be selfish which isn't allowed. Well, I'm not like any of you, and I'm going to set out on an adventure and take whatever I want from the world."

Cringing at Marguerite's words, I stood up and watched Becca, surprised she was doing nothing to stop Marguerite. There was no telling what she'd do with the book now. I couldn't believe Becca had given up without a fight, especially after vowing not to.

"So be it, Marguerite," Becca said. "If you can't find happiness in the simple things in life, your greed will never be satisfied. So go on, have your fun and wreak havoc on the world for entertainment. It won't do you any good."

Marguerite tossed her hair over her shoulder. "Maybe not, but it's going to be one hell of a ride." She paused, looking at Gabriel. "Are you ready?"

"I've been ready," he confirmed with a smile before letting out a loud whistle. Prince charged into the barn, stirring up a cloud of dust when he slid to a stop beside Gabriel.

Marguerite and Gabriel climbed onto their horses, the book still in Marguerite's hands. They kicked the horses' sides and galloped out of the barn, the last image of them ducking through the doorway twisting my heart with fear. If Becca had been telling the truth about the book, the world would never be the same.

31

"Are you crazy?" I asked Becca as soon as Marguerite and Gabriel disappeared. "How could you give in to her? After all that talk about how awful the book is, you're going to let them get away with it?"

"They won't get away," Lucian stated as he opened the stall door and led Gypsy into the aisle. He dropped the reins, letting them hang over her neck, and gave her a gentle pat. Rope burns had rubbed her neck and ankles raw, but like my wounds, the angry red marks were gone, the healing process well underway.

Becca smiled with confidence, surprising me. "No, they won't," she confirmed before shifting her gaze to the doorway. Cadence and Shade galloped into the barn, their black and white coats as different as night and day even though they shared the same mission. They stopped in front of Becca, standing tall, their ears pointed at her while they waited for her next command. Shade tossed his head, shaking his long mane and snorting, the white outlining his eyes a sign he was on high alert.

Becca nodded at Cadence, and the mare lowered to the ground, allowing Becca to slide onto her bare back. As Cadence stood up, Becca looked down at me. "Get on, Gracyn. We have to hurry!"

My heart accelerating at the urgency in Becca's voice, I ran over to Gypsy and Lucian gave me a leg up. As soon as I settled into the saddle, I glanced down at him, still wondering why he was helping Becca after betraying me. But there was no time to ask him for an explanation. That would have to wait.

After flashing me a quick smile, Lucian ran to Shade and jumped on his back. The horses bolted out of the barn single file, Cadence in front. I ducked when Gypsy charged through the doorway behind Shade, a blast of cold air hitting me the second we raced out into the night.

A full moon lit up the black sky, its soft light reflecting on the snow covering the ground. The horses kicked up a cloud of powder, charging full speed ahead. I grabbed Gypsy's mane and hung on, hoping we wouldn't be too late to stop Marguerite. But doubts lingered in my mind, my optimism fading. Gabriel and Marguerite had left several minutes ago, and their horses were as strong as ours. I had no idea what Becca was planning to do, but just catching up to Marguerite and Gabriel seemed like a long shot.

We flew through the woods, dodging the trees and branches. I leaned down near Gypsy's neck, bracing against her while adrenaline rushed through my veins. Her hooves crashed through the snow, churning it up around her legs the faster she ran.

After a few minutes, we emerged into a clearing, and Lucian and Becca halted their horses. I rode up beside Becca and tugged on the reins to stop Gypsy, my jaw dropping at the scene unfolding before us. Gabriel and Marguerite sat astride their horses in the middle of the field, facing a line of about a dozen horses and riders who looked like a cavalry without uniforms. A white horse stood in the middle, Celeste sitting tall on the mare's back. Everett rode a bay gelding beside her, his gaze shifting to Lucian before locking back on Marguerite and Gabriel. I recognized several of the others, including Celeste's mother on a dappled gray mare and her father riding a bay gelding. Derek sat astride a black and white paint, its flashy markings making it stand out against the solid-colored horses.

Marguerite and Gabriel turned their horses around and started to head in our direction, but pulled up as soon as they saw us blocking their escape route. Then they whipped to the side and began to charge, only to be cut off by the others. This went on for a few minutes until Marguerite and Gabriel halted in the center, the riders closing in on them.

"What is the meaning of this?" Marguerite asked. "Let us pass, or you'll pay."

Whispers broke out amongst the coven members, but stopped when a figure in a black cloak walked between two horses. Approaching the pair at the center, Samira pushed the hood down behind her neck, revealing hair and skin as dark as the midnight sky. She stopped before them, raised her hands, and began to chant.

Snow swirled on the ground, gaining momentum the longer Samira spoke. It rose up like a tornado until it spun around Gabriel and Marguerite, trapping them. Their horses spooked, shaking their heads and pawing the ground. Whinnying, they twirled around, searching for a way out, but the wind blocked them, the force too great for them to break through.

Marguerite dug her heels into her horse's sides, causing the mare to rear up, her front hooves slicing the air. Marguerite reached up to grab the mane, but wasn't quick enough and fell to the ground, dropping the book before landing in the snow. As Samira ceased her chanting, the funnel cloud disappeared, and Marguerite leaped to her feet, her eyes scanning the area around her. As soon as her gaze locked in on the book a few feet away, she lunged for it.

In a flash, Lucian jumped off Shade and ran toward it, his movement a blur. He reached for the book before Marguerite could grab it, then stood up with it in his arms, a satisfied smile on his face.

"I think you dropped something," he said, a mocking tone in his voice.

Her face turned a darker shade of red. "You have no business with that. I paid the price to get it after spending two hundred years in a dungeon," she hissed while Gabriel dismounted from his horse and approached behind her.

"That doesn't entitle you to play with power and use these spells to cause destruction," Lucian stated before walking toward Becca as she slid off Cadence. He held the book in his outstretched arms, his gaze steady on her. "I believe this belongs to you."

"Thank you," she said, taking it from him.

He nodded, then shifted his attention back to Marguerite and Gabriel. Silence fell over the field, all eyes watching the redhead and her golden-haired accomplice.

Becca trudged through the snow, nearing them. "We will allow you to leave in peace under one condition. You must promise never to look for this book again. Can you do that?"

I nearly choked, wondering why Becca would give them a chance at redemption. But the look on Marguerite's face told me she'd never agree to Becca's terms.

Marguerite narrowed her eyes as though Becca had asked for the impossible. "After all this time, why would I believe you'll honor your promise? And you can forget it. I'm not about to live a meager existence like the rest of you. I'd no sooner give up my chance for a better life than agree to stop breathing."

Becca bowed her head. When she lifted her gaze, disappointment lingered in her eyes. "Then we can't let you go."

Becca nodded at the others watching from astride their horses, and they began closing in on Marguerite and Gabriel.

"No!" Marguerite shouted as she lunged at Becca.

Without hesitating, Becca threw the book behind her before Marguerite landed on top of her. They crashed into the snow, both of them struggling to reach for the book. Seeing my chance, I jumped off Gypsy and rushed toward it, grabbing it at the same time as Gabriel. I stopped, fear settling over me when my eyes locked with his sinister stare. Caught off-guard, I felt the book slip from my fingers, my heart sinking at my failed attempt.

Becca and Marguerite jumped to their feet, circling with their eyes locked, like two cats ready to pounce. After a few seconds, Marguerite raised her hand, launching Becca into the air. Instead of crashing to the ground, Becca landed on her feet, her arms raised. The snow swirled up into the air, creating a long rope, the end forming a loop. Becca tossed it over Marguerite, catching her around the shoulders. She tightened it, then tugged the end, dragging Marguerite toward her.

Marguerite dug her heels into the snow, but she wasn't strong enough to hold her own against Becca. "Let me go!" she demanded, earning herself a tighter squeeze from the rope of snow.

My attention focused on Marguerite and Becca, I didn't notice Gabriel rushing up behind me until he put his free arm under my chin, choking me.

I coughed and tried to kick him, but my energy had been drained after being locked up for over twelve hours. My efforts wasted, Gabriel tightened his hold on me.

"That's enough!" he shouted, pausing until everyone looked at him. "Becca, let Marguerite go or Gracyn will pay the ultimate price."

Becca glanced at me, losing her focus on Marguerite. Marguerite whipped her arms out to the side, causing the rope to disintegrate into snowflakes that swiftly fell to the ground.

"You wouldn't," Becca said, her eyes narrowed. "After all this time, you know how much she means to me."

He laughed. "Yes, I will, so don't test me."

Gabriel didn't budge, his arm still locked under my chin, pushing against my throat. Barely able to breathe, I remained still, hoping I could channel my energy and fight him.

"Why?" Becca asked. "You have the book, and I let Marguerite go. You got what you wanted. You have nothing to gain by hurting Gracyn."

After a moment of silence, Gabriel took a deep breath. "You're right," he said, a satisfied tone in his voice. He released his hold on me, shoving me forward. I took a few quick steps before recovering my balance and turning to see the book in his hands. He looked down at it, disbelief forming in his eyes.

Marguerite snapped her gaze to the book and approached him. "I'll take that," she said, her arms outstretched.

"Not so fast," Gabriel said, still staring at it. "I've got it, and I think it's time we see what we have here." He opened it and flipped through the pages until one of them caught his eye. Then he started reading in a language I didn't understand.

The ground began to tremble and dark clouds raced through the sky, blocking the moon. His voice grew louder, and the temperature dropped.

"Gabriel!" Becca shouted above the thunder roaring from overhead. "You have no idea what you're doing! Stop!"

Ignoring her, he continued to read as if in a trance. A mixture of snow and ice shot down from the sky, hitting me in the face and arms, the force nearly bringing me to my knees. The clear night was gone, replaced by a wicked blizzard that kicked in with winds howling and visibility dropping to nothing. A wall of white surrounded me as chaos erupted.

Marguerite's laughter rang out in the distance. "It's working! Everything I learned about this book is true! We're going to get everything we want!"

Just when I thought we had failed, that Marguerite and Gabriel had won with their evil tactics, the storm vanished. Samira emerged in the center of the field, her dark eyes taking on a red glow while she walked toward Gabriel. When she was ten feet away, the book flew out of his hands, pulled by an invisible force. "The book may be powerful, but I'm stronger," she declared when it landed in her arms.

Gabriel charged toward her, but she locked her eyes on him, causing him to stop in the snow and drop to his knees.

"No!" Marguerite yelled before charging at me. "Take the book, and I'll take this one." She grabbed my wrist, her touch burning me, sending a searing pain through my veins. Smoke sizzled from my charred skin, and I started to fall to my knees, but her grip kept me standing.

Lucian and Becca turned to face her, concern and fear in their expressions.

"That's right," Marguerite stated. "I'm in charge here. Either make that witch give me the book, or Gracyn will die. Maybe you can bury her next to Cassie. They'll be side by side, six feet under."

Silence came next, the seconds that passed feeling like hours. Pain continued to spread through me, numbing me. Hoping for relief, I waited for someone to do something. When nothing happened, fury erupted inside me, bringing my energy back in full force. Images of the wolf in the crypt flashed through my mind, the vision fueling my determination to defend myself.

With a power I didn't know I had, I ripped my arm away from Marguerite. I raised my hand and a ball of fire formed in my palm, growing big and bright.

My gaze locked with Marguerite's, fear and surprise registering in her icy blue eyes.

"I saved you," I told her. "If it wasn't for me, you wouldn't even be here right now. You said we're related. Well, where I come from, relatives don't hurt each other. They help each other. But since you obviously disagree, I shall cause you the same pain you caused me."

I was about to throw the flaming ball at her when Gabriel lunged for me. I fell to the ground, the fire in my hand going out as soon as it hit the snow. He rolled on top of me until I stopped on my back, looking up at his cold stare. He leaned down, putting his hands around my neck in a solid choke-hold.

Gabriel's fingers curled around my throat, cutting off my airway. Unable to breathe, I struggled, but it was like fighting an iron chain around my neck. Then I thought I heard Lucian scream "No!" before my eyes closed and the world started to go dark.

I thought I was dead until I heard screams and a scuffle beside me. Taking a deep breath, I opened my eyes and rolled out of the way just in time to avoid Lucian and Gabriel who were wrestling in the snow.

Powerless to do anything, I took a moment to catch my breath. When I stood up, Everett rushed over to Gabriel and Lucian, placing a foot on them, stopping them instantly.

"We've had enough. Get up. Now!" he commanded.

Gabriel and Lucian slowly rose to their feet, and Lucian backed up next to his father. Everett pulled the knife that had killed Cassie out of his inside coat pocket and placed the tip against Gabriel's throat. Shock registering in his eyes, Gabriel's face turned pale the moment he saw the dagger.

"Where did you get that?" he asked in a fearful whisper.

Everett and Lucian exchanged glances before focusing back on Gabriel. I swallowed, my heart nearly stopping in disbelief.

"What do you know about this knife?" Everett asked slowly, deliberately.

"It...it belonged to me, but was stolen three years ago," Gabriel stuttered.

"And?" Lucian asked.

"That's all I know. I haven't seen it in years," Gabriel insisted.

Everett held it steady, keeping the tip of the blade on Gabriel's throat. "Samira!" he called. "You're needed."

She handed the book to Becca, then rushed to Everett who nodded at her. "You know what to do," he said.

Samira took Gabriel's hand and looked directly into his eyes, hers now dark again, the red glow gone. "Tell us the truth," she demanded. "When was the last time you saw this knife?"

"I already told you. Three years ago."

Samira kept her gaze on him while she dropped his hand, her voice loud and clear when she said two words that would change everything. "He's lying."

32

ilence returned to the clearing as all eyes settled on Gabriel, the look of panic on his face giving him away. I held my breath, waiting for Lucian's reaction. Rage ran deep in his eyes, like dark storm clouds about to unleash their fury.

"You're going to pay!" Lucian exclaimed, his words cutting through the night. He charged at Gabriel and grabbed him by the throat, picking him up off the ground. Gabriel clutched Lucian's hands and tried to pry them off his neck, but he was no match for Lucian's strength fueled by anger. Instead, Gabriel gasped for air, his face turning a pale shade of blue.

"Put him down, son," Everett ordered.

"I can't," Lucian said between clenched teeth, his eyes locked on Gabriel.

Samira touched Lucian's shoulder, causing him to glance at her. "Do you want to know the truth, or do you want to kill him first and never know?" she asked.

Slowly, with a restraint appearing to take every ounce of his willpower, Lucian lowered Gabriel to his feet and released him. "Fine. I'll let you live, but you'd better tell us everything."

Gabriel's eyes darted from Lucian to Samira to Becca, then to the rest of the onlookers still mounted on their horses. "It wasn't something I planned, I swear."

"Is that so?" Lucian muttered sarcastically.

Tears welling up in my eyes, I took a deep breath and fought the lump growing in my throat. I couldn't imagine how Lucian must feel to finally have this moment of truth.

"Yes," Gabriel said, his eyes narrowing, his expression twisting with anger. "All I wanted was to get out of this God-forsaken town and away from the coven. Ever since I can remember, that's all I've ever wanted."

"What does that have to do with Cassie?" Lucian asked, his voice strained.

"I was at the graveyard when she and Angel saw me. They got in my way, and I did what I had to do," Gabriel stated, not a shred of remorse in his voice.

"So that's it?" Lucian asked. "That's all you have to say?"

"Why were you at the graveyard?" Everett asked Gabriel, his voice calm but firm, anguish lingering behind the tears in his eyes.

"Does it really matter?" Gabriel retorted.

"You obviously had a knife with you. So tell us what you were doing there," Everett demanded.

"Fine," Gabriel relented with an irritated sigh. "You might as well know. I was going to attempt a spell to resurrect Marguerite. It required the blood of a relative and, since I didn't have Gracyn, the only one I could get was Gypsy. I had the knife to use on her, but before I could cut her, I heard a commotion in the woods. When I looked over, I saw Cassie and I knew she'd seen what I was about to do. I started to chase her, but Angel charged at me and I killed two birds with one stone. I saved myself from being trampled and from being ratted out by a little girl. But Gypsy escaped, so at least one of them wasn't harmed. And there you have it. Mystery solved."

Becca stepped forward, a disappointed look on her face. "Why?" she asked, shaking her head. "We had a good life. I thought you were happy."

"I wanted more," he said with a shrug. "And don't patronize me. I know you looked down upon me for being weaker, for not having as much power as the others. So I wanted out. But you made one very big mistake. You should have been more careful with your journal. As soon as I read about the book of spells and Marguerite, I knew I had to have them both. Besides, dear Becca, I was never the one you really loved."

"I stood by you," Becca said. "I took an oath, and I kept my promise."

"But your heart belongs to another man," Gabriel said. "So save it." He turned and started walking away.

Lucian ran after Gabriel, grabbing his arm when he was within reach and jerking him around to a stop. "You're not going anywhere," Lucian said. "Not after what you did. You took an innocent life. She was only a child. And then you let everyone believe I killed my own sister. You would have let me rot in jail for a crime I never committed. I ought to end your sorry existence right here."

Lucian lunged for the knife in his father's hand, but Marguerite intercepted with lightning speed. She raised an arm, and the knife flew out of Everett's grasp with an invisible force, shooting toward her. She caught it, wrapping her fingers around the handle before lunging at Everett and touching the tip of the blade to his heart.

"Now that the cat's out of the bag, I've had about enough drama for one night," she announced. Turning her attention to Becca, she commanded, "Give me the book now, or he dies."

Becca remained still, not moving an inch.

Samira stepped forward, her gaze locked on Marguerite and her dark eyes turning red again. Smoke rose up from the dagger handle, a sizzling sound and the scent of burning flesh following.

"What the—" Marguerite started, dropping the knife and clutching her hand.

Samira approached Marguerite, her black robe trailing on the snow. "You may be stronger than many here, but you're no match for me."

Marguerite backed up, seeming unsure and hesitant for the first time. "Who are you?" she asked.

"I'm your worst nightmare. Threaten the man I love, and you will pay," Samira said before raising her hands and chanting.

Marguerite's eyes opened wide with alarm. Before she could run, snow lifted off the ground, creating a funnel cloud around her. She stood in the center of it, trapped. A whinny cried out in the background, and her horse charged up to the wind circling Marguerite. The mare struck at it with her front leg, but the force launched her into the air. She landed in a heap on the snow, her legs sprawled out in front of her.

Marguerite began to rise off the ground, her shape flickering in and out of focus until turning into the white wolf with yellow eyes. It let out a long, painful howl before its body became translucent like a ghost. The figure rose higher in the sky, wavering in the moonlight, reminding me of the night I followed it through the woods months ago.

The chanting stopped, and Samira whispered something. The wolf disintegrated into tiny white particles that fell to the ground.

"No!" Gabriel shouted, running to where what was left of Marguerite had fallen and sifting his fingers through it. Then he looked up, grief and anguish written all over his face. "You bitch! What have you done?" he directed at Samira before jumping to his feet and charging at her.

Like a flash, Everett ran in between them, stopping Gabriel before he closed in on Samira. "You'd better think very hard before you raise a hand to anyone," he warned. "If you want to live, that is. She's far more powerful than any of us. I think she just proved that."

I silently agreed with Lucian's father, realizing Samira had single-handedly sent Marguerite away without the use of her hair or blood which Becca had needed when she'd done it hundreds of years ago. I wanted to know how one witch could do so much more than us, but remembered magic wasn't an exact science, no matter how much I wished it was.

"Marguerite was the only thing keeping me going for years," Gabriel cried. "After I found a picture of her, I had to have her. I searched long and hard for a way to bring her back. Now she's been stolen from me before we had a chance at a life together."

"Marguerite was evil. She would have destroyed you," Everett stated.

"He's right," Lucian added. "She asked me run away with her. Some loyal girlfriend you had there."

Gabriel spun around, his eyes locked on Lucian. "I guess you got what you wanted. I took someone you loved, and now your father's friend has taken someone I loved. We're even."

"We're not even close to being even," Lucian said. He looked at the knife lying in the snow, and it rose into the air before snapping into his hand like a magnet pulled to metal. As soon as his fingers wrapped around the handle, he pointed it at Gabriel, then faltered. Lucian swallowed hard, a tear escaping his eye as he lowered the knife to his side.

"What's the matter?" Gabriel sneered. "Aren't you man enough to avenge your sister's death?"

Lucian glanced at his father and Becca, his eyes searching for approval. Becca stepped forward. "Gabriel, you know what the punishment is for taking the life of another witch. We can either banish you for an eternity of misery, or you can choose death. The decision is yours."

Gabriel rolled his eyes. "If I choose the first, you're the only witch in the coven who can cast the spell to put me away. Are you prepared to do that to me after all I've done for you?"

Becca drew in a sharp breath, her hesitation speaking volumes.

"That's what I thought," Gabriel said before turning and walking away.

"Oh, no!" Everett rushed after him, darting in front of him and blocking his getaway. "You're not getting out of here. Not after what you've done. You know the code. Killing is strictly forbidden."

Gabriel threw his head back and laughed. "And what are you going to do about it? No one here seems to have the fortitude to touch me. I could probably kill again and get away with it. This coven is weak. You all are more pathetic at being witches than I am. I'm out of here."

Gabriel took two steps before Lucian charged in front of him, the knife still in his hand. "My father's right. You're not walking away. Cassie's murder will not go unpunished."

With a snide grin, Gabriel pushed Lucian, knocking him to the ground. Everett lunged at Gabriel, not noticing the titanium ice pick Gabriel pulled out of his pocket and aimed at Everett's chest.

In a flash, Lucian was back on his feet. With the speed of lightning, he drove the dagger into Gabriel's heart the moment the ice pick was about to penetrate his father.

A look of shock crossed over Gabriel's eyes before the light in them died and he sank to his knees, collapsing in the snow, the ice pick still in his hand.

"Now you'll never hurt my family again," Lucian said, bending down to pull the knife out of Gabriel. He threw it onto the ground, cringing as though he never wanted to see it again. Turning to Becca, he bowed his head. "I'm sorry. I had to do it."

She nodded, her eyes filling with tears. "No, I'm the one who's sorry. I never would have guessed Gabe was behind Cassie's murder." She looked at her dead husband, sorrow in her expression. "If I'd had any idea he was involved, I would have come forward right away."

"We know," Everett said, approaching Becca. "You couldn't have possibly known what a monster he was. He was very convincing."

"Yes, he was," she said. "But Everett, are you okay? I can't believe Gabe would threaten you."

He smiled as Samira rushed to his side. "I'm fine," he assured them. "He hurt my pride more than anything." Turning, Everett placed a hand on Lucian's shoulder. "Son, you did the right thing."

Lucian nodded, a heavy look in his eyes.

Becca put the book in one hand and reached for Lucian's arm with her other one, reassuring him with a quick squeeze. After letting go, she fished the amber stone out of her pocket. She held the gem up, staring at it as the moonlight reflected off its shiny surfaces. "We have one last loose end to tie up," she announced before shifting her attention to the white horse in the center of the line-up.

"Celeste," she said. "It's time for you to work some magic."

Celeste looked at Becca, visibly surprised. "Me?"

"Yes," Becca said. "You. You're destined to watch over the script when I'm gone, so why not start now? You'll cast the spell, and then I want you to keep the stone. But I'll take the book. I'm not sure where I'll put it, but I'll hide it away."

"Okay," Celeste said, still seeming unsure.

"Come here," Becca instructed.

Celeste looked at her mother, waiting until she nodded to dismount. As soon as Celeste reached Becca, Becca put the stone in her hand. "You know what to do. Just as we practiced."

"Yes," Celeste said before closing her eyes. She held the stone up high and began to chant. Within seconds, the book Becca held flat in her outstretched arms flipped open. The pages rifled back and forth, first slowly, then faster, as though they were being pulled by a magical force. The words lifted off the pages, rising in the air to form a long ribbon of black particles. Celeste continued, and they were pulled toward the stone, disappearing as soon as they touched it, giving the gem a yellow glow for a moment.

When the stone darkened, Celeste opened her eyes and studied it, a perplexed look in her brown eyes. "It got hot, and now it's cold again. Did I do it?"

"Yes," Becca said, holding up the book to show off its blank pages. "You'll have to put the stone in a safe place and guard it."

"I will," Celeste replied. "You can count on me."

"I know," Becca said before giving her a hug.

When Celeste pulled away and turned to face the horses behind her, Derek dismounted and approached her. "That was incredible," he said.

"Thanks," she said, seeming flustered by his attention. "Well, I'd better go." She started to turn, but stopped when Derek spoke again.

"Hold up for a minute," he said, pausing until he had her attention again. "I know tonight was pretty heavy, but when things settle down, I don't suppose you'd like to have dinner with me one night, would you?"

Her face lit up with a bright smile. "I'd love to."

As they walked back to the horses, I looked over to see Lucian making his way toward me. Without any warning, he wrapped his arms around me and kissed me. When he lifted away, tears glistened in his eyes. "It's over. It's finally over," he whispered.

"Yes," I said, letting out a small smile before it collapsed and I pulled away from him. "But wait a minute. You have a lot of explaining to do. You really scared me when you handed me to Marguerite this morning. What was that about?"

"I'm sorry. I know it may have seemed a bit harsh, but I sent you in there so I could use my visions of you to find Gypsy. But I had to be convincing, so I couldn't risk telling you. You had to believe I wanted to send you away, or Marguerite never would have fallen for it."

"What if the vision didn't come to you?"

He sighed. "I didn't think about that possibility until after Marguerite dragged you into the woods. But I saw you when you got caught in the storm on your way home, and I also saw the night you were in the car with your friend's stepfather. I have a feeling I'll know where you are any time you're in trouble. I wouldn't have done it if I hadn't been confident I'd be able to get you back. The alternative of watching Marguerite torture you by inflicting pain on Gypsy wasn't a whole lot better."

"Okay," I rolled out slowly, finding it easier to forgive him than I'd expected. "But how did you make a deal with her?"

"It wasn't planned, that's for sure. I couldn't sleep, so I went out to check on the horses. Apparently, Marguerite got around, even in a blinding snowstorm. When she showed up from out of nowhere, the idea came to me, so I offered you up."

"Gee, thanks," I said with a deep breath. I remembered the few times Marguerite had seemed to read my thoughts and realized he had to keep his plan a secret, otherwise she probably would have figured it out. My frustration with him began to crumble. "Never again, okay? Next time, tell me what you're up to first."

"Let's just hope there is no next time."

"Agreed," I said, then changed the subject. "I saw you in a dream while I was trapped in the barn. I knew you didn't kill Cassie before Gabriel confessed. Although I've known all along, ever since I met you. I'm sorry I doubted you when I found the knife. I never should have stopped believing in you."

"It was a complicated mess, and I know being with me while everyone else cast their suspicions was hard. The fact that you weathered the storm by my side means more to me than you'll ever know."

"The day it happened, you were painting a picture of a woman about to jump off a cliff. It was truly a moving piece, but very sad. Who was she?"

"My mother."

Not prepared for his answer, I felt my heart drop, the sorrow buried in the painting nearly crushing me.

"That's how I always saw her, ready to give up," he explained. "I never knew when she might jump. I thought if I painted something like that, she might take one look at it and snap out of her depression. Unfortunately, it didn't work."

"Do you still have the painting? I'd love to see it."

"Yes. I'll show it to you one day. We have plenty of time now, you know."

I nodded. "So, I need to ask—"

He pressed a finger to my lips, hushing me. "I think I know what's on your mind, and maybe this will help clear things up. I'm in love with you. I think I have been since the first time I laid eyes on you. And now, there's nothing to stop us from being together. I know I'm not perfect, but I promise you I'll be there for you for the rest of our lives, however long that might be. Does that answer your question?"

I nodded, more tears blurring my vision. "I love you, too," was all I could say.

He smiled, grinning from ear to ear. "You know, we've never had a real date. What do you say? Will you have dinner with me this weekend?"

I bit my lip to keep my smile from taking over, my heart swelling. For the first time since I'd moved to town, Lucian and I would be able to go anywhere without people whispering and passing judgment. We didn't have to hide how we felt. All it took was one word for me to answer him. "Yes."

Then he kissed me again while we stood in the snow under the moon, not caring who watched.

33

The following days were a flurry of activity. The coven worked together to dig a grave under the snow in the witch cemetery, laying Gabriel and his horse to rest. Whimpering sounds came from the crypt, but this time, no one came to Marguerite's aid, especially not me. I had learned my lesson. The witches sealed off the area, putting another spell on it to keep anyone from entering and releasing Marguerite again. Although, as I had learned, only a blood relative would be able to set her free.

Becca filed a missing person report on Gabriel, then informed the hospital he had disappeared. The witches cast a spell on the town to erase all suspicions of Lucian's involvement in his sister's murder. Finally free from the whispers and accusing stares, he no longer had to hide in the shadows or keep a low profile.

I woke up Sunday morning feeling like I had a new lease on life. Sitting up in bed, I noticed the blinking light coming from my phone on the dresser. I rushed across the room and grabbed it, finding a text from Lucian. *I'm picking you up at nine o'clock. Make sure you're ready.*

Smiling, I shook my head, remembering how he'd teased me at dinner the night before about another mystery outing today. In spite of my pleading, he refused to tell me what he had planned. So I threw on a pair of jeans and a sweater, brushed my hair, and ran downstairs to get breakfast before he arrived.

When I reached the kitchen, Becca scurried about, whipping eggs in a bowl, the counter cluttered with bread, butter, and milk. "Good morning," I said, heading for the coffee pot.

"You seem to be in a good mood today," she replied, pouring the eggs into a skillet on the stove and stirring.

"Yes. Lucian's picking me up soon," I told her as I filled a mug with coffee and splashed some creamer into it.

"What do the two of you have planned for the day?"

I turned and leaned against the counter, my fingers circling the warm mug. "I'm not sure. He won't tell me. He said it's a surprise."

"Sounds interesting."

"Everything with him is," I said, raising my eyebrows as I remembered the last time he surprised me with a day out at the pumpkin farm. At that moment, standing in the kitchen with Becca, another thought banished Lucian to the furthest corner of my mind. Something had been nagging me ever since the showdown with Marguerite, and I might as well bring it up now. "Becca, I know a lot has happened over the last few weeks, but since things have settled down, will you please tell me who my parents are? I've been patient and I haven't bugged you about it too much, but I think I have a right to know."

She sighed, shifting her gaze away from me to look down at the eggs. "You're right. It's time you knew," she replied softly before glancing back at me. "You might want to sit down for this."

"No," I stated, stepping up to the island to stand beside her. "I'm okay. Just tell me the truth and get it over with. I'll be fine."

"I hope you're right. I'm your biological mother."

I felt as though the wind had been knocked out of me for a second. Drawing in a sharp breath, I remembered some of the signs. The picture on Becca's dresser of her holding a newborn baby, Marguerite's reference to me as a relative, Becca's hesitation to even discuss this with me. "Why didn't you tell me?" I asked.

"It was complicated. I told you once before that Gabriel wasn't the strongest witch. His insecurities concerned me, and now I know I was right to worry. I didn't want any attention I gave you to cause him to become jealous, which is why I gave you up in the first place. Gabe and I grew close right after I got pregnant with you, and he helped me through a rough time. He wasn't all bad."

"That's it? You chose him over me?"

"It's not like that at all. You're different than most of us since your father is human. I wasn't sure if you'd be more human or more witch, so I wanted to give you a chance at a normal life. When you hurt your friend's stepfather, I knew you were more witch than human and realized you belonged here with us."

"Were you ever afraid I'd turn out like Marguerite?"

Becca smiled. "No, not at all."

"Okay. Good." I paused, taking in this new information. As much as I felt like I should be shocked, it gave me a sense of peace. I couldn't think of anyone else I'd want as my mother besides Becca, even though she'd always seemed like more of a sister to me.

"So," Becca began, sounding hesitant as she continued stirring the eggs. "I'm afraid to ask, are you okay with this?"

"Yes," I replied, meeting her gaze. "I am. But do I need to start calling you Mom? Because that would feel really weird. You're Becca to me."

"No, please don't. That would take too much getting used to, and I think I'm a bit too old for a change like that."

"And my father?" I asked with sigh. "I think I can guess who he is."

Becca nodded. "He's on his way over here right now."

"He is?" I asked with a gasp. "Wow. Um, okay, I guess that's one way to break the ice. Does he know about me?"

"Yes. We had a long talk last night. It turns out he was starting to put the pieces together before I told him."

"Does he know about us? I mean, about our magic?"

She nodded with a deep sigh. "Yes. He's known what I am for a long time because I had to tell him why it wouldn't work out between us." She paused, glancing at her watch. "He should be here any minute."

Before I could say another word, I heard a car pull into the driveway. My gaze snapped to the front door, my jaw falling. All my life, I'd thought my father was dead. The idea that he was alive seemed surreal, but if I could get used to being a witch, I could probably handle getting to know my father.

I placed my coffee mug on the island and rushed across the room, my sights set on the front door. Without bothering to grab a coat, I ran outside onto the porch while a silver sedan pulled up next to Becca's SUV. As soon as the engine turned off, Mr. Wainwright stepped out of the car wearing jeans and a dark green jacket, his normally scruffy jaw clean-shaven.

I ran down the porch steps and stopped in front of him. "Hi," I said. He smiled. "Hello."

An awkward silence stretched between us for a minute before I broke it. "Becca told me everything. How long have you known?"

"Honestly, I think I figured it out the night you and Becca helped me get up to my apartment. Something that night just clicked. I hadn't suspected a thing until then. When you told me you were her sister the night we met at the bar, I never questioned it. I've always known Becca's life is full of secrets, and I knew anything was possible. But I never imagined...well...that you were my daughter."

"Are you okay with it?"

"Yes, definitely. I thought I'd never have children, and it turns out I have a wonderful daughter. But I should be asking you the same question."

I smiled hesitantly. "It's a bit of a shock. I never had a father. Ever since I can remember, I was told he had died. So yes, I am. Although it's going to take a little getting used to."

He nodded. "I understand. You've had a lot dropped on you lately, although you seem to take it all in stride. Most people wouldn't."

"I guess I'm not like most people."

"No, you certainly aren't."

"I'll take that as a compliment," I said before gesturing to the house. "You should go in. Becca's making breakfast."

He glanced at the house, a look of amazement on his face. "I still can't believe it. I never thought this day would come."

"What? You and Becca?"

"Yes," he replied. "She kept me at bay ever since she married Gabriel. Even though I knew she never truly loved him, she remained faithful to him. She took her vows to heart, no matter how difficult it was."

"But now that's over," I said.

"Yes, finally. I'm still surprised it happened in my lifetime."

"Then what are you waiting for? Get in there and make her happy."

"Just one minute," he said, holding up a finger as he approached me. "I have to do something first." Without any warning, he hugged me, then let go. "Whatever happens, I'm always here for you. We'll spend some time together soon."

I smiled. "Does this mean I have to call you Dad in class?"

He laughed. "That might be a little weird. You can stick to Mr. Wainwright in class. But outside school, call me Aidan, okay?"

I nodded. "Got it."

The front door opened, and Becca stepped out onto the porch. "Everything okay out here?" she asked.

"Yes," I said. "We're fine."

"Good," she said as Aidan hurried up the stairs and into her arms. After he kissed her, he lifted his head. "Just so you know, I'm never letting you go. I may grow old and leave this world, and then you can find someone new because I'd never want you to be alone, but until then, you're stuck with me."

She smiled at him, her eyes lighting up. "I can't think of a better way to spend the years to come." She paused, shifting her attention to me. "Gracyn, why don't you come in and join us for breakfast?"

"Okay," I said, about to head up the steps when Lucian's Range Rover appeared in the distance. "In a minute. You two go on in."

They disappeared into the house as the black SUV rolled to a stop on the snow in the driveway. Lucian hopped out and approached me, a happy look on his face. "Good morning," he said before kissing me eagerly, passionately.

Sensing the urgency in his kiss, I pulled back. "Lucian! You're a little bold today."

"Where you're concerned, always. You can expect a greeting like that from me for the rest of your life."

"But," I started, gesturing to the house. "They could be watching."

"Let them. For the first time since we met, I don't have to hide my feelings for you," he stated before kissing me again.

A few seconds later, I untangled myself from his embrace and started to head for the porch steps, but he held my hand, not letting me go. "Not so fast," he said. "I need to ask you something."

"Really? What's that?"

"What are you doing for New Year's?"

Smiling, I raised my eyebrows, realizing I hadn't thought much about the holidays. "I have no idea. Right now, I just want to make it through the next week of school. Why?"

"I was wondering if you'd like to go to Hawaii with me. I want to spend some time with my mother, and I'd like her to meet you."

"I'd love that. How's she doing?"

"Better, although I'm still worried she'll fall again. I think she'd enjoy getting to know you, especially when she sees me happy for a change. I talked to her late last night, and she seemed more like herself. She's just as relieved as the rest of us, knowing justice has been served to the one responsible for Cassie's death." Lucian paused, his soft smile caving into a frown. "I also promised my father I'd try to get her to sign the divorce papers."

"Really?" I asked. "I'm sure he appreciates your help." Over the last few days, Lucian had been more receptive to Samira since she not only banished Marguerite, but also helped draw a confession out of Gabriel. Now that Lucian seemed to accept her, I had high hopes he'd make amends with his father. Helping him get the divorce papers signed was a step in the right direction.

"I don't think I have much of a choice. He's happier than I've ever seen him. He lights up when Samira walks in the room. He was never like that with my mother and, unfortunately, he never will be. Now, knowing how I feel about you, if I had to stay with Zoe for the rest of my life, I think I'd go crazy. So the best thing I can do is ease my mother through this. Maybe someday she'll find someone she loves as much as I love you. But she won't be free until she gets over my father and gives up the drugs. It's going to take time, and I want to be there to help her."

I nodded, a smile spreading over my lips. "I'm sure she'll appreciate that. And yes, my calendar is wide open for New Year's, so I'd love to join you."

"Great. It's a good thing, too, because I already bought our tickets," he said with a sly grin.

"Why doesn't that surprise me? Now come on," I said. "Becca's making breakfast. Let's eat before we leave."

"Sounds good," he said as I led him up the steps.

"Wait," I said, stopping at the top and turning to him. "First, tell me where we're going today."

"I already told you it's a surprise," he said, a twinkle in his eyes.

"Hmm," I mused, stepping closer to him. "Maybe I can convince you to give me a hint." I kissed his lips gently, running my hands up his arms to his shoulders. Sifting my fingers through his hair, I trailed more kisses down his neck. "Just one tiny clue."

"Okay," he said, giving in at once. "You win. In all the craziness of the last few weeks, I haven't gotten a Christmas tree yet. I figured it's about time to take care of that. So make sure you wear snow boots. And I hope you're good at decorating because we have an attic full of ornaments."

I laughed, realizing in that one moment how much I loved him.

"Is that okay?" he asked, sounding unsure.

"Yes," I assured him. "It's perfect. I can't wait."

With a smile, I threaded my fingers through his and led him into the house.

Epilogue

Ten years later...

A spring breeze whispered through the trees surrounding the backyard behind the white farmhouse Lucian and I bought eight years ago after our wedding. I stopped at the picnic table, placing a tray of lemonade on it as I drew in a deep breath of fresh air. Gypsy and Shade grazed in the pasture extending from the weathered barn we were planning to fix up as soon as we had enough money saved. His job working for his father had allowed us to move out on our own, but we watched our finances carefully, making sure the mortgage was paid first. My position as an Art teacher at the high school helped, but not much.

My dream of going to a top notch school to pursue an engineering degree had proven to be attainable when I'd been accepted to MIT, but as soon as it became a reality, my perspective changed, leading me to art. Painting and creating new masterpieces challenged me, and when I thought about having a family of my own, I sought out a career that would give me a balance in life. Teaching art allowed me to have the summers off, and I loved helping the students express their creativity.

With a smile, I removed the glasses of lemonade from the tray, only to look up when my daughter ran over. At five years old, Claire was the spitting image of Cassie. Her long blonde hair hung in two braids, her green eyes lighting up when she saw me and ran up to the table. "Mommy! You have to come quick! There are two new calves in the field!"

I let out a soft chuckle. Claire inspected the herd every morning, counting the calves and letting us know right away when one arrived.

"Claire, honey, there's a new calf just about every day right now. I'm sure your father will check on them later."

She huffed, but her attention was quickly averted to the side of the house. "Grandpa!" she shrieked before taking off.

I turned to see Aidan in blue jeans and a white button-down shirt approaching the table, his eyes bright and clear. His face had added a few lines and his hair a few shades of gray since I'd first met him. Both he and Becca were beginning to age, but I'd never seen either one of them happier since they'd been reunited. Becca's headaches hadn't been too bad over the last ten years, possibly because she hadn't needed to use much power since peace had returned to Sedgewick. But she was aging, her days apparently numbered, and I savored the time I had left with her.

Aidan beamed, his face lighting up as it did every time he saw his granddaughter. "What is it?" he asked, kneeling in front of Claire.

"There are two new calves! Want to come see them?"

"Sure. Just let me say hi to your mom." He stood up and walked over to me, greeting me with a hug. "Hello, Gracyn. You look like you're glowing today."

"No more than usual, I'm sure," I replied. "How are you?"

"Ready for summer. Only one more month until school's out."

"I know the feeling," I said with a grin.

Claire tugged on his hand, causing his smile to grow. "Well, I'll let you get back to work," he said. "Becca went in through the front door. She wanted to put the potato salad in the refrigerator. And I guess I have some calves to check on. We'll be back."

"Okay. But don't spend too much time out there. Lucian's going to get the grill started soon."

"Mom!" Claire groaned. "You know we have to make sure everyone's okay first."

"Of course. You take very good care of the herd. Where's Destiny?"

Claire whistled and a pure white horse trotted into view from the trees. The mare approached Claire, then stopped beside her and nuzzled her head. Claire laughed, reaching up to pet her horse. "Right here!"

"Good. As long as she's with you," I said, stroking the mare's neck. Claire and Destiny had been practically inseparable since birth. The mare was very special, watching over Claire like a protective mother hen. "Okay, the three of you can go check on the cows. But be back in an hour."

Aidan raised his hand in a mock salute before turning around. He lifted Claire onto Destiny's bare back, then walked beside the mare as they disappeared down the trail leading to the pasture where we kept our small herd of cattle.

Alone again, I started to pick up the empty tray before two arms wrapped around my waist. Lips nibbled at my neck, and I laughed, turning around to face Lucian. At that moment, a nauseated feeling came over me, causing my smile to fade.

"What's wrong?" he asked, suddenly concerned. "You're not feeling well."

"No, I'm not," I said, backing away and touching my stomach. "But I'll be fine. I'm pregnant." I felt a smile slide onto my face as I watched his reaction.

His jaw fell open, his eyes lighting up. "Are you sure?"

"Yes. It would be hard not to be sure about this," I said. "I never get sick, remember? But morning sickness gets me every time, just like it did with Claire. Besides, I took the test this morning and it was positive."

He took a deep breath, the news registering in his expression as he took it all in. "We're going to have a new baby?"

"Yes."

Shaking his head, he touched my abdomen, then looked up, a worried look in his eyes. "Oh, no, what if it's a boy and he's just like me?"

"Then I would consider it a blessing."

"We don't need another dark, brooding Dumante in this world."

"That's not how I see you. You're a gentle, caring man. There aren't many men I know of who would go traipsing out into a muddy cow pasture in the pouring rain to save a cow and her calf. And yet you did that a few weeks ago. So if it is a boy, I hope he's just like his father."

Lucian smiled, seeming bewildered. "You always see the good in me, don't you?"

"I always have, and I always will," I declared before moving into his arms and kissing him. When I pulled away, I smiled. "We'll share the news with everyone at lunch. Are your father and Samira on their way?"

"Yes. They should be here soon."

"Good. Celeste and Derek are also coming."

"Oh, no," Lucian said with a groan. "I'd better go hide the hoses. That little boy of theirs is quite a handful. We can't let him soak us again."

I couldn't help laughing at the memory of four-year-old Ryan squirting everyone at our Fourth of July barbeque last year. "Yes, please do. And then hide anything else he might get into. There's no telling what he'll do next."

"Good idea," Lucian agreed, rolling his eyes.

"Now if I know Becca, she's cleaning up the kitchen for me which means I need to get inside and help, or I'll feel guilty."

Lucian nodded. "Yes, you should. Tell her I'd come in to say hello, but I need to save us from a five-year-old terror," he said, mock fear in his eyes. Before he turned to leave, he kissed me again. "Have I told you today how much I love you?"

"No, but you don't have to," I said, realizing I couldn't be any happier than I was at this moment. "Now go before we all end up drenched this afternoon."

As Lucian headed toward the barn, I carried the empty tray into the house. Once inside, I stopped in the hallway, the picture of Cassie and her horse hanging on the wall capturing my attention as it did every time I walked by. Reminding me of Claire, Cassie's smile never failed to tug at my heart. She might have been gone, but the memory of her lived on, never to be forgotten.

Acknowledgments

I always start this section by thanking everyone who has emailed me, stopped by my table at an event, or picked up one of my books to read. Thank you for your interest and taking the time to read my stories!

To my mom, thank you for you for reading this manuscript and giving me your honest feedback. I love discussing the plot twists and every last detail with you.

To my editors, Amy and Kate, thank you for taking time out of your busy schedules to work on this project for me. I learn something new from every editor I've used, and it was a pleasure working with both of you!

Once again, to Jennifer Gibson for the beautiful cover and bookmark designs. Your work has been noticed by so many. Someone compliments your work at every show I go to!

Lastly, to my family, coworkers, and friends as well as everyone mentioned above. Thank you for listening bearing with me as I continue on this incredible journey. It wouldn't mean as much to me if I didn't have all of you to share it with!

About the Author

Tonya lives in Northern Virginia with her husband, son, two dogs and two horses. Although she dreamed of writing novels at a young age, she was diverted away from that path years ago and built a successful career as a Contracts Manager for a defense contractor in the Washington, DC area. She resurrected her dream of writing in 2013 and hasn't stopped since.

When she isn't writing, Tonya spends time with her family. She enjoys skiing, horseback riding, and anything else that involves the outdoors.

More information about Tonya and her writing can be found at www.tonyaroyston.com.